Praise for
The Double Cross

"[*The Double Cross*] packs a full story with plenty of frontier action and believable, sympathetic characters. I'm already looking forward to the next entry in the Spanish Brand series, but until then I will content myself with rereading *The Double Cross*."
—Heather Stanton, All About Romance

5 Star Top Pick: "If I were to choose a time and place to read about, it would not be New Mexico in 1780. I prefer my locations and society to be settled and civilized. Why then, would I choose this book? Two words – Carla Kelly. I have yet to be disappointed by anything she has written, and this is no exception. She weaves historical facts so tightly and so interestingly into her stories, you don't even realize how much information you're absorbing.... Life at this time was hard and unpredictable, and this beautiful love story interwoven with history makes for an outstanding read."
—Lady Blue, Romantic Historical Reviews

"Kelly skillfully invites readers to share in this romantic adventure that is played out amidst scenes depicting the harsh landscapes and living conditions on the frontier–all punctuated with an assortment of unsavory characters pitted against the heroic."
—*ForeWord* magazine

"Each of these characters' personalities are portrayed so endearingly that at the end of this unforgettable story of honor, love and redemption, we are sad to let them go, making us eager to see what is in store for the next installment of the series"
—The Historical Novel

"Engaging and high
best. I can't wait for the
—Carla Neggers, New

"*The Double Cross* contains clever chapter headings and endearing repartee. The characters, even the secondary ones, are real and lovable. Even through some darker themes, Kelly's smart writing breaks through and the adventurous heart triumphs. The characters evolve and Kelly hints that the world of the Spanish Brand may be evolving as well."
—Tara Creel, *The Deseret News*

"One of the things Ms. Kelly does best is show ordinary people living lives of extraordinary grace, and that's a treat. I also enjoy how she shows widows and widowers finding love again, much as real people do. I look forward to more Spanish Brand stories in the future."
—Darlene Marshall's Blog

"Carla Kelly's vivid storytelling plunges the reader into a tense, hypnotic tale of love and courage in *The Double Cross*. A dangerous land filled with memorable characters springs to life and stays with you long after the final paragraphs."
—Diane Farr, bestselling author, Regency Romance and Young Adult fiction

MARCO AND THE DEVIL'S BARGAIN

MARCO AND THE DEVIL'S BARGAIN

THE SPANISH BRAND SERIES

CARLA KELLY

CAMEL PRESS

Seattle, WA

Camel Press
PO Box 70515
Seattle, WA 98127

For more information go to: www.Camelpress.com
www.carlakellyauthor.com

Cover Photograph by Charles Dobbs, www.charlesdobbs.com
Cover design by Sabrina Sun
Map and brand by Nina Grover

Marco and the Devil's Bargain
Copyright © 2014 by Carla Kelly

ISBN: 978-1-60381-229-0 (Trade Paper)
ISBN: 978-1-60381-230-6 (eBook)

Library of Congress Control Number: 2014935357

Printed in the United States of America

10 9 8 7 6 5 4 3 2 1

To Nina Grover,
21st century friend
and 18th century mapmaker

Books by Carla Kelly

Fiction

Daughter of Fortune

Summer Campaign

Miss Chartley's Guided Tour

Marian's Christmas Wish

Mrs. McVinnie's London Season

Libby's London Merchant

Miss Grimsley's Oxford Career

Miss Billings Treads the Boards

Mrs. Drew Plays Her Hand

Reforming Lord Ragsdale

Miss Whittier Makes a List

The Lady's Companion

With This Ring

Miss Milton Speaks Her Mind

One Good Turn

The Wedding Journey

Here's to the Ladies: Stories of the Frontier Army

Beau Crusoe

Marrying the Captain

The Surgeon's Lady

Marrying the Royal Marine

The Admiral's Penniless Bride

Borrowed Light

Enduring Light

Coming Home for Christmas: The Holiday Stories

Marriage of Mercy

My Loving Vigil Keeping

Her Hesitant Heart

Safe Passage

The Double Cross

The Wedding Ring Quest

Non-Fiction

On the Upper Missouri: The Journal of Rudolph Friedrich Kurz (editor)

Louis Dace Letellier: Adventures on the Upper Missouri (editor)

Fort Buford: Sentinel at the Confluence

Stop me If You've Read This One

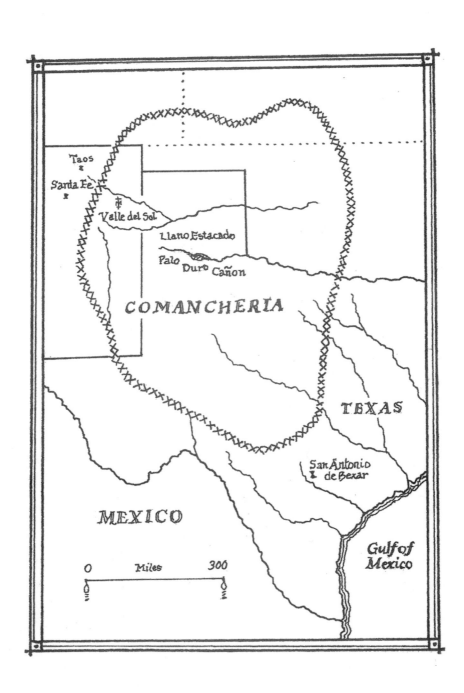

Taos

Santa Fe

Valle del Sol

Llano Estacado

Palo Duro Cañon

COMANCHERIA

TEXAS

San Antonio
de Bexar

MEXICO

Gulf of
Mexico

0   Miles   300

Te deum laudamus: te Dominum confitemur
Te aeturnum Patrem omnis terra venerator

O God, we praise Thee,
and acknowledge Thee to be the supreme lord,
Everlasting Father, all the earth worships thee.

—A portion of a prayer of joy and thanksgiving, circa 400 A.D.

Juez de campo

An official of the Spanish crown who inspects and registers all brands of cattle and sheep in his district, settles disputes, and keeps a watchful eye for livestock rustlers. In the absence of sufficient law enforcement on the frontier of 18th century New Mexico, a royal colony, he also investigates petty crimes.

Contents

Prologue

In which Anthony Gill is a rare man who would like to ask directions

COULD HE TRUST A dying man? Reason told Anthony yes. Why would a dying man lie? On the other hand, the man was a trader, and traders seldom told the whole truth about anything. Besides, even though Anthony had performed the most menial of tasks during their months of association, this particular trader had never been satisfied with his work. *You'd have thought he wanted me to bury his offal with formal ceremony*, Anthony thought, still angry with the man who lay dying in the eerie emptiness of the Staked Plains. The others were already dead. Now it was just the two of them.

As near death as he was, the trader had refused to lead Anthony Gill toward that hidden canyon in Comanchería that every trader wanted to exploit, providing it actually existed. Even a dying trader, covered with pox, oozing and rotting from the inside out, wouldn't be so small-minded as to send a fellow white man to his certain death among the Kwahadi, the Antelope Eaters.

On the other hand, who was to say the Kwahadi weren't all dead, too? Smallpox, always around, had struck with stunning ferocity. Praise God—if there was a god—he had been inoculated years ago.

Anthony sat beside this impromptu deathbed of Texas earth, staring ahead into the distance that looked exactly like every league they had traveled for weeks, and decided to trust the dying man's directions toward the colony of New Mexico. Anthony knew he was only with the traders on sufferance, never mind that he did have one useful skill.

"You there, attend to me," the man croaked. Even in his ultimate extremity, the trader was no more polite than he had ever been. With unexpected strength, he tugged at Anthony, forcing him to breathe deeply of the reek that constituted a man about to succumb to smallpox, *la viruela*, as the Spaniards called it. Viruela sounded more melodious than smallpox. Call it what you will, in this killing season of 1782 it devoured nearly everyone—young, old, poor, rich, good, bad, Comanche, trader, this trader.

"But not Anthony Gill," Anthony said in English to the wind that blew ceaselessly from the west and north.

When Anthony's ear almost touched the trader's mouth, the man had described the one landmark that would get him to Santa Maria, a garrison town perched on the edge of Comanchería. "Look for the tree," he whispered. Anthony shuddered as pus flew out of the man's ruined mouth.

"A tree?"

Wearily, the man nodded. "One tree, fool. Line up on it. You will see the slightest cut in the rocks ahead. Go that way. Go straight."

He coughed again. *I hate this trader*, Anthony thought, *but by God, I have a duty.* He dipped his filthy handkerchief into his canteen. He wiped the man's ruined face, reminding himself that there wasn't anything he couldn't wash off his hands, providing there was enough water. He had almost no water left. He sighed.

Anthony poured a little more water on the disgusting scrap, the final handkerchief remaining to him that belonged to Mrs. Gill. He dribbled the water in the trader's open mouth, where it pooled and ran out the corners. *Ten minutes, no more*, Anthony thought.

"In a day, you will find the river. Follow it north."

"I would rather you gave me directions to that secret canyon where the Kwahadi hole up in winter," Anthony said. "You've been bragging that you know the way."

"Estúpido," the man muttered. "I want to save your worthless hide."

The trader was right; Anthony's hide was worthless. He couldn't even remember his last sensible plan. "Tree. Gap in the rock," he said. "Supposing I actually get that far without being skewered, peeled, and probably unmanned by the Kwahadi, what then?"

"Find Marco Mondragón," the trader gasped, his time almost up.

"Very well. Anything else, you stinking lump?" Anthony said in Spanish, not caring now if a man staring at death heard another's opinion of his faulty character.

"Bury me deep, you fool," the trader whispered, then died, kindly putting Anthony out of his personal misery, too.

ANTHONY DIDN'T BURY HIM; too much bother. He did scrape some of the trader's pox into a screw-on tin. Maybe this Marco Mondragón, if he found such a man, would be interested in inoculation. It was the one gift he could give, dubious at best, because some died from the cure, too. That was what had gotten Anthony Gill in trouble in the colony of Georgia.

He considered the matter. Perhaps his gift could also be a bargaining tool. He had lived too long on the hindquarters of ill fortune not to consider all the angles.

Anthony pocketed the disgusting sample, kicked the dead man for good measure, then stared down with a frown. "Why in God's name did I kick him?" he asked the wind. "What have I become?"

He expected no answer, no burning bush, no thundering from on high, and he was not disappointed. Anthony Gill mounted his horse that staggered under even so light a burden as he had become. He hoped he could spot that tree and line himself up with the stone gap in distant rocks. Finding little Pia Maria Gill might have to wait for a season; he needed Marco Mondragón more.

Chapter One

In which the Mondragóns go their separate ways with some reluctance

"**H**USBAND, IF I DIDN'T know you to be a dedicated and resourceful officer of the crown, I might think that you are putting off your visit to the garrison," Paloma Vega said into her husband's bare shoulder. She softened her criticism, if such it was, with a delicate nip on that shoulder.

The dedicated and resourceful officer of the crown tightened his grip on his wife when she tried to ease to one side. Paloma stayed where she was, both arms around Marco Mondragón's neck and her fingers massaging his head. She knew how much he liked that. Amazing what a woman learned in fifteen months of marriage.

She kissed him, one of many similar kisses she had distributed here and there last night and just now, when the late dawn of early January lightened their room. "You're not stalling because you'll miss me, are you?" she asked into his neck. "You're coming to get me in three days."

"I will count the hours, Paloma," he replied, his voice drowsy now. And no wonder—neither of them had slept much last night. It was going to be embarrassing enough to troop into the kitchen at the Double Cross so long after the hour of breakfast, and know that Sancha and Perla, *la cocinera*, would chuckle about them later in the morning. How was it going to look when she arrived at her sister-in-law's hacienda this afternoon and yawned through dinner? It wouldn't hurt to mention the matter to him now, since he was obviously mellow. "My love," she started, then laughed. "Never mind. If I start to yawn, your sister will understand why."

Marco kissed her shoulder again, and then her neck, and then she didn't really care how much she was going to yawn that afternoon, or what the servants or her sister-in-law thought.

A little later, she said, "Husband, explain to me again just what this is I have gotten myself into?"

Traitorous man, his eyes were starting to close again. January it might be, but a summons from the visiting lieutenant at the garrison in Santa Maria couldn't be ignored. "Marco, you have to go to Santa Maria and I have to leave, too."

He sat up. "What have you gotten yourself into? Fifteen months of marriage and you ask me that?"

She thumped him in a tender spot. "Did you give Felicia this much trouble?" she asked, citing his first wife, one so beloved.

"This and more. Well, maybe not more," he amended. "*Oye*, you are referring to your visit to my sister, and not my nearly supernatural powers in bed?" He tickled her. "If you roll your eyes like that, they'll get stuck."

"Seriously now. I go to your sister's hacienda and we knit socks?"

"*Claro.* Luisa has been doing this for years because she gets bored in January. She summons her friends to join her for several days of knitting, and what I suspect is non-stop gossip."

"Oh, never," Paloma teased, feeling more than mellow now herself and wishing for a long nap before breakfast—or was it lunchtime now? "Did Felicia go?"

"Every year until … well, you know."

"I know," she said softly, treading delicately around his feelings about Felicia, who had died nine years ago along with their twins in a cholera epidemic while he was away.

He was silent a moment, tightening his grip on her shoulder. "You and Sancha have spun my best mohair into yarn," he said, businesslike. "Knit socks for me, for you, for servants." He lay back against his pillow and grabbed her, blowing into her neck until she shrieked. "You're so much fun. The outriders who go along get together in the stable to drink and gamble. I get a year's worth of socks."

"Supposing I just want to stay here with you?" she asked, happily tucked into that spot that she liked so well between his chest and his arm. "She didn't invite me last year."

"We were newly married and—"

"Be honest now. Luisa didn't think too much of me. I know some called me your sudden wife."

"They don't now," he reminded her. "She's learned a lot in a year, too."

Paloma kissed his chest. She knew he was right, although she was still shy around women from Santa Maria and other ranchos she had met at church but seldom saw. "I'd rather stay here."

"You need to meet your neighbors, my heart," he told her. "They already know how brave you are—finding old Joaquin Muñoz in the snow storm and saving the Comanche." His expression grew more tender. "Are you worried about your cousin?"

She nodded, thinking of the abominable Maria Teresa Moreno, who had married Alonso Castellano, one of Marco's neighbors. Maria had already paraded her growing belly in front of Paloma during Christmas Mass, her self-satisfied smile a constant reproach to Paloma, who mourned her own childless state.

"She will taunt me about … you know," Paloma whispered.

"I know," he said, and hugged her closer.

"Marco, why me?" She stopped. They had suffered through this conversation before.

"I wish I knew, my heart." Marco sat up, and pulled her with him. "Up! Up!" He tugged her from the bed. Suddenly shy, she turned away when he appraised her from hair to heels. "Ah, yes. You're not the skinny girl I married last year."

He wrapped her in his generous embrace. "Luisa only invites those she likes, so I doubt Maria Teresa will be there. You should know this—word is getting around about her. You yourself told me that would happen."

"Maria Teresa always muddies her nest," Paloma said.

SANCHA MADE NO COMMENT when they finally strolled into the kitchen. Paloma thought the housekeeper rolled her eyes at Perla. She couldn't be sure, since it was only the tiniest glimpse; better just to brazen it through.

"Sancha, you're better at this than I am. How much yarn do you think I should take with me to the hacienda of the widow Gutierrez? What did Felicia do?"

She knew Sancha liked to be reminded of her late mistress, and was rewarded with a smile.

"I can gather what you need, señora," Sancha said, "if you will get breakfast for this lazy ranchero and officer of the crown."

Perfect, Paloma thought, as she nodded to the housekeeper. *He is not lazy in bed, but no one will hear that from me.* "Thank you, Sancha. I can scrape some mush from the bottom of an old pot for this lazy man."

After Sancha and Perla left the kitchen, the lazy man patted her rump. "I could pick you up after two days."

She filled his bowl with mush and chilis. "Oh, no, my love. Three days! I have so much to knit, in addition to stockings. Remember please, that I tried to measure you for a *chaleco* before bed. It took me all night because you were not helpful."

They both laughed, then ate in companionable silence, Paloma still relishing every bite. She wondered if it would take months, or even years, to lose the fear every morning when she woke that today there would be no food. The thought made her sigh and look down at her already empty bowl.

"I know that sigh," Marco said, pushing back his partly finished bowl.

She couldn't help it; her eyes followed his bowl. When he saw that, he pushed it in her direction, then picked up her hand, spoon and all, and kissed it.

"My heart, just remind yourself that those days are over. Anytime you want more to eat, you just take it. I'm full."

"No, you're not," she said just as gently, and pushed his bowl in front of him again.

He pushed it between the two of them. "Everything I have I will share. Don't ever forget that." He clicked her spoon with his, dipped it full and held it out to her.

They alternated bites until his bowl was empty, too. When they finished, he went to the cupboard and took out some *carne seca*. "Let's take this with us. I get hungry between here and Santa Maria."

"You do not!" she scolded, so pleased with her man.

"But *you* do, and it matters to me. Get on your riding clothes, Paloma. I have to visit the garrison"—he made a face—"and you have to knit stockings."

MARCO KNEW HE WANTED Paloma beside him in Santa Maria's garrison. They had been married long enough for him to appreciate her calm assessment of problems. Before Christmas that first year, Paloma had watched Señora Chávez arrange the nativity scene, the *belén*, outside the church. She saw how the widow tucked in the Christ Child with the swaddling bands she had knitted from Marco Mondragón's wool. Marco had told Paloma how the Holy Babe had disappeared some years back. On a hunch that the widow grieved for her recently dead son, he found the Cristo in Señora Chávez's house. She had wanted to keep the Babe warm, because her only child was cold in the earth.

"It's her job now to keep the *belén* tidy," Marco told Paloma. "Shouldn't that be enough?"

His wife had asked him gently, "Tell me why, then, does she stand in the cold and rock back and forth?"

"I don't know, except that I don't question how people mourn," Marco told her finally with a certain amount of painful understanding. "What more can we do?"

"I'll think about it."

Paloma had thought about it for a week, going about her usual tasks in her quiet way. She denied him nothing, but he knew her mind and heart were on the widow Chávez. He had almost hated to mention over supper one evening that a barn cat had been snatched by a coyote, leaving four kittens not even old enough to have their eyes open.

"I suppose Emilio will have to drown the little things," he told her. "Seems a shame."

Paloma had put down her spoon and looked at him in triumph. "That's it," she said, as she left the table, pulled her shawl around her and ran out the kitchen door.

He followed, curious, and then not terribly surprised to find her on her knees in the horse barn, her hands full of mewing kittens that groped about blindly, their mouths open, hungry. In another minute they were arranged carefully in her shawl and carried through the snow into the kitchen.

As Marco watched, she warmed some goat's milk and sat on the floor with a rag, which she dipped in the milk then dribbled into each kitten's mouth. After a long time, their bellies were full and they slept in a heap. "This is how I kept Trece alive, that expensive and rare yellow dog of yours," she told him. "Tomorrow we will take these orphans to the Widow Chávez."

"Paloma, she's old and forgetful," he reminded her. "Four kittens! She'll be up all hours."

"She's a mother," was his wife's simple reply.

So it had proved. The Widow Chávez had been only too happy to take the babies into her house and nourish them. That was the last time that Christmas season anyone saw the Widow Chávez mourning her own son in the snow beside the *belén*.

Considering all that, if Paloma came with him to the garrison, Marco knew he would have an ally when the sergeant started to blather and apologize and blame the king of Spain for every wrong his pitiful cadre of soldiers suffered. And there would be the visiting lieutenant. *Ay caray!* Marco said as much to Toshua—their Comanche who would not leave—as he saddled his horse and then Paloma's.

Toshua shook his head. "You're growing soft, señor. What did you do before Paloma came?"

"I complained and went by myself."

"Well then." Toshua folded his arms. "She said she would knit me a pair of socks, too. Me, I have never worn socks, but you do not hear me complaining. I want socks."

"You could be a little sympathetic, Toshua."

"I doubt it."

THEY LEFT FOR SANTA Maria, Paloma riding beside Marco and followed by a mule carrying a sack of yarn and other gifts for Luisa, as proud-stepping as if his wife had promised him socks for each of his four feet, too.

Toshua came next, riding behind, and then beside them, then ahead, always looking to the right and left, even as Marco did. His four guards looked as pleased as men could look. They knew they were escorting their master's admirable wife to the hacienda of the Widow Gutierrez, where, while the ladies knitted, there would be wine and card games and gambling.

As much as he liked to ride with Paloma on the same mount, Marco had quickly discovered how pleasant it was to watch her control her own horse. She had a sure hand, even when the mare sidestepped a few times, shying from winter birds hunkered down in the brush along the trail.

"Did you ride with your father?" he asked her.

"Whenever he let me. He gave me my first horse when I was six."

Marco knew the look in her eyes was the same one in his, when she had assured him she did not mind if he mentioned Felicia. *Why is it that no one thinks we want to speak of our beloved dead?* he asked himself, not for the first time.

His mentioning her father had given Paloma permission to ask a question of her own. "Marco, how did your sister's husband die?" She glanced at Toshua, who rode farther ahead of them now, his lance across his lap.

"A sad story. It was a summer seventeen years ago when the Comanche moon never set. We were all forted up throughout Valle del Sol. One of Manuel's best milk cows wandered away, and he went to find it, even though Luisa pleaded with him. He could see the cow tethered to a bush, just a stone's throw from their walls, with no one in sight."

"That means nothing," Paloma said.

"Manuel knew that, too, but all he could see was the cow. When he was too close to the cow to back away, he saw the feet of the Comanche clinging to the cow on the other side. Then, Luisa said, there seemed to be *indios* everywhere."

"She watched the whole thing?" Paloma asked, her voice low so Toshua could not hear.

"From the wall. They stripped Manuel, ripped off his privates, staked him over a low fire and cooked him for two days. They made him eat his own flesh." He glanced at his wife's pale face and leaned over to touch her hands. "He pleaded with Luisa to shoot him, and she did. She was carrying their younger son and went into labor that night."

"We have all suffered," Paloma said. She looked in Toshua's direction. "But so has he. When will it end?"

He had no answer.

Santa Maria came in sight too soon to suit him, and maybe Paloma, too, if he correctly interpreted her little sigh as they came to the garrison, around which the village had been constructed. *Neither of us wants to do what we have to*, he thought. *I could assure my lovely woman that she will have a good time at Luisa's, but she will not believe me.*

While his guards busied themselves and Toshua, too, looked away, Marco leaned over in the saddle and kissed Paloma. "We'll ride for you in two days, Toshua and I."

She kissed him back, her eyes merry. "It's *three* days, my dearest. You can *say* that, but I will wager you another evening measuring you for a sweater that Toshua heads for Hacienda Gutierrez once you two ride home."

"I doubt you will be any more successful with *that* sweater, if you lose! Be a good girl and knit socks."

Chapter Two

In which there are uninvited guests

ANOTHER HOUR SAW PALOMA and her escorts safely to Hacienda Gutierrez. She surveyed it with a critical eye. The typical red-colored adobe and stout gate made her doubly grateful for Marco's stone walls and guards on constant patrol. She thought of death's visit here seventeen years ago and better understood her sister-in-law's farseeing eyes. *Could I do that?* she asked herself. *Could I shoot my husband to end his torture? Pray God it never comes to that.* She looked around, hoping no one was watching, and crossed herself.

The gates swung open and there stood Luisa Gutierrez, her sister-in-law, her hands outstretched in welcome, even though the day was raw and snow threatened.

They kissed, and Luisa took Paloma by the hand as they hurried toward the hacienda. "You're the last, my dear," her sister-in-law said. "You live the farthest away. Everyone else is hard at work." She laughed. "Well, no, not exactly. They are all gossiping."

A servant opened the door, but Luisa hesitated, then shook her head slightly. The door closed on silent hinges. She turned to face Paloma.

"I have to tell you: your cousin Maria Teresa got wind of this gathering and invited herself. I don't know how she heard about it."

"I feared she might be here," Paloma said, wanting to leave, wishing she could have stayed in Santa Maria with Marco.

"I never invited her, but since she came, I owe her the hospitality of the Gutierrez family," Luisa told her.

"I understand, sister. At least I needn't sit next to her."

Luisa tapped on the door and it opened again. They walked inside, but Luisa hesitated once more, as if mulling over what she wanted to say.

"Go ahead." Paloma heard laughter and many voices in the *sala*.

"She's boasting that she is with child," Luisa said, her face red. "I hope this doesn't upset you."

"I have seen her at church. Luisa, I would be foolish if I allowed that to upset me," Paloma told her, wishing again that she could leave this place. She couldn't help her sigh, just a small sigh that made Luisa frown, then kiss her forehead.

"I suppose Marco tells you to be patient, eh? My brother is so deliberate. He's right, though."

I know, Paloma thought, as she followed her sister-in-law into the *sala*, even though every part of her yearned to be elsewhere. *Easy to say.*

Maybe it was all those hard years in her aunt and uncle's house in Santa Fe that made her want to turn away when every woman in the *sala* looked at her. Whatever confidence Paloma had already earned as the trusted wife of a landowner and officer of the crown seemed to dribble away. She hesitated in the doorway.

Luisa understood. She simply held out her hand and announced, "Paloma Vega de Mondragón. You all know my sister-in-law."

Marco thinks you are brave, she reminded herself, as she gave the medium-sized elegant curtsey that Mama had taught her so long ago.

"Paloma, the sudden wife," Maria Teresa Moreno de Castellano said. "My cousin." She tittered behind her hand.

Paloma took a shallow breath and held it, afraid to look around. *Marco thinks you are brave*, she thought again, and looked up.

What she saw put the heart back into her breast and started it beating again. She saw smiling faces, kind ones, and generous hearts, as the two lovely Borrego sisters rose and each took her by the hand, tugging her over to sit between them. Dazed, she heard other comments: "Oh, now, you must share!" and "We get a turn, too," and gentle teases: "You Borregos did that because you know the Mondragón wool is the best and you're going to snitch some," and "Paloma, how did you snare the man every mother in del Sol sought for her daughter?"

"I had a yellow dog he wanted," Paloma teased back, enjoying the laughter that followed. Obviously everyone in Valle del Sol had heard the story of the runt for which the *juez de campo* paid one whole peso. Rumor flew on mayfly's wings in eastern New Mexico, apparently.

Paloma looked around the circle, recognizing the women she saw in church when she and Marco were able to make their way through the snow to *la iglesia*. Something else became immediately obvious—Maria Teresa sat on the edge of the circle, no one near her. Some odd force was at work here that Paloma didn't understand, even though she felt grateful for it. She took a deeper breath and smiled.

"I have not managed a household before the Double Cross, but I have noticed that one of my husband's stockings always seems to disappear between the bedchamber and the laundry room. Why is this? Is there some *diablillo* at work in Valle del Sol?"

The ladies laughed and returned to their knitting. Chaca Borrego declared that she would make three stockings for each match, from now on, because she had the same problem. The others smiled and nodded.

Her heart easier, Paloma took out her knitting needles and the mohair that she and Sancha had spun into yarn only a week ago. She had noticed that Marco was getting a corn on his little toe. Maybe extra-soft stockings would help, and maybe Maria Teresa would say nothing more.

When Maria cleared her throat quite loudly, the needles all stopped, then resumed their work as each woman in the circle ignored Paloma's cousin. *What is going on here?* Paloma asked herself. She could have told the knitters that her cousin never allowed herself to be ignored. Paloma tensed because she feared what was coming. She would have given the earth to suddenly vanish and find herself back at the Double Cross kitchen.

Maria Teresa cleared her throat with even more volume. "I hope you all will give me lots of baby advice in the coming months," she declared, then gave Paloma an arch glance. "Too bad everyone is not as blessed as I am."

The knitters stopped again and the silence seemed to circle the room like a bad odor. *She made me cry in Santa Fe, but I cannot let her make me cry in Valle del Sol*, Paloma thought, wounded in the softest, most vulnerable part of her heart, that place where she had never let Maria Teresa touch her before.

She could barely bring herself to glance around the circle, but to her relief, she saw only horror followed by a firmness around mouths and a narrowing of eyes. She could also tell that no one knew what to say, how to respond to such rudeness. Paloma continued knitting, thinking how much her husband wanted children, even though she knew he would never tell her. She put down her knitting because her hands were starting to shake. Not for the world did Paloma want her own cousin to see how harshly her words harrowed her soul.

Consider this part of the adventure. Hadn't Father Damiano told her that very thing in San Pedro? She thought of her bloody sandals tacked to the wall of the *sala* at the Double Cross, put there by her husband to remind him what bravery was, and how a woman would walk to a dangerous place just to return a yellow dog. Her dowry to him was courage; it was time to show some.

"It *is* a sorrow to me, Maria," she said, her voice so calm that she surprised herself. "We hope and pray that we will be as blessed as you someday. We leave it in the hands of Our Lord."

There now. She picked up her needles, and with steady hands, continued to knit her husband wonderful mohair stockings. It was as if everyone except Maria heaved a sigh of relief. Luisa herself started the conversation again, effectively shutting out another word from Maria Teresa, who sat there with a frown on her face, wondering what happened. Obviously she hadn't yet figured out that she'd left her allies behind in Santa Fe—if indeed she had any there—and that Valle del Sol was different. If there was something more, Paloma didn't know.

In a few minutes, Paloma chatted with the others, silently reminding herself that this was far from the worst day of her life. That had certainly been the day her entire family was tortured and then butchered by Comanche raiders. Compared to that day, Maria Teresa was a frog peeping by a pond, a rooster crowing at false dawn, a grasshopper sawing its hind legs. She took a deep breath, knowing that however this knitting marathon ended, she would go home to the finest man in Valle del Sol—something of hers that Maria Teresa could never have. She was content.

AS HE SAT IN Santa Maria's garrison on the other side of a desk from Lieutenant Xavier Roybal—of His Serene Majesty's forces in Santa Fe—Marco wondered whether Paloma could look in this man's eyes and find the honest man.

He decided she could, if for no other reason than that the lieutenant was young and had not yet learned to disguise his emotions or his motives. Ah, Marco wasn't being fair to his wife, who had enough skill in discernment to select the honest man among the politicians. Xavier Roybal was no challenge to her already considerable skills. The officer looked like the worried man he was.

While the lieutenant went through the formal motions of greeting that prefaced any visit by authority, Marco looked down at the wine in his goblet. It was a heady wine that Roybal must have brought with him. The usual garrison libation was sour and tasted like vinegar. Perhaps the young lieutenant had more experience with visiting far-flung garrisons than Marco gave him credit for. This obviously wasn't his first such *visita*. He sipped and smiled.

"I amuse you, señor?" the lieutenant said, with just enough bite to assure Marco that if the man lived beyond his lieutenancy, he might learn to command.

"Amuse me? A little, I suppose," Marco said, seeing that honest man he knew Paloma would see. "If you want to cut through the bureaucracy and just tell me what is on your mind, with no frills, I have no objection."

Lieutenant Roybal gave him a genuine smile, the kind that showed most of his teeth, all of which appeared to be original. "We are of the same mind, Señor Mondragón. More wine?"

Marco shook his head.

"You might want more, after I have gone through the list I bring from Governor de Anza," he said, which made Marco laugh.

"I know the governor well enough to ask that you skip any blandishments that protocol might deem necessary. What is on the governor's mind?"

Lieutenant Roybal permitted himself a smile. "The governor told me you would ask that very question." The smile left his face. "Grave times are ahead, señor."

"I thought as much. Every autumn when I go to Santa Fe, the list of useless laws to obey gets longer and longer. That tells me that our Serene Majesty or perhaps the Council of the Indies wonder what to do with us."

Roybal refilled his own cup. "*Sí y no*, señor. As you are aware, King Carlos has been backing the Americans against the British …"

"Ah. You aren't calling them colonists now? That tells me something. What news?"

"Good news for them. Before I set out on this *progreso*, word came of an American victory at Yorktown in Virginia last autumn. The British remain in New York, but they are weaker."

"Well, well, and what does that mean for us here in Nuevo Mexico?" Marco drained his cup after all, and held it out to his host.

"It means our king is hopeful of some benefit when a treaty is actually signed with … let me see … I believe they are calling it the United States of America."

Marco nodded. "I would wager that our king has pulled all the troops he can into his possessions along the Gulf of Mexico, the better to cement his interests."

The lieutenant gave him a look of respect, which made Marco add, "We aren't rubes here on the edge of nowhere, lieutenant."

Roybal blushed and looked suddenly younger. "I would never assume so." He became more serious. "Then you know what follows."

Marco did. He sat back with a sigh. "I have feared for some time that the few troops on the edge of nowhere—here, for instance—will be withdrawn and sent east."

"You would be right."

Marco looked around at the room with its big desk, which should have been the office of a lieutenant, at least, perhaps a captain. It had been empty for years. The garrison's highest ranking soldier was a *sargento* who spent most of his time a sodden drunk.

"You're taking our miserable soldiers with you, lieutenant? Please do."

Roybal winced; the charge had struck home. He was too honest to deny it. "They are as foul and useless a company as I have seen anywhere." He clasped his hands together and looked Marco in the eye across the desk that separated them. "Everyone here in Santa Maria tells me that you are the law."

"A *juez de campo* has that title, whenever there is no effective law present." He leaned forward, too. "Lieutenant, there is no effective law here."

Roybal sat back with a sigh, but he did not break eye contact. "I know. I will say that these troops are not being withdrawn yet, but soon. As you know far better than I, you in Valle del Sol are the last law until San Antonio de Bexar in Texas." He asked, "Does that frighten you?"

"All the time, lieutenant. I have land, cattle, sheep, goats and a wife most dear, and—"

"Children?"

"Alas, no, or perhaps that is a good thing right now. Who can say?"

"When some other poor lieutenant or sergeant comes after me and takes these miserable troops, how will you manage?"

Marco drank deep and then smiled. "As we always have!" He stood up and went to the window, looking down at Toshua in the courtyard. The Comanche had situated himself as a cat in a room with several doors would. Toshua had found the vantage point from which to survey all entrances, looking from one to the other and back again, his hand light on his lance. Several soldiers stood inside their barracks at the window, not leaving the building. Toshua held them hostage without doing a thing.

"Lieutenant, we are making little gestures toward the Comanche, whom we defeated two years ago fifty leagues north of Santa Maria. Governor de Anza himself has told me to forge what alliances I can, and I shall do this."

"Do you have enough authority?" the lieutenant asked. It was not a challenge, but a genuine question wanting—perhaps even craving—a sensible answer.

"Out here, I create the authority I need," Marco said bluntly. "We are too far away to depend upon help, so we make our own laws when we must, and trust Our Celestial Father and His Son. Does that shock your military sense of law and order?"

Lieutenant Roybal shook his head. "I rather think it reassures me."

Marco sketched a little bow, gratified. "You can write in your ledger that Valle del Sol is well-aware of the dangers it faces and looking to improve the odds."

"*Claro*, señor." Roybal closed the ledger. He gestured for Marco to sit again. "There is one thing more. I must warn you that we have an unwelcome guest coming this way."

"Who would that be?"

"*La viruela.*"

Marco sat down with a thump. "*Dios mio*, smallpox."

Chapter Three

In which another guest arrives at Hacienda Gutierrez, as unwanted as Maria Teresa

MARCO LEANED BACK IN his chair, unable to look the lieutenant in the eyes. The younger man waited for him to regain his composure.

"We always have this unwelcome guest in our colony, lieutenant," he said finally, hoping the officer of the crown could not hear his heart racing. *I told Paloma I could protect her from everything but disease,* he thought. *I was a fool to open my mouth.* "This smallpox is different?"

"It is worse. Those men who dare to trade with the Comanche have been hurrying west, telling tales of whole villages empty of the living and stinking of death." He shrugged. "*La viruela* might never come to Santa Maria, or it might drop in for a lengthy visit. God alone knows."

They sat in silence for a moment. Perhaps the lieutenant, young as he was, had his own demons. *La viruela* had never been a respecter of persons.

"Is there a surgeon or physician in Santa Maria?" Roybal asked. He pushed the decanter toward Marco, who poured himself another glass.

Marco laughed. "A surgeon? Here? We don't even have a barber."

"So you have not been inoculated?"

"I have, actually, and my sister, as well." Marco sat back, remembering the trip to Santa Fe when he was a young boy, just for that purpose. The other *hacendados* laughed at his father for such an expense, when everything was in God's hands, anyway. Good thing Papa had been of a more scientific bent than his friends. He sighed. "My younger brother, also, but he died from the inoculation."

"It happens," said the lieutenant, with sympathy. He sighed, too, then. "My mother died of the inoculation." He crossed himself, then blushed, as though officers of the crown were not to mention their mothers. "Maybe someday there will be a better method. Then you have nothing to fear, personally."

"I have a wife, that one so dear. I've never noticed any scars on her from *la viruela*, or from inoculation, either." As he sat there drinking the lieutenant's wine, he was suddenly filled with the greatest urge to ride like a maniac to his sister's hacienda, strip Paloma past her shift, and take a good look at her. God knows he had looked closely at her before, but not for scars. *And do what, you idiot*, he asked himself. *Santa Fe is so far, and how do you know there is a surgeon there with access to enough pox right now to inoculate?*

"What is your advice, lieutenant?"

"Just this: be on the alert for diseased *indios*. Avoid gatherings. I already advised the useless sergeant here that he kill any *indios* who approach Santa Maria …." His voice trailed away, and he again appeared suddenly young and uncertain.

"That would not make Governor de Anza happy, since he has told me to send out peace feelers to the east among the Kwahadi," Marco reminded him. "Just *how* bad is this particular smallpox?"

"Reports say it is the kind that leaves dark blood spots under the skin and kills before the pustules actually erupt. No one who has not been inoculated survives this pestilence."

Marco stood up again and walked to the window. "Lieutenant, I would advise you to draft a letter to be read during each Mass for the next month. Warn about gatherings and any wanderers from the east." He couldn't face the lieutenant because he suddenly felt so discouraged. "Of course, with ten days before any symptoms set in—if I remember correctly—this will turn us into most suspicious and unkind hosts, if we kill random Indians. I can't advise that."

"I am composing just such a message for your priest right now."

"Very well. How much time do we have before this unwelcome guest arrives?"

The lieutenant shrugged. "It may never come."

"And it may be here tomorrow." Marco drained the rest of his glass and started for the door. "I have work to do. Good day, Lieutenant Roybal. Remember me to the governor, when next you see him."

After a few more pleasantries neither man had the heart for, he left, summoning Toshua, which probably relieved the entire garrison. Marco must have been wearing his unease all over his face, because the Comanche wasted not a moment as they rode from Santa Maria to ask what the problem was. Marco's answer didn't so much as alter his expression.

"From the East, you say?"

"Your territory, Toshua. Your home."

"They threw me out, remember?"

"Yes, but your people …."

Toshua's answering stare reminded the *juez* all over again that this man was Kwahadi, and no mere Indian. "Ask your woman if she would lift a hand to help her horrible aunt and uncle in Santa Fe! *She* will understand if I seem not properly concerned about my own people."

Marco was silent for the remainder of the ride to the Double Cross. As they approached his fortress of a hacienda, he could not help the little lift the first view always gave his heart, no matter what his mood. His pleasure passed quickly this time, as the old, gnawing worry came back, the one he was so certain Paloma had banished forever. It was dreadful enough when Felicia and their twins were dead of *el cólera* and buried before he returned from a brand inspection trip. Now there was Paloma, and she was not here to hold out her arms in welcome. He barely restrained himself from wheeling Buciro about to ride through the darkness to Hacienda Gutierrez, just to see Paloma's lovely face.

He didn't try to hide the groan of anguish that escaped him. Startled and then amazed, Marco bowed his head when Toshua leaned over and placed his hands firmly on Marco's. The Comanche gave them a little shake.

"Do not fear, señor," he said. "You are too seasoned here on the edge of Comanchería to borrow trouble from tomorrow."

"But Paloma is not with me." Marco couldn't help it.

"She is safe at your sister's hacienda." Toshua patted Marco's hand as though he were a child, and not a man grown, a landowner and officer of the crown.

"I will ride there tomorrow and bring her back," Marco said, knowing he sounded stubborn and childish.

Toshua laughed then, a low rumble that commanded Marco's attention because the Comanche never laughed. "While it is true my three wives kicked me from the lodge, I do remember other days when they merely frowned and pouted if I tried to change their plans! Take my advice: Showing up early to a women's gathering will earn you no kisses from Paloma."

Marco couldn't help his own smile. He sat on Buciro in the gloom of night as the guards on the roof continued their steady pacing and his *mayordomo* closed the gate until morning. Marco's heart was not easy, but Toshua was right.

Why had he shown such weakness to a Comanche, *por dios*? "I should take your advice."

"*I* would," Toshua replied. "I seldom give any."

Still, Marco had trouble setting the guards for the night, then walking around his own compound, as he always did after dinner. He could think only of his wife, and the trouble from the east coming her way. He sat for a long time in his office by the horse barn, just staring at a handful of complaints and a packet of new ordinances and laws that Lieutenant Roybal had handed over with a wry grin of his own before he left.

"We officers of the crown should have no illusions," Marco muttered out loud, forgetting that Toshua sat by the fire. When the Comanche looked at him, Marco grabbed up a handful of paper. "If I threw this in the fire, no one would know or care, and the course of the empire would proceed in exactly the same way. What should I do?"

"You wait two more days, then ride to your sister's hacienda, where *I* am not much wanted."

It had only been a rhetorical question, but it touched him that someone took him seriously. *So my sister does not like you? Ride there anyway tonight, my friend,* he told himself. He knew he could not ask Toshua to do that, but in the year they had known each other, he had learned to respect the Comanche's instincts.

He left Toshua in the office, already unrolling his bedding by the fireplace. For reasons unknown, he had claimed the office as his sleeping room. Marco looked back at the office, then thought of Toshua in the garrison at Santa Maria. For the first time, he realized that the view from the office commanded all the entrances to the Double Cross. He couldn't help his rueful smile. "My friend, you would know instantly if I tried to leave tonight, eh?" he asked the wind. He decided he wasn't desperate enough to find out what Toshua would do.

He spent a long time on his knees in the chapel, then returned to the kitchen, no easier in his mind. Under his housekeeper Sancha's disapproving eyes, Marco took a bottle of wine from its bed of sawdust in the storeroom.

"At least take a glass with you," she said, giving him no chance to sneak away with his vice. She reminded him uncomfortably of earlier, darker days. He dared a look in her eyes and saw no sadness this time. Maybe things weren't as bad as he thought.

He went to the *sala* and sank onto the *banco* against the wall. With a frown in the general direction of the kitchen, he popped the cork and drank from the bottle. Trouble was, tipping his head back put him in a direct line with Paloma's bloody sandals tacked on the wall, testimony of her willingness to walk to a dangerous place to return his dog. After a year, the blood had turned to vague dark splotches, but he knew what it meant. He had married a brave woman. What would she think if she could see him drinking from the bottle in the *sala*?

He turned a little, not wanting such a visible reminder of bravery, not when he was feeling so weak and powerless. "How in the world can I protect you?" he murmured, supremely dissatisfied with himself.

Marco took another swig from the bottle, then looked down in surprise to see Paloma's cat twining around his ankles. Chica had arrived on the premises after Sancha shrieked about a mouse in the pantry. He had seen his lovely wife chatting with Señora Chávez after Mass, and sure enough, soon after there was a kitten from the litter they had originally given to her when their barn cat died. Small world.

Chica had a ball of yarn in her mouth, which she dropped at his feet, a clear indication that the only one tired and discouraged was Marco. He picked it up and tossed it across the *sala*, but Chica only looked at him with that evident disdain of cats, as though wondering why her mistress had ever aligned herself with someone so ignorant as the man swigging from a bottle.

Marco fetched the yarn ball himself, annoyed by the ingratitude of cats. He remembered that when Paloma threw the yarn ball, she always accompanied it with a sound, "Shew!" Feeling supremely silly, he looked around to make sure there were no servants within earshot. "Shew!" he exclaimed, and threw the ball.

The cat returned it promptly and dropped it at his feet again, even as she glanced here and there for the person obviously better at the game than he was.

"Looking around won't do any good," he told her. "We must be patient, you and I."

To his secret delight, Chica heaved herself down against his stocking feet and settled in, apparently for as long as he intended to drink in the *sala*. After another pull, Marco set down the bottle and picked up the cat. He found her purr so soothing. Perhaps if she purred in his ear on Paloma's pillow, the night wouldn't seem so long or the bed so empty.

BY KEEPING HER HEAD down and knitting quickly, Paloma finished one sock before Luisa's housekeeper announced dinner. There was a dining room, of course, but she knew Luisa preferred the kitchen, as her guests did.

All of her guests except Maria Teresa moved toward the kitchen. Her cousin murmured something about "always eating in *our* dining room," low but not quite out of earshot.

When Maria Teresa said that, in addition to the other not-quite-inaudible pricks and barbs she had delivered *sotto voce* all afternoon, Paloma watched the others. There was no mistaking that Luisa's other knitters were ignoring Maria Teresa.

The worst moment came when they began to file into the kitchen at Luisa's kind invitation. Teresa sidled up to her, grabbed Paloma's hand, and placed it on her swelling belly. In a loud voice, she exclaimed, "*Mira*, cousin, you can feel my baby!"

Shocked, the other women looked at each other, as though they had no antidote for such blatant unkindness to a woman—a relative, no less—already whispered about to be barren. Hadn't Paloma Vega been married to the obviously fertile *juez de campo* for more than a year? It was not a subject to be discussed, especially when that second wife stood right there.

Paloma felt the blood drain from her face and saw the triumph in her cousin's eyes. An afternoon of slights was about to be avenged.

Only if I allow it, Paloma advised herself. What would Marco have me do? He would have me kill you with kindness.

She pressed her hand against her cousin's belly and felt the child within kick back. Paloma smiled, because it *was* a miracle, no matter how unpleasant the vehicle. She patted Maria Teresa's obvious evidence of her own fertility. "How sweet. I hope someday that I will be as fortunate as you are. I pray to the Virgin daily over the matter." Paloma removed her hand and walked into the kitchen with her head held high, even as her heart broke.

"SUCH FORBEARANCE," HER SISTER-IN-LAW said much later, as the two of them prepared for bed. "If you had snatched out every hair on her head, you would have had a roomful of willing accomplices." She unbuttoned Paloma's dress. "Why oh why did Maria *say* that?"

"I would never give my cousin the satisfaction of knowing that her darts struck home," Paloma replied, pulling on her nightgown. All she wanted to do was crawl into Luisa's bed and not wake up for three days.

"*Pobrecita*," Luisa murmured. She pulled back the covers for Paloma. "I didn't fetch my first son until seven months of marriage, if that is any consolation."

It wasn't, but Paloma loved her sister-in-law. She settled into bed with a sigh. With a yawn, Luisa joined her.

Luisa laughed. "Funny how no one wants to share a room with your odious cousin. Did you see how fast the Borrego twins and their sister Refugio insisted that they enjoyed sleeping three to a bed?"

Paloma had noticed. She also noticed how the light went out of her cousin's eyes when everyone paired off and left her all by herself in a room for two. Anyone would acknowledge that the woman only got what she deserved, tit for tat, but Paloma couldn't help—and barely understood—her own sympathy. "She is not a happy woman."

Maybe this was a good time to ask Luisa about the afternoon's treatment of her cousin. "Everyone ignored her. Some even laughed behind their hands. What is it that amuses everyone about my cousin?"

Luisa stared at her. "You don't know? You, of all people?"

"Me, of all people, I suppose," Paloma replied, puzzled. "What did she do?"

Luisa looked around as though the room were full of scribes taking notes, and whispered the tale of how Maria Teresa Castellano had evacuated her bowels right on her own doorstep last year when Marco and her husband Alonso brought the news that Comanches had been killing their cattle.

Paloma sat up in bed and stared at her sister-in-law through the gloom. "I never heard a word of this from Marco!" She sank down in bed, remembering the incident of the cattle. "But ... but ... only a few days later, Alonso's own herder confessed to the deed. It wasn't Comanches."

"No, indeed, but the damage was done." Luisa giggled, then turned her face into the coverlet. "So Marco never said a word?"

"You know my husband—your brother—is too much of a gentleman to mention such a thing." She thought a moment. "The servants!"

Luisa nodded. "The word spread from the housekeeper, who delegated two servants to clean up Maria's mess." She counted on her fingers. "Up and down Valle del Sol it went, everywhere but the Double Cross, I gather."

Paloma slowly let out her breath. "I was so afraid of Maria Teresa when I came here, but I knew that at some point she would muddy her nest." She laughed into her sister-in-law's shoulder. "Never did I think she would do it literally!"

They chatted a few more minutes in companionable conversation until the sentences stretched farther and farther apart and then stopped. *I miss you, Marco,* Paloma thought as she closed her eyes, *but think of all the socks.*

SHE WOKE AS THE room was beginning to lighten, startled to see Luisa dressed and bending over her. There was an unreadable expression on her face that had Paloma reaching for her dress as she threw back the coverlet in one quick motion.

"Luisa, what—"

"The guard sent an alarm to my housekeeper. Hurry."

Even in the low light of dawn, there was no mistaking Luisa's pallor. Paloma yanked on her dress. Barefoot, she let Luisa Gutierrez drag her down the corridor and out the front door. Paloma shivered, but noticed that Luisa had not bothered with her cloak, either. Luisa ran to the wall and scrambled up the ladder, Paloma close behind her, every nerve on edge.

The guard pointed over the parapet and Luisa nodded, her eyes serious. She gestured to Paloma, who saw her fears and knew she was thinking of other desperate days.

"*Mira!* Is it your Comanche? Tell me quickly or my guard will shoot him."

Paloma squinted into the distance. "Don't shoot," she said. "I cannot tell yet, but it might be. Please don't shoot."

"He's too close. I'm shooting him," the guard said and raised his musket.

Paloma shoved him and the gun discharged in the air over her shoulder. Paloma reeled from the concussion and lost her balance when the guard jerked her around, his eyes wide with fright and something more. They steadied themselves, staring at each other.

"The *juez* was a fool to marry you!" the guard shouted in her face.

From beyond the gate she heard a man's voice call out, "Paloma, help me!"

"It's Toshua," Paloma said. The look she gave the guard must have been fierce because he backed away. "Open the gate."

She hurried down the ladder, not caring if every guard in the courtyard saw her bare legs and beyond. When the guard wouldn't lift the heavy bar, she yanked the smaller bar off the smaller man gate and stooped through the narrow opening. To her terror, it slammed shut behind her.

"Paloma, stop! It could be a trap." Luisa pleaded with her from the parapet.

She knew Luisa was right; she still couldn't see clearly. The Indian had called her name, but she was known in the valley now. She peered closer as she walked toward the man carrying a lance and stopped, thinking of her mother and remembering how Mama had squared her shoulders and walked toward an entire horde of Comanches. *Mama, you were braver than I*, she thought, her mouth suddenly dry. Staying where she was, she moved from one bare foot to the other, because the winter grass stubble hurt.

The Indian had a man slung over his lap, head down, hands trailing. The darkness began to lift, and she let out the breath she must have been holding since she opened the man gate, grateful to God. It *was* Toshua.

"Paloma, does this make four times you have saved my life?"

She ran closer now, unafraid, even though the danger wasn't over. "Make it five, Toshua," she said as she stopped directly in front of the horse and rider, her hands out in what she hoped was a commanding gesture to stop the guards who had not lowered their weapons.

Paloma looked over her shoulder at Toshua and the burden he bore. She sniffed. The man had either been dead for days or smelled worse than a herd of javelinas. Gingerly, she patted the foul lump of rags.

"I'm alive," the man said in Spanish so poorly accented she wondered where he had come from. Did they speak Spanish on Mars?

She was on sure ground now. "You are headed for a bath, señor," she told him, then smiled at Toshua. "You remember your own bath, I trust?"

"I remember," her Comanche said. "You need not remind me. You cut my hair, too."

"Open the gates," she called up to the guards, still poised to shoot. Even though she was barefoot and trembling, and her nighttime hair wild around her face—Marco would have laughed—Paloma willed herself tall and brave.

Her heart went out to Luisa Gutierrez, too soon a widow because of a morning much like this one. Her sister-in-law stared at her from the parapet, then put her hands over her face. *I am sorry, my dear*, Paloma thought.

"If the *juez de campo* were here, he would tell you to open the gates in the name of the crown," she said, speaking most distinctly. "This is *my* Indian and there is a wounded man. Do as *I* say."

Chapter Four

In which a stranger is too close for Toshua's comfort

WHEN THE GATES OPENED, Toshua handed her the reins and she led him and his stinking burden through the gates. As frightened women and servants began to fill the courtyard, he bent down and spoke to her alone. "You are the *juez* now? Your man will know about this before another day passes. I know you Spanish. Word travels faster than smoke."

"Don't be silly," she whispered back, not surprised that everyone in the courtyard kept their distance, including the guards. Paloma looked at the man in Toshua's lap. "Who is he? Where did he come from?"

The Comanche dismounted. "He was staggering around in the *arroyo seco* beyond the hay stacks." He ignored the crowd that had gathered as he took Paloma by the arm and kept her moving toward the stables. "To show you the measure of his desperation, he did not back away from me."

Luisa's guards stood their ground by the stable door until Paloma fixed them with a stare that she borrowed from her absent husband, the stare that made people do what he ordered. *Please let it work*, she prayed silently. *My arsenal of stern looks is limited.*

Maybe it had worked. One guard turned away, his shoulders high with disapproval. The other gestured them inside the stables, his hand on his sheathed dagger.

The stranger was a small man. Toshua took him by the back of his filthy coat and slid him off the horse, while Paloma steadied him, turning her head away because he reeked.

The stranger shook his shoulders, which Paloma took as a sign to let go.

Happy to oblige him, she backed away, but not too far, because he swayed, then held out his hand to her. She took a shallow breath, then put her arm around his waist and led him to a grain bin, where he perched, looking around and blinking his eyes.

"I have not been inside a building in six months," he told her. At least she thought that was what he said.

"What is your name?" she asked.

"Antonio Gil," he replied.

"Antonio? I doubt that," she said. "I really do. Your Spanish is awful."

In spite of his obvious exhaustion—she saw no fear—the stranger managed a smile. "Should I say Anthony Gill instead? I am from Georgia."

"Gill. Gill. Guh?" She couldn't even pronounce it.

As it turned out, Anthony Gill couldn't manage ten steps on his own. With Toshua on one side and Paloma on the other, he made slow progress toward the hacienda, where Luisa stood, eyes wary, her mouth pressed in a firm line that reminded Paloma of Marco.

"Please, dearest, he needs food and a bath," Paloma said to Luisa, then stepped back in surprise as her cousin Maria Teresa ran from the hacienda, screaming, pushing the other women aside in her panic.

"Where did everyone go? What is wrong?" Teresa shouted. "Why is everyone …." She gasped, her hand to her mouth, and stared at Toshua.

Paloma gaped at her cousin as she flattened herself against the wall of the hacienda, her eyes huge, her thin face draining of color.

"Teresa, there is nothing to fear," she said, wondering at so much terror for no reason. Her cousin had missed the whole crisis, and look at her. What harm could one dirty man and an Indian cause, in a hacienda full of Luisa's guards and all the guards who had come with the other women?

Before Paloma could defend herself, Teresa darted forward and grabbed her hair, loose around her shoulders. She yanked on it, jerking Paloma away from the stranger and the Comanche. Paloma's eyes filled with sudden tears from the pain. She tried to grab Teresa's hand as her cousin's fingernails dug into her scalp. Why was she doing this?

"Teresa, he is harmless! So is Toshua. Please let go," she pleaded. "You're hurting me."

Her cousin gave her hair another yank, which sent Paloma to her knees, her hands clutching Teresa's fingers, trying to lessen the pain. Toshua dropped the stranger in the dust and unsheathed his knife in one smooth movement, his eyes intent upon the hysterical woman. Paloma felt strands of hair pull loose from her scalp as she reached for Toshua—now to stop him. "No, Toshua, no!"

Teresa screamed again, looking around wildly as her audience gaped at her. "You see? You see? Paloma's Comanche wants to kill me! I have witnesses!"

"He wants you to let go of Paloma's hair," Luisa said as she finally grabbed the distraught woman. "What is the matter with you, Señora Castellano?"

To Paloma's relief, Teresa let go of her hair. She sank back, patting her head where it hurt the worst. "There is nothing to fear," Paloma said, wondering how to reason with this cousin whose torments she had endured for years, this cousin she thought she knew—unkind and vengeful but essentially harmless.

"My dear, you should lie down," she said, wishing she did not sound so timid. This was not the voice of a *juez de campo's* wife. Maybe she was foolish to think she could borrow some of her husband's power.

"You *would* say that!" Teresa shot back. "I let down my guard and this Comanche devil murders us all! You would like me to lose this baby, would you not? This is your fault. You are barren and you are jealous of me." Her cousin looked around again, as if to seek approval from people already turning away in disgust. Two of the braver women—older women who had lived their entire lives on the edge of danger in Comanchería—had helped Anthony Gill to his feet and were leading him inside.

Paloma saw the sympathy in their eyes, but all she felt was shame that Maria Teresa was a relative, and horror that her cousin thought her capable of such meanness. "You know I would never even consider such a thing," she said, keeping her voice soft as she sought to reason away her cousin's lunacy.

"You planned this whole thing!" Teresa clutched her belly and backed away from Paloma. "Rodrigo! Saddle my horse!" she shouted to her only guard, who stood there as stunned as everyone else. "I will tell Antonio how dangerous you are and he will pay a visit to your husband!"

"That is enough," Luisa said. She tightened her grip on Maria Teresa. "Let us gather your possessions. You should leave."

"You cannot reason with a crazy woman," Toshua told Paloma, helping her to her feet. For good measure, he turned to stare at Teresa as her hostess dragged her inside. Whimpering under his glare, Teresa hurried ahead of Luisa. "I could ride ahead and kill them both before they were a league away. Just say the word." His face hardened. "I doubt even her husband would mourn her."

"No, Toshua. That will not solve any of my problems," Paloma said firmly.

The Comanche shrugged. "It would solve the main one." He looked around. "We are all tired of Señora Castellano."

"Just let her go and do no harm," Paloma said. Her head ached, but it was nothing compared to the ache in her heart. *Tell the world that I am barren?* she asked herself, wretched. *The world already knows.*

They stood together in the courtyard, nearly shoulder to shoulder, waiting while Rodrigo, looking like the most put-upon of men, saddled his mount and

Maria Teresa Castellano's horse. He kept his head down as the other guards teased him, making whooping noises that turned Toshua's expression sour.

"My People do not sound like that," he muttered to Paloma.

No, you don't, she thought, remembering the day the Comanches rode through the open gates of her father's hacienda near El Paso, silent, painted men sitting so carelessly on painted and masked horses, careless because the men in the field—her father and brothers among them—were already lanced and scalped. She glanced at Toshua and looked away, uneasy even after more than a year of his presence on the Double Cross.

When she didn't say anything, he turned away. She looked toward the open gate, yearning for her husband with a fierceness that surprised her, even though only a day had passed since they kissed goodbye in Santa Maria. She knew he would sit her on his lap until she was calm. It was what he already did every four weeks when she went to the storeroom and returned with her monthly supplies and tears on her cheeks. "Patience, *chiquita*, patience," he used to tell her. Now he just held her in his arms. She wanted him right now.

Maybe Toshua understood. "She said some unkind things to you, Paloma," he said, his voice softer now. His eyes never left Maria Teresa's outrider as he led the two horses into the courtyard. "Hard words."

"Just words."

"Will she cause you trouble?"

"If she can." Involuntarily, she stepped even closer to Toshua as Maria Teresa hurried from the hacienda, her satchel in her hand and yarn trailing behind her. It would have been a funny sight, except that Paloma saw real terror on her cousin's face. *I doubt she has a single easy day in Valle del Sol,* Paloma thought, wondering at her own pity for her cousin.

Maybe her cousin misinterpreted her expression. Maria Teresa glared in her direction and Paloma steeled herself. All her cousin did was shake her finger. Maybe Toshua standing so close had something to do with that.

Maria Teresa threw her satchel at the guard, who made a face as he turned away to tie the bundle behind his saddle and stuff the yarn in here and there while the other men laughed. When none of the idlers in the courtyard offered to help her mount, she shrieked at her guard for being dead to duty.

"How terrible a thing to work at the Castellano ranch," Toshua said. "I hear that Señor Castellano cannot keep men on his property." He gathered the reins and stood there, indecision on his usually impassive face.

"Perhaps you should return to the Double Cross," Paloma suggested, feeling uneasy, because Toshua never appeared indecisive. He had the look of a man who had just realized something unpleasant. What, she did not know.

"I have four guards," Paloma reminded him gently.

"I wish you had not touched the stranger from the east."

"You needed my help," she said, puzzled now.

"All the same …." He turned away with his horse toward the horse barn, where the other guards moved far away from him. When he was close to the barn, he turned around again and mounted, riding his horse to Paloma, no indecision on his face now.

She stood her ground as he halted the big bay directly in front of her and held out his hand. "Come with me to the Double Cross. I fear I have done a bad thing in taking this stranger within Señora Gutierrez's walls." He gestured with his fingers, edging closer, coaxing her. "Do you trust me?"

It was the question Paloma had asked herself for months now. Her mouth felt strangely dry. She looked into his eyes, still seeing the honest man through all the layers of her own fear.

"Please, Paloma. Just drop everything here."

"The yarn. My stockings. Luisa."

He shook his head and leaned closer, his arm extended, ready to gather her onto his horse.

She stepped back. "I do not trust you, Toshua. God help me, but I do not."

There was no disguising the hurt in his eyes, which brought tears to her own, as she tumbled into the dust whatever trust they had so tentatively forged. He leaned down, and she backed farther away until she was under the shelter of the portal and practically in the doorway. "I do not," she whispered. "God forgive me if I am wrong."

The guards of the hacienda were edging closer, themselves, sensing a threat to Paloma that she knew was not there. *This is a matter between me and Toshua*, she wanted to tell them, but she knew they would not understand. Someone made a move toward the open gate. "Please leave, Toshua, before you cannot," she begged him.

He edged closer. "Do this and do not doubt me. Stay far away from this man I have brought here and probably should have killed."

Paloma nodded, not able to look at him, because she was already feeling remorse so deep that there probably wasn't a word for it. "Ride, Toshua."

Chapter Five

In which a stranger ponders his situation and Paloma regrets hers

HER HANDS TO HER mouth, Paloma watched Toshua wheel his horse and dig his heels into the animal's flanks. The guards had gathered closer, some of them as indecisive as she was, and others with their swords already drawn. Another began to run toward the open gate, where a small boy stood, pushing against one of the massive doors, which slowly began to shut.

Dios, what have I done? Paloma asked herself as her heart thundered in her breast. In a few seconds Toshua would be trapped and surrounded. She knew he would fight, but there were too many.

She watched in horror and then amazement as Toshua, guiding his horse with his legs, reached for an arrow behind him, fitted it to his bow in one motion and shot at the boy.

The child wore a loose-fitting poncho. The arrow slammed into the fabric and nailed him to the gate so he could not push. His mouth opened and closed in terror as he tugged on the poncho, the gate forgotten.

As soon as he had loosed the arrow, Toshua dropped to the far side of his horse, away from the hacienda's guards, until only his heels could be seen. They had no target, and the boy at the gate was powerless to trap him. One second, two seconds, and the nearly invisible Comanche raced through the gate and vanished. Even his horse's hooves seemed to be silent.

Paloma sagged against the doorframe. She put her head down in shame, knowing that she would see the hurt and disappointment in Toshua's eyes in her dreams. *What have I done?* she asked herself again.

She dragged herself inside the hacienda, her misgivings multiplying with every step she took. *Don't show it*, she ordered herself, as she looked in the *sala* where the women had tidied themselves after a hasty awakening and were beginning to knit again. It would have been easy to skulk down the hall and hide herself in Luisa's room, but she could never do that to Marco Mondragón, the husband she adored.

She stood in the doorway, her hands clasped in front of her, as her mama had taught her. "I deeply apologize for any disturbance that my cousin may have caused," she said, holding her head high, looking around the room at the ladies who had suddenly given her all their attention. She looked for meanness and found none.

One of the Borrego twins—she must learn to tell them apart—put down her knitting and patted the empty space beside her. "You have been too busy to knit socks for the *juez*," she said. "Sit here and knit, or he will have bare heels this summer. Is that your yarn over there? Fetch it, Dolores," she asked her twin.

Ah, then this was Chaca. "Thank you, Chaca," Paloma said and sat down, her heart full. She smiled her thanks at Dolores and continued where she left off.

"Paloma, take it from me," said an older woman, someone from an outlying hacienda she did not know. "A year and few months is no shame or crime. You will yet give the *juez* a child or two."

"Or three," said Cecilia Chávez, from her seat closest to the fireplace, as suited the oldest among them. She looked around at her friends. "Some say the water from Rio Santa Maria explains why there are so many children here, but we do not think it is the water." The other ladies chuckled, the crisis of Maria Teresa over. "As for your regrettable cousin, too little cannot be said about her."

Paloma winked back her tears in the face of such kindness. *And the Comanche who thinks he must protect me? How do you feel about him?* she wanted to ask, but hadn't the courage. She turned her attention to the mohair stocking. If she couldn't be wise, at least she could be diligent.

She began to relax as her fellow knitters returned to idle conversation and laughter, and marveled how much more cheerful everyone seemed, now that Maria Teresa Castellano had left. *She will probably whine and cry and nag Alonso until he pays a visit to my husband to complain about me or Toshua, or the cold weather, or the axis of the earth, or some other imaginary slight,* Paloma told herself, as she dropped stitch after stitch. She put her hands in her lap, telling herself to stop her crazy-making thoughts.

It seemed that the only thoughts she had were ones determined to send her walking up and down in the *sala*, if only she dared. She was not certain if she had angered Toshua or saddened him. "Just go back to your plains," she whispered, barely moving her lips. "That's all I want."

She stared at the stocking in her lap. She was making a muddle of it, and mohair was too dear to waste. When Luisa's *cocinera* came into the *sala* with a pitcher of steaming hot chocolate, followed by a little child staggering under a mound of tasty *pan dulces*, Paloma used the distraction to excuse herself.

Luisa must have known she would do precisely that. She stood in the hall as though waiting for Paloma, her face solemn.

"Come with me, dearest," she whispered. "I do not know what to make of this man."

WASHED CLEAN AND FULL of posole and buttered bread so tender his eyes filled with tears, Anthony Gill felt his eyes begin to close. The bed was soft, the room was warm, and he had not been warm in weeks. There was no wind to blow snow and dirt into his eyes and chap his lips. He even wore a man's nightshirt, something that had not dignified his body in more months than he could count. He sniffed at the collar, which smelled of camphor. Whoever wore this nightshirt had not worn it in years, if the camphor and permanent creases were any indication. It was much too large for him.

The woman had introduced herself as Luisa Gutierrez. When he finished eating, she had gestured to the servant to remove the dishes he had practically licked clean. He almost stopped her from whisking away the one slice of bread he couldn't finish, then reminded himself that if he ate so well now, there would probably be more food later. This was not a poor house.

When the servants finished, she followed them, returning behind other servants, who carried a wooden tub and brass buckets of hot water. When the tub was full, she left a towel and cloth beside it, an Indian pot with soft soap, and the nightshirt. He stripped himself naked before the door had barely closed. The water was bliss, and the soap a scarcely remembered luxury. Even though the soap stung cuts and scrapes he hadn't even been aware of, he gritted his teeth and scrubbed himself until he must have removed a layer or two of epidermis. He thought of earlier years and better times, and shook his head at his own foulness.

Anthony knew he had lice and wasn't sure what to do about it, until he noticed a pair of sheers and a fine toothed comb beside the nightshirt on the bed. He had quit blushing years ago, but the knowledge that this obviously gentle lady knew his predicament made his face hot. He dried off and wrapped his towel around his middle. Leaning over the well-used tub of water that had a shiny film on it now, he combed and cut. It was a poor job, to be sure, but the lady of the hacienda was too hospitable for him to leave a host of unwelcome guests for her, once he quit the place.

She had thoughtfully left a small pot of white salve. He sniffed it, discerning more camphor and something tart and grassy. Maybe it was sage. Whatever it was bit into the nicks on his scalp, but he rubbed it in, relieved to be free of the little pests that had accompanied him all across Texas.

He undid the towel and looked at his hairiness down there, wondering if his privates should receive the same treatment. He decided they should, and cut more carefully. He knew his balls were going to itch like billy-be-damned when the hair came in again, but maybe that was the price of being a guest in the Gutierrez hacienda.

When he had done all he could without resorting to the finer tools in his leather medical satchel, Anthony shrugged into the nightshirt and crawled between sheets smelling of more sage and civilization, and the fine hand of masterful housewifery.

"Oh, this is better," he whispered and closed his eyes.

He had almost composed himself for sleep when the door opened and Mistress Gutierrez came in again, followed by the younger woman who had stood so bravely in front of the Comanche's horse, when things weren't looking too sanguine for him or the Indian. From under his eyelids, he assessed the woman more closely, admiring her slim shape. His professional eye had already told him that the older woman had been made a mother several times over. This younger one, probably not.

She had wonderful brown hair, maybe even with a touch of bronze in it. She kept her distance, but he could not mistake her vivid blue eyes. For so many months he had seen nothing but black hair and dark eyes. Not that he had minded dark hair and olive complexions—after all, Catalina and Pia Maria looked more like the Gutierrez woman. This one was different, and he appreciated the difference.

Anthony watched them as they conferred at the doorway, their heads together. They didn't appear to be related, but they obviously stood on good terms with each other. They both looked at him, and finally Luisa Gutierrez came closer.

"The servants will remove all of this," she said. "I intend to burn your clothes and I will have no argument."

Her Spanish was precise and easy to follow, and he did not doubt that she would do exactly as she said. He was clean and comfortable and did not want that set of circumstances to change, at least until he had a good night's sleep. He had been thrown out of meaner establishments because of the sin of being English.

He nearly smiled as Mistress Gutierrez picked up his foul garments with forefinger and thumb and held them away from her. The other woman came into the room far enough to take a well-darned sheet from the carved chest by the door. She spread it out, and the mistress of the household dropped his disgusting smallclothes in the center. His shirt and breeches landed next on the reeking pile.

There was no disguising the distaste on her face when she picked up his coat, the leather one he had patched and re-patched and then patched the patches as he had made his slow way across Texas's winter landscape with the traders. She hefted it, then gingerly reached into the pocket and pulled out his smaller surgical kit, the little leather pouch that contained his few knives, bistouries, a flensing box, and his sole remaining needle.

She didn't untie the leather thongs that secured the heavy cloth around his knives, but put it on the table next to his satchel. She reached in again and pulled out the little tin that contained pus and scabs from the last dead trader.

"Stop, stop!" he said in English.

Startled, she looked at him, probably not understanding his words, but aware of his obvious concern. She set the tin next to his knives.

"Is there anything else of worth you wish to keep?" she asked in Spanish, her eyes wary now.

Anthony shook his head, and she finished gathering his remnants. She held up his pathetic socks and waved them at the young woman who had retreated to the doorway again.

"Do you want to give this raggedy *estranjero* one pair of socks you have knitted for your man?"

Ah, she was married. Well, of course she was, he told himself, wondering how it was that he could be three-fourths dead and wasted and still think about lovely women.

The little one nodded and left the room. When she returned, she held the socks out to him, then knotted them and lofted them toward the bed. He caught them one-handed, deciding to put them on after the ladies were gone. No one needed to see how skinny his hairy legs were.

Maybe it was time to try that Spanish that the little one already knew was accented so poorly. "Why do you not come closer?" he asked, doing his best.

"Señor, where are you from?" she asked.

"I'll tell you, if you come closer," he coaxed.

She shook her head. "Toshua told me not to."

"The Comanche?"

"Yes. Nurmurnah, Comanche, The People, what you will."

She stood her ground. Maybe he could tease her a little. "You prefer a Comanche to a white man?"

"*That* one."

So much for his charms. This one wasn't impressed. He thought she would leave, but she stood in the doorway and looked him straight in the eyes. She seemed to be measuring him, studying him. To his disappointment, she shook her head. It was only the slightest shake; he doubted she was even aware he had noticed. On some scale he did not understand, he, Anthony Gill, had been weighed in the balance and found wanting. *Well, join the line,* he thought, suddenly weary. *I haven't impressed anyone lately.*

He smiled at her, hoping she would stay, because he liked her. He had noticed her wedding ring; maybe he just couldn't help himself. "There is a husband to be reckoned with, eh?"

"Oh, yes. He would kill you as easily as look at you, if you prove dangerous."

Why couldn't he let this go? He shuddered elaborately. "I had better avoid him."

"I do not believe you can, señor. He is the *juez de campo* of this district. He will take an interest in you, because you are so obviously not from here."

That was plain enough. Anthony remembered the dying words of the pox-ridden trader. Was it time to inquire the whereabouts of one Marco Mondragón? Perhaps Señor Mondragón would keep him safe from nosy officials. He could ask a servant later, someone who might be more sympathetic than the pretty wife of the *juez de campo*, whatever that was. It appeared that his luck was as bad as ever. Or he could ask her. What harm would it do?

"Señora, I have been told to find Marco Mondragón. Do you know…?"

Her eyes widened, her amazement quickly replaced with wariness. "Marco is the *juez* and he is my husband."

Anthony sighed. His luck had not changed.

Chapter Six

In which a Comanche confesses and there is no absolution

CAUGHT IN THE ACT. Why couldn't it have been one of his servants, instead of Toshua? And why, after more than a year of the silent man's presence, was he still trying to impress a Comanche? It couldn't be done.

Blame the cat, who followed him about, now that Paloma was knitting socks and probably having a good time, and not even thinking about her husband pining for her. Only two days? He was lonely and put upon and now Toshua had caught him playing fetch with a cat.

"Shew, señor?" was all Toshua said, after he let himself go quietly into his office by the horse barn. "Shew?" And *de veras*, he was almost smiling.

It was too late to brazen it out, not with Chica carrying that little yarn ball in her mouth and dropping it at Marco's feet for another throw. "It's what Paloma says when she throws this little bit of yarn. Call me a fool and get it over with."

That was a definite smile, even if it was brief. Marco threw the yarn ball without benefit of *Shew!* and Chica ignored him. Marco shook his head and turned back to the latest brand report he was copying to take to Santa Fe in early autumn. He looked up after a moment. Toshua had not moved.

"What is the matter?" He tried to speak casually, but there was something he did not like in the Comanche's expression, some uneasiness around the eyes. "Paloma …."

If Marco expected reassurance from Toshua, he was doomed to disappointment. *Calm, calm,* he told himself. *You are an officer of the crown.* Easy to think, except that he was a husband first. He cleared the paper to one side and pointed to the chair Paloma usually occupied, when she knitted while he worked. "Sit."

Toshua sat in that funny, splayed-out way of someone still unaccustomed to chairs. He opened his mouth to speak, then closed it and looked away. "I have done a bad thing," he said finally.

Marco grabbed the Comanche's arm. The measure of the Indian's distress showed, because he did not resist Marco. "First tell me. She lives?"

"For now," Toshua replied, his face impassive, but his eyes far from it.

"*Dios mio*," Marco whispered. "*Dios mio*."

He sat in stunned silence as Toshua, looking him in the eyes now, told of finding a man staggering around the *arroyo seco* near Hacienda Gutierrez, and taking him to Señora Gutierrez. Marco closed his eyes when Toshua told of Paloma standing in front of his horse to ward off the archers from the parapet.

"I can never be out of her debt, señor, and what have I done?" Toshua did not even try to hide his own devastation. "Not until we were inside the walls, and Paloma and I had led the man inside the hacienda, our arms around him, did I remember what you told me about *la viruela* coming from the east."

"Did you tell Paloma about smallpox?"

"No. I tried to get her to leave with me, but then Maria Teresa Castellano, her horrible cousin, started making a racket because I was there, blaming Paloma for everything." His eyes narrowed. "I am missing more opportunities to kill that woman. This doesn't make me much of a Comanche."

"Maria Teresa! I doubt that my sister invited her." Marco walked to the fireplace. With some force, he tossed in another piñon knot. "Was this man … do you think he was diseased?"

"How can I know?" Toshua shook his head. "He was hungry and smelled bad, but I do not know …."

Who can tell? Marco asked himself as he stood by the fire, suddenly cold. Ten days or two days, and then the stranger might come down with smallpox, with Paloma sure to follow. "He could already be infected, and we wouldn't know, would we?" He spoke out loud, but the words were directed more to himself.

Apparently the Comanche grasp of incubation was non-existent, if Toshua's puzzled expression told Marco anything.

He didn't want to look at Toshua, or say another word. All he wanted to do was ride to Hacienda Gutierrez and confront this stranger. *I will kill him myself*, he thought, remembering Lieutenant Roybal's warning about people from the east. *At the very least, he will be jailed.*

But here was the Comanche, remorse scarring every inch of him, from the sorrow in his eyes to the way he slumped in the chair. "There is more?" Marco asked, not wanting to hear it, when all he wanted to do was ride to Paloma. "Come, Toshua. Tell me."

It took a long moment, reminding Marco all over again how different he was from the Indian. "I tried to get your woman to ride out with me, but she backed away. Said she did not trust me. Señor, I would never hurt her!"

Certainly you would not, but you are Comanche, Marco thought, stirred by Toshua's anguish. As he made an appropriately sympathetic face, Marco wondered if he would ever trust Toshua, either. *And yet we must learn to get along.*

He stared at his desk, the piles of papers going nowhere during the winter, but which still had to be filled out and stashed until his next trip to Santa Fe, where they would be wrapped in red tape and stashed somewhere else. Shuffle here, shuffle there—it was a fool's game in a land where Spain was losing control. Maybe control was gone already, and the news hadn't worked its way to the edge of the empire yet.

Irritated with himself, he stood up and went to the window. It was late afternoon and time to shutter the window against the night's cold. The sun was sinking low now but the moon would be full. They could see well enough to ride to his sister's holdings. They could be there by midnight. As he watched the sky, mulling over everything he had to do before he left and discarding all of it, the gate opened and in rode Alonso Castellano.

"*Dios,* I do not need that man in my face," he muttered. Too late. The closer Alonso rode, the more obvious was his former friend's indignation.

Toshua came to the window to stand beside him. He grunted, "Just say the word, señor."

"You know I will never do that," Marco assured the Indian, or maybe he was assuring himself. He waited, unwilling to open the door. Let Alonso bang on it. "I will give him five minutes, and then we will ride."

Bang, bang, then bang again, when Marco couldn't steel himself to open the door. If she were there, Paloma would be laughing and calling him a big baby. Later on, though, she would soothe away her words as she best knew how. He closed his eyes, remembering his puny assurance that he could keep his dear one safe from everything except disease. Why had he tempted the devil?

With Toshua right beside him—maybe he understood Marco's reluctance— the *juez* opened the door. Marco stepped aside to let the man enter, then gestured to Toshua. "Saddle our horses. We're riding," he said quietly. Without another word, he pointed to the chair the Comanche had vacated.

Sitting behind his desk, hoping to give himself some hint of power, he listened to Alonso Castellano rage and complain about the Comanche who terrified Teresa on purpose. Scarcely pausing for breath, he turned his attack on Paloma, who was unkind and jealous because his wife was with child and she was not. Marco did not believe a word of it, but he let the man spout forth until five minutes had passed. Then he stood up, interrupting Alonso mid-sentence.

"That's enough. You have dredged up everything you can possibly have to say against my wife and the Indian who protects her." He didn't raise his voice, or flail about with his hands, as Alonso was doing. An officer of the distant crown, all Marco hoped for was a tiny share of that majesty. It must have worked, because Alonso was suddenly silent.

"I will mention your concerns to Paloma," he told Alonso. "As for Toshua, I do not govern him. I also doubt that he deliberately set out to frighten Maria Teresa." He took a chance then, mainly because he was weary right down to his bone marrow of Alonso Castellano. "If your wife remains so terrified of Indians that she fouls herself, I would remind you: we live in a dangerous place and I cannot change that."

The reminder of Maria Teresa's reaction to Comanches last year brought Alonso up sharp. His indignation turned to embarrassment. After a few more muttered words, he turned on his heel and left. The dramatic effect was marred because the man fumbled with the door latch, unable to make the simple thing work. Marco crossed the room and flung open the door. "Go with God, señor," he said. Go with God, indeed! The Castellanos probably complained to Him, too.

The rudeness of his own thoughts sent him to his knees immediately, asking the Lord's pardon for such pettiness on his part. But he knew that wasn't why he had fallen to his knees. He crossed himself and prayed silently for his wife, petitioning Padre Celestial to do whatever He could to keep her safe. He crossed himself again but remained where he was, leaning his forehead against his desk. "I ask too much," he whispered, "but please, Father, someday a child."

THEY ARRIVED AT RANCHO Gutierrez at midnight—two cold, stiff, and silent men. Toshua had answered his questions about the stranger then added something of his own, before the cold made it hard to speak.

"Señor, he spoke Spanish, but not well. *I* have a better accent than he does."

"What does he look like?"

"Under all the dirt, he might have lighter hair than I have ever seen. His eyes aren't blue like hers, but they aren't green, either."

That was all either of them said before the cold drilled into Marco's forehead and Toshua pulled his poncho over his face until only his eyes were visible. Marco forced himself to think about practical matters: the spring lambing, coming in another six weeks and followed by new calves; his promise to send for the cobbler to make Paloma a pair of red shoes with heels. He had promised her red shoes after a particularly rousing celebration of his affection for her. "You've never seen me dance, my love," she had whispered into his chest. "Red shoes, and I will dance for you."

He couldn't help the groan that escaped him, then glanced at Toshua, embarrassed. He knew the Comanche had heard him, because he turned his head quickly before once again facing into the wind.

Snow was falling lightly when Marco forced his mouth to work and shout an announcement at the gates of his sister's hacienda. They opened immediately, almost as if Luisa—or Paloma, for that matter—had told the guards they would be arriving. Hands less stiff than theirs relieved them of horse duty in the barn. His face serious, Luisa's *mayordomo* ushered them both into the hacienda, not even blinking at the Comanche. That was a good thing, Marco decided. He doubted Toshua would have remained in the courtyard.

Luisa met him in the foyer, kissing his cheek. "You're too cold, little brother," she murmured, then stepped aside when Paloma, in her nightgown and her hair tangled, threw herself into his arms. He held her close, feeling her flesh and bones, assessing her as though she had been gone a month and not a mere two days. He could not help himself from thinking, *Are you strong enough to withstand a killing pox?*

Not even giving him time to shuck off his wool cloak and leather jacket, Paloma took Marco by the hand and towed him to Luisa's *sala*. He looked around, curious. On other years when he had dropped in on Luisa during the marathon sock knitting, the *sala* had been littered with individual mounds of stockings done and unfinished, ready for the women to begin again in the morning.

"Where are your knitters?" he asked Luisa, who had followed them into the *sala* but was looking over her shoulder at Toshua behind her. "Don't fear him, sister. Please. Not now."

"I will always fear him," she said, keeping her voice low. She looked around the *sala*, too. "After Teresa created such a scene this morning, no one felt like knitting." She gestured toward the shuttered and barred window. "And then it began to look like snow, so we ended early." She rested her hand on Paloma's back in a protective gesture not lost on Marco. "That woman ... that woman ... took all the fun out of our gathering."

"I assume then that you did not invite her."

"I would never have invited her!" Luisa said. She lowered her voice. "But once here ... oh, little brother, I do not have to explain the rules of courtesy to you."

"No, you do not."

Though tamped down to glowing coals, the fire still warmed the *sala*.

Marco removed his cloak and Paloma took it from him, much as she would have done at home. He unlatched the silver toggles on his leather *chaqueta*, then gestured for her to sit on his lap. He knew it was a forward thing to do, something he would never have done even in his own *sala*, if there were visitors, but Luisa was his sister, and he did not think she would mind. It hardly mattered; Paloma in a chair even right next to his would have been too far away.

Luisa gave them both a half smile. "So you see, brother, perhaps you did not need to make your cold ride. Matters are well in hand now because the troublemaker is gone."

He exchanged a look with Toshua, who squatted on his haunches by the door, far from Luisa. Alert, Paloma looked at them both. "I can tell there is more and it is worse," Paloma said. "Toshua insisted that I leave with him. Why was that?" She put her hand inside his *chaqueta*, against his shirt. "It has something to do with the stranger, does it not?"

"When I went to Santa Maria to confer with the lieutenant from Santa Fe, he warned us of smallpox heading our way from the east."

Paloma shivered and tightened her grip on him. "He was foully dirty and hungry, but that is all ...." Her voice trailed away as the implication struck her. "He could be infected? *O Dios.*" She looked across the room to the Comanche. "Did Toshua know this?"

"I told him after we left Santa Maria. He was not privy to the lieutenant's information."

"Why didn't you warn me?" she asked Toshua. "You just told me to stay away from him, but it was already too late, wasn't it?"

His eyes as troubled as hers, the Comanche nodded slowly. In one graceful motion, he rose from the floor and left the room. In a few moments they heard the outside door close.

"I do not know how much he understood, Paloma," Marco said, even as he wondered why he defended Toshua. "I suspect that The People have no idea of incubation periods." He gathered her closer. "I am afraid now."

She nodded then inched herself even closer to him like a small, burrowing animal. She sat up with a start, her eyes wide, her expression anxious. "But Luisa! She has been tending him. After Toshua told me not to go closer, I never went into his room at all. Luisa!"

Silently, Luisa left her chair and knelt on the floor by Paloma. She pushed up the long sleeve of her nightgown to expose her forearm and show what seemed to be a small incision. Turning her head slightly, she lifted the hair from her neck to expose pock marks left behind by *la viruela.*

"This incision?" she said, pointing to her arm. "I have been inoculated, which sometimes leave pock marks, too. Not always." She put her hand on

Marco's knee. "Have you not noticed similar scars on Marco's arm and hip?"

Paloma pressed her face to his chest now, her voice muffled. "He has all kinds of nicks and scars, Luisa." She couldn't help her sob. "What was one more to me?"

He kissed her hair, rocking with her, but he had to ask. "My love, what about you? I have never noticed such a scar on you. Have you been …?" He couldn't even finish the question.

She shook her head and he had her terrible answer.

Chapter Seven

In which Marco learns, if he had any doubts, how kind a woman can be, how cruel a man

PALOMA TOUCHED HIS HEART in a way that, if he lived to be an old man of sixty, he knew made him more fortunate than most men. She gave a great sigh that he felt all the way to his backbone as her tight grip on him turned into a caress. "Well, then, the Saints be praised that *you* are safe," she said. "I could not bear it if something happened to you."

He couldn't help himself then, as he bowed over her head and cried, the deep, wracking sobs he had not cried since returning nine years ago to his hacienda and finding Felicia and the twins dead of *el cólera*. Her arms tightened again, as she comforted *him*, soothed *him*, with little obvious thought to herself.

Through his misery, he heard Luisa leave the room and shut the door. His wife held him in her arms as he wept, then wiped his face with her nightgown.

"That's enough now, my love," she said. She gave his shoulders a little shake. "It won't matter now if I am in that stranger's room or not, will it? I want to talk to him. And it won't matter if you and I just curl up in bed and wait for dawn. No need to bother the stranger, is there?"

Whatever damage he has done to my love is already done, he thought in total misery. "We can let him sleep."

Weary in his body, heart, and mind, Marco shucked off his clothes and crawled into bed beside his wife. With hands quite practiced now, she massaged him until he forgot how cold and discouraged he was. They made slow and thoroughly pleasant love. The part of his brain that jumped up and down, tugged at him, and called him a churl for using her dear body to relieve his own pain was effectively quashed by the part that shrugged and fell wholeheartedly into Paloma's willing plan for his total comfort.

"There now. I dare you to stay awake," Paloma said, as practical as ever. Cold as it was, she didn't appear interested in hunting for her nightgown, which suited him. She wore too many clothes.

He couldn't help laughing at her. She shrieked when he grabbed her and blew a rude noise on her stomach. "Suppose someone hears us?"

"Who cares?" He pulled her close, gave her a more genteel kiss, then fell asleep holding her.

He woke up an hour later to the sound of weeping. She had turned away and muffled the sound with the blanket, but he heard her and it broke his heart.

"*Cálmate*. We'll think of something."

"What?"

"Something."

THE NOVELTY OF A bed with sheets and blankets meant that Anthony Gill slept later than usual. The blankets smelled of sage instead of manure, and no one kicked him awake. He was hungry, to be sure, but he knew there was food somewhere.

He sensed a man's presence in his room, so he kept his eyes closed. Only a few months with the traders from East Texas had taught him wariness. Suspicion had been his fickle companion for several years and he knew better than to tempt the fates that had already turned their backs on him.

He wondered about the man. At some point last night he had been roused from slumber by a woman's shriek. It brought him immediately upright in bed, every nerve on edge, until the laughter that followed made it obvious two lovers were hard at play. The lonely part of him wanted to listen, but he was too discouraged. Was this the lover?

Anthony lay there silently, then opened his eyes just enough to see. A man sat beside his bed, staring at the wall. From the frown on his face, he was looking inward rather than at anything. He had an elegant profile, with a handsome Spanish nose, straight and long, and deep set eyes. His high cheekbones hinted at a bit of *indio* in his background, but he was dressed as a Spanish rancher would dress, in leather breeches with a wool shirt.

As the room lightened, the man sighed and shifted his weight in the chair. He glanced toward the bed, and Anthony noticed eyes of an unusual light brown. *He knows I'm awake,* Anthony thought. *Could this be Marco Mondragón? He must have been the man sporting in the next bedchamber late last night. Lucky man to have such a pretty wife.* Anthony Gill's wife had been pretty, too, before the Comanches came. What they had left behind had made him recoil and run into another room, anything to avoid looking at so much brutality visited on one so fragile.

"Señor?"

Anthony happily left the past for the present. "I am Anthony Gill," he said. "Is there some water?"

Anthony watched the man's face and saw his slight smile at what he knew was his terrible accent. The Spaniard said nothing, but poured him a drink of water and handed it to him. Anthony tried to sit up, expecting no help, but found his heart touched when the man put his hand behind his back and raised him into a sitting position. He piled up two pillows, then sat back in his chair, watching Anthony with those unnerving light eyes.

Anthony drained the cup and handed it back.

"*Más?*"

Anthony shook his head.

"Then tell me about yourself, and it had better be the truth."

How will you know if it is not? Anthony asked himself. The man had a way of looking at him, measuring him. Best to tell the truth, or as much of it as seemed plausible. He knew he was a good liar.

Anthony opened his mouth then closed it as the older woman came into the room with a tray, followed by the one he knew was Paloma, the wife of this Spaniard. She sat down beside her husband, her hand naturally seeking his. She was calm and lovely, but her eyes looked troubled. There it was—she gave him a shy glance, then looked at him full on. She had done the same thing last night. He found himself appraising her as a physician would. That initial tentative glance told him she had not always been treated kindly. Her fortunes had evidently changed, if she was the woman who shrieked last night and then laughed. He thought she was.

"Eat slowly," the older woman said. Señora … Señora Gutierrez, he remembered from last night. She touched the younger woman's shoulder. "Dearest, should you be here?"

"It doesn't matter."

She spoke so quietly, then turned her face into her husband's sleeve. After a moment calming herself, she stood and followed Señora Gutierrez from the room. Anthony looked at the man, who seemed to be caught up in the same emotion as his wife, and suddenly he understood.

"I am Anthony Gill, late a resident of Louisiana," he began. Georgia could wait, until he knew how the wind blew. "Who are you?"

"The man you think I am. Apparently you have been looking for me. I am Marco Mondragón, this district's *juez de campo*. You're not telling the whole truth."

Damn, but he was good. Anthony knew he was only alive this far because he could lie. The *juez* seemed to have more skills than other of his countrymen. "I am from the colony of Georgia, on the coast of the Atlantic."

"That's better, but tell me now: exactly what did you see as you crossed Texas?"

"Bodies in heaps, dead of smallpox." Anthony had lied so long that he couldn't resist exaggerating.

The *juez* didn't even blink, but his naturally downturned mouth seemed to droop farther. When Mondragón leaned back in his chair as though all the bones in his back were gone, Anthony knew he would win this one, his first victory in years. He never thought he would be grateful for that last trader who died full of smallpox inside and out, but the dying man had sent him to the right person. *Maybe I should have at least spread a little dirt over that miserable piece of human wreckage*, Anthony thought. He waited for the question he knew was coming, because this was an intelligent officer of the crown.

"Are you inoculated?"

Ah, yes. "I am, señor. That is why I am not dead."

Was that a look of disappointment? Was it the look of a husband who wonders why a smelly trader should be so blessed, while the dearest treasure of his heart was not? More than likely.

The *juez* took his time. "We have been warned of *la viruela* approaching from the east, and here you are," he said finally. "The officer from Santa Fe on his annual *progreso* gave me full powers to prevent any Indians from coming into Santa Maria, and to kill them at my discretion. You, too, Señor Gil. Tell me why I should not do precisely that."

Here it was; better pause and take his time. "Señor Mondragón, I have been searching for my young daughter, Pia Maria. She will be four years old now. A year ago, my wife was raped and tortured by Penateka Comanches, who stole Pia Maria."

Anthony stopped, easily reading an expression that wasn't so inscrutable now. The Spaniard sighed. "We have all suffered. And did they trade her to other People farther west?"

"Aye, sir," he began, lapsing into English, which earned him a puzzled look. "*Sí*, they did. I allied myself with traders and went in search of her."

"Really?" Mondragón asked, his skepticism evident. "All hard living aside, I have never seen an ally of Spanish traders in such sorry shape as you."

"I was not precisely an ally of the traders," Anthony admitted. "I did their menial work. They kicked me and beat me whenever they felt like it."

Anthony said it matter-of-factly. There was no point in whining about his mistreatment by men who traded, gambled, and whored in the same room with him, filthy and foul.

Señor Mondragón had obviously heard tales similar to his, because his expression did not change. "And have you located your daughter?"

"Quite possibly. The traders knew of a deep and long canyon controlled by Kwahadi." He laid out his whole hand. "Señor, I have been searching for you because I have been told you are the man who can get me there."

Mondragón shook his head, much as Anthony thought he would. The man was no fool.

"I know of no white man who has ever been there. Granted, we are improving relations with the Kwahadi since the death of Cuerno Verde, but our good intentions are still as shaky as a baby trying to stand. Maybe in a year or two I can help you. I'm sorry, but that's where the matter must rest, especially while *la viruela* stalks the plains."

Draw it out and make him suffer, Anthony thought. *You know you don't like him any more than the others.* "*La viruela* is going to kill your wife."

Anthony may have overplayed his hand. He hadn't thought the *juez* would move so fast, and with his knife drawn. Anthony hadn't even heard it leave its sheath, but there it was, the point against his throat. He held his breath.

"Damn you, Señor Gil," Mondragón said, his voice practically quivering in his anxiety. His hand, however, was rock steady. "Tell me why I should not push in this blade and silence you?"

"Because I am a physician, *un médico.*"

The knife clattered to the floor, and the *juez* sank back into his chair with a noticeable *whoof* of the leather cushion. He passed a shaking hand in front of his eyes. Anthony rubbed the spot where the blade had left a nick.

He watched Mondragón, interested to know this man, and how he could play him. He knew the *juez* was not stupid. There it was—the relief gone, the bleakness back.

"What good can you possibly do my darling? Can you cure *la viruela* when it strikes? I doubt it supremely. No one can."

"I cannot," Anthony agreed. This had to be good, and he took his time. "What I *can* do is prevent it. I scraped some scabs from that trader. Over there in that tin box. I can inoculate your wife."

The air went out of Marco Mondragón in a *whoof*, as it had gone out of the chair. "Thanks be to God," he said, his voice barely above a whisper. "How soon?"

Anthony slapped down his last card, the winning card. "As soon as you promise me you will take me to that canyon so I can find my daughter."

Silence. Anthony knew he was being weighed and found seriously wanting. The shame of it might have bothered him two years ago, but nothing bothered him after seeing Catalina Gill crammed onto a Comanche lance, probably while she was still alive, the iron tip coming out of her skull. He matched him stare for stare.

"There is no honor in you, is there?" Mondragón said finally.

"None whatsoever."

"If I do not agree, you will withhold treatment."

"Most certainly."

"Damn you."

"I assure you that has already been taken care of. Take it or leave it. If you think to try the inoculation yourself, you will kill her."

The *juez* flinched. He picked up his knife, fingered the blade and sheathed it. "I have no choice."

"I see none. I want Pia Maria. I will do anything to find her."

Anthony saw the defeat in Mondragón's eyes, also contempt that made his blood run in chunks. Obviously the Spanish had made contempt a fine art, more than the British who had driven him from Georgia. Maybe it was the light brown eyes that made the *juez* look so sinister. Anthony doubted Paloma ever saw that expression.

"Suppose you inoculate my wife for certain, and Toshua most probably, and my servants, and I change my mind after they are protected?"

Anthony had to give the *juez* credit. The man knew he had lost at the same time he had won his wife's life, but he wasn't going down without a struggle. Better now to flatter him a bit, if flattery it was. Probably it was just the truth, something Anthony had not considered for a long time. He had kicked truth aside on the Texas plains.

"Change your mind?" Anthony asked. "How can you? You are an honest man who would never go back on his word."

Another sigh, followed by a wry sort of smile or grimace. "You've trapped me."

"I was hoping to."

The *juez* stood up. He sheathed his knife and turned toward the door. His hand on the latch, he looked back. "Let me understand you better, since we are to be partners in a game so dangerous my courage almost fails me. You could have inoculated those traders, couldn't you?"

"Yes, once I had some live pox. By the time we reached the Clear Fork of the Brazos, I could have harvested scabs aplenty from dead Comanches." He shuddered. "They lined the banks, half in and half out of the water they thought would give them relief."

"Don't you doctors take an oath that compels you to treat the sick?"

"I hated those men and they mistreated me."

Mondragón nodded. "I can almost understand that. There are men I dislike, too. But you took an oath. You would also withhold inoculation from my dear wife, who never would harm you?'

"Most certainly, unless you oblige me, as you will now."

"You're a monster and a discredit to your profession."

Anthony did not flinch. "I am, indeed. I am a father and I will find my daughter."

With no hesitation, the *juez de campo* held out his hand to seal Anthony's devil's bargain. "You have my word, you bastard. When do we begin?"

Chapter Eight

In which Paloma and Marco realize they have married idiots

PALOMA BRACED HERSELF TO show a cheerful face to her husband when he came from the room of the stranger, Anthony Gill. She would tell him, if he hadn't already thought of it, to bar the Double Cross from any strangers and perhaps keep her safe that way. She could remind him that *la viruela* might not even reach their district. She could put a smiling face on the matter and tease him about borrowing trouble from tomorrow.

Her smile vanished even as she saw the latch going up. She could not fool this man who knew her inside and out, this man who seemed to breathe in rhythm with her. All she could do was stand there like the Spanish matron she was now, her head up, her hands clasped at her waist, wondering what would happen to her, and wondering how this good man could possibly cope with another death—hers this time.

The door opened. She thought she knew him, but there was such a look in his eyes. His mouth was set in what she feared was rage so barely contained that she took an involuntary step back. What on earth had Anthony Gill told him? She hesitated, then held out her hand to Marco.

He must have noticed her hesitation, because he calmed himself, even as she watched. He took her hand and it trembled in hers.

"What, my love? Surely there is nothing worse that Señor Gill could have told you than what we already know is coming our way."

Alert now, wary even, she watched his expression change into precisely that look of false good will that she had been thinking of practicing on him. This would never do. She grasped his hand and tugged him down the hall into

Luisa Gutierrez's *sala*, which she knew was empty now, all the knitters gone. He did not resist as she towed him along, a little woman dragging a tall man who put up no resistance. Good thing the governor could not see his *juez de campo* now.

She closed the door behind them and sat down on the earthen bench that was part of the inner adobe wall. She patted the spot beside her. When he sat down, she took his hand and clutched it to her breast. "What is it, Marco?"

He tried to smile, then obviously gave it up as a bad business. She could almost see him thinking something through; she knew him that well.

"I have very good news, my love. That man"—he nearly spit out the word, then collected himself with great effort—"that man is a physician. He has the capacity to inoculate you, and he will."

Paloma closed her eyes and felt herself melt like butter, so great was her relief. "*Gracias a Dios,*" she murmured, and touched her forehead to his shoulder. She opened her eyes and looked at him again, mystified by the expression of vast disquietude. Surely he should be happy at this news. True, inoculations themselves could be dangerous, but that was a chance everyone took. There must be more.

"What else?" she asked.

"Nothing else," he said too quickly. "We'll take him with us and see how many of our people, Toshua included, will agree to inoculation. We'll probably have to wait here a day while he inoculates my nephews, but then—"

She put her fingers to his lips, stopping the flow of words. "What else?" she asked again.

"Nothing else."

"Don't you dare lie to me!" She hadn't meant her words to come out with such force. He winced, and Paloma knew he had never heard that tone of voice from her before. Well, too bad. He was not telling her what was written so clearly in his eyes and in the way his hands still trembled. "Not to me, Marco. Not ever to me."

He leaned back against the wall, something he seldom did, this man who sat so straight, as though he were always in the saddle. He banged his head gently against the wall with increasing force until, horrified, she put her hand behind his head to cushion the blows. He stopped.

"What is he making you do?" she asked.

"Nothing."

She shook him. "If you don't tell me the truth right now, you can … you can sleep in the *sala* when we get home. I didn't marry a liar, and I certainly didn't marry a coward!"

He winced and put his hand over hers. "Paloma, you have a grip. Suppose I have a bald spot now?"

She let go, then deliberately stood up and sat on his lap, straddling him so he had no choice but to look her in the eyes. "Well?"

Her presumptuous action in a place not remotely close to their own bedroom startled him, a man of typical Spanish dignity and some rectitude. Maybe that was what he needed, Paloma reasoned, to yank him out of his peculiar state of mind. He blushed like the newlywed he wasn't. "I am not as brave as you are, Paloma Vega. We already know that. It's not *my* bloody sandals hanging in our *sala.*"

She sat back, hoping no one would come into the *sala* and see them like this, but less worried about propriety than she would have thought possible. She willed herself to sound conversational now, in light of his obvious distress.

"I'm staying here just like this until you tell me the truth. You think I cannot manage whatever you have to tell me? I watched my mother and my unborn brother die by degrees as I hid under her bed and tried not to scream. God help me, I could not look away. What can you possibly tell me that I cannot face?"

He made no effort to coax her into a less compromising position. His hands went to her bare thighs and finally stopped shaking.

"Are you so certain?" he asked, challenging her in his own turn. "It is this: in order for that, that *excuse* for a physician to do what he swore to do as a man of healing ...." He stopped and took several deep breaths. Paloma slid off his lap, tugged down her dress, and seated herself beside him now, her eyes intent on his.

"In exchange for your inoculation, I am to take that man onto the Staked Plains among the Comanche, our sworn enemy, to find his kidnapped daughter."

She just naturally went into his open arms. This was the man she knew. "How did you think you could ever hide that from me?" she scolded, but gently. "When you tipped your sombrero and rode east onto the Staked Plains ...." She took a deep breath and his grip on her tightened. "When you did that, did you think I might not notice?"

"You married an idiot, Paloma," he said, with something resembling his usual humor. "I could have warned you, but I didn't want to. I *wanted* you to marry this idiot."

She willed herself calm. "This is simply solved, husband," she said. "I will not be inoculated. He will have no power over you then."

For a long, long moment, he said nothing, just cuddled her close and kissed her ear. "This is puzzling, indeed, wife of my heart, body, mind, and soul. Shh. Shh. I did not know *I* had married an idiot. This is news to me of a startling nature. You *will* be inoculated if I have to tie you to our bed, sit on you, and not let you up until that foul physician finishes. Do not argue with me. In this I will not be moved."

What could she say? She knew he meant it. She took an equally long time to answer him, choosing her words just as carefully, because there was no telling if a man as stupid as he was would understand. "It appears we are both idiots. I will go along with this supreme silliness on your part only—and I mean only—if I accompany you onto the Staked Plains, too. Toshua and I. We will help that man of no character whatsoever find his daughter."

"I won't consider it," he said quickly. "You will *not* accompany me to the Llano Estacado."

"Then I will not be inoculated. If I die, you can remarry, and maybe your next wife will give you children."

Marco gasped and Paloma knew she had gone too far. She was the bigger fool. She knew it when he grabbed her hair in turn and yanked on it, as though to call her to her senses. When he spoke, it was in that low, passionate tone he reserved for lovemaking, only he was not wheedling or coaxing in a playful way. Her heart pounded in her throat as she suddenly grasped just how ferocious love could be.

"Understand this once and for all, my love, because I will not say it again. I did not marry you to get children. I married you because I love you. I will always love you, whether we are blessed with children or not. Don't say anything like that ever again." He let go of her hair and gathered her close.

"I won't," Paloma promised, her words muffled in his chest. "But I will go with you."

"Nothing terrifies you more than Comanches," he reminded her.

There now, the roughness was gone from his voice, but not the passion. She knew he was considering his own demands, this man who had been pummeled sorely by a physician, this man who wasn't used to being pummeled by anyone.

"One thing terrifies me more, my love—the thought of you without me and me without you. We are in this together. If we die, we die. Didn't Father Damiano say something about that when he married us?"

"I don't remember. All I could think of was how pretty you were in that green dress and white mantilla." He reached under her skirt and pinched the inside of her thigh. "And maybe other things."

"You realize you are hopeless."

"I know. Very well. I just made the devil's bargain with a bad man. I'll make a better one now with a good woman."

DIOS, REMIND ME TO make every moment count with Paloma Vega, became Marco's unspoken prayer for the day they remained at his sister's hacienda.

Luisa's sons offered no objection to their inoculation, but Marco did not allow any more until Anthony Gill assured him that there was plenty of live pox in the small tin for him to inoculate all of Luisa's servants who were not already immune to the pox, and then Paloma and all the servants of the Double Cross household.

Even though he knew she would not go back on her word, once given, Marco was dismayed when Paloma shook her head at Antonio Gil's summons to join him with Luisa and her sons. She went down the hall on silent feet and Marco listened for the door to Luisa's chapel to open and close.

Hands in his pockets, the physician watched her, then shrugged, turning away. Marco wanted to throttle him for his lack of empathy.

Marco eyed the small tin in his hand, and a little three-tined tool that resembled a fork. "That tin cannot hold enough live pox to do all you say."

"It does. Trust me."

"I don't trust you at all."

Antonio shrugged again. "Have it your own way, then. Once these inoculations have produced pox, I will have new scabs to harvest. I can inoculate all of Santa Maria. Watch me."

Marco nodded. "Inoculate Paloma right now, after you finish with my nephews. I'll be able to get her home, won't I?"

"Certainly, provided you can coax her out of the chapel." Once more, the physician looked in the direction Paloma had gone. "I used to believe in God," he said, more to himself than Marco.

Since she had burned all his rags, Luisa had given the tattered man clothes that had belonged to Ramon, her husband dead these seventeen years. The clothes didn't fit; Ramon had been a man of substance, and Antonio Gil had been starved for a long time.

Still, they were well-cut clothes, and the thin little man seemed to stand a bit taller. To Marco's skeptical eyes, Antonio Gil almost looked like what he claimed he was.

"The incubation period for smallpox is about ten days," he was saying, as he nodded to Juan and Tonio to pull up their sleeves to the shoulder. "For some reason, inoculation usually brings on the symptoms in five days. You can easily get Paloma home and I will come with you."

"And those symptoms are ..." Marco began. "I was young when this was done to me and I do not remember."

"A pain in the head, aching bones, nausea, fever," he recited. "The eruptions begin on the third or fourth day of symptoms and the scabs follow. With good luck the matter is resolved and the scabs drop off after a week. It is longer with a real case of smallpox. No one knows quite why."

Marco's nephews eyed the little man with identical expressions of terror and distrust. He almost smiled when his sister sat between them on the bench, the three of them crowded close together, as though they were much younger. She put an arm around each son, her expression brave, she who had been through so much.

"No one who hasn't been inoculated comes in this room now," Antonio said, screwing off the cap. "Who goes first?"

Chapter Nine

In which Paloma is more persuasive than she realizes

PALOMA WASN'T READY TO see him when Marco opened the door to the chapel. He knelt beside her on the cold tiles, as he did so often in their own chapel. Her eyes closed, she breathed in the familiar odor of his body.

"I would rather do this thing on the Double Cross," she said, when he rocked back on his heels and held out his hand to her.

"Señor Gil says it must be now, since he has uncapped the pox. We'll leave for home when he is done. He is coming with us. He just inoculated my nephews and the servants who have never been so treated, or already survived an encounter with *la viruela*."

"I don't like him."

"Nor do I."

Paloma saw how hard it was for him to be so helpless. She touched his cheek, and he instinctively turned his head to kiss her palm.

"No matter how we feel about this man, I am depending on you to convince Toshua to be inoculated," he said.

She couldn't help the tears that welled in her eyes suddenly, tears that had nothing to do with the smallpox. "Marco, I hurt Toshua's feelings when I refused to leave with him yesterday. How can I convince him to do something he probably doesn't understand?"

"You must try." He gave her a level look. "He must be inoculated and he must come with us onto the Staked Plains. If he does not, we have no chance of success."

Of course he was right, and she did owe Toshua an apology. "Where is he right now? I will not be inoculated until I have apologized to him and convinced him to be inoculated, too."

"You're not just stalling?"

"No. I have given my word. I will let the physician do what he must," she reminded him.

He took her gentle rebuke with a wry smile, that smile she liked so well, because it was part of what made him so dear. "I last saw him heading for the horse barn. Shall I come with you?"

Paloma shook her head, kissed his cheek, and left the chapel. In the hall, Antonio Gil was just closing the door on her nephews' room. He gestured to her, but she shook her head.

"I have to convince Toshua to be inoculated. When I have done that, we will both return and then you may do what you will."

Poor man. He seemed not to be able to manage the slightest resistance to his will. "You will probably not convince him. What then?"

"I will convince him."

Antonio rolled his eyes and turned away, which irritated Paloma. For years she had suffered that kind of response from her horrible relatives. This time she decided not to let it go by. She raised her voice and spoke his name, so there could be no mistaking who she addressed. To her small satisfaction, he did look surprised.

"I mean what I say." She came closer. "Let me tell you: I don't like you for putting my husband in such a vice."

He shrugged, and she knew he mocked her. He turned to go again. Again she stopped him, but this time she kept her voice low.

"One more thing. Let me assure you of this: if you stay around me and my husband, especially my husband, you will become a better person."

He laughed. To her ears, it wasn't a mean laugh, but the laugh of someone taken off guard.

"You've been warned," she told him serenely, and continued on her way to the horse barn.

She found Toshua squatting on his heels in that Comanche way, against the outer wall. The thought crossed her mind that he was sitting outside in the cold just to feel sorry for himself. She took a deep breath and squatted beside him, so close that he could not ignore her.

"Forgive me," she began, with no preamble. "Should I have taken your hand when you tried to get me to leave here yesterday? Certainly. Can you be patient with me?"

He still wasn't looking at her, but Paloma knew she had his attention. She wanted to touch his arm, but her bravery did not extend that far, despite Marco's assertion that she was the bravest woman alive. *But I must be brave,* she told herself, and proved as much by reaching out slowly. She touched his upper arm and had to swallow down tears when he put his hand over hers and kept it there.

"Forgive me," she said again.

He did something then that took her breath away. He inclined his head toward hers until they touched. It was the briefest contact, but it moved her in ways she could never explain. *I need not fear this man,* she told herself.

With his hand still covering hers, she told him of the evil bargain that the physician had struck with her husband. "He is not a good man, but Marco and I must bend to his will. And if I must, you must. Toshua, we need you with us on the Staked Plains, if we are to have any chance of success." She sighed. "No, *any* chance of returning alive at all."

He was silent a long time, but she expected that. Several servants came and went from the horse barn, obviously surprised to see a Comanche and the wife of the *juez* crouching there together in the raw January wind. One of them stopped, but the fierce look Toshua gave the man sent him scurrying on. He would probably hurry inside to find Marco, but she knew Marco would leave this up to her.

"You know I have no power with my tribe anymore," he said finally. "My wives threw me over for a younger husband and told lies. I have been banished. How can I help you?"

How indeed? It was a good question. "I just believe you can," she said, not bothering with logic. "As it stands now, Marco and I and the physician will travel to the Llano Estacado after I have recovered from my inoculation."

"I am surprised that Señor Mondragón would permit you to accompany him."

"It was my bargain for my own inoculation. I cannot—I will not—allow him to go without me."

"Are you not afraid, little sister?"

She knew it was a slip of the tongue. Toshua's grasp of Spanish was good, but he had his lapses. "I am terrified," she said, and then could not hold back the tears any longer. She had been determined to persuade this man without resorting to womanly subterfuge. "I am even more terrified of a long life without Marco. We go together, and we need you."

"Even though I have no standing with my own people?"

She nodded. "Toshua, from what that foul physician has told us, there are Kwahadi, Penateka, and other Nurmurnah dead all across the plains from *la viruela*. We don't know what we will find, but the doctor might be a bargaining tool for you, too." She shrugged. "Or we could all die the first night on the plains."

Toshua grunted. She shivered, and for the first time he seemed to realize how close they were crouching together, facing the wind from the north and west. He stood up and held out his hand to her. With no hesitation this time, she took it. He led her inside the horse barn and they sat on the nearest bench. He looked around, a slight smile on his face.

"You are a careful woman, and not inclined to gamble," he reminded her.

"I will risk anything for Marco Mondragón," she said simply. She turned businesslike then, because time was passing. "I will be inoculated, and then you will be inoculated. And then we—"

He stopped her with his hand on her arm this time. "You will not think me less Nurmurnah if I say to you to I fear this thing?"

"I am afraid, too. We could die from this treatment, but if we live, we need never fear *la viruela* again."

"Tell me what that devil man will do."

She described the process as best she could. "This does not sound like a hard thing to do," he said.

Paloma hadn't considered that aspect. "I suppose it does not."

He sat back and folded his arms, suggesting to Paloma that he was about to strike his own bargain. She was not wrong.

"Señora Mondragón," he began quite formally, "although I do not understand how such a cut and mere thread can stop the Dark Wind, I will agree to this on one condition."

"Which is…?"

"When you have been inoculated, *you* will inoculate *me*. I trust no one else, and certainly not that foul sack of dung I rescued."

If this was a rebuke of her own failure to trust, so be it, Paloma decided. Minute by minute they were being drawn deeper into Antonio Gil's web. It was useless to struggle. She understood the greatest issue and nodded, even though she quailed inside. If he were here, dear Father Damiano would only remind her that her adventure continued.

"Very well. Let us go inside. I am cold."

DOESN'T THIS SILLY WOMAN know that we must hurry?

Anthony couldn't help himself. As he paced in the hall, he wondered if he would ever look at medicine as anything but a business. Probably not. Why was she taking so long?

He heard a door open and close, and then the *juez de campo* stood there at the end of the hall, just watching him. It was hard to tell about Spaniards, with those heavily porched eyes that could look so menacing. Maybe he didn't mean to be menacing, because Spaniards were a strange breed. What wasn't hard to tell was the man's utter devotion to his wife. Anthony felt a momentary pang, because he knew he had gotten in the way of that devotion with his demand. The moment passed, as he knew it would.

The man wasn't going to say anything. *Damn him for making me uncomfortable*, Anthony thought. "Where's your wife? I have to do this."

He hadn't meant to sound so peremptory. All it earned him was the type of stare only a Spaniard could exhibit effectively—one that "looked down the long nose." Catalina Gill had raked him with a glance like that when he didn't measure up.

"She's convincing Toshua to be inoculated. He's the Kwahadi who saved your nearly useless hide."

"An Indian? Who cares?" God help him, why could he not keep a civil tone?

"You do, if you have any plans to survive more than a day or two near the sacred canyon, provided we live long enough to find it." Señor Mondragón's expression changed to tender as he looked over Anthony's shoulder. "Ah, my love, who goes first?"

Anthony turned around, happy to admire the pretty lady. For a small woman, she had quite an air about her.

"I will go first," she said, faltering slightly. "Only if you will hold me, Marco."

"I was going to insist upon that," her husband said.

Anthony felt like stepping out of the way of the glance the two shared. "And the Indian?" he asked, striving for a professional tone. True, the love was not directed at him, but it had been a few years since he had seen any at all. Toward the end, Catalina had been anything but kind to Anthony Gill.

"He has a name, and it is Toshua," Paloma replied with no little dignity. She took a deep breath and looked as young as he suspected she might be. "He will be inoculated if I do it, not you. I will watch you closely, Señor Gil."

She pronounced it "heel," as he was used to hearing, without a hard gee in sight. Maybe, if he cared enough, he could teach these two some English. It was obvious they had no idea what was probably going to come their way, once the colonies became the states and more people like him started moving west.

Anthony looked from the woman to the Indian, who only raised one eyebrow. It was enough. "Certainly," he said, easily convinced by that simple expression, mainly because there was nothing remotely tame in Toshua's eyes.

"Where will you do this?" Paloma asked. She stood beside her husband, her hand in his.

"Where did you sleep last night?" Anthony asked. "That might be the most comfortable place."

She gestured, and Señor Mondragón opened a door. She turned to include the Indian. "You, too, Toshua. You should watch, I think."

The Indian surprised Anthony by hanging back. He shook his head. "This is your private place," he told her, as though she needed reminding.

"You have my permission," the *juez* said. "Who do you think is going to look after you two, as *la viruela* runs its course?"

Like most white men, Anthony had come to believe the myth that Indians had no feelings. And after seeing what Comanches had done to Catalina, he would have been the first to confirm that myth. This was different; these people were different. The Indian gave a small sigh that thankfully served to cover his own. What kind of people were these? Likely he would have leisure to explore the matter as the disease played out.

They all looked at him expectantly. He told Paloma to sit down on her bed and decide where she wanted the inoculation.

She looked at her husband. "Did you say yours was on your arm?"

He rolled up his left sleeve and turned his arm so she could see the scar on the inside of his upper arm. She touched it.

"I thought that was an arrow wound."

He laughed, a low sound probably not intended for anyone's ears but his wife's, but there they all stood. "We've never taken an exact census of my scars, Paloma."

She grinned at him and rolled up her own left sleeve, pointing to her forearm. "If I have to watch so I can inoculate Toshua, it had better be a convenient place."

As she sat completely still on the edge of the bed, Anthony spoke to a servant hovering in the hallway. He brought in a little table, pulled it up to the bed, and picked up a stool another servant had brought into the room. Before Anthony could do anything, Señor Mondragón gestured for him to stand aside while he picked Paloma up and sat down on the bed, holding her on his lap. She let out an enormous sigh and leaned against him. Anthony envied them for one irrational moment, until he reminded himself that nothing in life was fair. Mooning around wasn't getting him one step closer to Pia Maria. Ask any American. Time was money.

Chapter Ten

In which Paloma and Toshua receive a medical education

"REST YOUR ARM ON the table, Señora Mondragón."

"Paloma," she whispered, "just Paloma." Her voice was hoarse and she hated to show her terror, but she did as he directed.

Noticing that she hunched over because she sat higher than the table, Marco spread his legs and settled her between them. "Better?" he asked, his voice close to her ear.

She nodded, her eyes on the tin container that the *médico* pulled from the shirt Luisa had given him. *This could kill me*, she thought, and leaned back against Marco, by instinct wanting to distance herself from the poison. His bulk reassured her, reminding her that only this morning they had made love on this same bed. He knew her so well.

Paloma recognized the linen napkin he spread on the table, one of Luisa's. *This is no banquet*, she told herself irrationally. She glanced at Toshua, wondering how he was digesting this. He leaned over the doctor's shoulder. Antonio frowned at him, but did not have the courage to say anything.

"Just sit next to Marco," she told him.

"I should not do that. It is your private place," he said in protest.

Paloma blushed. "Not here at Luisa's. Sit."

He did as she said. He grunted as Antonio Gil took out a small tool that looked like a tiny fork with three tines.

"It's wicked sharp," the physician said, speaking in a conversational tone now, reminding her of Father Eusebio back in Santa Fe at San Miguel. Several times she had escaped from her aunt's grasp long enough to accompany the priest to some of the huts in his parish of Analco. He washed grit and gooey matter from children's eyes while she held their hands. She could not imagine two men less alike, and yet they both were healers.

"I'm just going to scrape this for one inch, but hardly below the surface. Hold still now. Steady her arm, señor."

Marco did as Antonio asked. She held her breath, then let it out slowly, even as Marco did. They breathed in unison. It felt no worse than a mosquito bite. A little blood pooled to the surface, but only a little.

"I've cut off two two-inch lengths of thread, one for you and one for our Comanche friend here. Ordinarily, I would ask you to look away, because I do not want you breathing and scattering anything from the scabs. You need to watch, though. Señor, would you just put your hand over your wife's nose and mouth? Lightly."

Marco did as the physician asked. His hand trembled only a little.

As she watched, Gil gently tamped the thread into the tin container. When he raised it, bits of matter clung to the twisted cotton. With an economy of motion that told her he must have done this many times, he set the tissue-laden thread directly over the furrow on her forearm. In the next moment he wrapped her arm with a strip of linen from another of Luisa's napkins, splitting the ends and securing the knot. He sat back.

"Keep it dry." He glanced at the Comanche seated next to Marco. "Your turn. You want Paloma to do what I just did? *I* can do it, you know."

Toshua grunted. "I trust her more than I trust you." He appraised the physician for a long moment, until Gil tugged at his collar. "Maybe I do not trust you at all."

"Your choice." Gil nodded to Paloma. "You sit here."

She did as he said, after patting Marco's leg. He moved after she did, standing beside her now, as Toshua slid into her former spot. Paloma regarded him seriously, ashamed of her own lack of trust, in light of his. But here was Antonio Gil, bending over her, pointing out the little fork.

"Just the lightest touch."

"Should I wash it first?"

The physician laughed and looked at Marco. "Your wife, sir! We're inoculating the most dangerous thing in the world, and she worries about cleaning off the tool! I love women, I truly do."

Paloma blushed and looked down. Other than from her own cousin, she had not heard hurtful, mocking words in a long time. She looked up quickly at the soft whoosh of a knife leaving its sheath, then held her breath as Toshua placed the tip right against the point of the physician's jaw. He pushed it until blood appeared in little drops.

"If she wants to wash it, let her wash it," Toshua said. He looked at Marco, who seemed also to hold his breath. "I can kill him right now or wait until we are on the Llano Estacado. It's a big space."

She had to give all credit to her husband. He appeared to be considering the matter, as the physician looked from one to the other with terrified eyes. "Oh, let's wait a bit."

The knife went back into its sheath. Toshua nodded to her. "Since I do not understand anything that you are doing, it doesn't matter to me whether you wash that thing or not." He rested his forearm on the table. "Let us begin."

Paloma nodded and picked up the fork. She held it to Toshua's arm. And did nothing more.

With a wry smile, the Comanche took the fork from her and gently scraped the skin on his own arm. "Now you do the rest."

Relieved, Paloma picked up the thread and tamped it into the scabs. When she thought she had enough matter on the thread, she looked at the physician, who nodded. It was a simple matter to place the thread into the bloody furrow and bandage Toshua's arm.

"Done," Marco said. "Come, señor, and inoculate two of Paloma's outriders. The others have survived *la viruela*. When you finish, we will ride."

Paloma held up her arm. "Señor Gil, what will happen now?"

"Probably you and your lord and master would call it God's mystery," he said, but this time, there was nothing in his voice that mocked her. Obviously, Antonio Gil was a quick study. "I call it medical science. What happens? Give yourself five days, and you will come down with smallpox."

She couldn't help but shiver while Marco took her hand.

"You'll be safe and warm in our bed and I will watch over you," he told her. "Toshua, too." When he spoke to the physician, he used his voice of command, the one that everyone in Valle del Sol obeyed. "When you have finished on the Double Cross, we will see how many of our neighbors you can inoculate."

"What about Señora Gutierrez here?"

"Luisa will take care of her sons." He still held Paloma's hand, so he tugged her to her feet. "Come, my dear. You and I will ride the same horse, and the physician will ride yours. Gather what belongings you possess, Antonio Gil. We're leaving as soon as possible."

Toshua left the room as quietly as he had entered it. Paloma smiled at the way he held up his arm and stared at the bandage.

"I wonder what he thinks it will do," she said to Marco, then sighed. "I suppose the same thing had occurred to me."

She was silent as the physician capped the tin, gathered his tiny instrument in the napkin, and left the room.

Marco released her. "I will take Señor Gil to your horse and come back for you. Gather your things, my love." He smiled. "And are there stockings?"

"Certainly there are," she assured him, striving for her normal tone. "Even a pair for Toshua."

To think I came here to knit stockings and gossip, Paloma thought as she gathered her satchel and the stockings. Finding Luisa sitting with her sons, she knelt and kissed her hand as a good sister-in-law should.

"We will be the lucky ones," Luisa whispered, touching her forehead to Paloma's.

She returned to the bedroom she had shared with Marco and lay down, looking at her arm and wondering. "What goes on in there?" she asked no one in particular. Not for the first time she wondered what business went on below her skin. Was there a nook or cranny that kept her from conceiving? It was the dearest wish of her heart to know. Obviously her heart and her loins weren't on speaking terms. And now she was going to get smallpox. Just the thought made her shudder.

When Marco returned, he lay down beside her and gathered her close.

"You know Luisa will scold you for lying on her bed with your boots and spurs on," she teased.

"We'll be on our way before she notices," he replied with a little laugh. He sat up and ran his hands over her body, with a light pinch here and there. "I don't know, Paloma. When we came to del Sol more than a year ago, we shared a horse and you were much skinnier. It's going to be a tight fit."

She thumped him, which made him wince—to her mind, far more dramatically than the thump warranted.

"You are heartless! Up you get."

MARCO DIDN'T MIND THE tight fit. He enveloped her in his cloak and she settled into his arms as she always did, with a tiny sigh of contentment that never failed to touch his heart. They chatted idly for a few minutes; then her comments came at wider and wider intervals until she slept.

The physician rode beside him, no great shakes in the saddle, but then, Antonio Gil wasn't a Spaniard. What was he? Time to find out.

"Why are you here in Nuevo Mexico?" he asked. "Where did you come from?"

"Do I have to tell you anything?"

"As a matter of fact, you do," Marco replied. Staying affable required an effort. He was tired of this man already. "This is my district and I am *juez de campo*. It's perfectly within my power to torture you for answers, or maybe just because I want to, then send you to prison in Santa Fe. Let me ask again: where are you from? And don't tell me East Texas."

He watched the little man shrink inside himself and felt uncomfortable playing the bully. This was obviously a man who had been sorely used. If he had been in the rough company of traders for many months, there was no telling what they had done to him. He sought for a kinder tone.

"Come, come, if we are to be traveling companions in the Llano—even though it is the most stupid scheme you could have concocted—I deserve some answers."

Gil nodded, but with no visible enthusiasm. Either he didn't understand the jibe, or he knew it was true on some level. Marco reconsidered. Perhaps it wasn't the stupidest thing the man beside him had ever dreamed up. *You haven't told a truth in such a long time that you wouldn't recognize one*, he thought, uneasy.

"I am from the colony of Georgia, on the Atlantic Ocean. Have you heard of it?"

Why did the man always rub him the wrong way? "We're not entirely ignorant here in Nuevo Mexico," Marco replied. "Georgia is a buffer colony between the Carolinas and the colony of La Flórida, which I believe the British control right now." Might as well give the man a little more news. "According to a lieutenant passing through Santa Maria, the British were defeated at a place called Yorktown. Maybe your Georgia will be a state soon, and your country independent."

If he had thought the news would spark an enthusiastic response, there was none. Obviously this fellow was no patriot. He wanted to ask him more, but something about the set of the man's mouth told him that he, Marco, the *juez* who could demand almost anything of his district, was only allowed a question or two at a time, and he had reached his limit. Perhaps he would allow a comment.

"If your colonies are to become states soon, when you find your daughter, you can return there in safety."

Antonio only turned bleak eyes on Marco, as if wondering what he was talking about. Though probably younger than Marco, he looked worn out.

Suddenly Marco understood. He had felt much the same after Felicia and the twins' death: getting from one day to the next took all the energy he possessed. Until he met Paloma—a meeting that had happened so much by chance—he was no better than the little man in borrowed clothes, riding a borrowed horse, with a grandiose plan that only a desperate man would attempt. He leaned toward him, overlooking the way Antonio shied back.

"We will find your daughter."

Chapter Eleven

In which Antonio revives his bedside manner

DARKNESS CAME EARLY. THEY rode through stout gates just as the light faded entirely. So long facing into the wind, Anthony's horse—Paloma's, actually—perked up, and with dainty, mincing steps took him directly into a horse barn. The earthy odors and sudden protection from the wind relieved his heart, or at least what remained of it. He couldn't help smiling at Paloma's loud yawn from the depths of her warm cocoon on her husband's lap. Marco bent his head close to hers and she giggled. *My Lord, they are childish*, Anthony thought, but he knew it was envy.

He dismounted with a groan and looked around, impressed with the solidity of the buildings and the height of the palisade, made of stone and not adobe. Everything appeared as capable as Marco Mondragón himself. Maybe the dying trader had steered him into a safe pasture, after all. *And maybe I could have pushed a little dirt over his body*, Anthony thought.

He smiled to himself, remembering Paloma's words about becoming a better person the longer he was around them. He knew it was folly. The only thing that kept a man alive was cunning.

Arm in arm, the Mondragóns moved toward the hacienda, with Toshua walking beside them, not behind. Anthony smiled to see how he kept his bandaged arm carefully held with his other arm. Perhaps he feared the whole thing would fall off, if untended.

Señor Mondragón turned to make certain he was part of their group and gestured Anthony nearer. They walked through what was probably a kitchen garden and into the kitchen itself, bypassing what he assumed was the more formal entrance.

The fragrance emanating from the kitchen was both warm and welcoming. Although he probably would have committed lewd acts just for the pleasure of eating a homely roast of beef and Yorkshire pudding—or even lowly spoonbread, a Carolina delicacy—Anthony took a deep lungful of chilies and pork. He sniffed something else, turkey, and let out an exclamation of pleasure, which made the *juez* gesture toward the table. He needed no formal invitation to sit down.

Silent, he paused while Señor Mondragón made the sign of the cross over the meal on the table; then he fell on the food like the famished man he was. As he ate, he noticed Paloma watching him, sadness in her eyes.

"My love, we should have seen that he had something to eat before we left your sister's house," she told her husband. She passed a cloth-covered plate. "Tortillas?"

Toshua finished first. He smacked his lips and belched, then nodded to the Mondragóns. When he stood up, Paloma held out other plate of tortillas and the Comanche took it. He nodded his thanks, then left through the door they had entered.

"Where does he stay?" Anthony asked.

"He likes my husband's office by the horse barn," Paloma said as she took a tortilla and swiped it around her empty bowl, snagging the last tiny bits of meat.

Stupefied with food, Antonio sat in silence. Paloma finished her meal and watched her husband, who was talking to a woman with her own bunch of keys at her waist, possibly a housekeeper. Another woman with flour on her hands listened. Their faces serious, they nodded, then left the kitchen, one heading outside and the other through an interior door.

"To the *sala*, my dearest," the *juez* said. "You come as well, señor."

Anthony followed them to a larger room, where a fire already glowed in the corner fireplace. Paloma lighted a straw from the fire and lit the candles in their sconces.

Anthony admired the room, which looked little used. In Georgia, the Gill house boasted a far grander salon, with chairs and a table from England and wallpaper made of leather. Still, that salon did not possess anything as ornate as the cabinet with delicate carving around the top, all painted red and green with gilt outlines. It must have come from Spain.

He glanced at the crucifix and then what looked like sandals hanging below it. Curious, he went closer, then looked at his hosts for an explanation. Paloma turned away, her face rosy, but Señor Mondragón come to his side.

"My wife's sandals."

Puzzled, Anthony peered closer. "Is that dried blood on the footbed?"

"Yes. It is a long story, but she was trying to return a yellow pup to me, and was ready to walk from Santa Fe to here to deliver it." Señor Mondragón touched the sandals with the sort of deference that some Spaniards probably reserved for relics of the church. "I like to be reminded of bravery, living as we do on the edge of Comanchería. Have a seat, señor."

Anthony sat on the adobe outcropping attached to the walls—built-in benches with cushions. Paloma spoke to her husband and he nodded. She left the room. When she returned, he saw that she had traded her riding boots for moccasins. She sat next to him on one of the two chairs in the room, tucking her legs under her in a childlike, endearing way. He saw her for what she was: a young wife with responsibilities, but still playful. The two chairs represented a certain subtle power that the Spaniards excelled in.

No one spoke. He could tell from Señor Mondragón's expression that he must be weighing something. When the room began to fill up with servants, Anthony knew what it was. He wished suddenly that he had on a good suit of clothes that fit, and that he could have found a barber somewhere in this region of open spaces. He was about to be introduced as a useful man of some importance to these people who lived on the edge of danger. For the first time in several tense years, it mattered to him what they thought.

When the room was full, the *juez de campo* wasted not a moment. "My dears, we are about to be visited by a most unwelcome guest—*la viruela*."

Several servants gasped. One woman burst into tears. Paloma knelt by her side and took her hand, telling Anthony worlds about the relationship the Mondragóns enjoyed with those who served them.

When the low voices were silent and Paloma was seated beside him once more, Mondragón raised his hand and continued. "We are most fortunate that this man, Señor Antonio Gil, is a *médico* with the power and ability to inoculate those of you who have not already been inoculated or who have not already survived *la viruela*."

The look of fear was replaced by a soft, "Ahhh," which made Anthony smile a little. All eyes turned his way. For the first time in a long while, he wished he truly was the man they thought he was. But even as shabby as he looked, no one seemed skeptical. He heard none of the titters or saw any of the arch glances that had been burned into his brain following his last encounter with the English, who thought everyone inoculated would live until they learned otherwise. Better to head this off right now.

Marco beat him to it. He held up his hand and all were silent again. "My dears, as wonderful as is the promise of a life free of *la viruela*, the cure sometimes demands a high price. A few of you may remember that my younger brother, Tomás, died of the inoculation when he was four years old.

Life is uncertain and we all take our chances. Never forget that, please."

The servants turned to Anthony again. He saw calculating looks, worried frowns, and even sympathy, as though El Padre Celestial had given Antonio Gil a heavy burden not of his choosing. He did something then that he had not done in years: he looked at each face—all of them unknown to him at this moment—and reminded himself that they were all his patients. The knowledge rendered him silent for a long moment.

"I will do my best," he told them at last. "Señor Mondragón, when do we begin?"

"MY LOVE, IT APPEARS you caught Antonio off guard. Why is that, I wonder?" Paloma asked Marco as they prepared for bed an hour later.

Half in and half out of his breeches, he sat on their bed. She came to his side and kissed his head. "This is going to be hardest for you," she told him, her lips close to his ear.

"You're the one with the bandage," he said, sliding off his breeches.

She folded them neatly and placed them on top of the chest. "You and Sancha and others who are already safe will have to tend to us."

"In the morning while Antonio inoculates everyone, I will make a list of who will tend whom, during these next few weeks." He smiled at her. "I'm a *juez de campo*. You know we love our lists. Come back here."

His tidy brain—the one that loved lists—told him that at some point, surely, their lovemaking would settle into routine. A year and several months had passed since their marriage, but that hadn't happened yet. Logically, he knew that the giddiness and sheer delight would move into something calmer, but so far Paloma Vega remained a great adventure. He felt something different this time in her sexual fervor, and it saddened him. She seemed to be extracting every scintilla of pleasure, as though this would be her last opportunity. He knew that the white bandage on her arm was working on her brain, trying to convince her that not everyone survived inoculation. He wanted to reassure her, but he was no diviner.

"We don't know what lies ahead, my love," he said finally, when she had settled herself against him, skin on skin, warm and heavy. "I could ask you not to worry about the outcome, but words are cheap."

Paloma sighed and made little circles of the hairs on his chest. "I want to be brave and not disgrace you. Suppose my bowels lose control? Suppose I rave like a lunatic? Or stink and sweat?"

He put his leg over her. "And suppose I live to be really old, and you have to take care of me when I lose control and rave?"

He didn't say anything else. In another moment, he felt her silent laughter.

"Go ahead, tell me I'm the silly one, to borrow all this trouble," she said, her voice gruff.

In answer, he kissed her head. "Go to sleep, my heart. You're only a little bit silly."

THE INOCULATIONS WENT SMOOTHLY, and Marco made his list. To keep Paloma busy, he instructed her and the women to make up pallets in the chapel, the largest room in the hacienda, once the benches had been moved into the interior courtyard and covered with canvas to protect them from newly falling snow. Ten pallets. Toshua said he wanted to remain in Marco's office, and Paloma would be in their chamber.

The next day, Paloma, Sancha, and *Perla la cocinera*, sporting her own bandage, cooked pots of cornmeal mush to store outside in the kitchen garden, where the cold would preserve it until needed. Mush would be easy to heat again and eat, when everyone was too busy tending the sick. They soaked and reconstituted dried apples, which they mashed with honey and cinnamon.

Another day passed and Marco tried, without her knowing, to watch Paloma for the symptoms that Antonio Gil described: aches, fever, sore throat, exhaustion, and a certain looseness of the mind or anxiety that heralded the arrival of the most dreaded disease in all hemispheres. He also watched Antonio, who looked fine-drawn and worn, still suffering the effects of starvation and abuse at the hands of traders.

"I was fair game," Antonio told them one night, as they sat around the kitchen table. "A curse here, a kick there. 'Let's make the Englishman's life a living hell.'"

"Englishman?" Paloma asked. "I thought you were American."

The doctor seemed confused for a moment. "It is hard to say what we are. Perhaps Americans now." He chuckled, but it was not a pleasant sound. "My living hell changed when a mule kicked one of the fouler men and I splinted his broken leg." He shrugged. "They saw I had a skill they needed, but why did I bother? He was dead of the pox in a month."

Marco saw the sympathy on his wife's face. She had suffered her own mistreatment at the hands of relatives who should have cherished her. "I used to make myself small in a corner of the kitchen and pretend I was invisible," she said.

Antonio nodded in understanding. "It never worked, though, did it?"

A rueful shake of her head, then for a moment the two of them stared into the distance. Paloma looked at the doctor, hesitating. "You splinted his broken leg because he was in pain, perhaps?"

"Perhaps," he replied, but Marco heard all the doubt in his voice, as though he were merely humoring Paloma.

This is a man of no sympathy, Marco thought. *He should learn some, but must we be his teachers?*

Toshua cleared his throat, as if preparing to speak. The sound roused Paloma, and she nodded her encouragement to the Comanche. He looked at the physician.

"Did you see any Kwahadi?"

"I saw Comanches. You all look alike to me," Antonio said with a shake of his head. "You have your secret places in the Staked Plains."

"We do. For all you know, the smallpox has not reached those of my tribe."

"Who can say?" Antonio asked with a shrug. "Do you know of some who have survived *la viruela* and are immune now?"

"A few. One of my wives, some old men who lived through an earlier Dark Wind. There are some in every band, as there are here."

They sat in silence. Paloma was the first to leave, getting up without a word, not looking at Marco. She threw a shawl around her shoulders and walked into the kitchen garden. In a few minutes, Toshua followed her. Marco started to rise, but Antonio put a hand on his arm.

"Let them alone, señor. I see this in people who have been inoculated and who are waiting, just waiting. They share a certain … knowledge."

Marco went to the window and gazed at his wife and the Comanche standing together, not touching but staring in the same direction, as wind tossed the snow around. They didn't appear to be speaking, but after a long while, Toshua left the garden for Marco's office and Paloma turned toward the kitchen, her face troubled. She came inside and just stood there, watching him, until her expression changed to something wry.

"It's hard not to borrow trouble," she said simply, before she left the room. He knew she went to the chapel, probably just to stand there and stare at the pallets, ready for whatever was to come.

MARCO WATCHED HER THE next day, and the next, not fooled for a moment by her studied serenity. She went about her usual tasks all day, collecting eggs for Sancha, working steadily, but with a certain detached air.

On the fifth day, she rose as usual to dress and gather eggs. He lay in bed and watched her, unwilling to get up, because she had left such a pleasant warm spot. When he didn't move, she said, "Lazy man," with a laugh, pressing both hands to her lower back.

He went back to sleep and came into the kitchen later—after Sancha, rubbing her eyes, had opened the food safe and Perla was laying the fire. He looked around.

"Paloma?"

"I thought perhaps she decided to sleep late," Sancha told him.

He ran out the door, calling her name, not bothering with his cloak. The sun was only beginning its ascent, but he could see the door to the henhouse swinging open. Ducking inside, he found Paloma in tears, a basket of broken eggs messing her apron. She was trying to scoop the slimy whites and yolks into the basket. She looked up, fear in her eyes, suddenly the old Paloma in the kitchen of her relatives.

"I didn't mean to drop them! They were so heavy all of a sudden. Please don't be angry."

He looked at her, thinking what Antonio Gil had told him about exhaustion and anxiety and other symptoms. Did she not remember that this henhouse belonged to the kindest man in all of Nuevo México? Was some part of her mind back in Santa Fe? "Paloma, don't worry about the eggs. Give me your hand. Let's go inside."

Obediently she held out her hand and he pulled her easily to her feet, only to have her fall to her knees as though they were made of jelly. Her eyes were wide with terror. "*La viruela?*" she whispered as he swung her into his arms and carried her from the henhouse.

"It's beginning, my love," he told her as he picked his way carefully through the snow.

With a sigh, she rested her head against his chest. "I'm sorry about the eggs, but I ache everywhere."

Antonio sat at the kitchen table when Marco shouldered the door open, carrying his wife. He got to his feet, a ragged thin man in borrowed clothes, but suddenly possessed of something that had been lacking. For the first time, Marco saw real purpose in his expression.

"Get her to bed," Antonio ordered. "Sancha, find a warming pan. She will shiver and then she will burn."

The *médico* did something then that warmed Marco's heart. He leaned forward and kissed Paloma on the forehead. She closed her eyes with something near to relief—if Marco was any interpreter of his wife's moods, and he thought he was.

Marco tried to carry her through the door into the main hallway, but she grabbed the sill, stopping him.

"Toshua. Someone look after Toshua. Oh, please."

Chapter Twelve

In which Antonio walks through his own valley of shadows

PALOMA THOUGHT SHE KNEW how gentle her husband was, but why had he placed her, naked, on a bed of spikes? Thank God he had not been distressed by the broken eggs. How could she shiver one moment and cry out from heat the next? Who was this smelly, sweaty person?

It was a puzzle, because the next moment she was perfectly reasonable, dressed in her best nightgown, fragrant with lavender, her hair nicely brushed and spread across her pillow. If only her back didn't feel like someone had taken an axe to it.

She was dimly aware—one day later, two days?—when Antonio removed the bandage from her arm and stood there looking down at her for a long moment. As she held her breath, he finally nodded, as though pleased with what he saw. She looked, too, and saw red grains of rice just under the surface of her skin. Her neck itched. When she raised her hand to scratch, Marco pulled it down, then dabbed on a salve that cooled the fire there, but only just; she still wanted to scratch.

She glared at both men, obviously in cahoots to make her uncomfortable.

"You have a line of pox," her traitor husband said.

"Right on schedule," her equally unpleasant physician added.

She wanted to argue, but the words wouldn't come. She sighed and slept, instead.

She woke to a raging thirst, wanting water more than anything. She could have cried when Marco brought her a cup with blessed ice in it. "Icicles everywhere outside," he told her, raising her up for a long drink.

"I'm sorry I said such horrible things to you," she mumbled.

"Which time?"

And then he *would* kiss her forehead, even though she knew she smelled bad. What was a woman to do with a husband like that?

Paloma had no sense of time, knowing it was night only when her husband came to bed. During the day she had vague recollections of him in her line of sight, back and forth. He fed her mush and applesauce. She cried with shame when he cleaned her after her bowels moved, but he only told her not to be such a goose.

One morning she woke to the knowledge that someone else besides Marco was in the room. Painfully, she raised up on one elbow and looked around. To her relief, it was Toshua. He lay on a pallet in front of the fire, so for one odd moment she wondered if Marco had moved her into the office because she was too much trouble in their bedroom.

When her mind cleared, she knew he had brought Toshua into their own room, the better to watch over him, too. Paloma lay back down, strangely satisfied.

Finally there came the day when she opened her eyes, certain it was morning, and felt hungry. She turned her head, waiting for the pain to come. Nothing. Cautious, she touched her neck, feeling scabs. She counted them. One, two, three. Only three. Thanks be to God.

Careful of herself, she turned on her side. Her husband lay beside her. She studied his face, noting that the hollows were deeper under his cheeks. *You have had a hard time of this, my lord*, she thought. As he lay on his back, his deep-set eyes closed, his eyelashes impossibly long, she admired his elegant profile. She studied him, because there had been more than one moment in the past few days when she feared she would never see him again. With a gentle finger, she traced the outline of his forehead, nose, and lips. He opened his eyes and shifted to face her.

"Paloma?" he asked, hesitant, as though he didn't know what she would say, or if she would even be rational.

"Who else would be in your bed, señor?" she teased, which brought tears to his eyes.

"*Gracias a Dios*," he whispered.

With his help, she struggled into a sitting position and looked toward the fireplace. Toshua lay there, breathing deeply and evenly.

"He came to himself last night around midnight." Marco smiled at her. "He did what you are doing now, wanting to know if *you* lived."

She lay back down, exhausted by such a simple effort. "How long have I been like this?"

"About seven days," he said, drawing her closer.

She wanted to resist his embrace, because someone smelled foul, and she didn't think it was Marco. "You're still being a goose," was all he told her, so she let herself be cuddled.

She insisted on sitting up for breakfast in bed—chilis in mush and hot chocolate sweetened with honey and cinnamon. The first few spoonfuls went down easy enough; then she hadn't the strength to finish. She set down the spoon, perplexed at her own weakness. Marco picked it up and fed her, keeping his voice low so Toshua would not wake. When she finished the entire bowl, he pulled back the covers and picked her up.

"H'mm. Lighter," he whispered, hefting her easily. "Now, dearest, you are going to the laundry room for a bath. While you are soaking, the servants will change our sheets and you will then go back to sleep."

She offered no objections; just eating had exhausted her.

His sleeves rolled up, Marco washed her from hair to heels, treating her like fine china.

"A girl could like this," she teased, when he dried her. She leaned against him as he knelt to dry her legs. "And you'll bring me hummingbirds' tongues and mulled wine? Perhaps Valencia oranges."

"Silly wife," he teased back, taking a little longer drying between her legs than she thought necessary. The sensation soothed her, reminding her that she was still alive. "Marco," she murmured. "Marco, I didn't die."

* * *

ANTHONY SAT BACK, HIS tired brain still analytical and wondering why it was that nowhere in Spanish America was there a comfortable chair; not here, not in east Texas, and not in Florida. He had found himself envying Marco Mondragón's impossibly fine posture, and could only credit chairs like this and many hours in the saddle. He thought of a pleasantly rump-sprung armchair in the study in Savannah, wondering what had happened to his possessions when he bolted and ran for his life.

He also envied Marco his wife, sleeping now as he watched. Lucky woman, she had survived with only a few pockmarks on the side of her face and her neck, plus that mark on her forearm. She breathed evenly and peacefully now, as her body marshaled its forces and returned her to health. By the end of the week, she would be up and about, no worse for the experience except for those few reminders.

He glanced back at Toshua, who watched him. Devil take the Comanche! No matter how soundly Toshua slept, if anyone came into the room besides Marco, he woke, maintaining his vigilance until the interloper left. His doctor's mind was certain the Indian was weak as a kitten; his self-serving side—the greater side, Anthony admitted—wasn't so certain. Anthony wondered if

Paloma had any idea what a protector Toshua was; probably not. She wasn't a woman overly concerned with herself.

There were probably other patients he could be checking, but he hadn't the energy to move. Blast and damn them, it was as though an army of patients demanded his attention day and night. Hippocrates and his stupid oath. When was a physician to sleep? He closed his eyes.

He woke when he heard rustling from the bed and remembered what Marco had told him before he left that morning to visit his neighbors. "She'll try to get up when she feels better. I trust you will see that doesn't happen." It was no suggestion. Besides, Anthony didn't want her moving, either. He had seen too many relapses that led to death, when patients called themselves healed before the disease finally let go.

He opened his eyes, admiring Paloma's trim legs before she tugged down her nightgown.

"And where do you think you're going?" he asked, trying to sound frosty.

Ah ha, caught in the act. He tried not to smile at the guilty look on her face, and failed. "Paloma, you've been warned," he reminded her. She opened her mouth to protest, but he swung her legs back in bed, covered her with the blankets again, and tucked them firmly under the mattress, as though to trap her there. "You're not going anywhere until two or three more days have passed."

The mutinous look did not disappear. "You let Toshua go back to the office," she accused. "He has been up and about."

He glanced at Toshua, who was listening. "My dear little patient, I *never* argue with Comanches." He could try a little cajolery. "Besides, I promised your husband you'd stay right here, and so you shall. You don't want to disappoint such a nice man, now, do you?"

Resignation replaced mutiny. Paloma lay back and yawned. "Well, maybe just this once." She raised up on one elbow. "You'll need to entertain me, then."

He had all sorts of ideas, all of which would have resulted in at least two men slitting his only throat. "What do you have in mind?"

She sat up and pulled Marco's pillow behind her own, then settled back, her hands folded on the coverlet over her belly. "Tell me how on earth you ended up here. Where are you *really* from, Señor Gil?"

Anthony regarded her a long time, but her glance did not waver from his. For a brief moment, he wondered if the colony of New Mexico was far enough from Georgia, and if he would ever feel safe.

"Tell me," Paloma coaxed. "You are far from trouble and in a safe place." She smiled to herself. "That's what I discovered when Marco brought me here."

He could have reminded her that Marco couldn't keep her safe from smallpox, but that would have been petty of him. Why not tell her what she asked? At the very least, she would discover what a fool he was.

"You have to stay awake."

"I will," she promised. "You are the first American I have ever met."

"I won't be the last."

"How is that?"

He tried out the word. "Americans. Americans are ambitious and land-greedy. You will see them here, eventually."

"Marco's land grant is safe."

He heard the pride in her voice. *I hope to heaven it is*, he thought. He merely nodded and squirmed himself into as comfortable a position as he could find in the unyielding chair. "I'm no revolutionary. All I ever wanted to do was heal people, and maybe make some money." He shrugged. "It seems I could do neither."

* * *

HE SPOKE FOR AN hour, discounting the time she slept, even though Paloma had said she would not. Maybe it was a good thing he had caught her trying to get up, because she *was* tired. Paloma listened to his tale of an up and coming physician, back from acquiring a medical degree in a colony named Pennsylvania, setting up his practice in Savannah, a little town he thought she would like. "The ocean is beautiful there. Have you ever walked barefoot on sand and felt the waves lap at your feet?"

"No. There isn't much water around here, if you haven't noticed."

He leaned forward to ruffle her hair. He stopped, his hand almost on her head, when Toshua sat up.

He described how war came first to the northern colonies and then gradually seeped south like an ever-widening wound, setting families at odds with each other. "I thought I could keep out of the whole mess," he told her. "Physicians can be neutral, I thought. I can tend to both sides, the British and the Americans, can't I?"

Poor, skinny little man, Paloma thought. She stopped his narrative—she could see it was painful for him—and asked him to bring her something to eat. "I really want *biscoches* and maybe some wine. Tell her we need two glasses. Toshua?"

The Indian shook his head.

Antonio seemed grateful for the interruption and left the room quickly. Paloma sat up and looked at Toshua, who lay by the fire, his hands behind his head and a thoughtful look on his face.

"What do you think?" she asked him.

He grunted. "I think it is impossible to be a person in the middle."

Paloma nodded. She looked at the doorway and crawled to the end of her bed. "Have you ever seen Americans?" she asked him, keeping her voice low.

"I have."

"Wh—what did you do to them?"

He didn't answer, which was all the answer she expected.

"I remember this: There are many of them. Perhaps the little doctor is right," he said finally.

"I wonder." She couldn't help herself then. She leaned closer. "Toshua, do you believe he is telling the truth?"

A slow shake of his head answered her question.

She heard footsteps in the hall and hurried under the covers again, just in time to see Antonio with a tray. He set it on the table and handed her the plate. She took two *biscoches* and told him to take some, himself. He did not argue.

"Where was I?" he asked, even though Paloma was certain he remembered.

"You were trying to stay out of trouble, which I don't think you managed to do."

He shook his head and ate both *biscoches*, washing them down with the diluted wine. Paloma watched him, determined to tell Sancha to see that he had all he wanted to eat.

"What happened?" Her prompt was as gentle as she could make it, even as she wondered at Toshua's slow shake of his head.

He took a deep breath. "Two British officers came to me, wanting inoculation." He made a wry face. "Two big, healthy men. They were eating better than the rebels, I gather. I inoculated them both." Another deep breath. "One lived and one died."

"My goodness. But you told them it was dangerous, didn't you?" Paloma asked.

"Certainly." He stood up and went to the fireplace, stepping around Toshua. He added several sticks of wood. "It's cold in here."

"No, it isn't," Paloma said. "What happened then?"

"Can't you guess?" he burst out. He shook his head, angry at himself, when she gasped in fright. "Sorry." He sat down again. "The British were furious, certain I had caused the one death because I was sympathetic to the rebel cause. The Americans got wind of what had happened, and rumor spread that I caused that death on purpose because I was on *their* side. I was on no one's side. I was a doctor, for God's sake!"

"All you were doing was your job," Paloma said. She rubbed her arms. Maybe the room *was* cold. "Did the British hear that rumor?"

"They did. Since they controlled Savannah, I was at their mercy."

He lowered his voice, as if the bedroom of Marco Mondragón was filled with British sympathizers. "My housekeeper heard they were coming, so she warned me. I snatched up my medical satchel and whatever money I could find, and fled. Just ran out the back door and down the street, when soldiers were banging on the front door. It was that close."

"That's a relief," Paloma said, her eyes on her hands, because looking at the little man's bleak face was beginning to sadden her.

He let out a harsh sound then—somewhere between a laugh and a growl—which made her flinch. "No relief for my housekeeper. The British," he spit out the word, "tortured her and hanged her naked from the lamppost in front of my house, because she would tell them nothing. She didn't *know* anything!"

He put his head between his hands and sobbed, a fearful sound. Paloma felt the tears start in her eyes. She leaned close to him and touched his head. "*Pobrecito*," she whispered.

He left the room then. Paloma pulled the blankets higher on her shoulder, because she shivered. "Where is Marco?" she asked Toshua.

"He knew you were better, so he went to visit your foul cousin and her weakling husband."

"Why?"

Toshua sat up. "He has been traveling through the district, offering the *medico's* services." He made a face. "He wants everyone to be sick and uncomfortable and mess their beds for a week, and then feel better. I do not understand your medicine. The Dark Wind blew over us, but we were still sick."

"I know. It's hard to understand." She sighed. "I wish Marco were here."

"I can find him."

"No, you can stay in bed and behave yourself!"

He smiled at that. He put his hand to his forehead and knuckled his fingers, like a servant obeying her.

"You're trying my patience," she said, reminded of her older brother, dead these twelve years at the hands of men just like the Comanche on the pallet by the fire. Life was strange.

"Did you notice?" he asked, when she thought he was asleep.

"Notice what?"

"When the little man cried, there were no tears."

Paloma felt that same chill at his words, but exhaustion ruled her again. She closed her eyes and went to sleep immediately, worn out with such a sad story. When she woke, shadows lengthened across the bed and Antonio was seated by her again. Wordless, he put his hand to her forehead and nodded.

"Cool." Next, his fingers went to the pulse in her neck. "Regular." He must have traveled through the kitchen, because he handed her a chicken leg. "Eat."

She did, famished, even though she had polished off the rest of the *biscoches*. She glanced at Toshua, who had chicken, too.

"I made my way south to what you call La Flórida," he began, picking up his narrative. "It wasn't safe, either, because the British controlled a big fort there in Saint Augustine. Fort Saint Mark, they called it."

"Castillo de San Marcos," Paloma said. "I have heard of it."

"I worked my way west, offering my services at little towns and plantations. The British controlled West Florida by then, so I moved on. Everyone always needs a physician. You know, like everyone always needs a blacksmith. I ended up in Natchitoches, Louisiana, French territory, but I was safe enough."

His shoulders relaxed then, and the harsh lines of his face seemed to soften. Perhaps Louisiana had better memories.

"Is that where you met your wife?" Paloma asked finally.

He nodded. He didn't speak for a long time, but Paloma was patient.

"Catalina Maria Rosas, the daughter of a merchant in Natchitoches. He was Spanish, yes, but that far on the frontier, no one seemed so concerned about governments. I cured her father's piles and he invited me to dinner, in his gratitude. She was a pretty lady." He looked at the wall, seeing through it. "I had a miniature painted of her, but I lost it, just like I have lost everything."

He made to rise, but Paloma put up her hand to stop him. "Tell me, please."

"You want the rest of my story?" he asked, as if impatient with her. "You want to hear how we married, had a daughter, named her Pia Maria, and how I got greedy and tried to buy land, and ended up cheated and on the run again, because I can do nothing right?"

He was on his feet now and backing out the door. "That story?" he shouted at her as he left the room, slamming the door behind him.

Paloma stared at the closed door, stunned at Antonio Gil's ferocity, sorrowful that it was all directed at himself. She looked at Toshua, who shook his head.

"Yes, that story," she said.

Chapter Thirteen

In which Marco is reminded how hard it is to do good deeds

NO ONE WOULD EVER hear it from him, but Marco couldn't help his own sigh of relief to be in the saddle again and away from death, contagion, and even recuperation. Good thing he was not ordained to be a physician. He pointed Buciro east and south toward the Castellano holdings, thinking that even some doctors—Antonio Gil came to mind—didn't appear overly joyful about their profession.

He looked back at the Double Cross, feeling crass and suddenly wishing he could save everyone. Paloma would have to find out sooner or later, but her little yellow dog—the one her foolish husband had paid a fortune for in Santa Fe—was masterless. Perhaps Andrés was too old to survive the rigors of inoculation. Poor Trece whined and sniffed at Andrés, Marco's *mayordomo*, as he lay so still in the chapel. How could anyone explain to a dog that the old, dear man who spoiled him was mere clay now and destined for the cemetery? It was hard enough for humans to understand that not everyone survived inoculation. Maybe Paloma would have a solution.

Paloma. He closed his eyes and crossed himself, relieved that she had survived. He wished she rode with him right now, even though he knew how much she dreaded visiting her reprehensible cousin Maria Teresa. Even now, he still felt the occasional worry that Paloma would somehow be gone or dead when he returned. He had left her in good health but grumpy this time, because she was tired of staying in bed. Grumpy, he could handle.

It especially chapped her thighs that Toshua was up and about again. Marco chuckled to himself. Try to stop a Comanche from doing whatever he wanted? Impossible. The greater surprise was that Sancha even asked Toshua to help her with some mundane kitchen duties, because Perla was still on her pallet in the chapel, and so was the little boy who helped with the cutting and dicing. Marco couldn't help but wince inwardly to see how good Toshua was at slicing things into small strips. He had never asked the man just what tortures he had administered to the unwary who had traveled through Kwahadi territory, and he knew he never would.

And how will I fare on the Llano? he could not help asking himself. There was no way Paloma was going to accompany him and Antonio Gil, no matter what she thought. If it meant deception up to and including locking her in their bedroom until he was a day away, he would do it. *He* had made the stupid bargain with the Englishman or American or whatever he was, not Paloma. True, he had done it for her, but that was hardly the issue. There wasn't anything he wouldn't do for the treasure of his heart.

As he rode along, he did something he didn't usually do: he compared Felicia with Paloma. Marco could scarcely imagine two more different women in looks, temperament, body, and even mind. Felicia was the loveliest olive color, with snapping brown eyes and high cheekbones, betraying her Tewa side. Even before the twins came, she was abundantly shaped and enough to make a man sigh out loud, just to look at her fully clothed. And when she was bare? *O Dios.* She was kind, she was generous, and she could get angry enough at him to stand on his feet and poke him in the chest. Felicia never was interested in learning to read or write, but just recalling her lovely voice when she sang to the twins still brought tears to his eyes.

And here was Paloma, still too thin for his total personal taste, but so lovely to look at. She may have lacked Felicia's curves, but there was just enough of breast and hip to excite him in a deep sort of way that Felicia had never touched, if he was honest with himself. Light brown hair, blue eyes and freckles, especially on her shoulders, made her a rarity in his part of Nuevo Mexico. And *ay caramba!* how she had suffered last summer when they had gone riding, stripped, swam in the Santa Maria, made love and baked in the sun too long. Never again. She could read better than he could, and more and more, it was her lovely penmanship that entered brands and records into his ledgers for the governor.

That Paloma was brave, he had no doubt, even though she shrieked when she found mice in the grain stored in the horse barn and crossed herself every time she saw a bat. She had already endured the worst that life could throw at her, without becoming bitter. There was no one like her.

Could she sing those achingly beautiful lullabies to their children? He might never know, and that was a sorrow, no matter how he tried to put a cheerful face on it every twenty-eight days, when he found her in tears. Maybe when he and the physician were riding on the Llano Estacado, he could ask the man about such a dilemma. It wasn't a subject to broach when anyone else was around.

Did he love one wife more than the other? Was it something a man widowed and married again could ever understand? No philosopher or saint could have explained to him how it was possible to love so much twice. Possibly this was God's most tender mercy, but he was no theologian.

Such idle musings served to get him to the Castellano hacienda without dwelling on the frosty welcome, if one could even call it a welcome, from his former friend Alonso and Maria Teresa. January was the month when he delivered the 1782 forms to fill out, enumerating all the calves, lambs, kids, piglets, and foals as they came. The crown wasn't much interested in chickens. He knew everyone lied because no one wanted to pay that much tax, but these were the forms he took to Santa Fe every autumn. He was pretty certain that the governor's *fiscales* added a certain percentage to each calf, lamb and foal list, considering human nature.

He had taken Paloma with him in December to visit Pedro Cárdenas, who wanted to register a new brand. She was better at drawing than he was, but even more to the point, the Cárdenas family never heated their bedchambers; he was tired of being cold when he went alone, and Paloma had kept him warm.

Thinking of her particular warmth reminded him of the little yellow dog again, so sorrowful because the man who spoiled him was dead. Marco thought of birds he found dead on cold winter mornings, and calves born too soon, and loved ones cold in clay. *No wonder we New Mexicans carve such bloody crucifixes of the Christ*, he thought. *We are wedded to death.*

Last Sunday, when he finally did not fear for Paloma's life, he had taken Antonio to Mass with him in Santa Maria. With Father Francisco's approval, he had stood up, drawing Antonio up with him, to tell the other parishioners about the danger coming their way. His friends and neighbors had chuckled behind their hands as Antonio's accent grated on their ears; no one was laughing when he finished.

Marco could only leave it up them to decide whether or not to risk inoculation, but when the Mass ended, more than half of the congregation put their names or X's on the paper he carried. The Castellanos were not among them. Alonso had started forward, but Maria Teresa had yanked him back. They had left in a hurry, before Marco could discuss the matter with them. Perhaps he would have a chance to try again, he reasoned, as he swung himself from the saddle. He nodded to his outriders to take their horses to the barn, where Alonso's *mayordomo* might grudgingly provide skimpy amounts of grain.

He knew better than to expect any kind of welcome from Alonso and Maria Teresa. At his own hacienda, and others that he visited, the door would already be open, with the master of the house waiting with open arms to give him a friendly *abrazo* and a kiss on each cheek, if the man happened to be a relative. Since their wives were cousins, Marco could have expected such kisses, but he knew better than to look for affection. He sighed and knocked on the door, already dreading what was to come.

He had waited a long, long time in the cold before the door finally swung open. He smiled at the little maid, who just looked worried.

"Señor Castellano?" he asked.

She pointed to the *sala* and darted away before he could hand her his cloak and hat. Dropping them in a pile by the front door, he took a deep breath and entered the *sala*. Both of the Castellanos stood before him in front of the fireplace, effectively blocking any stray warmth that might have taken off the January chill. Marco wished he had kept his cloak on.

No smile. No mulled wine or hot chocolate. No *biscoches*. No idle chatter. Just the two of them frowning at him, almost threatening him to utter anything resembling a pleasantry. He tried anyway.

"Lovely to see you both in good health," he began, with a little bow.

They stared. Marco gave an inward sigh and drew himself up to his official height. He took out the form with its royal stamp and handed it to Alonso.

"Just the usual, my friend," he said, and then more formally, because he was the *juez de campo*, after all, "To be filled out as appropriate throughout this year of Our Lord 1782 and returned to me by next September."

There was nothing more to say, but he knew he had to try once more. He chose a kinder tone. "My dears, I wish you would reconsider the opportunity to be inoculated."

He addressed Alonso, noting the wistful look the rancher gave him. He also knew Alonso was a weak man who would dance to Maria Teresa's tune. "With your wife's consent, perhaps *you* could be inoculated. Alonso, you could stay with us during the procedure, and Maria Teresa and your child-to-be would never be endangered."

"Out of the question," Maria Teresa snapped. "He would never leave me for such a thing."

"Before God and all the saints, he should. Even *one* of you inoculated would be better than no one," Marco argued. "And if some of your servants would follow suit, you would all be much safer."

Alonso opened his mouth to speak, then closed it.

"Please, Alonso. Any one of us could stay here with your wife, so she is not alone, while you are inoculated and quarantined from her in a safe place."

"I cannot," Alonso replied, his voice dull.

Might as well try, Marco thought, stiffening his own spine, in the face of Señora Castellano's bitter-eyed intractability. Amazing how a woman like that could dismay even a *juez*. He tried to choose his words carefully, knowing even before he started, that what he said would be touchy, at the very least.

"You could be inoculated, too, Maria." He held up his hand when she started to speak, and miracles of miracles, she remained silent. "I know, I know! This could very well endanger the child you carry. Or it might not. *El médico* told me that he does not know, either."

"Not another word, *juez*," she said, daring him.

"I will speak," he said, each word distinct. "It is a terrible risk. The alternative is worse. Yes, you could lose this child if you are inoculated. Antonio Gil just doesn't know." He held up his hand, knowing in his heart that he would never again be invited onto Alonso's land. "You also know that you are capable of bearing another child. Please, Maria Teresa, at least consider it."

Her voice was high and tight when she spoke. "Did your wife send you to give me this message?"

Marco stared back, startled. "She … she doesn't even know I am here."

"Liar."

He turned away, stunned at the anger than welled inside him. He forced down his angry words, wishing with all his heart that he could just scoop up Alonso and drag him away from this viper. He breathed in and out, but he could not bring himself to turn around.

"Señora, I know that what I have suggested goes against everything that we believe in our Holy Church. You can complain to Father Francisco about me all you want. But let me tell you: I am a realist and this is a hard land. Good day to you both and God protect you, because I cannot."

Marco stalked to the door and flung it open, and then he could not help himself. He turned around and glared at the two of them, fixing his gaze finally on Maria Teresa. It gave him a sick sort of pleasure—he knew he would regret it almost immediately—to see her actually quail before his glance.

"And you! You and your family have robbed my wife of her land, her cattle, and her dear mother's brand. Mistreated Paloma and robbed her, and I cannot do a thing about it."

He slammed the door after him, tears in his eyes, then bowed his head in shame as he heard Alonso's wife laugh and laugh.

Chapter Fourteen

In which the Mondragóns listen with love

FURIOUS AT HIMSELF FOR letting that wretch of a woman play him like a guitar, Marco shouted for his guards. In minutes they were mounted and ready to ride, even though the wind had picked up and snow filled the afternoon sky. Ducking through the open door of the horse barn, he watched Alonso hurry toward him. Marco waited, unwilling to stay one more minute on this land, so great was his shame at allowing himself to be goaded by that *hechizera*. He was supposed to be a *juez de campo*, a wise man.

He stared ahead, not even willing to look at the man on foot.

"Don't come back here ever again," Alonso mumbled.

"I won't," Marco snapped, his eyes on the gate. "I will send someone else in the fall to retrieve that document I gave you. I will send others to handle any business of the crown I might have with you."

"You have cast aspersions you cannot prove upon the whole Moreno family."

"It's the truth, Alonso," he said, finally looking his former friend in the eyes. "Your wife's father somehow acquired a brand that belongs to Paloma Vega, and her land near El Paso del Norte, after the death of her family in a Comanche raid. She was but eleven years old and had not an advocate in the world. Eleven, Alonso, eleven."

"You have no proof," Alonso replied, his tone less certain.

"You are correct," Marco agreed. "I stand by my accusation, though."

"Go!"

Marco wheeled Buciro around and gestured to his outriders to precede him. He followed, sick at heart at his own foolishness. Any yet .... Before he passed through the gate, he looked back at Alonso.

"Tell me something. Among your wife's jewels and trinkets, have you ever seen a little star and a V on a chain? A child's necklace?"

The look on Alonso's face told Marco everything he needed to know. "That's what I thought."

Alonso surprised him them. With a glance back at the hacienda, he walked to the gate. He put his hand on Buciro, patting Marco's horse in an absentminded way. "I would be your friend again, Marco. Perhaps when *la viruela* has passed, we can discuss this brand."

"If you survive," Marco said. Maybe brutal words would sink in; a *juez* could hope.

"Yes, if we survive. I would be your friend again," Alonso repeated.

"And I, yours," Marco said, reaching down to touch Alonso's shoulder. "*Vaya con Dios.*"

"*Y tu.*" Alonso backed away from Buciro and held up his hand, after another glance at his house.

Relieved—after all, who likes to lose a friend?—Marco rode through the gate, his head high.

His dignity lasted until he was out of sight of the hacienda. He blew out his cheeks and slumped in his saddle, which made his outriders frown and look at each other, uneasy. He managed a weak smile and a joke. "Sometimes I do not shine in this *juez de campo* business," he said to the nearest man.

"If I may, señor, I have heard that no one shines, who comes from the Castellano holdings," the man said, looking at Marco with some sympathy. He laughed. "Maybe you should receive a commendation from the governor for not murdering them both."

Marco managed a chuckle, because it was expected of him. "You have it, Pablo. Perhaps I *did* show remarkable restraint."

HE DIDN'T GET HOME a moment too soon. The Castellano holdings were not quite a league away from his own, but Marco felt the growing reality that the only thing that was going to make his debacle of a visit even slightly palatable was his wife's sympathy. Maybe she could kiss away the hurt to a man's pride, like a mother with a child.

When they arrived at the Double Cross, he didn't argue when his men told him they would curry his horse, Buciro. "Only this time, and *gracias,*" he said as he hurried to his house.

Kitchen smells could wait. He tossed his cloak and hat on a bench in the hall and hurried into their bedchamber. Paloma sat there with her knitting, which she put aside at once. She held out her hand to him, and he saw that she was pale and fine-drawn in that way of someone recuperating, leaning back against her pillow and his. Her eyes were on his face, and they were full of concern.

"Paloma, I blundered so badly with the Castellanos. What I said! *O Dios mio.*"

"Take off your boots," she said as she patted the space beside her and raised the blanket.

He did as she said, tossing his belt and knife after the boots. Without a word, he lay down beside her and rested his head in her lap. He closed his eyes, home again.

"Your ears are cold, my lord," she told him quite formally, the way she always spoke when she was ready to scold him for some infraction or other. Her mild admonition turned into a gentle croon when he started to cry. She put her hand over his ears as though to shelter him from the sound of his own failure, if that's what it was. Heaven knows *she* had never measured up in Maria Teresa's eyes.

"Poor man, did you try to convince them to be inoculated?" she asked when he was silent.

"I failed. I thought perhaps if only Alonso were inoculated, that would be some protection, at least. She wouldn't hear of it."

"Then you have done all you could. No tears over that, my love," Paloma said. She took the pillows out from behind her head and inched down closer to him.

"It was worse. I was so angry, or maybe I was frustrated, but I accused them of stealing your brand and your family's land near El Paso del Norte."

She sucked in her breath, probably upset with him, but she didn't draw away. He waited for her to speak, but she was silent.

"Forgive me for losing my temper." His apology sounded so feeble to his ears. "She taunted me and I rose to the bait like a trout in a stream. Fool!"

"Maria Teresa can be provoking," was all Paloma said. She went to work on the buttons on his shirt. "Why don't you just get comfortable and go to sleep?"

"That's your solution to my stupidity?" he asked, relaxing a little.

"Well, no, but *el médico* told me not to exert myself," she said, sounding most practical.

Marco smiled at that and did as she said, even though it was only early afternoon and he had much to do. He got into a nightshirt only because he did not know when the little doctor might wander through to check on his patient.

He composed himself for a nap, nothing more. When he woke, it was dark and someone—something?—was licking his face.

He sat up, and Trece tumbled into his arms. He patted the space beside him. Paloma wasn't there, and then she was, sitting beside him on the edge of the bed this time, wearing her robe over her nightgown.

"I disobeyed you and the doctor," she said, sounding not even slightly repentant. He heard the sorrow in her voice, and he knew where she had been.

"Andrés …."

"Ah, yes. I walked into the chapel and Trece was whining and sniffing and turning in circles. You won't mind if he sleeps in here for a few nights? I know I was supposed to stay in bed, but …."

Marco rested his head on her leg, as Trece turned around a few times and settled down with a grunt. "I'll miss the old man. He taught me so much, after my father died."

"We all will miss him. Sancha tells me he went peacefully." He felt her sigh more than heard it. "And Sancha told *me* to get back to bed before she swatted me." She put her lips next to his ear. "Are you just a little afraid of her, too?"

"You found me out, Paloma. Better do what she says."

In another moment she was out of her robe and pressed close to him again. "I walked just down to the chapel and back, but I'm tired."

He held his wife close until she slept, only a matter of minutes. When her breathing was deep and regular, Marco got up, dressed again and left Trece curled up next to Paloma. When he opened the door, he nearly jumped back, startled, because Antonio was raising his hand to knock.

"She's sleeping. Just so you know, she disobeyed us and went to the chapel."

"I was there, too. I am sorry about the old man."

To Marco's ears, Antonio didn't sound sorry. He wondered again why the man had gone into medicine in the first place. Wasn't it one of those higher callings, like the priesthood? Obviously, he was too naïve for his own good.

"Let her sleep," he told the doctor.

They walked down the hall together, Antonio telling him who was on the path to recovery and who still lingered in what he called "the shadows." Perhaps he should not judge the little man so harshly, Marco told himself. He looked tired and fine-drawn himself, and still too thin. And he thought he would ride onto the Staked Plains like this?

Marco said as much to Toshua, who had resumed his usual place in Marco's office. He lay on his pallet, not entirely awake, his eyes half-closed, looking very much like Paloma and the other recovering patients in the chapel. "H'mm," was all Toshua said in reply to his rant, designed to cover up the irritation that still smarted from his visit to the Castellanos.

Not that Toshua ever had much to say, Marco reasoned. He shuffled the papers on his desk and arranged them into more efficient piles—like the good bureaucrat he was, he thought, with some distaste. Maybe it was time to turn over the thankless job of *juez de campo* to someone younger. He was thirty-two now and starting to feel it.

"There are ways we can travel on the Llano and attract little notice."

Marco looked up, startled. He had forgotten that Toshua was even in the room, and now the Comanche stood right next to his desk. Damn, but the man was silent.

"Are you saying we might actually do this thing for the doctor—we must, you know—and even survive?" he asked, when his heart had settled back where it belonged.

"I will take you on secret paths and you will have to trust me, because one rise of ground looks much like the other. You will be lost."

"How is it that you can find your way through such a place?"

Toshua shrugged. "I just can. And maybe you should ask yourself if you trust that little man."

"I trust him not at all, but I made his devil's bargain for Paloma."

"I could kill him for you. Paloma knows how to work the magic to defeat the Dark Wind. You don't need him."

"Don't tempt me!"

Toshua gave him that wry look that signaled he did not understand. He walked to the fireplace, added a few more piñon knots and squatted there, facing the flames. He looked back at Marco, and his expression was deadly serious, even menacing.

"Don't even think to sneak away to the Llano with me and the medicine man and leave Paloma behind." He jabbed his finger. "And don't tell me it has not crossed your mind."

I'm guilty as charged, Marco thought, embarrassed. "She must not come."

"You know what she would do—she would follow you anyway, all alone on the Llano."

Chilled, he looked down at the paper in front of him. Toshua was right. He didn't pry in Toshua's life, but he had to ask. "Would any of your wives have done something like that?"

The Comanche looked around elaborately. "Do you see *them* here?"

* * *

PALOMA CAME AWAKE SLOWLY, still turning her head to test for pain. Nothing. Only then did she open her eyes to see Marco watching her from the chair by the bed, Trece in his lap. She wanted to look out the window, but it was shuttered to keep out winter. How was she supposed to know what time of day it was? Her days had always been regulated by duties, but the inoculation had left her as clueless as a child. A week had vanished from her life, and it puzzled her.

"Marco, I don't know if it's morning or night," she complained.

He grinned at her, which made her want to throw something at him. She said as much, and he laughed.

"You are too easily amused," she said, her voice crisp.

"And you are grumpy and therefore recovering, thanks be to God."

She wanted to be angry at him, but he reached under the covers and tickled her foot, which meant she could not stay angry at such a man as a husband, especially if he invoked the deity.

"Señor Gil said two more days in bed, and if the weather isn't too cold, he wants to take you with him while he inoculates our friends in Santa Maria."

"I can't imagine why. I wasn't brave enough to make that cut in Toshua's arm. You will come, too?"

"He didn't invite me, but yes, I will."

Someone knocked. "Speak of the devil," Marco said, with no amusement now.

Antonio opened the door and stood there until Marco nodded. *What makes a man so frightened of his own shadow?* Paloma asked herself as she folded her hands in her lap.

"Did you tell her what I want?" he asked, with no preamble, which made Paloma shake her head. *Poor man!* He would probably never learn the rhythm and nuance of dealing with people like her or Marco. Not for this Englishman or American—whichever he was—the leisurely inquiries about health, general comments and other non-topics that led up to the real reason for the visit.

From his frosty tone, Marco was having similar thoughts. Or Paloma reasoned that a visit to her obnoxious cousin was going to ruin her husband's day far beyond the actual visit.

"I do not *tell* her anything," Marco replied. "If she *chooses* to do as you say, she will. If not, you will find someone else to donate pox."

Antonio looked at him, mystified, and then he shrugged and addressed her, after an elaborate bow that irritated Marco further—he was determined not to be cheerful—and amused her. "My dear Señora Mondragón, would you—or do I ask too much?—would you consent to let me scrape your neck for its truly excellent scabs so we can inoculate the village of Santa Maria?"

"Certainly, you may," she replied. "I would ask something of you in exchange."

"Anything up to one half of my puny kingdom," Antonio teased.

"You may scrape away at my neck once you have finished telling me what happened after you married your wife and settled in Louisiana."

The smile left his face. "You can imagine the rest," he told her, his eyes troubled. "Would you be satisfied if I just admitted that I was a fool and the poorest husband in all of North America? We all have our hard stories."

"We do," Paloma agreed. "Still, I would have *your* hard story, señor."

Chapter Fifteen

In which Antonio unburdens himself

WHEN HE FINISHED, ANTHONY knew the Mondragóns would not look upon him so kindly, as they were doing now. Just wait, he will put down the silly dog and his wife will edge over on their bed and give him room to sit with her. I doubt she would mind if he kept his boots on, spurs and all. Oh, no; he knows better than to try that. I see before me a well-trained husband.

The dog minded no better than most little dogs, whining until Señor Mondragón reached down and scooped him up. He angled the little yellow dog toward the foot of the bed, and although it whined again, it was not allowed to squeeze between the two of them.

The doctor sighed inwardly. In the last four months of her life, Anthony Gill's wife was edging away from him, obviously unhappy. On the other hand, Pia Maria always gave him her complete attention—at least all the attention a three-year-old is capable of—which was almost enough to take away the pain her mother was causing. Whether Catalina knew it or not, he couldn't have said.

"Pull that chair closer," Mondragón told him, which gratified Anthony.

"Where did I leave off?" Anthony asked Paloma, even though he knew full well where he had stopped the narrative earlier that day.

"You and … and Catalina had a daughter named Pia Maria," Paloma prompted.

"Yes, Catalina," he said, enjoying the sound again. "Catalina."

"I used to do that," she said.

"Do what?"

"Say my brother Claudio's name out loud over and over, when I knew my aunt and uncle could not hear me," she told him, her eyes on her hands. "There was Rafael, too, but it was Claudio who liked to put me in front of him on his horse."

"You never told me much about Claudio," Señor Mondragón said.

It's my story, not hers, Anthony wanted to say, but they were looking at each other. He watched them, envious again.

"I've wanted to, as you talk about Felicia now and then." Leaning closer, she gave her husband a kiss, then remembered Anthony, blushed, and drew back.

Anthony held his breath as Señor Mondragón touched his wife's cheek and she leaned toward him again. It was a lovely gesture. The *juez* whispered in his wife's ear then, and she nodded, her eyes down. "If we have a son," she whispered.

There is more here than I know, Anthony thought, wondering, for the first time in a long while, about the lives of others.

But they were looking at him now, or Señor Mondragón was. "Tell us," was all he said, but in a peremptory fashion, as though this was a subject that needed changing.

"We were barely managing," Anthony said, feeling as though he were trying out the words. "Catalina seemed content enough, but I wanted more."

No need for them to know that for some reason, Anthony had always wanted more, a larger slice of bread, a bigger dog, a better education, a grander house. On and on, until there was nothing; that was the trouble with wanting.

"I had been putting a little by, here and there, and I had the misfortune to listen to a land scheme."

That wasn't entirely truthful. Some of the citizens in Natchitoches talked about large tracts of land for sale to the west, and a man among them who claimed to be a surveyor and an agent. Anthony had sought out the man. He had walked right into the scheme like a particularly stupid fly wandering into a web.

"He told us of land to the west in Texas, where cattle roamed wild, and mission Indians were tame and willing to work for little. He represented himself as an agent for a Spanish grandee who owned the land."

"It isn't done like that," Mondragón said.

"I know that now. I believed him then, maybe because I wanted to." Anthony thought it might hurt to say that out loud, but he felt a surprising relief. "I wanted more." He couldn't help the catch in his throat. "I convinced my father-in-law to join my scheme. I lost all our money and most of his, and he threw me out of town. He had that kind of power."

He closed his eyes, remembering the awful scene: Catalina in tears, Pia Maria distressed and moving back and forth between her parents, his father-in-law shamed and reprimanded by those in authority above him. To this day, Anthony wasn't sure why Catalina had followed him.

He glanced at the Mondragóns, wondering at their reaction. It was what he suspected he would see: Paloma's eyes were filled with sympathy, whereas Marco looked skeptical, wearing the thoughtful expression of a man unlikely to be taken in. Anthony plunged on. Better to bare all, now that he had started.

"I couldn't go east, because word had spread through official channels that I was a schemer. And the British and the Americans were still slugging it out. There was one more Spanish presidio just west of the French in Natchitoches."

"Los Adaes," Mondragón said. "Wasn't that where, years ago, the governor had forced the settlers to go farther west to San Antonio de Bexar? And some objected?"

"Ah, yes. Eventually some of them straggled back toward Rio Trinidad. They had their fill of dust and Comanches."

"What kind of people lived in Los Adaes when you got there?" Mondragón asked.

"What you would expect: discouraged folk, some French, runaway blacks, confused Indians." He managed a laugh. "I treated malaria and sore eyes, mostly, and all kinds of venereal disease."

Paloma made a little sound and turned her face away. She was such a tender soul.

"We had one common denominator, though."

"Comanches."

Anthony nodded. "They knew a weak settlement when they saw one. I suppose it was just a matter of time."

Paloma made another sound, one that brought Mondragón's hand to her neck as he pulled her face into the hollow of his shoulder.

"We know enough of that," the *juez* said. "Say no more."

"Oh, no! You get all of it," Anthony said, his voice rising. "I was in the presidio, treating someone's case of the clap, for God's sake! The Penateka raped and tortured my wife and impaled her on a lance that came out of the top of her head. I think she was still alive when they did that. They snatched away Pia Maria."

He looked at them and saw only confusion, then realized he had spoken in English. Well, never mind; they had imaginations. He was silent.

"Penateka," Señor Mondragón said, repeating the only word he had understood. "Honey eaters. They took your daughter and sold her farther west? That would be their style."

"Yes."

"How do you know for certain?"

"After I buried my wife, I rode with some soldiers to San Antonio de Bexar." He made a face, remembering how the men had treated him, an *inglés* who spoke poor Spanish. "Everyone needs a surgeon, señor."

Mondragón nodded. "And a good blacksmith," he added, which made Paloma chuckle.

Anthony thought he would be a bigger man and overlook their gentle humor at his expense. "We passed a settlement that had forted up and defended themselves. They mentioned seeing a little girl no more than three, with long yellow hair. Pia Maria. They said the Indians were not Penateka, but Nokoni, so she had been sold."

"The Nokoni live north, not out here."

"In San Antonio, I joined with traders who had come from a Nokoni camp where they said a blond child was traded to Kwahadi." He couldn't help the bitterness in his voice. "The Kwahadi traded twenty buffalo robes for her."

Apparently Señor Mondragón saw the matter differently. "Twenty, eh? That tells me they are taking very good care of her. Twenty!"

For the first time since he had stared in horror at Catalina, Anthony felt the tiniest comfort. He looked at the *juez*, seeing nothing but sincerity in the man's expression. There was no false hope there; Señor Mondragón believed what he was saying. "You think so?"

"I know it," he replied simply.

The Mondragóns looked at him now with kindness in their eyes, all teasing aside.

"I must find Pia Maria. I have nothing left," Anthony concluded. He knew that among the traders, it had been a sign of weakness to let his desperation show on his face. He thought the Mondragóns were susceptible to bare pleading. "You have so much, señores. I have so little."

Paloma nodded. "You may do what you will to my neck now. I hope it will not hurt."

A safe topic again. Anthony sighed inwardly; he understood scabs. He motioned Señor Mondragón to move, and he did, but not far. The *juez* stood beside the bed, his eyes intent on the process. For a brief moment, Anthony held his bistoury in the flame of the fireplace, then walked back to them, waving the little instrument in the air to cool it.

Paloma eyed the blade with some trepidation and leaned back when he approached her.

"Come now! You're the lady with her sandals tacked on the wall in the *sala*," he said.

"That wasn't so hard," she replied, her eyes still on the bistoury. "I was astoundingly in love with this man with light brown eyes."

Anthony glanced at that man and smiled to see him blush. He gave him a moment to kneel beside the bed and whisper in Paloma's ear.

"Well, I was," she whispered back, her voice gruff. "Still am." She took a deep breath and sat forward, turning her head to expose her neck and its line of scabs.

Deftly, Anthony pressed the sharp blade against the edge of the scab and popped it onto the cloth in his hand. One more and two more, and the thing was done.

"There, now. I didn't hurt you," he told his patient. "Hold still another moment. I'd like some of that ooze, too."

She shuddered, and Marco laughed, which earned him a hard stare from his wife. When he had extracted all the runny matter he wanted, Anthony folded a small square of linen and dribbled some wine on it. He handed it to Marco, who diligently dabbed at the red spots on Paloma's neck until the oozing stopped.

"Very good." Anthony closed the tin container and tossed the linen squares in the fire. He pointed an admonitory finger at his patient. "One more day and night in bed with no exertion, then your life will be your own again, Señora Mondragón. I now declare you immune from *la viruela* for as long as you live."

Tears came to her eyes, and she reached for the hand of that husband who laughed at her, twining her fingers through his. Anthony glanced at him and looked away. The *juez* wasn't doing any better at schooling his own feelings. What a bunch of crybabies; the Spanish were like that.

He held up two fingers. "Two days from now, *con su permiso, juez*, I will take your wife—and probably Toshua, because he will insist—and inoculate all of Santa Maria who signed your paper."

"I will go, too."

WHEN DARKNESS CAME, THE Mondragóns lay in bed, Paloma's nightgown more north than south.

"You heard the *médico*, dear husband: a day *and* a night with no exertion."

"Is this exertion?"

"Perhaps not."

He whispered in her ear. She laughed softly and wrapped her legs around him.

"Only once, because I am still recuperating."

Later, Marco closed his eyes, soothed into that comforting sort of relief that making love to his excellent wife gave him. He held her close. "I meant it, dearest, every word. Someday we will name our son Claudio."

He felt her silent sigh and clapped his arm tighter around her, giving her a shake. "Have a little more faith, Paloma, just a little."

He felt her nod against his shoulder. "Do twins run in the Mondragón family?"

"No. They ran in Felicia's family. You and I will eventually have babies one at a time."

Feeling the sudden dampness on his shoulder, he swallowed the boulder in his throat. "Just a little faith," he whispered.

Chapter Sixteen

In which people have their reasons

TWO DAYS LATER, THE sun shone but gave off no warmth as the four of them, plus their ever-present outriders, rode to Santa Maria. Paloma took a deep breath of the frosty air, wondering how long the sensation would last of relief and reprieve from sickness and death. In her heart, she knew she owed the little *médico* a debt she could never repay, even if he was a scoundrel and she wasn't entirely certain she would ever trust him.

They had come from the funeral for Andrés, partly Catholic and partly Tewa. As he lay dying, the old man had told Sancha specifically that he wanted only prayers from his master, the *juez*. After the trip to the family burying ground—Paloma watched Marco's eyes linger on the three graves most dear to him there—the others had divided up the old retainer's possessions, Tewa fashion, telling stories and joking. When all that was left was Trece, Sancha stepped forward. She looked around as though daring anyone to stop her, and picked up the little dog.

"He is a valuable dog, Sancha," Marco teased. "Probably from the court of the emperor of China, considering how much I paid for him."

"He will eat well in my kitchen, señor," was all she said. Trece licked her ear as she carried him to that kitchen.

Without wasting another moment, they mounted and rode to Santa Maria, Paloma happy to be in the saddle. She noticed her husband watching her carefully, worried for her. And there was Toshua, glancing at her now and then, too. Did a woman need so many protectors? At least the *médico* appeared unconcerned about her health. She watched him, instead, understanding him for what he was: a man who cared for nobody except himself. For the first time, Paloma wondered why he was so intent upon finding Pia Maria. She made a small sign of the cross on her chest, taking back such a wicked thought. Certainly he cared for his child; why else would he be here?

"Are you feeling good?" Marco asked, leaning toward her.

Heavens, the man must have seen something sour in her expression, with such a wicked idea. "I am fine, dearest," she assured him. "I just had the strangest thought."

"Care to share it?"

She shook her head. "You'd think I had cotton wadding for brains."

"Don't you?" he joked. "You married me," which made her gasp and prod him with her quirt.

Dear God, it feels good to tease and be teased, she thought, as she put spurs to her horse and chased Marco across the wintry landscape. It also relieved her not to have to express her strange thoughts about Antonio Gil.

BY THE TIME THEY arrived in Santa Maria, snow was falling and Paloma was hungry. Maybe Marco was hungry, too, because he led their little group directly to Santa Maria, their church. She knew he had sent riders ahead to let Father Francisco know they were coming for the inoculations and would be staying in the church's humble answer to a guesthouse. A warm fire would be welcome, Paloma told herself, maybe even more welcome than tortillas.

Father Francisco met them at the side door, his hands tucked economically into his long sleeves, his face serious. His expression didn't change when Marco asked if their rooms in the guesthouse were ready, but he did gesture them off their horses and into the stables.

When their horses were curried and grained, he handed Marco the key to the little house that connected to what passed for a rectory, in such a small town. "There is room for you all, except the Indian will have to sleep in the barn," he said, which earned a grunt of satisfaction from Toshua, who had told Paloma earlier that was what he planned to do, anyway.

"When you are settled, Señor Mondragón, come to the rectory, please," the priest said, and turned on his heel.

Paloma looked at her husband. "That was not the warmest welcome in the history of our polite society," she said, trying to tease.

He turned the key in the lock and ushered her inside, Antonio following. "No, it was not. I have a feeling I know why." His put his arm around her shoulders. "Last year, Toshua told me he would have been happy to kill your cousin for me. Like a fool, I ignored him."

She gaped at him. "What in the world …."

After motioning Antonio toward his room and seeing him inside, Marco pulled her into their little chamber and shut the door. "The Castellanos probably rushed here as fast as they could to tell the priest that I had urged her to be inoculated, even if it meant losing her child. She will have told our priest that I encouraged her to commit a mortal sin."

"Dear God," she whispered.

The room had nothing more than a bed with a crucifix above the headboard, a charcoal brazier, cold now, and a *reclinatorio* for the penitent. His arm still around her, Marco sank down on the bed. "*Madre de Dios*, how did it come to this?" he asked. "All I have tried to do is serve these people, my friends—"

"You don't have to face this alone," she told him. "I will come with you."

"You needn't be there," he said, with no conviction.

She didn't bother to reply, but stood up and pulled him to his feet. "March, señor."

Easy to be tough; harder to knock and stand in front of Father Francisco's closed door for an inordinate length of time, behavior that struck her as rude.

The door finally opened. His face a study in discomfort, Father Francisco ushered them in. He hesitated to let in Paloma, but she pretended not to notice.

"Where my husband goes, I go," she said, her head high.

They seated themselves in front of the priest's desk. He looked at Marco a long time, his glance wavering before Marco's, troubled.

"Let me help you, Father," Marco said, as kindly as he could. "The Castellanos came to you to tattle that I had encouraged her to be inoculated against *la viruela*, even if there was a danger from inoculation that she could lose the child she carries."

Father Francisco's relief was almost palpable. "Yes, that is what they did. Marco, Marco, how could you *say* such a thing?"

"Truly, Father, our little *médico* is not certain that would be the result. He doesn't *know*! Before Christ, he is also fully aware of what he asks." Marco shook his head. "You know me, Father. I am not a man to go against any teachings of our Catholic faith."

Father Francisco sighed and stood up, pacing two steps forward and two steps back in his tiny office. He stopped and held out his hands. "What can we do, if *la viruela* visits us? Some will die anyway."

"But not as many! And truly, it may not even visit us, but I fear it will. Antonio Gil has seen its ravages across Texas." Marco stood up, too. "Father, I will encourage inoculation among all the people on my list. If women who are with child ask us, what do we tell them?"

Father Francisco clapped his hands together in frustration. "Tell them, oh, tell them what you told the Castellanos, but do not encourage such women to be inoculated! Holy Church cannot tolerate that." He pointed his finger at the *juez*. "And *you* would be in danger of excommunication, and worse, if the news traveled to Santa Fe and the bishop."

His words hung in the air. Paloma held her breath, full of new fear. How had it come to this? *Does my cousin hate us so much?* she asked herself, appalled.

"I will do as you say, Father," Marco said finally. He knelt. "Bless me, please."

Tears in his eyes, Father Francisco did as he asked. When he finished, he kissed Marco's forehead. "You have been placed in a bad position, but I do not know what we would do without you, señor. It must be that you have to do our dirty work." He clapped his hands again, but quietly this time, as if he wanted to change the subject and clear the air. "And now, please join me for our noon meal, the *médico*, too."

Paloma took Marco's hand as they walked back to get Antonio. She leaned against his arm, saying nothing. "All I really want to do is raise my cattle and sheep, live in peace and love you," he whispered, staring straight ahead. "Is the burden of *juez de campo* too much?"

She had no answer for him, stung because he had been forced to agree to Antonio Gil's devil's bargain in the first place. A lesser man would ignore it, but she knew she had not married a lesser man. Her cousin Maria Teresa had done that.

MARCO DID HIS BEST to maintain normal conversation over *la comida del mediodía*, grateful that Paloma kept up a steady commentary with the priest. Father Francisco's words had stung far more than the old man knew. Marco sat back—which made Paloma give him a startled glance—and considered the matter, remembering a time when a rancher, long dead now, had raked his own father, *juez* before him, over the coals for some misdemeanor or other. When the man left, still full of righteous indignation, Papa had only shrugged. "That's what it is to be *juez* de campo, *mi hijo*. Don't let anyone talk *you* into tackling such a thankless burden. You *know* better."

If only I hadn't had such a good example, dear Papa, he thought.

Antonio had been darting him quizzical glances. Once the meal was over and they began their rounds to the homes that had requested inoculation, Marco explained to the doctor just what had happened at the Castellanos and why the priest had talked to him in private. All he received in return for his explanation was a shake of the head, and "You Catholics," from Antonio, who was probably a total heretic, or worse, a Methodist.

Supplying balm to Marco's sore heart, they were well-received in Santa Maria, with entire families submitting to inoculation. There were frowns and tears, but it helped that Paloma was willing to hold the little ones on her lap and cuddle them while Antonio did his work. Even old Emilio Blanco, the blacksmith, had no objection when she held his hand. He blushed, but he did not draw away. While Antonio bandaged, Marco looked at his list and paired the patients with those who would help them while they suffered.

"I have to admire your lists," Antonio said as they passed the house of Señora Carmen Saltero, the mad seamstress. "You're a better bureaucrat than most."

"Is that a compliment or not?" Marco protested, but not with any vehemence.

"A compliment. Wait now, is this house on your list or not?"

Marco had stopped to face Señora Saltero's house. "It is not, but I want to try once more." He touched Paloma's arm. "And I have a gift for you here."

His wife smiled at him, her eyes lively. "Something for me? Is there an occasion?"

"Do I need one?" he asked in turn, remembering what old Andrés had said a year ago, about Paloma not being a woman who would ever make demands. He was right; too bad Andrés was not alive for Marco to remind him of his observation. "Perhaps there is an occasion. Let's stop."

Señora Saltero met them at the door with a smile wreathing her already wrinkled face and a tape measure around her neck. "Come, come," she said, ushering them inside to warmth and the fragrance of cinnamon.

Marco watched the doctor as they stepped into the *sala*, where Carmen Saltero kept her collection of ladies' mannequins, life-sized and grouped in cliques, as though they spoke to one another. Eyes wide, Antonio leaped back and swore in English, so no one was offended.

"I'll explain later," Paloma whispered to the man, giving him a little shove in the small of his back, because in his sudden terror, he had nearly collided with her.

While they stood in the *sala*—Antonio edging inch by inch toward the front door—Carmen went to a side table. She picked up a cloak and handed it to Paloma.

"He said you needed the warmest cloak I could make," Señora Saltero said, and looked at Marco for his approval. "Will this do, señor?"

With an exclamation of delight, Paloma shook out the handsome brown cloak, with its attached hood. She hefted it. "My goodness, Marco, it's so heavy! I'll be warm forever."

Marco nodded at the seamstress. "Perfect. We're going on a little winter trip, and I want my dear one to be warm."

"She will be, and then some," Señora Saltero said, pleased. "And now you two, what else can I help you with?"

Marco came close and put his arms around the dear lady, who let him fold her into his embrace. "Now why have you not consented to be inoculated? I will worry about you, if you are not."

She pulled away far enough to see his face but did not step out of the circle of his arms. "Twenty years ago in that last Comanche raid, I lost everyone." Her eyes filled with tears as she looked at Antonio, the one she did not know. "Señor, a husband and five children! I miss them," she said simply.

Marco pulled her close again. "Who will make dresses for our lovely ladies in Santa Maria?"

"I have been training Aldonza Rivera," she said. "She is even now in my sewing room, hard at work." She touched Paloma's cheek. "She made that cloak."

"It is a lovely cloak," Paloma said. Marco thought she might try to argue with the seamstress, but she did not.

People have their reasons, he thought, giving Señora Saltero a kiss on both cheeks. "Go with God, dearest," he said.

"And you, señor. Good day now."

"You could have put up more of a fight," the doctor said, when they closed the gate and stepped into the street again.

"No."

"That's all? No?"

Maybe he spoke out of turn, but Marco stopped and put his hands on the doctor's shoulders. The man flinched at his touch, and again he wondered just how badly the traders had used him. "Señor Gil, when you had a practice back there in Georgia, did you really get to know your patients?"

The man bristled and shook off Marco's hands. "Of course I did!" He paused and looked away. "Well, I tried. Now and then. I was busy."

So I thought, Marco told himself. "I am their *juez* and I know these people. I know that woman's pain. I would never argue with her. Trust me, it would be futile."

"If only I were as wise as you," Antonio snapped. He hurried ahead and Marco watched him go, shaking his head.

But here was Paloma, wearing the lovely new cloak, putting her arm through his arm. "I'll be warm when we ride to the Llano."

BUTCHER, BAKER, SOLDIERS, THE town beggar, Indios, prisoners in the presidio, the only *fiscal*, widows and orphans. Antonio inoculated most of them, but made Paloma do one for every three persons. The first cut had been difficult, considering that she had not had the courage to cut Toshua's arm. After that, she took her turn.

Two more houses and they would be done. The sun had long since left the sky and the snow had stopped, which meant that the cold settled in. Paloma pulled her new cloak tighter around her, relishing the warmth and wishing Antonio had such a cloak. The little man shivered, which didn't escape Marco's notice.

"I have something warmer for you at the Double Cross," he said as he knocked on the second to the last house. "We'll be warm and welcome here at the Mendozas."

Paloma gave him her questioning look.

"Rico and Luz Mendoza live here with their four children," he whispered in her ear. "I'm surprised the gossips in the knitting group didn't already do my work for me. I came so close to marrying this good woman, two years after Felicia …. Ah, Rico, may we come in?"

Rico the tinsmith. She should have known. Elaborate tin sconces with candles burning made their kitchen brighter than anyone else's. She would have to ask Marco to let her buy more sconces for their *sala* and perhaps their bedroom. She had no objection to eyeing him in bed.

Children and servants went first, except for two older women who already bore the scars of smallpox. While Paloma helped Antonio, she noticed Marco and Luz Mendoza deep in conversation and felt the tiniest twinge. *My love, if you had married this woman, you would have such a family now*, she thought, unable to help herself. *Ay de mi.*

Rico was next, his face serious. Intent, he watched Marco and Luz, too, and Paloma wondered what he was thinking. She glanced at Luz, who nodded before resting her head for the briefest moment on Marco's arm. She looked at Rico, worried, but he had a look of such relief on his face that Paloma was astounded.

"*Gracias a Dios*," he whispered, unmindful of the nick on his arm. He held out his other hand to Luz, and she hurried to his side and kneeled, kissing his hand.

"I know what I have to do, my love," she said. "The matter rests between us alone."

Rico nodded and flashed a huge smile to Marco, who sighed and turned away, overcome by something that Paloma did not understand. Never mind; he would tell her later.

Then it was Luz's turn. She sat on the stool her husband had vacated and dutifully held out her arm. "Señora Mondragón, would you?" she asked, her eyes bright, her expression resolute. "You were so gentle with Pepe and Celestia's inoculations."

"With pleasure."

Marco said nothing all the way back to the church, so she did not pelt him with questions. This was something he must not want Antonio to hear.

The doctor walked beside them, moving more slowly. Sympathetic to his exhaustion, Paloma slowed her steps. Marco now noticed they were hurrying too quickly for the little man and so began to move at a more leisurely pace, even though it was so cold.

In the frigid hall of the guest house, they said goodnight to each other. Paloma put her arms around Marco's neck as soon as he closed their door. "You had better tell me!"

"Of course. I think I can trust you," he said, which earned him a jab in the ribs from his loving wife.

"What was that all about?" she asked, shedding her cloak because the charcoal brazier had been lit and burned down to coals that warmed the little room. "Tell me now, or I won't ...."

"Won't what, my dove?" he teased.

"Oh, you know." Funny how the dratted man could still make her blush.

"Only if it goes no farther than these walls." He unbuttoned her basque and cupped his hands around her breasts. "My hands are cold."

Paloma turned her face into his chest so she would not shriek. His hands *were* cold, no denying. Apparently it was her task to warm them, even though she had planned to do precisely that, once they were in bed.

"All right, you scoundrel, they're warm enough!" she said. "You and Luz Mendoza were talking so privately and I'll admit it gave me a twinge." She frowned. "Rico didn't seem too worried, though. Oh, please! What happened?"

She shucked off her basque and skirt and darted under the covers, where she wriggled out of her chemise and removed her wool stockings. The smile on her husband's face, where earlier he had been so glum, cheered her heart. When he was bare and beside her, he kissed her shoulder and pulled her close, serious again even though they were in bed, a time when he usually was not so serious.

"Luz told me she was just barely with child, and begged my understanding that she still wanted to be inoculated. She thought I would object, because I am an agent of the crown. Bless her simple, honest heart. Dear God, objection was the farthest thing from my mind! I'll leave that to priests and popes. God forgive me if I have sinned."

Paloma heard the wonder in his voice. "I assured her that I dealt in brands and inspections, and neighbors' quarrels, and served as the law where there was none, but there my power ended. I told her whatever she decided was between her and *el padre eternal*, no one else. She believed me, because she wanted to. Paloma, Father Francisco must never hear of this."

He rolled over on his back and pulled her with him, his arms tight around her. "And who knows? Perhaps their tiny child will be unaffected by what we did tonight." He kissed Paloma. "All she wants to do is raise her children. Is

God so unmerciful as to prevent that? I doubt it supremely. Love me, Paloma."

"That's easy," she assured him, kissing his chest. "So you nearly married her?"

He laughed and rolled her over again. "I sat in her father's *sala* for a few nights, until she kindly told me she was desperately in love with Rico the tinsmith. Even if I was a rich landowner, I was too old." His hands on her breasts were warm now. "Am I too old, *chiquita mia*?

"Silly man," she said.

Chapter Seventeen

In which Paloma shares her uncertainty, maybe even her pain

THEY LEFT FOR THE Double Cross at noon the next day, after Antonio insisted on another, more rapid tour of the village, checking everyone he and Paloma had inoculated the day before. One stubborn jailer had changed his mind. Blushing, he asked Paloma to do the honors. Her face warm, too, she did as he asked, then impulsively kissed his forehead. Tears came to his eyes.

"No one has ever been so kind, señora," he said. "How can I thank you?"

"Don't beat your prisoners," she replied. "I am certain they are miserable enough, already."

"You have a soft heart, my love," Marco told her as they rode toward home. "I fear our trip to the *llano* is going to toughen you."

She nodded, uncertain what to say, so she said nothing. *It's all part of the adventure,* she wanted to tell her husband. As she mulled over that idea, another thought struck her with more force—maybe all of life was part of the adventure, the good times and the bad ones, the terror and peace, joy and sorrow. *If I look on it all as an adventure, I hope it makes me kinder, not tougher,* she told herself. Maybe she could explain this to her man some day.

He had turned to talk to Antonio, riding on the other side of him, so she slowed her horse and waited for Toshua, riding behind and watchful. She realized with a start that it was the first time in their many months' acquaintance that she had sought him out. He must have had the same thought, because he looked surprised.

"Would you be disappointed in me if I told you that I am afraid of this journey to the Llano Estacado?" she asked, wondering why she hadn't been brave enough to tell Marco the same thing. She knew Toshua would not answer quickly, and was patient.

"I am afraid, too, little one."

She looked at him with perfect understanding. "You just made me a little less afraid, Toshua. If I am afraid and you are afraid, we will be more watchful. Thank you."

He grinned like a boy then reached over, pulled down the hood of her cloak, ruffled her hair, and pulled the hood up again, so fast she might have thought it never happened at all, except that her hair was now a mess. He spurred his horse ahead, and she could see his shoulders shaking, which made her laugh, too.

Then he stopped and rejoined her, his face serious. "There is one thing: you have to trust me, Paloma."

Toshua had also never called her Paloma before. Always it was señora. She nodded, knowing he was right.

"I will trust you."

She knew she spoke too quickly when he gave her a stare. "I will try," she amended.

HOME HAD NEVER LOOKED so good to Paloma. Although Marco had assured her over and over that everything she saw now was hers, too, she still couldn't grasp the idea, not after years of discomfort and fear in Santa Fe with her relatives. Once the gates swung shut, she looked around, pleased, already picturing flowers in the porch's hanging baskets and tender shoots to coax along in the kitchen garden. In a mere two months, if God was good, the *acequia* would gurgle with water again, and the summer birds would return.

Even now, in the clutch of winter, the Double Cross was all she could ask for. Marco still wouldn't let her curry and grain her own horse, so Paloma sat on the railing in the horse barn and watched him. She contemplated the capable way he stroked the horses and thought for a moment—before it made her blush—how capable those same hands felt on her body. *Dios mio, Paloma,* she warned herself. *Someone would think you had only been married two weeks, and not nearly a year and a half.*

"A peso for your thoughts," Marco said.

She could lie and giggle, but why? She hung onto the post and leaned closer. "I was just thinking about your hands and how nice they feel."

"Just my hands?" he teased.

She did put her hand to her mouth and giggle, even though Antonio watched them both from the next stall. "Be quiet, Marco."

A slow wink from her lord and master followed, and then he turned back to the business at hand. In another minute, he was whistling like a boy, and not a *juez de campo* with huge responsibilities. She watched him seriously now, grateful beyond measure, wishing her parents could know how well things turned out for her.

She asked Marco about that, several hours later when they were in bed and winding down for sleep. "Father Eusebio would probably say, 'Thilly girl, you are no Bible thscholar,' but Marco, do you think the dead have any way of knowing how things are going, here on earth?"

"I hope they do," her husband said as he settled into his favorite position, with her back tucked up close to his chest. He kissed several vertebrae on that back, and she felt a little fizz, even as her eyes closed. "It would be a fine thing if Felicia knows I am happy. I wasn't, for eight years."

"And I would like my parents to know that their daughter is alive and well and content."

"Very content, I think." He kissed her again, but he yawned, too. He ran his hand along the ridge of her hip. "It begins tomorrow, Paloma. We'll prepare for our trip. You and your kitchen ladies will make *carne seca*, and Toshua and I will consider which pack horses to take."

"And our little *médico*?"

"He told me he's going to harvest some more scabs." Marco shuddered. "I'll find him warmer clothes, but how do you think he will fare?"

"He got *here*, didn't he?"

Marco chuckled. "I'm a dolt! Paloma, it's your fault. Loving you must addle my wits. He's probably tougher than we are."

Paloma settled in for the night, secure in her husband's arms. "Maybe rage has kept him alive. It kept me going in Santa Fe." She kissed his arm. "Now love sustains me. Good night."

Marco stayed awake long after Paloma slept, his satisfied body reminding him that nature had taken its course and he should sleep now, but his mind paying no attention. He knew how to make plans; he knew that when they saddled up and rode east into the most dangerous place in all of King Carlos's New World domains, he would be ready. What his mind couldn't agree to was taking his wife with them, simply because she refused to stay behind.

He knew he could order Emiliano, his old steward, to lock her in a room and not let her out for three or four days. By then, he and Antonio and Toshua would either be dead or swallowed up by the Staked Plains. Paloma would not know where to look or how to begin, all by herself. What nagged him was that he did not know what she would do. His head told him that a sensible woman would remain at the Double Cross and give him the scold of his life when or if he returned. His heart told him that this complicated, tough-beyond-fear woman he had married would follow anyway. He dared not take that chance.

The moon was high, so he moved carefully to his side and watched her sleep. She was right—his eyelashes were longer than hers, a fact that she frowned about, when she slowed down long enough to look at herself in the mirror. He could find no fault with her anywhere, from her brown hair, to her freckles here and there, to her graceful shape. Not for the first time, he wondered what was going on inside her body to keep a baby from beginning. It was a mystery and it chafed him. He needed sons and daughters for all this land. He craved another little one or two—oh, the twins!—crawling around his stocking feet in the office and trying out a new tooth on his big toe. He never minded the burp smell, or the other odors of little bodies. And there was Felicia with her deep brown eyes, loving every moment of their constant needs. He closed his eyes in utter pain, and must have cried out, because Paloma opened her eyes.

She seemed to know his sorrow, because her eyes filled with tears, too—something he never wanted to see, and never wanted to cause. His insides writhed.

"Maybe one of us can work up the nerve to talk to *el médico*," she whispered into his neck. "Marco, I am so, so sorry."

What could he say? He hugged her tight.

PALOMA WOKE UP EARLY, sad to her heart's core, knowing that somewhere deep down in her husband and lover's generous heart, there was a spot she could not fill. She dressed quietly, not bothering with shoes, and let herself out of their room. Dark shadows filled the corridor, but she paid them no mind as she tiptoed to the chapel.

The benches again replaced the pallets, now that everyone was recovered from inoculation. She knew her way around the chapel, even in the dark, so she walked to the front, genuflected, and found the row with the candles. Pleased with Marco for being so up-to-date, she found one of the newfangled lucifers and scratched it against the railing. The little flare and the smell of sulfur brightened the space and briefly drowned out the incense. She lit a candle and knelt there, praying for what, she did not know.

It was wrong of her to think that Felicia would disappear from Marco's heart—she knew that—so Paloma pleaded with the Virgin to ask her Son to forgive that vanity on her part. There must be a saint somewhere for barren women, but Paloma didn't know who it might be. Instead, she pressed her forehead against the smooth rail and wept for herself.

She knew she dared not bargain with the Virgin Mary or promise the Lord that she would never ask for anything else, because she already asked for nothing, except for a child. She had so much—a loving husband, a beautiful home, food, warmth, clothing. It was more than she ever thought would be hers. She closed her eyes tighter and pressed her lips even tighter, remembering that eternity of lying scrunched into the corner under her mother's bed, terrified almost to the point of madness, as death ruled her peaceful home and slammed down her parents. She remembered wanting desperately for everything to be exactly the same as it had been earlier that morning, except that she knew it never would be again.

She whispered the *Ave* over and over until her mind calmed, until she could reflect on that long-ago day with a certain detachment, and not horror. She considered what it was that had kept her from crawling out and surrendering herself to the Comanches. Something had kept her where she was, even when the building caught fire and flames crackled in the *vigas* high overhead. She had heard no voice, no miraculous reprieve from a saint or *Padre Eternal* Himself, who obviously had bigger fish to fry elsewhere, even as her entire world crumbled. What was it?

To her infinite relief, she felt it again, kneeling there in the darkness of the chapel, lit by one tiny flame. Paloma watched the flame, small and bravely burning. Truly, there was not a baby inside her yet, but there was something else, some bit of strength that she knew, just *knew*, was powerful enough to rule her universe. Where it came from, she had no clue. It had always been there, even in her deepest despair. It burned there now; maybe she had just forgotten.

With a shuddering sigh, she rocked back on her heels, then bowed forward until her forehead pressed against the cold tiles. "*Gracias*," she whispered into the floor, and kissed the tile. No prayers to the Virgin were futile. If anyone understood babies, longing, and courage, it must be Holy Mary, Mother of God.

When she sat up, she knew she was not alone. She knew it was Toshua, and for the first time, she felt nothing but relief. When her eyes accustomed themselves to the gloom, she saw him sitting, Comanche-fashion, almost close enough to touch. Without a word, she moved over and sat the same way beside him. She leaned against his shoulder, which made him take a sudden deep breath.

They sat there in silence, Paloma knowing she would have to speak first, because he was a shy man. She cleared her throat.

"I was feeling sad because I do not have a baby inside me." There, she had said it to someone besides Marco. "I came here to think about the matter. Why are you here?"

"Because you are here."

She glanced at him in surprise. "But you … you sleep in Marco's office."

She felt him nod. "I also wander this Double Cross at night, checking if all is well." He nudged her shoulder. "All was not well."

"But the guards—don't they see you?"

"No one sees me unless I want them to."

There was nothing of braggadocio in his words; it was a statement of fact, so she nodded. "You wanted me to see you now? Why?"

"So you will know you are not alone."

She was silent, just leaning against this man who was her protector in more ways, perhaps, than she would ever know. To her deep satisfaction, his arm slowly went around her shoulder.

"Call me *pabi*."

"Pavee?"

"Close enough."

"What does it mean?"

"Older brother. You need one now, I think. Will I do?"

Paloma had thought she was through with tears. Apparently she was wrong.

Chapter Eighteen

In which three travelers begin a winter trip with a man they don't trust

MARCO KNEW PALOMA HAD left their bed, and he thought he knew why. He also reckoned she might want to be alone with herself. He lay there in his suddenly empty bed, wondering if he could explain to this blessed woman that somehow, in a way he could not understand either, there was room in his heart for both of his beloved wives.

He wondered what he would find in the kitchen when he finally got up, dressed and went there: Paloma sad, or Paloma happy?

What he found was neither, but better. She sat at the table sorting beans while Sancha, trailed closely by Trece, moved from fireplace to table, preparing breakfast. Still weaker from her inoculation than anyone cared to see, Perla the cook sat close to the fire, huddled in her shawl.

When he came in, Paloma looked up and smiled at him. That was all. She probably knew he was headed for the horse barn, his usual destination before breakfast, because she didn't pat the bench beside her. She just smiled at him in a most serene way. There was suddenly less of the new bride about her, and more of the matron. It was the smile of someone made newly confident—by what, he did not know. It touched his heart in comforting ways.

He rested his hand on her shoulder, throwing caution to the winds to run his thumb up and down her neck, which made her head turn toward his hand. To his further amazement, even though servants watched and they *did* come from a reticent society, she kissed his hand. *O cielo!* Too much of this and his head would swell so large that even turning sideways wouldn't get him through most doors.

Toshua waited for him in the horse barn, looking as though he had something to say, which made this morning even more unusual. Still, there was that Indian hesitation, so Marco spoke first.

"Did you talk Paloma out of coming to the Staked Plains with us?"

"I didn't even try, señor."

"What then?"

"I adopted your wife this morning in the chapel. She is my little sister and I am her brother."

Marco just stared at him, which made Toshua smile. "I did. Told her she could call me *pabi*. This makes me her older brother. She misses one named Claudio." He sighed. "I cannot replace him, but she still needs an older brother."

"She has a husband, I would remind you," Marco said.

"Brothers are different and she needs one," Toshua insisted with some finality, which told Marco the matter was taken care of and needed no more commentary.

Marco sat down on the grain bin, gesturing to Toshua to join him. "Was she sad there?"

"Very much sad. She cried, and then she stopped crying, and sat back. It was dark—she didn't know I was there—but I could see a little lift to her shoulders. Then she leaned forward to the floor and kissed it. I did not understand, but it was not my business to question her."

"She is sad because we have no children." There, he had admitted it to someone besides Paloma.

"She told me."

"*Dios*, really?"

Toshua nodded. "That was when I adopted her. I am her *pabi*, her older brother. Your wife's troubles are mine, too, now." He took a long look at Marco. "Now I am adopting you. You are *tami*, my little brother."

Marco thought of his own little brother who had died of inoculation so long ago. Marco nodded. "I accept, pabi." Maybe he needed an older brother, too.

MARCO KNEW HE WAS short tempered and troublesome as they prepared to leave, and could not understand Paloma's serenity. Didn't she understand how dangerous this was, she, who knew the worst that Comanches could do? On their last night at the Double Cross, as they prepared for sleep, he asked her.

"Why should I fear? It would be worse to never see you again," she told him, her lips against his cheek as she spoke. "It's that simple. Don't complicate things, Marco. You do that sometimes, you know."

Paloma was right; that had ended the argument.

That afternoon, he had spent a long moment in the horse barn with Buciro, his favorite mount, but an elderly gent. "Don't give me sad eyes," he whispered to Buciro. "I know you would carry me to the ends of the earth, but better not to the Staked Plains."

He and Toshua had decided on two pack horses for the two tents, rope, ammunition and probably more *carne seca con gris* than anyone wanted to eat. "Pemmican, pemmican," he said, trying out the Indian word that Antonio Gil had used. Listening carefully to Perla's instructions as she still sat by the fireplace, Paloma and Sancha ground the dried beef, added dried tomatoes and spices, then doused the whole thing in beef fat. They hadn't really needed Perla's instructions, but both women knew the old cook had to feel useful.

Since tortillas would never keep, the little doctor had talked them into what he called "hardtack," consisting of nothing more than flour, water, and a little salt. "It never goes bad," he assured them as he demonstrated, wrists deep in flour.

"Hardtack," Marco repeated in the horse barn. "Hardtack." He would have to listen to Antonio carefully, to learn how to pronounce his rrs without rolling them. The sound was harsh to his ears.

The men weren't so particular, but Paloma insisted upon a change of clothing for herself. Blushing, she asked Marco for a leather pouch for her monthly supplies. He found one for her, and earned himself a slap on the head when he suggested she label it, so no man would open it by mistake. They ended up laughing about it. One thing led to another, and dinner was late, that last night.

Their usual gathering in the chapel before bed was as solemn as those nights he remembered from his childhood, when the Comanche Moon had risen and he and his brother and sister slept in the hollowed out space under the chapel floor. Everyone crowded into the chapel this night, even his Navajo beekeeper, who was skeptical about religion. One more time, Marco went over his instructions slowly and carefully. He hadn't bothered to write them down, because no one could read. After the last *Ave Maria*, he did take Sancha aside and hand her a folded sheet of paper.

"If only Paloma returns, burn this," he whispered to his housekeeper. "If neither of us returns, see that my sister gets it."

Sancha took the folded paper with its wax seal, a question in her eyes that she was too polite to ask.

"In this, I am deeding my land grant to my younger nephew. His brother will inherit his father's land, and Julio will receive mine."

Sancha made a face, crossed herself and tried to hand it back, as though the document burned her fingers. "Master, I cannot even bear such a thought."

He put his hands on her shoulders and drew her close, as he would his mother. "My dear lady, we must be realistic."

From the shelter of his arms, she nodded. "Better you kill that doctor than do as he asks. God will not hold you accountable to a devil's bargain!"

"If I did that, how could I face that same God some day?" he whispered back, then kissed her cheek. "I will do my best to stay alive, and keep Paloma alive, too."

MARCO STARED ALL HIS fears in the face and rode east in the morning with his dearest Paloma, a doctor he did not trust, and a Comanche he needed more than words could express—his older brother. He wasn't sure that Toshua would have consented to return to the Texas plains where he had been cast away by his own people, if Paloma were not along. In fact, he doubted it.

They left after the sun rose, snow falling lightly. He led both pack horses, docile creatures that probably didn't even need a lead. Paloma rode beside him, pretty in her new warm cloak and precise in her posture, as efficient in her side saddle as she was anywhere else. Again, he silently thanked her long-dead parents for teaching her to ride so many years ago. Toshua ranged around from side to side as he always did, alert. The little doctor frowned with the concerted effort of a man who might ride well enough, but would never be easy in the saddle.

True, they rode into danger, but Marco couldn't help but feel his heart lift to be in the saddle for a long trip. Winter usually confined him to the Double Cross, and he didn't mind, not really. The last year and a half had been a wonderful time to use winter as an excuse to go nowhere and devote his free time to Paloma. *I have turned into a lazy lover,* he thought, with no remorse. Better to be a husband having a hard time prying the mattress from his back than to repeat those horrible eight years when the space beside him on that mattress was cold and empty.

Marco couldn't deny the pleasure of a good ride. When Toshua got within earshot, he gestured him over. "Remember that time a year ago when Paloma and I rode to Santa Fe and you were supposed to stay behind where it was safe?" he asked.

The Comanche laughed. "How did you know?"

"You're not the only smart man on the Double Cross." Marco leaned across his saddle. "But tell me, *pabi*: how did you hide from us after the fork in the Chama and the Bravo?"

"I turned back at the fork. You didn't need me the rest of the way." He turned so serious then. "But I will stay with my brother and sister now, no matter what."

February was no time to leave the shelter of the mountains and head across the plains, but a promise was a promise. They rode steadily, with no complaint from Paloma. She never complained. Why would this ride be different? How bright her eyes were! Marco could have sworn she was enjoying the freedom of the open spaces, too.

"Tell me, husband, why is it called 'the Staked Plains'?"

"I have heard that in the days of Coronado, the conquistador planted stakes within eye-view of each other, so he would not get lost," Marco said. "There is a sameness you will start to notice tomorrow."

Antonio squared around to look at Marco. "Señor, I have seen the view of these plains from the east. *That* is a sight."

"True," Toshua said. "I hear that when you travel from where the sun rises, you face a high wall, an *estaca*. Right, little man?"

"We would call it a 'cliff' in English."

"Cleef, cleef," Marco repeated.

"Close. It goes for miles and miles."

"Think of it as a stockade," Marco told Paloma, "*una estaca*."

"How much of it have you seen?" she asked.

He wished he could be wise and all-knowing. He also knew it was impossible to fool this woman. "Only what we see now, my dearest."

She swallowed and gave him such a look then, fear followed by calm determination. He imagined she had looked just like that when she had stared at the mountains between her and the man whose yellow dog she was trying to return.

He felt his own pulse pick up speed, and he began to breathe faster. Everything from now on was new to him. He had spent his life on this bit of plain, tucked against the more familiar mountains. He wanted to grab Paloma's bridle and turn around. The only thing that stopped him was the look she gave him just then, as if she understood his sudden terror and his fervent wish to protect her.

She angled her horse closer to his until they were almost knee to knee, and she stayed that way through the long afternoon.

Paloma already knew one consequence of that great plain. When she had to make water, all she could do was gesture for them to turn around. He knew how modest she was about her functions, and how this mortified her. "Not even a bush," she grumbled, when she finished. By the same token, she looked the other way when it was their turn. Hopefully, it would be dark when they had to squat. If not, well, that was the journey.

THEY MADE THEIR PUNY camp smack in the open plain, an act that went against everything Marco knew about Comanchería. There was no alternative, not with miles of emptiness all around them. Marco's small fire of brush and dried buffalo dung struggled against the wind, even though the snow had stopped and bone-rattling cold clamped down. Paloma retreated to their tent, once he and Toshua set it up.

He and the other men stood by the fire, pretending to warm their hands. "Let me tell you now, if it gets too cold on this journey, we will be four in one tent, the better to stay warm," Marco said.

"I'm supposed to cozy up to that Indian?" Antonio said.

"It would be better than freezing to death, *médico*."

"You would like that, wouldn't you? Then you could turn right around and go home."

Marco rolled his eyes. He remembered a night by the fire with Father Damiano at the monastery where the Chama joins the Bravo—the spectacled priest telling him about pilgrims who complained about everything. "It's like this, dear boy," Damiano had said as they toasted cheese. "In each group of pilgrims that comes to this monastery, I look at them and wonder which one is the complainer. It never fails."

"Which one, indeed," he said out loud, which earned him a glare from Antonio Gil. He walked beyond the limit of the fire—if one could call it a fire—made sure the wind was blowing right and unbuttoned his breeches in the dark. He looked down at his barely visible stream, probably the warmest thing around.

To his horror, a hand reached out for that same warmth. Marco leaped back, shoving his member into his pants, his heart pounding. As he stared in fright, a naked man covered in pox flopped into the dampness he had left.

Chapter Nineteen

In which the travelers see what Antonio knows

"STAY IN THE TENT, Paloma!" Marco shouted as he staggered into the feeble firelight again. He gestured to Toshua, who came immediately to his side. Wishing his hand didn't shake, Marco pointed into the darkness.

Toshua walked to the same spot. Same reaction. He leaped back, his mouth opening and closing like a fish. Marco took another deep breath and came closer. He just looked at Toshua, and the two of them walked into the darkness to kneel by the figure lying there face down. Tentatively, Marco put his hand on the man's ruined neck, finding a pulse so puny he had to hold his hand there longer than he wanted, to be certain.

"He's still alive," he said. "Help me."

They both hesitated, then gently, with hands under armpits, dragged the man into the light and turned him over.

"Nurmurnah," Toshua said.

By now, Antonio had joined them, his face registering all his disgust at the sight of the Comanche. Her eyes wide, Paloma looked through the tent flap.

"Marco?" she said, her voice quavering.

I cannot shield her from this, he thought. "Come here."

She did as he said, her reaction the same as theirs. It changed quickly as she knelt beside the man. "*Pobrecito*," she whispered. "*Pobrecito*. What can we do?"

She was looking at the physician. They all were.

"Nothing. I cannot help him. I wish I could."

I believe you mean that, Marco thought, surprised. "Isn't there something, *anything*?"

"Of course there is," Paloma said, taking charge. "Marco, get the sheet in our tent. We don't need it. Let us at least cover his nakedness. How cold he must be! Toshua, can you tell him we will take care of him?"

"You, señora, are out of your mind," Antonio snapped.

"No, I'm not," she said quite calmly. "I just decided that I can forgive these people. Don't get in my way!"

Antonio looked at Marco with a pout, almost like a petty child wanting a reprimand for a bully. Marco could only sympathize. "*Médico,* when she speaks in that tone of voice, I do what she asks."

"Oh, Marco, you do not," Paloma scolded gently.

He brought the sheet to her. To his amazement, when he returned, she already had her arms around the dreadful sight that used to be a man. Even Toshua stared in disbelief.

I will never be worthy of Paloma if I live to be an old man of sixty, Marco thought as he draped the sheet around the dying man and tucked it under his wasted body. He smelled as foul as he looked; thank God it was winter.

"Can we give him something to drink? I remember feeling so thirsty," she said, looking at Antonio.

"You can try, but good luck to you."

"You can do better than that!" she snapped back.

Without another word, the doctor poured some wine into a tin cup. He knelt beside her. "Hold his head higher," Antonio said. "He won't be able to drink it, but he will taste it."

Paloma did as he said, sighing when the wine just dribbled out the sides of his mouth.

"His throat is clogged with pox. That is the best he can do," Antonio said. Tenderly this time, he dabbed at the man's chapped lips.

Marco squatted beside his wife, close enough so their shoulders touched. He felt the tremble in her body that seemed to come from some deep core, and knew how terrified she was. He stared, transfixed, as the Comanche opened his eyes and looked around, obviously startled at what he saw. Paloma patted his chest and he sighed so long that Marco was certain it was his final breath.

But no. He looked at Toshua with something close to recognition, Marco thought. He spoke and Toshua nodded.

"He cannot sing his death song," Toshua told them. "I will sing mine for him."

Toshua began to sing, high and unearthly and weird, similar to the chorus of songs Marco had last heard when Governor de Anza and his soldiers—

Marco among them—cornered Cuerno Verde and his Kwahadi at the Rio San Carlos nearly three years ago.

Marco felt the shivers travel up and down his spine, remembering. Toshua sang with his eyes closed; he sang with his whole heart.

"Please stop," Paloma said, her voice soft, but cutting through the song. Toshua did as she asked.

"I think it is not good for you to sing your own death song, *pabi*," she said, and began to sing a different song, one so familiar to Marco. She graciously took the burden from her adopted brother with a hymn of her faith. *O God we praise thee; we acknowledge thee to be the Lord.*

He already knew how sweet and pure her voice was. She had sung to him a time or two, late at night when no one else was listening. "*Te deum laudamus,*" she sang, "*te dominum confitemur.*"

In the cold and snow of a feeble fire that gave off little light and no warmth, his wife sang praise to God with a dying Comanche in her lap. Marco joined her on the "*Sanctus, Sanctus, Sanctus,*" and then hummed with her when she was too teary-eyed to sing anymore.

When they were finally silent, the Comanche opened his eyes again, but only partly.

"His shoulders aren't quite so tense," Paloma whispered to Marco. "I wish we could do something."

"You just did, my love," was all he could manage.

The Indian spoke again to Toshua, who nodded and unsheathed his knife. Paloma looked at him in alarm, but Marco was already tugging her gently away.

She let him pull her from the dying man. He picked her up and carried her to the edge of the light, where she shuddered as Toshua released the Comanche from terrible suffering. Marco kept his back to the fire until he heard the sound of a body being dragged into the darkness it had come from. When he set Paloma down, she sagged to her knees, then stood upright, hanging on to his belt.

"This is a terrible journey, and we have only begun," she said.

HOW COULD SHE SLEEP? She did, finally, huddled so close to Marco that it was a wonder the man could breathe. When Paloma made some sleepy remark about that, he just chuckled and kissed her forehead.

First light brought another terror, if not worse than the one the night before, at least as frightening. She left the tent first, hoping to have a tiny private moment before the men were up.

There before her, as far as she could see, was a carpet of the dead. She went to her knees again in absolute terror, then scrambled to her feet and backed up toward the tent.

"Marco!" she called, wondering if he could even make out his name, because it sounded like a gargle to her.

The tent flap flew open and her husband gasped. "*Dios mio!*" he exclaimed, his voice sounding no better than hers. He stood by her side, his arm around her. That wasn't enough, so he put both arms around her, pulling her close to his body that shivered along with hers.

Others had seen their puny campfire, crawling from … somewhere. No one moved. One pox-covered person—man or woman she could not tell—must have frozen to death with one arm raised, begging for help. Paloma started to count the bodies, then stopped, because she was just saying "*uno, dos, tres*" over and over again like a lunatic.

"Are we at the gates of hell?" she asked, her face turned into Marco's chest.

"Somewhere very close."

Rubbing his eyes, Antonio crouched out of his tent, then said something harsh in English. Toshua followed, staring and shaking his head, probably as stupefied as Paloma felt, if his expression told the truth.

He stared a long time, silent, then said, "There is nothing we can do except eat, break camp and give the wolves time to work."

They did precisely that, mounting and riding in record time, all of them desperate to get away from their unseeing audience. Paloma tried to ride with her eyes straight ahead, but she couldn't help noticing how Toshua rode among the dead, looking. She thought once he was going to dismount, with his leg half over the saddle, but he must have changed his mind. *Who do you know here?* she couldn't help thinking.

"Ten dead people," Marco said, when their horses, shying and skittish, had picked their way through the dead. "Toshua, where were they going?"

The Comanche shrugged.

Antonio spoke up. "In their delirium, they probably didn't know what they were doing. Just following a leader. Toshua, think of the days when *your* mind wandered from the cut on your arm. Paloma?"

She nodded, keeping her face resolutely toward the plains before them, not willing to see the dead frozen and unburied. "I probably did some strange things, too."

Marco chuckled. "Ah, yes. I had no idea I was married to a woman who liked to dance on tables."

"I didn't!"

"You tried." He laughed, and the sound seemed so out of place, until she realized how badly they needed to laugh. The other men laughed and Paloma patted her warm face. When they were silent, she leaned closer to Marco. "I didn't really do that," she whispered.

"You did."

Paloma shook her head, embarrassed, but relieved that for at least a few minutes, she wasn't thinking of death.

FOR THREE DAYS, THEY rode across a barren plain that soon began to look the same color as the leaden sky. It was gray everywhere, no matter what direction she looked. To her relief, there were no more dead bodies.

"Where are the buffalo?" she asked Toshua on the second day. He had been riding ahead and by himself for two days since they left the camp of death. She knew him well enough to understand his long silences, even though she had questions. Marco and Antonio were talking, so she rode closer to the man whose life she had saved several times, noticing how much longer his hair was now. She remembered how mortified he had been when they were forced to cut his hair because of lice.

But now she just wanted to talk to him, to have him reassure her that he knew where he was going. How to begin? "Where are the buffalo?" she asked again, when she rode beside him.

If he was irritated at her presence, he didn't show it. "Farther south." He looked around. "Not even animals like this Llano Estacado, as you call it. You know how little water there is, when we have to melt snow to drink."

"What do The People call it?"

"Big empty."

She didn't know if he wanted her company, so she asked. He nodded, which gave her courage to ask the question on her mind since the terrible night with the dying man.

"You … you knew who he was, didn't you?"

He gave her a look of something close to admiration. "You were watching me. I cannot say his name, because he most certainly wanders with the restless spirits now, and I don't want to call him back."

Paloma shivered. "I don't either. But … you knew him."

He turned in his saddle and propped his leg across his horse without his horse faltering. "He was one of the men who had me thrown from my band because my wives complained."

"So … those people back there. Was that *your* band?" She didn't think she made an exclamation but she must have, because Marco called, "*Qué es?*" She shook her head at him.

He watched her a moment, wary, then returned to his conversation with the doctor.

"I recognized them."

He couldn't have been more evasive. "Why did your wives complain?" She had wanted to ask before, but it was a nosy question, maybe even a rude one, the kind of question her cousin Maria Teresa might ask. "Oh, if I shouldn't ask …."

Toshua shrugged. "I think it was the young one, or maybe that wife of the Spanish settler. They had their eyes on another man." He made a cutting gesture across his abdomen. "Shaa! I would have let him borrow them, if he wanted."

She had heard that about Comanches before. "Just like that?"

"Certainly. We People share everything."

"If Marco tried either side of that *coin*, I would murder him," she said with some feeling.

He gave her a kind look then, as if he wanted to help. "If he had another woman, or maybe two, he might have children."

Sick at heart, Paloma turned away. In another moment, Toshua tugged her bridle and turned her horse toward him again.

"I should not have said something that wounds your heart," he told her.

Paloma nodded. It was her turn to ride ahead, not out of sight—she feared the Big Empty—but ahead far enough to wonder why, in all her helping of others, she could not help herself.

Chapter Twenty

In which the sky is no friend and the chase is on

PALOMA KNEW TOSHUA DID not mean to hurt her feelings; he was a practical man offering a practical solution to a problem. She told herself not to dwell on the matter because they had larger challenges at the moment: the horses were thirsty and there was no water anywhere.

"I suppose this is one reason game is sparse here," Marco said as they walked back to camp that afternoon after gathering buffalo chips for a fire. Her apron was weighed down and she walked slower and slower.

"I'm a dolt," he said and stopped her, lifting her cloak to untie her apron, which he gathered together and slung over his back. "Better?"

She nodded and started moving, but he stopped her again. "Is it too much, Paloma?"

"Yes, but here we are. I just wish I had a little privacy."

"It's the journey, dearest," he said. "Remember two Octobers ago when we came to Valle de Sol from Santa Fe? No privacy then."

She nodded. "We had our mountains then and not this ... this endless plain. I miss our mountains."

"I do, too." He looked around. "There is no protection here."

The sun had gone behind clouds and she was unsure of any direction. She fought down the panic, reasoning that her husband thought he had married a grown woman, and this was no time to show him otherwise.

They ambled slower toward the two tents, hobbled horses neighing from thirst, and the tiniest pinprick of a fire—the smallest speck in the immensity of the Staked Plains. She couldn't help her sigh.

"What was that for?" Marco asked.

"To return, we have to cross this again."

"But only once more." He looked at the night sky so rapidly darkening. "I will never travel this far from my mountains again." He put his lips close to her ear. "Between you and me, the Comanches can have it, and with my own *Te Deum.*"

She gave him her sunniest smile, and surprised herself by meaning it.

They walked slower, maybe both of them reluctant to return to a doctor who complained about everything, and a Comanche who knew more than he was letting on. Paloma tugged on her husband's hand, and he stopped.

"Toshua knew those poor people."

Marco nodded. "I thought so, too. I tried to get him to talk, but he was silent on the subject."

"I tried, as well. Why does he say nothing?"

"Comanches don't speak of the dead. Maybe he cannot say more."

She tugged on his hand again, pulling on it until he leaned down. She put her lips next to his ear this time. "Don't ever be that way with me. Be free to speak your mind."

"I already do. And you?"

Paloma nodded, then shook her head. She took a deep breath and told him Toshua's solution to her barrenness. There. Call it what it was, she was barren.

Marco winced. "A Comanche solution, not a Spanish one! Maybe I was not entirely forthcoming, either. When I rode with the *médico* this afternoon, I did tell him our ... our ... well, I asked if he had any suggestions. He's a doctor, after all."

"Did he?"

Marco shook his head. "He asked me some embarrassing questions, then he sighed, and said he wished he could see inside our bodies."

"*Dios*, that could get him in trouble with the Inqusition!" Paloma said, her eyes wide. Then she chuckled. "I'm the dolt now! He's not even Catholic. See inside our bodies? Imagine such a thing." She leaned closer, maybe thinking a priest would materialize there in the middle of absolutely nowhere. "Then I say it is too bad he cannot."

They continued in silence to camp.

ANTHONY GILL KNEW HE was not, by nature, an envious man. Envy required some thought, some observation, and here he was, observing. Maybe it was boredom. He looked around the little fire, watching the Mondragóns, actually watching them, Paloma so pretty, even though her nose and cheeks were red. He had never seen a more graceful woman. And there was Marco, a broad-shouldered fellow with a handsome, long Spanish face, and a close beard now, after only a week. Anthony knew it would take him a long time to grow even that much.

True, that face under the beard had reddened considerably as he had answered such probing questions that afternoon, reminding Anthony all over again that people of Spanish origin were, on the whole, shy. Anthony looked at Paloma again, wishing he could actually examine her. He thought of the surgeons he knew back in Georgia, those men who shaved and cut hair, and sometimes probed within the body. At least he could inoculate. He should be content with that, even as he wished he could help Paloma Mondragón.

Dinner was more of the dreadful pemmican and far-better wine. Anthony laughed to himself, watching Marco sweet talk Paloma into finishing her portion. Afterwards, Paloma went into their tent, and Marco spent some time with his hobbled horses. Anthony thought he even prayed among them, a rancher unhappy about no water for the animals that served them.

Determined to become a better observer, Anthony noticed that Toshua spent some time looking at the night sky. Was that how he knew how to navigate this sea of winter grass? Surely not; there was no daytime equivalent, unless it was the sun, itself.

He looked up, too, enchanted with the stars that seemed so close. He recognized Orion, that harbinger of winter, a man-god with a sword. It was the middle of February, and Orion dipped a bit lower. In a few months, he would make his exit and spring would come. Why did it seem so far away right now? That was the dilemma of February.

Later, in the tent he shared with Toshua, Anthony smiled to himself, amused as the Mondragóns tried to make love quietly in their own tent. Marco was less successful at silence, which made Anthony chuckle.

"I always wish them joy with each other," Toshua whispered.

"I thought you were asleep."

"No, no."

Antony heard Toshua turn over in the tight space. "I had a good wife once. I liked her more than the other two." His voice turned contemplative. "I wonder why she decided to listen to those witches." From contemplative to harsh—"Now those witches wander these plains forever, burning, freezing, scratching at their running sores."

Good Godfreys, were your former wives among the dead by our camp? Anthony asked himself. Frightened, he pulled his blanket higher, wondering just whom he shared this tent with. Thank God he did not believe such nonsense. Still, he also knew he would not stick his head outside this tent until morning; it paid to be careful.

* * *

"SEÑOR?"

Marco groaned. He had no earthly desire to leave his warm little cocoon of two blankets and Paloma. The sun was barely up.

"Señor!"

Aware of the urgency, he sat up, careful to tuck the blankets around his wife, who was stirring now, too. *Dios*, it was cold! He dressed as fast as he could and stuck his head outside the tent.

Toshua nodded to him and pointed. Marco squinted, then his heart began to sprint.

"Who are they?"

"From the south. Maybe Apaches, maybe Tonkawas."

"How long, do you think?"

"Hard to tell. They are far away right now, but they are riding, and here we sit."

The men looked at each other; there was nothing to say. Toshua went to his tent and yanked the tent pole. The doctor inside yelped and swore. Marco was a little kinder.

"Paloma, we have to ride fast. Hurry, please."

She asked no foolish questions, even as her face paled. He turned to saddle the horses, assessing them, aware of how thirsty they were, how cold.

By the time the horses were saddled, Paloma was dressed and already folding the tent. On her face was that set, determined expression Marco had seen more and more on this cold journey. She looked at him, a question in her eyes. He pointed to the south. She looked and took a deep breath, even as she crossed herself.

"Paloma, if you have anything of importance on the pack horses, carry it with you. If we need to, I'll loosen the ropes tethering them to us. We might need the distraction they can provide."

She nodded, her eyes going in sympathy to the pack horses. "They've been so good to bear our burdens," she said softly. She transferred another blanket and more pemmican to her horse, then let him help her mount. She settled her skirts around the side horn and turned resolutely away from the distant riders.

Even Antonio did not complain this morning. He usually rode on the far side of Paloma, as though wanting to remain separate from them all. This morning, he deliberately rode on the other side of Paloma, putting himself between her and the unknown riders, which touched Marco. The *médico* even leaned over to ask Paloma, "You have all your inoculating supplies, do you not?"

She nodded, and pulled back her cloak a little to expose the leather bag that hung from her shoulder.

"You remember everything to do?"

She nodded again, and they started at a steady clip, heading east as always, but faster.

"Let's see if they turn and follow," Marco told Toshua.

"They will."

THEY DID, ALTHOUGH WITH no increase of speed, loping along in a way that was more than maddening, as they paralleled the travelers. Marco observed his companions, wondering at their apparently unspoken agreement not to deliberately look south, even though everyone's eyes strayed that way when they thought no one saw them. The only time Paloma showed any fear was when he dismounted fast, and as they watched, untied the packhorses. She whimpered, then set her lips more firmly. All Marco could do was pat her leg before he mounted again. To his relief, the obedient animals continued to follow, although farther back. It chafed him, because he knew the unknown riders were now aware of what he had done, and why.

Damn them! He watched, hoping they would take the bait and veer toward the pack horses, which even now had paused to nose among the sparse vegetation. No luck.

He could ask Paloma to pray for a miracle, but he knew she was already praying. Her lips moved in a continuous *Ave Maria* as she rode, her back straight, her eyes only darting small glances.

It was a party of ten or twelve and they did not ride like Comanches. "I think they are Apaches," Toshua told him, then grinned. "At least Apaches won't eat our little doctor, like Tonkawas!"

"I've never dealt with Tonks," Marco said, speaking softly so Paloma would not hear. "They really are cannibals?"

Toshua nodded. "They have certain favorite parts."

Although he could see no change in the vastness around them, Marco felt they were traveling more downhill now, dropping ever so slowly in altitude. What it meant, he did not know, because he had never felt so lost in his life, so dependent on another human as he was dependent on this Comanche. His long-dead father would never have understood it; Marco barely did.

If that wasn't enough, Marco looked behind him in late afternoon, when the wind began to ruffle his hat. *Dios,* but a storm was bearing down. The suddenness of it startled him, who was used to watching clouds build and billow over the Sangre de Cristos. Were they not suffering enough? He tied down his hat before it blew away. He looked back to watch monster clouds rise higher and higher, as though a demon hand swatted them into the atmosphere. The sun had been weak all day, and now it seemed to surrender to clouds that grew darker and darker. He looked at his wife, who seemed unaware of the storm coming from behind. More and more, her glances were directed south.

He looked at Toshua, who smiled back, oddly cheerful. Had the Comanche lost his mind? What in the world was there to smile about? Marco distinctly counted twelve Indians now, close enough to know they were Apaches.

Then the sun vanished, snuffed by clouds. The wind bellowed like a gored ox, blowing hard enough to throw back Paloma's cloak and skirts, exposing her leg crossed over the side saddle. Grabbing at her cloak, she tucked it tighter, her expression anxious as she absorbed the immensity of the storm.

Toshua rode closer between the two of them, which angered Marco. "I ride beside my wife," he said, troubled by the man's smile, feeling the start of doubt about the Kwahadi's intentions.

"Señor, when I say so, will you ride as fast as you can?"

"Should we not stand and fight?"

"Unnecessary right now; maybe later." Toshua was shouting now, because the wind howled. The sky had turned an unearthly deep blue. Lightning began to flicker, little tongues of fire darting out from the massive clouds towering so high above them. Marco had never seen a storm like this one, so nearly a living being.

Marco watched the approaching Indians, amazed to see that they had stopped, their horses prancing in little circles. Were they preparing to rush them, or had the storm put some fear in their path?

Snow slapped them sideways, only it wasn't snow, but sharp-edged sleet that made their horses begin their own little dance of fear.

"Paloma, put your leg over your horse," he shouted. "Hang on! No telling what will happen."

She had already done that, even as her cloak billowed about her and bared her legs to the freezing rain mingled with ice. Pain replaced anxiety.

"Fast now!"

At Toshua's command, Marco touched his spurs to his frightened horse, wishing he rode the predictable old Buciro. He waved to Paloma, who struggled to control her horse, then followed him, the look on her face as fierce as any warrior's. Antonio had the terrified stare of a man not even slightly willing to be left behind. And still Toshua kept grinning, as he watched the storm even more closely than the Apaches, who had definitely fallen back.

Through the sudden gloom created by the devil storm from the north, Marco looked ahead and saw the canyon's edge. It was so close! The beautiful little "*Te Deum Laudamus*" his wife has sung a few days ago tumbled through his brain. He looked for some break, some way in, and saw nothing but an edge. *God help us*, he thought.

"There's no way down," Marco shouted to Toshua.

With his lips, the Comanche gestured toward the south, where the Apaches waited. "That's where it is, and we cannot go there without a fight." He dismounted. "Hand me that rope that tied your pack horse. "Do a *dar la vuelta* around your horn."

Suddenly Marco knew what Toshua was going to do, and he felt only relief. He dallied the rope and watched as Toshua pulled Paloma, protesting, from her saddle. As she cried and tried to dig in with her heels, the Comanche swiftly tied the rope around her and dragged her to the edge of the canyon.

"Not without Marco!" she shrieked. "I won't! I can't!"

"Do as he says, Paloma," Marco ordered, pulling back slightly. Maybe this horse was as good as Buciro, after all. Maybe he knew something about horses, although not as much as Toshua. The sturdy beast stood firm, unruffled by the storm, feeling the slight play of the rope.

She was pleading now, on her knees, desperate to stay with him.

"No, Paloma. Go over the edge. You can scold me later."

"See if I ever curtsy to you again!" she raged, as Toshua tightened the rope and picked her up.

Marco laughed. "I'll bow to *you!*"

Her courage failed her at the edge and she sank to her knees again as the wind blew ice in all directions. Her tears unmanned him and Marco started to dismount.

"No!" Toshua shouted. "I'll go with her."

Toshua grabbed the rope. "I am your older brother now. I am your Claudio. He would want you safe."

She turned a tearful face to him, and Marco felt his own heart break a little. "He couldn't help me twelve years ago. Please don't do this!"

"Claudio would if he could have, my love," Marco said to encourage her. "Trust *this* brother."

Her face a mask of terror, Paloma nodded and reached for Toshua.

Without another wasted moment, Toshua tightened his grip on the rope and dropped over the edge with Paloma.

Chapter Twenty-One

In which Paloma learns a valuable lesson

PALOMA COULDN'T HELP HERSELF; she screamed all the way to the bottom, her arms tight around Toshua's neck. She felt him chuckle and make strangling noises, and she wondered why Comanches were even allowed to exist in an orderly universe.

"Calm, calm, little sister," he said when they touched ground. "Your husband is holding the horse firm and you cannot fall." He laughed then, strangely exhilarated by what she knew right down to her marrow was a desperate situation. "Do not back up. We're on a trail only. The bottom is still a long way down."

Paloma held her breath in fright. When he loosened the rope and she saw it snake upward toward Marco, she went to her knees and crawled toward the rocks and solid wall.

"I will go to him now. Don't move. Wait, wait." He knelt beside her and she clung to him. "Still and silence."

She felt the vibrations of horses' hooves close to her. *Please, please let it be Marco*, she thought, even as she knew he was far above her, facing Apaches with nothing more than a wretched doctor to help him. Then the nightmare of her childhood became real as a horse masked with eyeholes and beadwork emerged from the darkness of the storm. She had seen such horses before, on that day when her world changed forever. She squeezed her eyes shut like a child and shrank against the stones that suddenly felt so comforting.

She whimpered when Toshua stood up, but he kept his hand on her head as he spoke to whoever stood above them on horseback. It was a low-voiced exchange, rising and falling with an intensity that made her open her eyes, when she realized the one on horseback was a woman.

Paloma stared as the icy sleet turned to rain so cold that her teeth chattered. Toshua moved closer to the horse. He moved with a stealth that made him more apparition than flesh. Paloma watched in surprise as Toshua put his hand on the woman's leg. The gesture was tentative, then it became a caress.

"Paloma, this is Eckapeta, my oldest wife," he said. "She says The People have been watching us." He said something in Comanche to the woman and her reply was sharp. "You stay here. We are going up the trail to help your husband, because all he has is a worthless little man at his side."

"Go then, and hurry," Paloma urged. "Your *wife*?"

Toshua shrugged.

Silent herself, Paloma shivered and tried to wrap herself in her sodden cloak, as the woman made a tsking sound with her tongue and let her horse turn around in that tiny space. She held out her hand to Toshua. Before he leaped up behind her, Toshua handed Paloma his knife. The woman carried a bow and quiver, too, slung across her shoulder.

"Use my knife if you need to. Don't hesitate, little sister," Toshua told Paloma.

Two other riders followed Toshua and the woman up the narrow trail as rain turned to snow and the wind howled like one of Toshua's restless spirits, roaming on the plain above. She closed her eyes and hugged the canyon wall. "*Te deum laudamus*," Paloma whispered. She was alone on the trail with the poor company of her imagination.

The storm raged, but she listened intently for war cries, shouts. Nothing. When the snow tapered off and the cold clamped down, she peeked out from the sodden hood of her cloak. She gasped to see a dark figure, a weird apparition of the storm, looming over her. Resigned to death, she closed her eyes, wanting to be brave, wanting one more glimpse of Marco. Sudden darkness enveloped her, and she wondered if this was death.

It was warmth, a buffalo robe. "Who ..." Paloma said. She struggled to look through the folds of the robe and saw a young woman standing there. Without a word, Paloma held open the robe.

After a moment's hesitation, the young woman came closer and then joined Paloma under the robe. She smelled of tanned hide and wood smoke and the faintest tang of sage.

"We'll just wait here until everyone is safe and we are all together again," Paloma told her, wondering if the young woman understood Spanish. It hardly mattered; she knew she was only trying to comfort herself.

"You must not scream like that ever again, as long as you stay with The People." Her Spanish was clear and she was obviously peeved.

"I promise," Paloma said, contrite. She knew her rescuer was younger, but there was that edge of command in her voice that branded her as Comanche. "Who are—"

"I am Ayasha. I rode with Eckapeta. We will stay here."

I had no plans to move, Paloma thought, grateful not to be alone. Under a buffalo robe in a storm might be no place to strike up an acquaintance in Paloma's usual world, but she had left that world. Unsure of herself, but desperate for human contact, she put her arm tentatively around Ayasha's shoulders, hoping she wasn't breaking some Comanche rule.

Ayasha moved into the circle of her arms as if she belonged there. They huddled close together, and Paloma closed her eyes. Like a child, she tried to blot out what was going on above them by simply shutting her eyes. *If you are dead, Marco*, she thought, *I will be as brave as I can be. I will never dishonor your memory, my love.*

She jerked upright at the sound of howls, yips, and puma-like screams directly above them. Ayasha made no sound but burrowed closer, if that were even possible. Paloma tasted blood in her mouth and realized she had bitten into the soft flesh inside her mouth; she spit out her blood. She pressed her hand against her mouth, wishing for a cloth, when she heard the sound of falling bodies, men shrieking all the way to the canyon floor. She gasped when one of them landed on the trail, still alive and clawing with bloody fingers to keep from sliding off. Paloma peered through the robe, every nerve alert.

His plain headband told her he was Apache. For one small moment, his desperate eyes locked on hers, and then he let go, the momentum too great. *Keep breathing, Paloma*, she told herself.

Feeling another body strike the ledge, she screamed, which earned her a slap across the face and sharp words from Ayasha. Paloma needed no interpretation. She pressed her lips together, Toshua's knife tight in her grip. In her life she had only used knives in the kitchen, but a survival instinct told her how to hold this one.

Both of them silent, Paloma heard labored breathing, then sudden cold and snow as the Apache yanked back their sheltering buffalo robe. In the dim light Paloma saw his upper arm pierced by an arrow and his scalp partly torn from his head.

Quicker than sight, Ayasha drove her knife into the Apache's nose. With a roar, he grabbed her and tried to fling her over the edge.

Paloma threw off the buffalo robe and grabbed Ayasha, tugging her back against the canyon wall. The man's grip faltered, giving Paloma mere seconds to yank her free and try to thrust her farther back, except that Ayasha was having none of that. The Comanche scrabbled close again, jerking on the arrow in the man's arm as he screamed in agony and flailed about.

With a grunt, he grabbed Ayasha's leg this time, pulling her toward the edge. With no hesitation, Paloma drove her knife through his wrist, twisting it. He yanked his hand up. Her knife clattered against a rock as she gave him a monumental push with a grunt of her own that sent him over the ledge.

Without wasting a moment, Paloma grabbed Ayasha and dragged her back from the edge, looking around in the failing light for the buffalo robe they had flung aside. She threw it around them again, pulling the girl into an embrace so close that they began to breathe in rhythm. She shivered, or maybe Ayasha shivered. They were bound together so tightly that Paloma could not tell.

There was no sound of humans above them now. *What a strange storm!* Last year, Marco had told her of lightning in winter, but she had put it down to a tall tale. Through a slit in the buffalo robe, Paloma blinked at the lightning, and then the close roar of thunder, as snow fell, and then icy sleet, as if the elements couldn't decide what to do.

"Just be alive," she whispered. She wrinkled her nose at the odor of blood and her own rank fear. She pressed her head against the rocks of the canyon wall and closed her eyes.

But there was Ayasha. The Spaniard in Paloma told her to make polite conversation. "Do you belong to the woman who rode away with Toshua?"

"I belong to no one," came the quiet answer.

"I have been there," Paloma whispered back. *Pray God I am not there again*, she thought.

BUCIRO WOULD PROBABLY HAVE handled the lightning better, but Marco had no other complaints about his mount. He shook his head when Toshua offered to show him the Comanche way to take a scalp, and could only hope that thunder obscured his retching at the wet sound as the Comanche finished his circling cut around the dying Apache's head, then grasped the deep gash at his neck and yanked away his entire scalp.

He heard the little doctor vomit when Toshua, with a certain savage flair, placed the scalp in his lap. All that earned Antonio Gil was a look of great contempt from the author of the butchery.

Marco couldn't help himself as he added his own meanness to Antonio's induction into life in Comanchería. "This is what you asked for, when you made your bargain with me," he snapped. "Would to God it was *your* scalp and we could go home." He winced as Toshua's woman—who *was* she?—took another scalp. "But I don't like it either," he muttered under his breath to the man still leaning from his horse, retching up his toenails now.

When the other Comanches finished their business of death meted out most painfully, two of them retrieved Marco's pack horses. The woman guided her horse around the carnage, paying no attention to the lightning, thunder, and snow. She nodded, evidently satisfied that they could do no more damage. Leaping off the back of the woman's horse, Toshua mounted an Apache stallion. The animal rolled its eyes in terror. After a few sharp jerks, it kept still, though it was hardly docile.

"Follow me," Toshua said, pointing south with his lips. "Let's find my little sister."

In single file, riding parallel to the rim of the canyon whose vastness was revealed by lightning, they rode to the place where the Apaches had waited, before so foolishly charging them. Marco leaned out over his saddle, relieved to see the trail below. It wasn't wide enough for two horses abreast, but he knew something of narrow trails.

Apparently Antonio Gil did not. Marco heard him whimper, but he followed, probably because the Comanches behind him were in no mood for cowardice. The storm lifted even as darkness came. They descended slowly, until Marco was able to make out a dark mound on the trail. He squinted closer, the bottom dropping from his stomach as he saw all the blood in the fading light. *Oh please no*, he thought, as Toshua dismounted, knelt by what proved to be a buffalo robe, and pulled it back.

Marco looked closer and sighed with relief to see his wife and another woman, their arms tight around each other, alive.

"Paloma," he said, and she looked up, her concentration so fierce that he wondered if she recognized him. Toshua helped her along the trail and lifted her into Marco's saddle, as Toshua's woman swung up the other one.

She still wore her heavy cloak, but it smelled of blood and death. She gripped a knife tight in her hand. Gently he tried to loosen her fingers, but she shook her head. Very well, then; he knew something of terror. The knife could wait.

"Paloma, my love," was all he said, even though he wanted to say so much more.

Marco reckoned an hour passed before they reached the canyon floor. By now the storm was a distant rumble, even though snow still fell. Darkness encircled them, until he noticed little points of filtered light here and there. He looked closer. They were in the middle of a Comanche village, and the mellow light shown through buffalo hide tipis. It was a small encampment, pitifully so.

He listened; no dogs. He sniffed; larger fires had burned here earlier. Ahead of him, Toshua dismounted and simply stood there, looking around him. The woman dismounted and stood beside him. As Marco watched, amazed, the Comanche put his arm around her.

"That's his wife," Paloma whispered, the first thing she had said since

Toshua put her into his saddle. "He told me her name but I can't remember it."

Marco tried again to take the bloody knife from her and this time she surrendered it. "I stabbed a man and pushed him off the ledge," she whispered again. "I have also learned to be very quiet."

He dropped the knife in the snow and put his arms around her, holding her tight until she stirred and looked around. "The other one with you?" he asked.

"Ayasha. She has no one."

Paloma leaned back against him, a sudden heavy weight. "I am so tired," she whispered.

She offered no objection when Toshua held out his arms for her. He carried her to the woman as Marco dismounted. After a low-voiced discussion, the two Comanches walked into the circle of tipis. Paloma looked around for him and held out her hand. Marco followed, stiff and sore, feeling every pain of the encounter with the Apaches.

"What about me?" Antonio Gil asked.

Marco ignored him, then remembered he was still a Christian, a *juez,* and a kind man, generally. "Come along, little man," he said. "Paloma would say we are having an adventure."

"I hate adventures!" he snapped.

Marco wondered again why God in His infinite wisdom had saddled them with an idiot. Where was this written in his charge as *juez de campo* from the governor and the viceroy in Mexico? *I swear that if I survive this, I will give up that job,* he told himself, not for the first time.

Paloma was on her feet now, reaching for him. Marco grabbed her and held her to him, doing nothing more than breathing. In a moment the woman touched his arm and gestured inside. He ducked into the tipi with Paloma and sighed with the pleasure of sudden warmth.

He thought Paloma would relax, but she stiffened, as if remembering something, and moved to the tipi flap. She stepped outside.

"Paloma?" he asked, following her.

She ignored him and walked to the horse where the younger woman was just dismounting. "Where will you go?" she asked.

"I have a place with the Old One," she said. With a little wave, she disappeared into the gloom.

"Paloma? It's cold out here," Marco said gently.

"Ayasha taught me to be silent in danger." Paloma put her hand in his, her expression troubled. "I knew that once before, and it saved my life. I suppose I had forgotten." Silent now, she let him lead her back to the tipi.

Once inside again, the woman—Toshua's woman, Marco supposed, but there was an explanation owing—unclasped Paloma's cloak with sure fingers and tossed it to one side. While Marco just gaped stupidly, worn out with terror himself, the woman worked fast, unbuttoning Paloma's wool sacque. She had started on Paloma's basque when she backed away. "Let Marco help me," she whispered, her eyes on Toshua. "Please, lady, do you speak Spanish?"

"*Claro*," the woman said. She turned to look at Toshua and said something sharp in Comanche.

Toshua nodded. He glanced at Marco with faint embarrassment. "Sometimes I forget how shy you people are," he said as he left the tipi.

The woman stepped back, and Marco finished undressing Paloma, who was visibly shaking now, perhaps from both cold and fear. The woman pointed to the pile of buffalo robes and pulled them back, motioning to him. He guided his trembling wife to the pile and helped her down, covering her.

"You, señor," she said next. When, in his own stupor, he didn't move fast enough to suit her, she yanked at his belt and started to tug on his breeches.

"I can do that," he said hastily.

She gave him a look faintly reminiscent of one from his sister Luisa, as if she wondered how someone could be as old as he was and yet so silly. "Do your own business then."

He knew she wasn't going anywhere, so Marco resigned himself to stripping in front of her. He smiled a little when she gave him a push on his bare bottom toward the robes. He lay down beside Paloma and gathered her close. They warmed each other until Marco felt his shoulders, so tense, begin to relax. He was aware of the woman gathering up their clothing and putting it somewhere. He felt a puff of cold air as the tipi flap opened and then closed. He heard low voices, then the sound of more clothing dropping, then silence.

Marco lay there a long moment, naked and defenseless and deeply unused to such feelings. The soothing sound of his wife's deep breathing calmed his heart, and he slept, too.

Chapter Twenty-Two

In which Toshua explains his wife

ALERT TO STRANGE SOUNDS, Marco woke once during the night, careful not to jostle Paloma, who had burrowed even closer. In the dim light from the fire, he watched her eyelids flutter. He had seen her do that early in their marriage, when he knew she suffered from nightmares. He had not noticed it in recent months, so the sight saddened him.

But she hadn't wakened him. He turned over slowly, facing toward the center of the tipi, curious.

They were doing their best to be silent, but Marco knew enough about Comanches to turn his back again, shy himself, even if they weren't. Paloma said the woman was Toshua's wife. Marco smiled to himself; all evidence did seem to point that way. As Toshua panted softly, and the woman sighed, Marco felt himself relax even more. Yes, he was shy. He hardly ever even kissed Paloma outside of their bedchamber, but there was something so oddly peaceful about what was happening in that tipi, deep at the bottom of a canyon in winter.

For the first time in his life, he was seeing Comanches as people. True, he had become used to Toshua far sooner than Paloma had, but there was always that wary separation he did not know how to overcome, because it was engrained in him since birth. One must fear the Comanche always and never let down any guards. To do so meant death, and not any ordinary death, but death so painful that he could not bear to think about it. The people in whose tipi he and his wife slept were masters of torture and intimidation. And here he lay with Paloma, calm, faintly embarrassed to have heard what he heard, but comforted. He suddenly knew, as deep as he knew anything, that Toshua meant him no harm. Paloma had begun the bond when she saved Toshua's life the first time, even if she wasn't entirely aware of this yet. It had come full circle in Marco's own difficult life, and he wanted to praise God.

Te deum laudamus, he thought, knowing that to even whisper those holy words would alert Toshua, because the man truly had powers that left Marco in awe. *Can you even hear my thoughts?* he asked himself. *If you can, please know that they are kind thoughts. I am in your debt forever.* In complete peace, almost as if he had received sexual release, too, Marco slept again.

When he woke, morning had come and the tipi was light. Someone had piled on more wood, because he was pleasantly warm for the first time since their journey began. He opened his eyes and looked directly into Paloma's.

"Great God, you are beautiful," he whispered.

Her gaze was just as serious as his. "And we are still alive, husband."

He laughed, and she put her hand over his mouth to hush him, but he just rolled onto his back in complete peace and stretched. He glanced toward the other side of the tipi. Toshua's woman was up and dressed. She turned around to look at him, and he understood why she was alive, and not even now a frozen corpse on the Llano with those who must have been forced from this tribe because they were diseased.

Smallpox had not been kind to Toshua's woman. Her face bore the scars of a distant encounter with what Toshua called the Dark Wind. To look at her gave him some idea how old Toshua might be, perhaps a little older than him, perhaps not. He—*juez de campo* of the most dangerous place on earth, bar none—looked into her eyes and saw nothing but kindness there. He could not have been more relieved.

"Thank you for saving us," he said simply, in his most careful Spanish, unsure of her language skills. "We owe you our lives."

She merely nodded, and he thought he had embarrassed her. He hoped he saw good humor in those expressive eyes set in a ruined face. Her hair was cut short in typical Comanche woman's fashion. She wore what appeared to be a much-used deerskin dress, with the high boots of winter. There was little beadwork on the dress, and it was patched in places. Recent years had not been kind to her.

Marco put his hands behind his head, completely vulnerable. "I would like to know your name," he said.

"Eckapeta," she replied. She dipped into a copper pot near the rim of the fire, poured what looked like broth into a wooden bowl, and held it out to him. "Sit up now, so you do not spill on my robes."

He promptly did as she asked, reminded again of his older sister and her admonitions. He nodded, after a sip of something that tasted faintly of meat;

he wasn't about to ask what kind. Eckapeta dipped another serving into a second bowl and held it out. "Tell your woman to sit up."

Marco shook his head. "Alas, I know she will not, because she is modest and shy and also naked."

"No matter how hungry she is?" the woman asked, more curious than irritated.

"No matter. Tell me, is that *camisa* she took off last, right before her bare skin … is that dry now? If you can find that, I might be able to coax her out of the robes."

Eckapeta set down the bowl and went to the far side of the tipi, where she must already have folded their dry clothing; he admired the neat piles. Taking out the *camisa*, she handed it to him. "Tell her not to be so shy. We have all seen breasts, and hers are probably no different."

Paloma was listening, of course, her face fiery. "Marco, I cannot," she whispered.

"Oh, you can," he told her quite firmly, almost in his *juez de campo* voice, but not quite. "This is their world, my dove, and we are guests."

Paloma watched him, still so serious. "Do you know what I learned last night, as the Apaches began dropping down onto the ledge?"

Marco shuddered inside to hear such words from his wife. "Tell me, please."

She looked at him, then at the woman, who was regarding them both with interest. "Exactly what you said. It *is* their world, but I might need reminding."

"I might, too."

She took a deep breath and sat up, instinctively crossing her hands over her breasts at first. She took another deep breath and put them by her sides. He thought he sensed a little pride, because she did have nice breasts. She took her *camisa* from him, raising her arms high to drop it over her head. She wriggled the *camisa* down over her hips, still covered by the robe—after all, she was Paloma and could not discard all modesty—then held out her hand for the bowl. She drank deep, even as he had, asking no questions.

She endeared herself to him forever by sitting there, practically naked by her own standards, but with her hands clasped in front of her on the buffalo robe, still a Spanish lady.

Eckapeta watched her, then leaned across him and pointed to her shoulders, not quite touching her. "I have never seen such things before," she said. "What are they?"

Paloma looked where the woman pointed. "Do you mean my *pecas*?"

Eckapeta repeated the word. "Do you have these little brown things all over you?"

Paloma blushed again. "Mostly just on my shoulders."

"Mostly," Marco teased, which made Paloma nudge him. The woman smiled and turned back to the fire.

"You can stop right now," Paloma whispered to him. "What must she be thinking of us?"

He was spared from any answer that would probably not have satisfied Paloma when the tipi flap opened and Toshua came inside. With a shock, the *juez* saw someone else now. Toshua had discarded the woolen pants and wool shirt he wore at the Double Cross. From his high winter boots, to his breechcloth, to the deerskin shirt and trade blanket around it all, he was what he had always been, a Comanche warrior.

Paloma swallowed audibly and clutched Marco's hand under the cover of the buffalo robe. All he could do was run his fingers across her knuckles and twine their hands together.

Toshua squatted by them in that easy way of his. "Our little doctor is complaining again."

Paloma had pressed herself close to him, and Marco felt her shoulders lose their tense lift at Toshua's words. "Please ask your, um, friends to humor him a little. Think of the good he can do," she said, her voice perfectly normal. The page that had turned in Marco's book of life a few minutes ago must have turned in hers, too.

Toshua nodded and stooped slightly to crouch his way out of the tipi.

"One more thing, my brother. Please tell us what is going on here." Paloma said.

"It is not a good thing." He opened the flap. "When I return with the little doctor, I will say more. Come with me, *tami*."

"When in Rome …." Marco threw back the buffalo robes that protected him, too. Naked, he walked with all the dignity he could muster to the folded pile of clothing, wishing that Eckapeta wasn't watching him so closely. Trying not to hurry, even though his face flamed, he pulled on his smallclothes, and then his breeches, wool shirt, stockings, and boots. When he finished, he beat a retreat for the tipi flap, but not before he heard Eckapeta say to his wife, "Your man has a lot between his legs."

He sighed, embarrassed beyond belief and certain he would never enter that tipi again, especially when he heard Paloma's low laugh. Toshua watched him with a lurking smile.

"My old woman will tell the other women and you will be much in demand."

Marco stopped and put both hands on Toshua's shoulders, something he had never done before. The Comanche started in surprise.

"*Pabi*, let us come to a right understanding here: I will not meet any woman's demands except Paloma's, and she will satisfy no man but me. I know what you suggest is the Comanche way, but it is not the Spanish way. On this, I am unyielding."

After only a brief staring match, Toshua nodded and Marco released him, wondering if he had committed some grave sin against a warrior by touching him that way. So be it. Toshua merely shrugged and gestured toward a tipi.

Marco looked around as they walked, and what he saw distressed him: few tipis, no dogs, a mere handful of warriors, and more children than mothers, apparently. No one looked well-fed. If exhaustion was something that could be put in a jug and sold, this village could supply all of Texas, he was certain. Granted, it was winter, and a lean time for everyone, but there was something more sinister here. He sighed to see what might have been a mound of burned tipis, some with the lodge poles sticking out like bones. He thought of the frozen dead outside their fire circle on the Staked Plain, and he wondered.

As they approached the smaller tipi, the flap flew open and Antonio Gil came out, his face a study in discomfort. Marco found himself wondering about this magic place called Georgia that el médico liked to talk about whenever things were not at their best, either on the plain, on the Double Cross, or apparently here. Even as he pasted a pleasant expression on his face, Marco decided that some people should only stay at home, where evidently things were perfect.

He held up his hand as the doctor stamped toward him. "One moment, little man. I do not care how aggrieved you are. Look around you. We are completely outnumbered and there are surely some here who would like to peel your skin from your body in little tiny strips. Granted, many are in a weakened state, but that is not so much a problem with Comanches."

Antonio stopped, suddenly fearful, and looked around. He said nothing, which Marco considered one of the great blessings of the day, and one achieved so early. He knew such compliance could not last, but he was going to savor it as long as possible. Marco put his hand on the doctor's shoulder and gave him a shake.

"I want you to look around you and see the suffering. Ask yourself if there is anything you can do."

Antonio surprised him. "I have already looked around. I confess that I do not even know where to begin." His eyes filled with tears. "How have they managed to come this far?"

"They are Comanches. That's all the explanation I have," Marco said, hearing something in Antonio Gil's tone of voice that gave him some hope. "Begin with the children. If they have sores, find something in your medical bag, some salve. It may do no good at all," Marco said, drawing close so Toshua could not hear him. "Let them know you care."

"Nothing is that simple," Antonio argued.

"Try it. That little fellow over there."

Marco turned away to follow Toshua. He looked back and smiled to see Antonio pick up a little boy who wandered aimlessly, wearing only a deerskin shirt to his knees and moccasins that had maybe seen better days a century ago. *Well, well,* he thought, as the doctor removed the trade blanket around his shoulders and wrapped up the child, before setting him on his feet again.

After checking the horses—it relieved Marco's heart to see a small stream flowing by the village—he took a sack of pemmican that had been plopped with their other possessions under a tree, surprised that no one had stolen it.

"Pick up the other one," he called to Antonio, who looked around, a frown on his face. "These people are hungry. Tomorrow I will go hunting with Toshua."

The doctor did as asked with no objection—another blessing—and trailed after them as they returned to the tipi.

Eckapeta had left the tipi, but Paloma was there, dressed now and her hair brushed and pulled back with a simple rawhide tie. She made a face to see the pemmican, but did not hesitate to take one of the misshapen balls of meat and grease when Marco handed it to her.

"No one is eating much here," she said to him as she stared at the pemmican, as though wishing it would transform itself into posole or tortillas. "The People are hungry because it is winter and many warriors are dead from *la viruela*. And the old ones ...."

"I know. When Eckapeta returns, will you help her distribute both sacks to the other tipis?"

"It won't be enough, but yes."

"I'll go hunting tomorrow." He looked at Toshua, who nodded. "*We'll* go hunting."

In that way of women, Paloma seemed to have claimed one half of the tipi. The buffalo robes were stacked in a neat pile. She had even hung her Rosary on a little notch in a tipi pole. She gestured to them to sit down, much as if they were guests in her kitchen on the Double Cross, or even in the more exalted *sala*. It touched his heart when she sat next to Toshua and leaned her head for the briefest moment against his arm.

"I know there is much to do, brother, but please tell us: how is it that you and Eckapeta ...." She let the sentence trail away, because she was not a prying woman.

Toshua eyed the tipi entrance, obviously wanting to finish his explanation before Eckapeta returned. "You already know how my women threw me over for a younger man. It happens sometimes, but I did not think it would happen to me."

Paloma nodded. Her hand was on his arm now.

He looked at Marco, apology in his eyes. "Forgive me, señor, but that second wife of mine—the Spanish one I stole from the rancher—what a horrible woman! She bullied my youngest wife, the pretty one with not a brain in her head. True, I had loaned them to the man because he was my friend."

Paloma stared open-mouthed at Toshua.

"It's a Comanche custom," Marco whispered.

"Maybe he *was* better." Toshua shrugged. "I cannot say my wives' foul names because they died there in the cold before our campfire on the plains. Eckapeta told me last night after we fought the Apaches that the other wives forced her to follow along with their scheme to dishonor me and throw me out."

Antonio folded his arms across his chest, skepticism writ large. "You believe that?"

"I do," Toshua said, after giving the doctor such a withering look that the little man seemed to grow even smaller. "When she comes back, look at her hand. Those evil women cut off two of her fingers and said they were ready to do worse if she objected. They told their tale and threw me out. You know the rest."

"You have forgiven this woman, who did you such wrong?" Antonio asked.

"She is my old woman and I feel better when she is near me," the Comanche said simply. He looked at Paloma. "My little sister, you have shown forgiveness to your cousin that I would still like to murder." His glance shifted to Antonio. "I did not know forgiveness until my little sister showed me." He patted the doctor as though he were a child. "You'll learn."

They were all silent then and Marco looked around. *We must act*, he thought. "How do we begin?" he asked finally.

Paloma stood up and gave him her kindest look, the one that always preceded some assignment for him. Felicia used to do the same thing. He waited, thankful for someone else to take charge, even if that didn't make him impressive in his own eyes.

"Dearest heart, you and Toshua need to go hunting *today*, not tomorrow. Eckapeta and I will hand out this pemmican. When you return with a deer or two, we will eat and talk about this."

"What am I to do?" Antonio asked.

"You will save these people," Paloma said simply.

Apparently Antonio was going to be a slow student. "This is just a small encampment. I am looking for the large gathering, somewhere in this canyon. They will have Pia Maria. We could ride out today."

Do you learn nothing? Marco asked himself. A sidelong glance at Toshua's narrowed eyes suggested that his friend, *pabi*, and totally necessary ally was having second thoughts about this entire expedition. Marco didn't dare look at Paloma for her reaction.

When she spoke, it was as though she spoke to a child, and not a bright one. "The People here have survived an ordeal of *la viruela*. Time is wasting and I want to get home to the Double Cross and plant chives in my kitchen garden. If you will not inoculate those who need it, I will." She looked at Toshua for reassurance, which relieved Marco; he was still stunned by Antonio Gil's callousness.

"If I said the word, little man, in five minutes there would be not enough left of you to gather into a small pile," Toshua said as he stood up. He held out his hand for Paloma. She took it without hesitation.

"Don't waste our time," Paloma told Antonio. It was simply said but with more power than Marco had ever heard from his wife.

They all stared at Antonio. Even behind his timid demeanor there was a look of desperation that gave Marco an unsettling glimpse of what a father would do for his child. *I can understand that*, he thought.

Paloma must have seen it, too. "If we do not help here, there will be no opportunity to find Pia Maria. If ever anyone needed friends and allies, we do."

Chapter Twenty-Three

In which Paloma marshals their skimpy forces, and learns more lessons

BEFORE THEY LEFT FOR the hunt, Marco surprised Paloma by planting a kiss full on her lips in front of everyone. When she felt her face grow warm, he did it again, then whispered, "Maybe I'll get into the spirit of the Comanche."

"You are a rascal," she teased, which earned her a pat on her rump. *Dios mio, my man had gone crazy*, crossed her mind.

Eckapeta seemed to appreciate the sentiment, if her smile was any indication. Her face clouded over a moment later. "I have not smiled in a long, long time," she said.

Paloma put her hand on the woman's arm. "Then I will make sure he does that again when he returns, if it makes you smile."

She took a quick glance at Eckapeta's hand, minus two fingers, as Toshua had said. She couldn't help her exclamation, which caused Eckapeta's pock-marked face to harden.

"Look at this hand, too," she said quietly, holding up her other hand, where the tips of three fingers were missing. She touched her face, drawing her hand through the smallpox scars to trace longer scars made with a knife by a woman in mourning. "Toshua and I had three children. All gone now."

Paloma felt her heart go out to the woman. "Perhaps I should not complain of my own trial," she said.

"We all know sorrow," Eckapeta replied. She held up her hand. "One fingertip for each child."

While Eckapeta watched, Paloma took a dozen pemmican balls from one sack and the same amount of hardtack from another. "We don't know if our men will find deer, but we won't go hungry in this tipi," she explained, setting them aside, happy to change the subject. Paloma handed one of the sacks to Eckapeta. The other pemmican sack went to Antonio, and she carried the hardtack. With her boots on and her cloak tight around her, she left the tipi.

Yesterday's storm had blown away and was probably over east Texas now. The day was crisp and clear, with nothing to stop the view that greeted her. Her mouth open in amazement, Paloma looked up and up to the canyon rim, even as she wondered how they had ever survived their descent in last night's storm and darkness. In the distance, she saw Marco and Toshua on horseback, following the stream. Hawks wheeled and dipped far above. She had never seen anything like this canyon.

"What is this place?" she asked in awe.

"It is our winter refuge," Eckapeta told her. She indicated the other tipis with a wave of her hand. "Usually we are much deeper into the canyon by this time, but the Dark Wind blew."

It was as Marco had feared. The band must have been traveling toward winter refuge when *la viruela* struck, forcing them to remain on the Llano Estacado. The dead they had encountered must have been cut loose, for the safety of the others. And so they had wandered.

Eckapeta gestured to what Paloma assumed was north. The canyon gave her no reference. She was as lost here as on the endless plains. "We are safe here, or we might be," Eckapeta said. "Who can tell? You can ride for days, until the rim is so high that the gods must perch there and look down on us." The woman sighed. "The gods have not been of much use lately."

Paloma nodded, taking in the shabbiness of the tipis. She knew that winter even made the Double Cross look a little rundown, what with no flowers in the hanging baskets, and the gurgle of the *acequia* hushed by a film of ice. But there was more than winter at work here. This was a village near death.

"How many have survived *la viruela*?"

"Three or four only survived, and they are so weak. Others seem not to have suffered, and we worry about them. Perhaps the Dark Wind will strike them yet." Eckapeta pointed to the scars on her face. "Those of us visited in other years by the Dark Wind are alive." Her voice hardened. "Others from farther in the canyon have forbidden us to come closer until we are sure the wind has blown over us. Meanwhile, we starve."

"I can understand that," Paloma said calmly, she who comprehended hard choices as well as the next woman. "We'll just have to change things."

For the rest of the day, they went from tipi to tipi with their modest amount of pemmican and hardtack. At first, her heart was in her mouth from the sheer terror of what she was doing, with Marco, her bulwark, nowhere in sight. By the end of the day, her heart was in her hand and she gladly offered it to The People.

She was no physician, but even to her untrained eye, the ones unaffected by *la viruela*—those who had developed immunities earlier—were also ill. She asked Antonio, and he shook his head. "Mostly they're hungry," he whispered to her. He looked her in the eye, maybe because to gaze too long on such suffering drained him. "I know how hunger feels. You do, too."

Paloma nodded, and turned her attention back to The People, admitting to herself that she could not argue with Antonio's shake of the head as he had wondered where to begin. *How can we make a difference?* she asked herself. *How can we keep The People alive?*

"I can help the little man."

Paloma turned around to see the young woman who had probably saved her life on the trail last night. "Ayasha?"

Ayasha nodded, obviously pleased that the Spanish lady remembered her name. "He seems afraid, but if you and the tall man tolerate him, perhaps he will be of use in some way."

"I believe he will be, and soon," Paloma said, happy to have Antonio Gil off her hands. After a moment's thought, she leaned closer to Ayasha, making them conspirators. "Actually, he is a man with powerful medicine, so powerful that he will save your people here."

Ayasha didn't try to mask her skepticism. "I do not see how that can be."

Stand up a little straighter, Señor Gil, Paloma wanted to tell him, because he did not look much like a savior. "Small and mighty. You will see," she told Ayasha. "Take him to those tipis and help him divide the food we bring."

Ayasha walked to Antonio, touching his arm lightly. When he jumped back in alarm, she turned her face to hide her amusement and rolled her marvelous brown eyes at Paloma.

"Very powerful man," Paloma said firmly, ready to thump Antonio.

She heard Eckapeta's chuckle. "Well, he is," she insisted. "When our men come back from the hunt, you will see."

They spent the day going from tipi to tipi, handing out what food they could. Paloma repented of complaining to Sancha that they would never need one more ball of pemmican, when the housekeeper had suggested they keep making more, back on the Double Cross. She had finally convinced Sancha, but as Paloma felt her heart grow heavier and heavier to see the dire need all around her, she wished she had listened.

Paloma finally lost all fear in the tipi where an older warrior with hollow eyes lay, frustration written all over his gaunt features. One of his hands clutched an arrow as the other patted for a bow just out of reach.

"Poor man. He knows he should be out hunting, and he is too weak,"

Eckapeta whispered to her. "His son and daughter are dead of *la viruela*." She touched his face, tracing earlier smallpox scars like her own. "He is starving and he has few teeth left."

As Paloma watched, barely breathing, Eckapeta bit off a hunk of pemmican and chewed. When it was soft, she took it from her mouth. With her finger against his lips, she coaxed the man to open his mouth and put in the food. It took him a few seconds to realize what was happening, and then he began to chew. Paloma knelt beside Toshua's woman, her heart full of an emotion she couldn't even identify.

"Some of The People might say I am wasting my time, that he will die soon," Eckapeta said. "Maybe I am, but I have not the heart within me to drive anyone else onto the Llano." Tears filled her eyes. "I should never have done that to Toshua two years ago, even if his other wives had threatened to cut off *all* my fingers!" She sobbed out loud, then clapped her hands to her mouth, shamed. "He's a good man, my Toshua," Eckapeta said finally. "Maybe I forgot."

"Toshua told me I am his little sister," Paloma said.

"He told me how you have saved his life over and over," Eckapeta told her. She shook her head mournfully. "I couldn't even do that once. No wonder he is your older brother now."

Without a word, Paloma took the pemmican from her and began chewing for the man lying there with something close to hope in his eyes now. When she finished with the pemmican, Paloma chewed hard bread and continued the meal, deeply aware she was probably performing a task more humble than even Father Damiano had ever attempted, and doing it for her enemies since childhood.

While she fed him, Eckapeta took water and deerskin scraps and cleaned the old fellow, despite his protests.

Paloma finished the puny feast with a swallow of water from her hand, the other hand behind the man's head to raise him a little. He smacked his lips in that way Toshua did when he ate with them in the kitchen of the Double Cross, and she knew he was satisfied. As the man she had fed looked at her and nodded, she wished that she had never scolded Toshua to stop smacking his lips.

"Sleep now," she whispered, her hand on his skinny chest. "My man will bring meat tonight."

She knew she would never be the same again, not ever, when she arrived at the next tipi and watched a young woman with exhaustion deep in her eyes and hunger practically sitting on her shoulder like a vulture nurse two infants. To say that she looked overwhelmed was to understate the matter.

"What is this?" Paloma asked, horrified.

"Her sister died of *la viruela*," Eckapeta said, "and she is trying to keep both of their babies alive. I think her husband followed my husband and your man on the hunt this morning. If they are successful, she gets the first meal, else how can she keep them alive?"

Paloma nodded. She knelt close to the woman, all fear gone. When one baby appeared satisfied, she picked up the child and gathered it to her heart, wrapping her cloak around the little morsel. "Would to God this were mine," she murmured into its hair. "Would to God."

Eckapeta looked at her, eyes alert. "I … I thought perhaps you had left your children with a nursemaid at that fortress with the stone walls that Toshua told me of last night."

"I have no children. I am barren," Paloma said. Only blunt speech would do in this place of nothing but terrible truth. "It is the sorrow of my life, perhaps even greater than the death of my family."

"We have all suffered," Eckapeta said quietly. They sat together, shoulder to shoulder, until the woman with the one baby now held out her hand for the pemmican. Paloma had to look away. The desperation in the young mother's face was as great as the desperation in Toshua's eyes, when she found him starving in Señor Muñoz's henhouse and rolled a rotten egg his way. She held the baby close, not caring when it wet on her and soaked through her cloak.

Content to her heart's core, Paloma sat cross-legged in the tipi. There was warmth and food for the mother, who made little mewling sounds as she ate. Paloma looked around to see Antonio come into the tent with Ayasha and kneel by a still form.

"Where do I take the dead?" he whispered to Eckapeta.

"Cross the stream by the two trees close together. You will see other bodies in the rocks."

He picked up the body and Eckapeta covered it with a worn blanket, the kind someone must have stolen on a raid into Spanish lands. Maybe it was even from her own parents' hacienda, snatched eight years ago. Never mind; what was done, was done.

When Antonio returned, his face stark, Eckapeta had finished feeding the young mother. The baby slept, too, so she covered mother and daughter with a trade blanket and held out her hands for the infant wrapped in Paloma's cloak.

Paloma shook her head and backed away. "No. I will keep this baby with me until it cries for milk, then I will bring it back."

"It won't cry."

"What do you mean? Babies always cry when they are hungry."

"Not babies of The People. When they cry, we ignore them. When they are silent, we feed them. It doesn't take long, even for a baby, to understand that."

And this silence keeps the whole village safe from enemies, Paloma thought.

She left the tipi with Toshua's woman. Snow fell again, and they stood close together as she told Eckapeta about last night on the trail, when Ayasha shook her by the chin and forced her into silence.

"You learned a good lesson, señora," the woman said. "Ayasha has no one now, which means she has every one of us."

"No parents?"

"Not for a long time. See the scars on her face? Last summer her husband was gored in a buffalo hunt."

"She's so young," Paloma said, wondering what she would do if Marco died. "Where does she go? Is there anyone for her?"

"Ayasha helps an Old One and we all spare what food we can. That is the way of The People."

"I have learned many good lessons today," Paloma said.

DARKNESS CAME EARLY IN the high-walled canyon as she returned the baby—not more than a month old—surrendering it with huge reluctance. She lingered there, watching the baby root and then grab at the mother's nipple. While she watched, Paloma tore off chunks of her last ball of pemmican and gave them to the woman.

"Which one is your baby?" she asked, hoping the young mother understood Spanish.

"The one sleeping," she said in Spanish at least as good as Antonio's, and indicated the smaller infant curled into the tight ball of a newborn. "My sister …." She looked down at the child who nursed, and her eyes filled with tears. "Her husband is deeper in the canyon, and I know he worries."

Weary with sorrow, Paloma rose to leave when she heard a horse galloping into the village. Startled, she opened the flap to see a warrior on horseback practically in front of the tipi. She turned around at an exclamation from the woman, who obviously knew the sound of that particular horse. Paloma stepped aside as a warrior with blood on his face crouched inside the tipi. He held out a lump of meat and wasted not a moment in cutting off small raw bites for the woman. He touched her face with a bloody hand. She gave him such a look as she chewed and swallowed.

Paloma cleared her throat, and he looked around, startled to see her. "Please, señor, is my husband …?"

He understood Spanish, too, to her relief. "Your man sent me ahead with this meat for my woman."

"He would do that," Paloma said, proud of her man. "Would you like me to slice some of this?"

Scarcely taking his eyes from his wife, the warrior sliced some smaller bits for her, then left the larger portion on a stone by the fire. He took another knife from a sheath tied to his waist and held it out to Paloma, handle first. Funny how only a few days ago Paloma would never have touched such a knife, the kind of knife she remembered with painful clarity as she hid under her mother's bed in terror. *What is done, is done*, she told herself again, and took the knife from him. She sliced the venison into thin strips, the same as she and Sancha had done with venison and beef on the Double Cross. For a moment, she longed for her clean, well-lit kitchen, with *ristras* of chilis hanging from the ceiling, and cloth-covered cheese and eggs. *Some day again, God willing*, she told herself as she sliced venison.

When she finished, there was a neat pile for the woman to cook on the hot rocks or parboil, once the babies were fed. Paloma took another long look at the child she had carried all afternoon and left the lodge.

She hadn't the heart to go far, because she yearned to gather the baby close to her again. Paloma stood there in silence, her hands clasped in front of her, waiting for her husband to return.

She hadn't long to wait. As the wretched village far below in the deep canyon lost the last bit of light, she saw Marco and Toshua coming, leading their horses burdened with two deer. She walked toward them, her heart lifting at the sight of his wave and smile.

She forgot her own yearning when she saw how tired he was. Still, there was a gleam in his light brown eyes, determination she was familiar with.

"You will eat and go directly to bed," she told him, trying the light scold she knew he was familiar with, from life with her on the Double Cross. It didn't work in the Indian village.

"We will finish butchering these deer, my love, and stuff ourselves like Comanche. They are thin from winter, but we will feast. We should also talk tonight about Antonio's gift of life."

She tried again. "It can wait for morning. Once everyone is full, everyone will sleep. Antonio would only be a cricket sawing on the hearth."

"I daresay you are right." He put his arm around her and walked toward the center of the ring of tipis, his horse following like a big dog.

By now, women had gathered with their knives. The men and children with any strength left helped Toshua and Marco pull the dead deer from their horses. Others led the horses away to the stream and what pasture remained. Everyone had a purpose. The work of reducing the deer to hide and bones went on by the light of a roaring fire built by Toshua and Eckapeta. There was nothing puny and defeated about this blaze, a far cry from the tiny pinpoints of light in the tipis last night, barely glimpsed through the storm. Paloma could tell they had starved before and survived. *I have, too*, she thought with pride that took the weariness out of her back and the longing from her heart. Her man was back and there was food. She gently tucked away the yearning for the Comanche baby and moved closer to help.

Chapter Twenty-Four

In which Paloma breaks Marco's heart, but can't help herself

T RUST A WOMAN TO *worry about her dress, even here*, Marco told himself as he stripped with his eyes closed, not even caring if Eckapeta and all the Kwahadi women in Comanchería stood in the tipi and stared. He patted his bulging stomach—ordinarily flat and his secret bit of vanity—amazed that he could cram down so much venison. He sank to his knees, stupefied with food and exhaustion and feeling every year of his three decades and a little bit more.

Paloma must have shooed out everyone else, because she was stripping, too, muttering to herself about the blood and brains on her dress. Or maybe it was just the two of them anyway. He crawled between the buffalo robes and reached for her.

"How in heaven's name do I clean brains from my skirt?" she asked, not unwilling to be towed to bed, but unhappy about her skirt.

"I haven't a clue." He patted her stomach, which bulged a little, too. "Have you ever eaten that much in your life?"

"No. And Eckapeta kept handing me more and more. Why do they *do* that?"

"The People eat when they can, and so do we now."

She started to tell him something about two babies and an exhausted mother, and he tried to listen, he really did, except that he could not keep his brain awake. He remembered a little sigh and someone kissing his chest—he assumed it must be his darling—and then he slept.

When he woke up, the sky was light and Paloma was gone. He lay there in perfect peace, all things considered. After several days of gloom, the sun finally shone. Was he one of those simpletons who needed sunlight to improve his mood?

He glanced across the fire pit to the other side of their temporary residence with Señor and Señora Toshua and saw two sleeping mounds. He got up quietly and dressed, sniffing at his own clothing with some displeasure. *I am getting ranker by the minute*, he thought. Paloma had said something last night about trying to clean her clothes, but all he could really remember was her warmth as she cuddled close.

As a good rancher ought, Marco checked his horses first, then went in search of his wife. The Indian camp was silent, everyone sleeping off a prodigious feed. No one stood guard, but what was there to guard but weary, defeated people and tired horses? The Comanche who had ridden with them yesterday—the man with a wife and two babies to feed—had explained the lack of dogs. "We only eat dog when we are starving," had been his simple statement. The warrior had been infinitely helpful. He knew the canyon as well as Toshua. He had been fueled by even more desperation than most as they hunted, considering his family obligations.

Marco stopped. The babies. He knew where Paloma was now. He walked to the trail and looked toward the little village, trying to remember where Paloma had been standing when he and Toshua walked in with their kills. "It would help me if you Kwahadi decorated your tipis," he said out loud. Each one looked the same—plain, wet, and sagging at this time of year. There wasn't much artistic sentiment in the average Comanche.

And there she was. Paloma had just crouched out of the tipi opening, a baby in her arms. He raised his hand in greeting and she walked toward him. It seemed to Marco that he probably could have seen her smile from the rim of the canyon, hundreds of feet above. She carried a child and she smiled; it was that simple, and yet complicated beyond belief.

"You were making some fearsome gurgling noises this morning," she said by way of greeting, so wifely. "Woke me right up."

He held Paloma close, the baby between them, and looked down to see bright brown eyes and a little mop of hair that probably was as soft as dandelion puffs to the touch. The child regarded him in silence, but with much interest. He knew the look because he had seen it many times on the faces of his dear twins, puzzling him out at first, because Felicia had been their tether through nine months. Somehow when the twins divined in some baby way his part in the scheme of things, they permitted him all sorts of fatherly liberties. The emotion struck him hard, and made him puff out his cheeks and blow to stop the tears.

"Kahúu just finished nursing her. She has ever so much milk this morning, thanks be to God and you and the deer."

"Is this Kahúu's child?"

"No, her sister's baby. Her sister delivered this little one, then died of *la viruela*."

We can't keep her, he wanted to say. *The Kwahadi would never in a million years permit such a thing.* He remained silent, but put his arm around Paloma's waist and walked with her along the stream.

"I'll take her back when she starts to squirm. She never cries, but she squirms and I know she wants milk."

There was something so wistful in his wife's words that he felt his heart crack. He knew she wanted more than anything to open her own bodice and nurse this baby, and it harrowed his soul in a terrible way that she could not.

"You're good to be so helpful," he finally managed to say, but it was a poor, poor attempt.

Her eyes filled with tears. "Would that I could nurse her," she whispered.

He hugged her closer and they continued their slow pacing.

She tried normal conversation, and failed. They walked in silence. She began to hum finally, and he recognized "*Te deum laudamus*," which had somehow become the anthem of this journey. He hummed along with her, comforted, as he knew she was, because she sang the words when she could.

When she finished, she stood still with a wry expression, the old Paloma again. "Do you think I am breaking some Comanche rule to sing such holy things to a baby of The People?"

He laughed softly, unwilling to wake up a baby. "I don't think The People take much interest in rules, do you?"

He sighed inwardly with relief, because the terrible moment had passed, and she was his again. He looked toward the distant camp now. He saw smoke rising from tipis, and women emerging, ready to begin another day, one with considerably more hope to it. He could almost sense a new optimism.

"Now is the time, my love. We have to gather The People and convince the rare few who have escaped *la viruela* that they need to be inoculated, which means they will feel sick and even nigh unto death for a few days, and that most will recover, but perhaps not all. I shudder to think of their reaction. Can we convince them?"

"You can do it, because everyone is in your debt, yours and Toshua's."

He kissed her cheek, a loud smacking kiss accompanied by a growl, that made a woman picking through the remains of the deer feast look up and smile. "I believe you, even though thousands wouldn't," he told her.

MARCO KNEW LATER THAT they owed their success to Toshua, a warrior rejected by The People, and Paloma, a woman who never should have cared so much. A skeptical man—after all, he was a *juez de campo*—Marco never would have thought they could have gotten the attention of thirty people accustomed since childhood to act independently. He remembered all too well the ferocity of every single warrior on the field of battle at Rio Carlos in 1779, each man doing his best, without regard to his neighbors.

He had never seen a band come together, but this one did, and with laudatory speed. Maybe they understood their great weakness. Maybe they knew that to survive meant more sacrifice. Or maybe they trusted him a little, he who had brought food and a kind woman.

It hadn't begun well. Marco should have known better than to give Antonio Gil the stage, once everyone was settled around last night's fire. It didn't surprise Marco that the Comanche chuckled and jostled one another at the man's poor Spanish. Even with Toshua translating, for those who needed it, everyone got lost in Antonio's explanation of small cuts and scabs, a waiting period and then illness. Marco could see that the little doctor was doing his best, but it was no way to talk to The People. Marco was at a loss until Toshua dismissed Antonio with a decisive chop of his hand. The little doctor sat back on a log, unsure of himself, the last thing Marco needed.

Toshua began to speak. Marco could follow only one or two words, but he understood Toshua's intensity. He caught the words "Cuerno Verde," the Kwahadi leader cut down in 1779 by Governor de Anza, and then "Señor Muñoz," the man who had enslaved him, Toshua—the Comanche who pleaded before them now. Trust an Indian to begin a story in precisely the right place: far from the beginning.

Toshua gestured of an evil wind, and people dropping and dying, which earned him nods and grunts from his audience. He gestured toward the doctor, then took Paloma by the hand, gently urging her forward.

Paloma looked at Marco, then handed him the baby, the last thing he wanted her to do, because he knew without a doubt that he craved the child as much as she did. He held the baby up against his chest, treasuring the feel of the little head as it turned this way and that, then found that comfortable spot just south of his neck that his twins loved, too.

He inclined his head toward the baby as Toshua traced the scar on Paloma's forearm, then pantomimed drawing a thread through something and applying it to her arm. A few swift circles, and he wrapped her arm with an imaginary bandage.

Paloma amazed Marco. She held out her hand with five fingers spread wide, then began to stagger and press her hands to her cheeks. As he watched, as fascinated as her Comanche audience, she drooped and languished, shaking her head from side to side and pulling at her clothes as though she burned with fever. After a long pause with her eyes closed, a wonderful approximation of time passing, she held out her hand again with five fingers spread, took a deep breath and smiled. His eyes on her, Toshua interpreted her actions and pleaded.

When she finished, Toshua gently touched her face and turned it toward him, so The People could see the row of smallpox scars trailing from her ear to her neck. His arm went around her as he kept talking and gesturing. When he finished, Paloma took his arm and pointed to his inoculation scar, going through the motions he had just described for her. Then she waved Marco forward. He looked at her, puzzled.

"Your turn, *juez*," she said. "Show off your inoculation scar."

She took the baby from him as he removed his doublet and unbuttoned his shirt, pulling it off his shoulder so they could see his own scar high on his biceps.

He buttoned up as someone asked a question. Toshua translated and Paloma started to laugh, that hearty sound he relished, even though he knew he was about to be embarrassed. *Dios mio*, who knew being a *juez de campo* would be this much trouble?

"Do I have to show them my pox scars?" he asked them both, and they nodded.

With a sigh, Marco unbuttoned his breeches and dropped his pants, pulling down his smallclothes just enough to show off the smallpox scars on his hip. The women whooped with laughter, probably the first thing they had laughed at in weeks, and even the warriors smiled. Eckapeta spoke up then, gesturing between her legs, and the women looked at him with wide-eyed respect.

"I won't show *that* off," he declared, which made Paloma put her hand to her mouth, her eyes lively.

When everyone had settled down again, Toshua continued. Marco sat cross-legged next to Antonio, Paloma beside him, lowering herself gracefully because she held the sleeping baby. "What is he saying, do you think?" she whispered.

"Probably asking for those who have not previously suffered smallpox to come forward. Say a prayer, Paloma."

"That is all I have done since we left the Double Cross."

As he watched, Ayasha stood up, her face serious, her eyes showing great determination. Paloma sucked in her breath. "Ayasha has been helping our doctor. Eckapeta said she had no one."

"Then you should inoculate her."

Others stood, looking around at each other, uncertainty on their faces. The warrior who had hunted with them stood up and spoke to Toshua at length. When he finished, Toshua looked at Marco, who came to his side.

"His wife Kahúu has already been visited by the Dark Wind, but he has not. He is his family's protector. If The People are inoculated and fall sick for many days, are they weak when it is done?"

"Alas, yes," Marco said.

"He wants to know, can they still travel to that place where the Kwahadi gather? Many warriors have assembled there, and he would feel safe for his family then."

"That's precisely where we want to go." Marco looked at Antonio, who came forward eagerly now, probably tired of being ignored. "What do you think?"

"Can we put them on travois?" Antonio asked.

Toshua frowned. "We don't use travois."

"Your friends the Kiowa do," Marco pointed out. "I know my packhorses are used to travois. We can carry those who are recuperating that way, and the rest on horseback, if they ride with someone else."

Still Toshua hesitated.

"And how much longer will we find deer in this part of the canyon?" Marco asked. He couldn't help his stern look, this *juez*. "And I mightily suspect that you have quite a few of our New Mexican cattle, the farther into this canyon we go. I *know* what good eating they are."

Toshua threw up his hands. "We will do it your way."

Chapter Twenty-Five

In which Antonio works more willingly

A NTHONY GILL HAD NEVER been particularly impressed with
Spaniards, for all that they had offered him refuge when the colony of
Georgia turned him out. He saw them as a superstitious, lazy lot, more inclined
to put things off. After casting his lot with the New Mexicans, mostly against
his will, he had been revising his opinion. The speed with which Marco and
Paloma organized the inoculations fairly amazed him.

He didn't think Paloma would consent to put down that baby, but she did,
handing the child to Eckapeta as she hurried into the tipi for her medical kit.
Marco wasted not a minute in securing lodge poles from the pile of unburned
ones someone had spared when they destroyed the tipis of The People stricken
with disease. He called for rawhide and was soon weaving a platform for that
space between the poles.

"We needn't hurry," Anthony said.

"We had to go quite a distance to find those deer, and tomorrow Toshua
and I will hunt again, probably even farther afield," he said, continuing to
twist and knot the rawhide. "Meat is scarce and we need meat. I'll begin this
today, so I can hunt with good conscience tomorrow."

This Spaniard could also do two things at once. As he worked, he called
to Toshua and Eckapeta and they sat with him as he told them to organize the
healthy to help those who would soon be inoculated.

"There are not so many strong ones," Eckapeta reminded them.

"Then Paloma and I will do all we can."

Anthony shouldn't have been standing there idly. He also shouldn't have thought for a single minute that Toshua's woman was slow.

"Why are you doing this, little man?" she asked him point blank. "I doubt you have any love for The People."

Anthony took his time telling her about Pia Maria, and how she had been kidnapped near Los Adaes, in the Louisiana territory. He thought it prudent not to mention the shocking death of Catalina Gill; Eckapeta was quite capable of drawing her own conclusions.

He wanted to see some compassion in her eyes for his plight, but there was none. Kidnapping small children was obviously part of her world she did not question. Why, he did not know; weren't there enough ready-made Indians? But she was looking at him for more explanation.

"The Dark Wind has been blowing strong across Texas. I proposed to the *juez de campo* that he accompany me to your lands where others have told me the child has been taken. In exchange for her release to me, I will inoculate The People against this dread disease."

He knew better than to glance at Marco Mondragón, the man he had coerced into this scheme. As it was, the *juez* cleared his throat impressively and turned slightly away.

Why did the woman have to be so smart? She looked from him to Marco, studying them both.

"You think the Kwahadi who have this daughter will release her to you?"

"If they want to avoid the total annihilation of The People, they will."

After conferring with Paloma, they decided on the open air as their medical bay. He asked Ayasha to roll the fallen log he had sat on earlier toward a taller tree stump, pleased with her willing help. He noticed that her pretty eyes had lost some of their desperation. Ayasha smiled at him, and he felt the heat rise to his face. She smiled at Paloma next, who rested the back of her hand briefly against her cheek.

You would think Paloma liked these savages, Anthony thought. *I will never understand women.* Still, Ayasha was helpful.

Enough of this. "I don't have any cloth for bandages and don't suppose these assassins do, either," he complained.

Paloma froze him with a look that unsettled his insides.

"I mean—"

"I know what you mean," she said, her words clipped and disapproving. "I brought along an extra skirt and bodice. Ayasha and I will rip them into strips."

He hoped no one had witnessed that little scene, but as in most of his life, his hope went unfulfilled.

"Whatever she said to you, I suspect you richly deserved it," Marco said, speaking from across a distance as he continued to weave the rawhide. "*Ay caray!* I hope I never see that look aimed at me!" He chuckled and went back to his business, a man secure in his affections.

"She said she is ripping up her one clean skirt and bodice for bandages."

"I thought she might."

So offhand, so casual. Anthony watched him, envious not so much for Paloma now, but envious that any one human being should have such trust in someone else. *He has led a charmed life,* he thought. *Nothing has even gone amiss for Marco Mondragón.* Logic told him that couldn't be true, but logic had never been a consideration in his messy life.

It was as if the Lord God Almighty, that fearsome Being who was thundered about from pulpits all through the colonies, had suddenly decreed that he, Anthony Gill, humble himself. This humbling took place less than an hour later in a hardscrabble Indian encampment in the middle of nowhere. As he considered the event later, Anthony decided that *humble* wasn't the right word. What happened before the inoculations began convinced him that a man could still learn, if he wanted to.

True to her word, Paloma ripped the material into serviceable bandages. When the ripping sound began, every single warrior in that camp—Marco included—whirled around, hand on knife. They all chuckled when Paloma looked up, startled, at their reaction, then continued. Ayasha's task was to roll each strip into a neat cylinder, then put them in another leather bag.

Paloma's tidiness in the face of mud and melting snow touched him. She was one of those rare women determined to improve her surroundings, no matter how filthy. Anthony wondered what it would take to discourage her, and decided that he would probably never find out. Paloma Vega de Mondragón seemed to be a flowing well of kindness. He looked at Ayasha, who watched Paloma, too, ready to imitate the woman who probably had no idea of her admiration. Smiling inwardly, Anthony remembered what she had said about Marco making him a better person, the longer he was in their company. *Do you ever take a thought to your own influence?* he asked himself, even as he doubted it supremely.

When Anthony signaled his readiness, Toshua and Eckapeta went to each tipi in turn and summoned the now less than willing patients. He had done this so many times now, but Anthony couldn't help but sigh to see how few there were. He remembered the frozen caricatures of the dead carpeting the plains and the burned tipis in this noisome camp. The People had suffered; he could not deny it.

But business was business. "Have someone begin, Toshua," he said to the Comanche. "Time's a-wasting."

Toshua gestured. No one moved. The Comanche walked toward his friends and fellow conspirators in making life miserable for white men; they backed away.

"Hellfire and damnation," Anthony swore in English. He hadn't the slightest idea what to do. This nonsense was putting more time between him and Pia Maria.

Paloma had been sitting beside him, ready to assist. She stood up.

"Good luck," Anthony muttered in English.

She gave him that look again—*Good God, twice in one day*—then walked to Toshua. They spoke; he argued; she shook her head; he yielded.

"Señor Gil, inoculate me again, so The People can watch it actually happening."

"You can't be serious," he said. It came out louder than he intended, because everyone stared at him.

"I have never been more serious," she replied. "They are afraid, and I don't blame them. Inoculate me again while they watch. It can't possibly do me any harm."

He opened his mouth to voice all kinds of objections, but couldn't think of any of them that made any sense. It wouldn't hurt her; she was already immune. Even more than that, she had such a fire in her eyes that he knew if he objected, she would probably do it to herself.

He glanced at Marco, who was paying attention now. Maybe her husband could straighten her out.

Damn the man. All he did was roll up his sleeve. "Do us both," he said. "There is not a Comanche alive who would admit to being less brave than a white man."

Anthony swallowed and did as they asked, Paloma first, while the women and children clustered around, and then Marco, for the benefit of the warriors. After that, they couldn't line up fast enough.

He probably should have felt a stab of envy when Paloma had more Comanches in her line that he did. The first warrior who came her way got a good ribbing from his compatriots, but she did have a knack.

"They prefer her to me," he remarked to Marco, with just a twinge of jealousy.

"So do I," he replied, which made Paloma cover her mouth with her hand and laugh.

When they finished, The People still squatted there by the fire that someone had built up again. The warmth felt good on his face. Antony watched them look over their bandages, holding their arms high, as Toshua had done weeks ago when it was his turn. He tugged on Toshua's fringed shirt and he turned around.

"Just … just remind them that in five days or so, they won't feel so good."

"I will." He nodded to Marco, who stood up and raised his hands.

"Toshua and I will hunt tomorrow. You must know that deer are scarce. You should make snares, for I have seen rabbits. I know you are weary but we all have to do our best."

The People nodded, looked at each other, and quietly left the campfire ground, "each to his own vine and fig tree," as Anthony remembered from a particularly windy sermon in Savannah. He stayed where he was, pleasantly tired now, pleased in a way he had not felt in years. He and Paloma had done the work. Pray God it would take. It was time Pia Maria went home.

* * *

TRUST PALOMA TO THINK she needed to apologize because she had not figured out how to get the blood and brains from her skirt. Long ago Marco had decided that was one of the many interesting things about women— sometimes they had trouble deciding what mattered and what didn't. He thought he might tell her so, but his prior experience as a husband warned him that she would not appreciate his observation.

Besides, he enjoyed just lying back against a mound of buffalo robes with Paloma's head resting against his stomach. He was full of venison, and knew she was bound to hear some disharmony as the venison meandered through his system, but she was used to him. He yawned, which made Eckapeta scold and call him ill-mannered.

Paloma laughed, a tired, satisfied laugh that told him worlds about her state of mind. His wife was oceans and mountains and deserts away from the timid woman he had first laid eyes on in Santa Fe, stuck in her uncle's house, barely more than Felix Moreno's property. Marco hoped he had also undergone some improvement since their marriage.

Eckapeta cleared her throat in that polite way that meant she wanted to talk, but only if he did, too. In a few short days, Marco had learned to recognize the language of the tipi, and how inhabitants remained civil to each other in tight quarters.

"Yes?" he asked.

She began in such a deferential way, but he already knew that Indians took their time getting to the point, even Comanches, who had low tolerance for folly. He listened for the gist of her remarks, and realized that she was a shrewd woman, a worthy match for Toshua, who lounged beside her.

"There is more to the little man's story," she said. It was a statement of fact, but he could answer or not.

"Much more."

She took her time, coming at the matter in leisurely circumlocution. "You are a wise man."

"I like to think so."

More time. "A wise man would never consent to travel to the secret canyon of the Kwahadi because he wants to do good to his enemy."

"No, I would never," he said, resting his hand on Paloma's head now, because she had stiffened. Probably as long as they lived, what he had bargained away to keep her safe would be a sore spot with her, because she thought more of him than herself.

"What did he hold over *you*, señor?"

Such a direct question. Wondrous how The People could circle around and around, then go for the artery.

"If I wanted him to protect Paloma against the Dark Wind, I had to promise to take him into your stronghold. If I would not agree, he would not protect her." He wasn't satisfied with that answer, but he couldn't think of how to improve a devil's bargain.

Eckapeta's eyes widened in surprise, then narrowed. "We should probably just kill him now," she said, as calmly as if discussing beadwork. "Paloma can do what he does."

"No! He has a daughter."

Paloma had joined the conversation. Marco couldn't help wishing she was less kind. Eckapeta's idea was sound to him. *Ay caray!* That made twice he had married sweet women.

"He thinks he will bargain with the Kwahadi who holds this Pia Maria?" Eckapeta asked so thoughtfully.

"I believe he does."

A long sigh from Eckapeta. "He will probably succeed. I want my people to live, but why does a man that evil win?"

"He is not so evil. I believe his trials have been tall mountains to him," Paloma said softly. She lay down again, then sat up, glancing at him shyly, then at Toshua and Eckapeta across the fire.

"My dears, you know I am a modest woman."

They nodded.

"It is this: could you two give us some time alone here? I want my man, but I am shy about it with others."

Marco knew if he had false teeth like Father Francisco, he would have swallowed them.

Eckapeta did not seem even slightly surprised. She stood up and held her hand out to Toshua, who bounded lightly to his feet, his expression less inscrutable than usual.

"Well, then," Paloma said when the tipi flap closed, her fingers on the clasp to that skirt she couldn't get clean.

Chapter Twenty-Six

In which Paloma becomes a new woman

MARCO AND TOSHUA RANGED even farther afield for deer the next day, returning with only two scrawny ones, ripe for winter-kill with almost no fat on them. Marco should not have worried. Newly energized, The People had been busy with snares and presented rabbits and mice to their tired hunters. It was all worth it to watch how Paloma eyed with vast suspicion a stew of mouse, then downed it with nothing beyond one heave of her belly.

She carried the Kwahadi baby everywhere, claiming that Kahúu needed rest from tending two infants. He knew it was true, having been through twins, even with a hacienda full of servants. He wanted to warn Paloma, remind her that the Kwahadi would never let her take one of their own. He didn't, because he enjoyed holding the infant when he could pry her from Paloma. Maybe baby smells were universal, because the memories flooded back and made him happy in ways that even Paloma could not touch.

When they weren't hunting, Marco worked on his rawhide lacing for the travois poles. One afternoon he came back discouraged from the hunt, with only one deer, and noticed that the lacing was nearly done. He looked around. The only Comanche in sight was the old man that Paloma and Eckapeta had fed from their own mouths. If not warm, the last two days had been less frigid, and he had seen the old man in front of his tipi, his ravaged face to the sun. Knowing the man spoke no Spanish, Marco just pointed to the lacing. With a dip of his thumb and forefinger, the Indian signed *yes*. *Thank you*, Marco signed back, his heart full.

They endured ten days of cold and hunger as the sickness took hold, worsened, and then passed. The sweetest moment came when Kahúu—her breasts showing evidence that even rabbit and mouse stew brought milk—asked him if he would allow Paloma to wear the cradleboard her sister had made, instead of just carrying her tiny niece.

Dios mio, are we part of The People now? he asked himself as he gave his consent. To his surprise—although why it should have surprised him, he couldn't say—Paloma agreed, apparently without even a thought or a backward glance at the great horror of her childhood.

She must have known what he was thinking. That evening before they slept, she whispered to him that she had let go of that terrible sorrow. "This is my adventure, my life," she said, her lips close to his ear. "Would I change things if I could? I honestly do not know. If those other Comanches had not destroyed my family, which left me at the mercy of my relatives in Santa Fe, would I have met you?"

He pulled her to him as the last, stubborn callus of his own loss sloughed away. Would he always love Felicia and twins? He knew he would, but he also knew that this life with Paloma was his adventure, too.

With a certain dogged determination, he and Toshua hunted large game and small, leaving early and returning at dark. Kahúu's husband suffered now from the inoculation, so he had remained behind. They drank water from streams as winter released its harsh grip, and ate the little bit of hardtack that resourceful Eckapeta had squirreled away for them. Marco knew his expectations were lower than ever, the day he tracked and shot a turkey that looked ready to fall over from starvation all on its own. The bird practically begged him to end its misery, flopping on one side so the shooting was even simpler. He could have just walked up and wrung its neck, except that he was tired. Toshua did a little dance. When he stopped, they stared at each other and burst into laughter.

While he did not think Antonio Gil took any pleasure in the days of sickness—why in God's holy name was the man a *médico*?—he had one moment of pride given to him by Paloma and Ayasha, who were generous with good will.

A complaint preceded the matter; perhaps it was jealousy. One of the women in camp had taken Paloma's leather medical bag and added beadwork. Paloma had been waiting for Marco at the head of their well-worn trail when he and Toshua returned with the single turkey. She fairly danced with the pleasure of showing off the exquisite circles and what looked like mountains. "Eckapeta tells me they represent The People's homeland to the north, have you ever seen anything more lovely?" she said in one breath.

Antonio had been waiting, too, with a complaint about the camp's general untidiness, as though he, Marco Mondragón, had any standing whatsoever in this Comanche village. Antonio looked at the beadwork. "Venetian beads," he told Paloma, eyeing them with something close to envy.

"How do you know?" she asked.

"When we traveled with the traders, beads very like these were in great demand."

Paloma had looked at him, puzzled. " 'We?' "

Antonio just shrugged, embarrassment increasing his ill humor. "You know how poor my Spanish is." His expression turned sour. "Even the savages laugh at my Spanish. *When I traveled*," he said, correcting himself and mocking her in the bargain. "Satisfied?"

I would thrash that man, if I weren't so tired, Marco thought. Some of what he felt must have communicated itself to Paloma, because she put her hand on his arm and shook her head. Still, he could not resist; well, he didn't try. "Antonio, I can't deal with your complaints right now," he said, probably with more force that he needed to exert. The doctor stalked away.

Ayasha had watched the unpleasant exchange, her brow furrowed. After Antonio left, she touched Paloma's arm lightly, the Indian way. "Antonio might become sweeter if I steal his bag and ask Owl Woman to bead it." Her frown returned. "I have nothing to trade her to do this work."

Marco watched, amused, as Paloma considered the matter, pursing her lips in that thoughtful way that would have led to a kiss and probably more, if they had been alone. A census of her belongings on this journey took little time, and she brightened. "I have it, Ayasha. Tell her that the big man's woman will trade her magic beads for the work."

Ayasha nodded and hurried to Owl Woman's tipi.

"Magic beads? Your rosary?" Marco asked. "Really, Paloma?"

She nodded. "I can tell the Rosary on my fingers. And … and the Virgin knows my needs." She gave him her sunniest smile. "When we return to Santa Maria, you can get me a new one."

"And what will you trade me for that?" he asked, after looking around and patting her backside.

"Probably just what you are suggesting," she said with matter-of-fact aplomb.

He gave a hearty laugh and draped his arm over her shoulder as they walked toward Eckapeta's tipi. "This is a real kindness for our little obnoxious doctor," he teased.

"He's not so obnoxious around Ayasha," she said. "Have you noticed?"

Marco had to admit he was innocent of that much observation. "She helps him at every opportunity, and he returns the favor by checking on the Old One that Ayasha tends. That's how they work in this encampment."

"I *have* noticed that," he said. "Everyone seems to be everyone else's keeper. I could tell Father Francisco, but he would probably not believe so much Christian good will from," he leaned closer to Paloma's ear, "savages."

Paloma nodded, smiling when he kissed her ear. "Maybe we colonists need to look closer and see the good."

"I believe we do." He looked across the encampment to where Eckapeta was helping Toshua with the pathetic turkey. "You could get a head start right now on bartering for the rosary I am going to buy you in Santa Maria."

"I could."

"I've also noticed that when the tipi flap is down in place, no one enters."

"I've noticed that, too," Paloma said with a blush.

"Big man's woman?" he asked as he closed the flap and helped her—such a kind husband—with her buttons.

"That's what Eckapeta says." She took over. "Marco, you're not so good with little buttons."

THE NEXT MORNING, ANTONIO complained that someone had stolen his medical bag. Paloma just glanced away with a smile, looking everywhere but at Ayasha.

Marco put his arm around the doctor's shoulders and drew him aside. "I think your bag will reappear soon enough. *Ay!* Like magic."

Two days later it was returned, arranged on the tree stump that had served as Antonio Gil's medical bay, the whorls and diamonds on prominent display. Marco couldn't help smiling at the delight on Antonio's face. "Owl Woman?" he asked Paloma, who nodded.

"Antonio, did you happen to notice Paloma's rosary in the Old One's tipi."

"I did, come to think of it," Antonio said, his eyes on the beautiful beading. "That was nice of Paloma."

"I thought so, too."

"You're a tease," Paloma said after Antonio wandered away, still admiring the beadwork. "Owl Woman did it. I asked her please to cut the straps and overlap them, because the bag is too long for him. I wonder, did she have time for that, too?"

They watched from a distance as Antonio slung the bag over his shoulder. His smile at the better fit answered her question.

"I'd like to drop him off the cliffs above us, but you and the others will kill him with kindness, eh?"

"Everyone needs a change in luck," she said simply. She gestured at the shabby camp. "Just look around you."

PALOMA HEAVED A SIGH of relief on the morning that Kahúu's husband sat up, blinking his eyes and probably wondering where the time had gone;

she remembered the feeling. Paloma had been tending both babies while the mother slumbered. She touched Kahúu's foot and the woman woke up, alert.

"He is better now."

To Paloma's amazement, Kahúu burst into noisy tears, which so startled the quiet babies that they cried, too. His eyes wide open, the warrior shook his head and lay down again, pulling his buffalo robe over his head, which made Paloma laugh.

The warrior's recovery from the inoculation was the first of several that day. By two suns later—Marco had no idea what day it was—the camp was recovering. To his astonishment, and even Antonio's surprise, no one had died.

"I don't understand. We're all hungry and I know discouragement when I see it," Antonio said.

Then you haven't looked hard enough, Paloma wanted to tell him. She had learned years ago that life was divided into small means. Little by little, she had watched The People grow strong in more ways than health. Maybe physicians in Georgia lived far better than she could imagine, and he just didn't understand.

"Can we leave in two days?" Marco asked the physician. "Will they be able to withstand the journey?"

A week earlier, Paloma thought Antonio Gil might have made some uncaring comment about trundling them up and who cared what happened. To her inward delight, he considered the matter. "If we are careful with them," he said finally, "very careful. There can be no exertion."

"We can manage that," Marco said.

Antonio nodded. "I really want to find the head chief, who might know where Pia Maria is."

"Where do you get the notion that there is a head leader, one man who controls everything?" Marco asked.

"There *isn't*?" Antonio's disappointment was almost ludicrous, but Marco didn't bother to laugh. He leaned in close to the man.

"These are *savages*. You have said it yourself. What do they know of organized government?" He did laugh then, but Paloma heard no humor. "We barely achieve that in our colony, Señor *Médico*!"

Paloma tugged him away, babbling something about Toshua needing a word with him. When they were out of earshot, Marco looked back, his eyes stormy. "Maybe I *should* have killed him."

"No!" She gave him a little push. "I think our doctor is genuinely concerned, but he also wants to find his daughter."

Marco grimaced and held out his hand. "Go ahead, slap it. I'm too suspicious of the man."

"Silly man," she said, her eyes merry. "Don't you see what's happened to *you*, my husband?"

"I'm a grouch?"

She shook her head. "You're a *juez de campo* here, too, always concerned about everyone's welfare." She kissed his cheek. "I like that about you."

He shook his head, rueful now. "*En realidad*, we should probably leave tomorrow. We have trapped and shot everything we can eat. I know, I know, patience. Don't I always tell you that?"

"For a different reason," she murmured, which meant he put his arm around her and kept it there, the *juez de campo* concerned about everyone's welfare.

She never understood how word traveled in an Indian camp, but by morning, The People who were strong enough were starting to pack. At this point Paloma had little to her name. She and Ayasha had ripped up her other skirt to make bandages and her petticoat was a muddy ruin. She debated whether to step out of the noisome thing, hoping it would crawl away and die somewhere.

Hands on her hips, she stood staring at the paltry contents of her other leather bag, when Marco cleared his throat and ushered Kahúu forward. Without thinking, Paloma held out her hands for a baby, but Kahúu had a beaded deerskin dress over her arm this time. Eyes down, she ran her hand over the beads in a loving way that told Paloma exactly whose dress this was.

"Oh, I couldn't," she started to say, then stopped when Marco, standing behind Kahúu, shook his head slightly.

I must accept this, she thought, as the weight of the honor settled on her so gently. "Nami?" she asked, trying out the Comanche word for sister, as she took the beautiful garment. Kahúu's brown eyes, as round and lovely as her daughter's, filled with tears as she nodded.

Paloma looked at Marco, who signed "thank you," extending his hands out and down from his heart. Paloma imitated his gesture.

Kahúu was just beginning. Next she handed Paloma a knee-high pair of winter boots. *I will not be cold*, Paloma thought. Another thank you followed, but when Kahúu gestured for her to come out of the tipi, Paloma gasped.

It was a woman's saddle, with a high red pommel and brass tacks for decoration. It was so lovely that she had to remind herself to breathe. Thank you with her hands wasn't adequate. She put her arms around Kahúu and they clung to each other.

Kahúu was the first to dry her eyes. She gestured to Eckapeta, who had watched the lovely transaction. Kahúu spoke in the language of The People this time, as if afraid that her rudimentary Spanish would not do the moment justice. Eckapeta nodded, and touched Kahúu's shoulder, before the young mother darted away, her hands to her face.

"What did she say?" Marco asked, when Paloma could only wipe her eyes and sniff.

" 'Ride proud. You are the woman of a warrior, too,' " Eckapeta told him.

Marco sucked in his breath and turned away. As Paloma watched him, he walked to the edge of the clearing, fell to his knees, touched his forehead to the ground, then stood again and kept walking until he was out of sight. Paloma turned to Eckapeta, worried.

The older woman touched her shoulder. She laughed into her hand, then whispered. "Give him a few minutes. Then take his hand and lead him back to the tipi. I promise you that Toshua and I will be busy helping The People pack." She made the sign for the sun halfway down, then dipped it lower. "Take buffalo robe time with a warrior."

Chapter Twenty-Seven

In which they travel through the wound in the earth, and find food

THEY LEFT IN TWO days, barely nourished by another bony deer and more mice, but having acquired something that resembled confidence. That morning in the tipi, Marco had proved little help in getting Paloma into the dress belonging to Kahúu's sister. Paloma insisted she should at least still wear her ragged chemise, even though he tried to take it off her, brushing his hands against her breasts.

"You are a rascal and we are trying to leave," she reminded him, but only in a halfhearted way, which told him precisely how satisfied she was.

"By all means, my dove. Just think of a hot bath and your own bed, which you so generously share with me."

She gave him a long stare then, and he knew when to suddenly become more helpful. "Hold up your arms, and I'll drop it down."

She did, and the soft folds of deerskin settled around her, falling almost to her ankles, because Kahúu's *nami* must have been a taller woman. No matter. The slits up the sides would accommodate a woman riding astride.

She had the same look of pleasure as when Señora Chávez had made beautiful dresses for her, twisting her head this way and that to look at the beading. She turned around a few times, just to watch the fringe sway. "You probably think I'm a big silly," she told him, faintly embarrassed.

"I think you're beautiful and I love you."

He sat her down and helped her on with the winter boots, glad to know she would be warm.

"They tie behind your knees," he said, and tickled the back of her leg.

"Marco, you're trying me!"

"Very well, *mi chiquita*. Let's help dismantle this tipi and ride."

He had to struggle to keep from laughing as she looked over her horse and the new saddle, a far cry from the side saddle she had ridden into the canyon … such a Spanish lady.

"Just put your foot in the stirrup like so and swing your other leg all the way over," he said, trying to be helpful without insulting her intelligence. Still she stood there. "I can adjust the stirrups, once you're up," he coaxed.

Her face turned red. She gestured to him to come nearer, even though the only thing close by was her horse, also looking at her expectantly. "Marco, I just have that scrap of a *camisa* on under this dress. What will happen when I swing my leg over?"

We'll all get an amazing view of what I normally see and no one else, he thought, amused, but he wasn't about to say that. He looked in the direction she pointed, touched to see her point with her lips, like The People. No one was watching. Before she could object, he picked her up and boosted her into the saddle. "Well? No one saw and the horse didn't bolt."

"I don't mean to be silly," she told him in that gruff voice he adored.

He just smiled and handed up her ragged cloak. "Wrap tight."

Paloma leaned over. "I really want to carry the baby. Will Kahúu let me, do you think?"

The eagerness in her voice pained his heart. "If she thinks you can manage, I expect she will."

His wife hadn't long to wait. Wearing the harried look of any busy mother packing for a journey, Kahúu came close and cleared her throat in that polite way of someone not wanting to invade privacy. Of course, she cleared her throat a little louder than necessary, which made Marco smile inside. Obviously she and Paloma stood on little ceremony now, and Kahúu needed her. He stepped back and Kahúu hurried forward, holding out the sleeping baby in her cradleboard.

"How do I get her on my back?" Paloma whispered to him.

"She'll show you what to do."

In practiced fashion, Kahúu stood on tiptoe and slipped one rawhide loop over the red pommel. The cradleboard dangled down from the saddle, and the baby's aunt arranged it just so, tucking the soft deerskin here and there. The child slumbered on. Paloma reached over and fingered the baby's hair in equally practiced fashion. She nodded to Kahúu and the woman patted her leg, then returned to her own horse, where her child slept, too.

At last The People were ready to travel. Unsure of his place in the greater scheme of Comanche logistics, Marco sat on his horse beside Antonio, who had located himself close to the two travois. An ancient elder—the Old One

Ayasha tended, who would probably not see too many more sunsets—lay on one of them, with soft packs all around her and a child perched next to her. An uncomfortably pregnant woman sat on the other travois, hugging another child to her. Her already short hair had been chopped even shorter, and her cheeks showed the tracks of recent scarring. Her warrior-husband had been one of the poor souls who died of *la viruela* on the Staked Plains, leaving her to an uncertain future.

The old man who had finished the travois lacing rode next to the woman so big with child, obviously keeping an eye on her. Antonio rode by the travois, too, his beaded medicine bag on proud display, his eyes on the potential patients. Ayasha rode beside him.

Paloma had fallen in line with Eckapeta, who carried a child in front of her, both parents dead of the Dark Wind. They rode behind Kahúu and her warrior, who rode his own horse which had been packed and padded until he couldn't fall off, if the strain of travel proved too great.

Marco counted thirty people, including babies, everyone shabby and makeshift-looking, with too much chopped hair and scarred arms and faces. The People had been mauled and bludgeoned, but they were riding at last to a safer place deep in the canyon. His pride at the sight would have astounded him a month ago, when the very last thing he wanted to do was Antonio's selfish bidding. As Paloma had said only this morning, "Stranger things have probably happened, but I can't imagine when or where."

Still Marco waited; they all waited, horses laden with people, tipis and poles, but little food. That bald fact gnawed at him, because he was used to providing for his own. At some point, The People had become his own people, and he chafed because he had not done better. Maybe he was their *juez*, and they just didn't know it.

As he sat musing over such a strange notion, Toshua rode toward him, two lances in his hand. The Comanche regarded Marco a long moment, then extended one of the lances. Marco took it, scarcely breathing.

"I should have told you last night. The elders in our band have named me war chief. They named you our peace chief, in charge of the camp and food. Let us ride."

Marco knew it wouldn't do for the newly appointed peace chief to weep, so he swallowed his tears with a mighty effort and watched how Toshua carried his lance, aiming for even a pale imitation. He glanced at Paloma, whose eyes were wide, her hand to her throat.

"*Te deum laudamus*," he said to her, raising his voice over the noise of animals and people he had come to know in good ways.

"Is that your peace song?" Toshua asked.

"Hers and mine. Lead on, brother. We follow."

THEY RODE ALL DAY, but slowly, following one stream and then another. The canyon was crisscrossed with streams breaking free from winter. Paloma thought they might stop to nurse the babies, but The People were far more economical. Kahúa simply opened her dress, pulled up the cradleboard and nursed her daughter as they rode along. When she finished, she handed the cradleboard to Paloma and lifted her niece from Paloma's pommel, the children trading places. When the baby had been fed, she switched them again. Paloma knew the babies were probably wet and messy, but they made no complaint, because that was the journey. When they stopped at night there would be time to take proper care of them.

She knew that as long as she lived, she would never forget the thrill of riding with people so at one with their horses. In the last month, she had become familiar with The People on land. They were not really tall—Marco towered over most of them—and not nearly as graceful as the Tewa and Navajo on the Double Cross. On horseback, they were transformed.

She vaguely remembered a book of Greek mythology that her father owned, and sitting on his lap and staring at pictures of centaurs—half man, half horse. Paloma was a skilled rider, but The People were centaurs. She rode now with the lords of the plains, and the knowledge made her sit taller.

As the day wore on, she observed that even lords had needs to meet. The men relieved themselves on horseback, except for Marco, who still wore his breeches. With a red face, the peace chief turned his horse aside and dismounted to take care of business. The People passed him with no comment, beyond a quick glance and a smile to see his bare rump as he pulled down his smallclothes.

With genuine amusement, Paloma noticed how some of the women craned their necks to look at that part of her man that Eckapeta had praised weeks ago. Paloma blushed when they regarded her with something close to respect. She would have to ask Marco if his jewels were something special. After all, she had no point of reference.

The day had begun cloudy, but the sun burned away the mists. Paloma stared upward at the height of the canyon walls, wondering if her fascination with this place would ever wane. The deeper they rode north—Antonio said it was north—the higher the walls. She stared upward, gawking at the sight, until the walls seemed to lean toward her, making her dizzy. She noticed Marco stared, too, open-mouthed and amazed.

"This is a wound in the earth. The People come here for protection," Toshua said, as he rode back down the line to assure himself there were no stragglers. "We will probably sleep in the caves tonight."

Caves came to Paloma's attention sooner than nightfall, when Antonio rode forward to Toshua and started gesturing, his eyes full of concern. Toshua indicated Marco, the peace chief, because he must have divined this was not a matter of war.

By now, several of the women had begun to keen, a low sound that sent ripples down Paloma's back. She turned around to see Ayasha leaning out of her saddle toward the old woman on the travois. Toshua halted the column and Marco, his face serious with responsibility, rode to the travois. He dismounted with Antonio and nodded as the doctor gestured.

"The old dear is gone," Antonio said. "I did my best …." His voice trailed away.

"What do we do?" Marco asked Toshua, when he joined them. The others drew closer until they had formed a circle.

Toshua stood looking down at the woman who had slumped sideways, her features peaceful on her last ride with The People. Paloma's magic beads were entwined in her deeply veined fingers. Toshua called another warrior over and they discussed the matter, pointing to the canyon wall, now a greater distance from them as the wound in the earth had widened. The warrior nodded and rode along the wall some distance as they watched, then stopped and swung his blanket.

Toshua turned to Marco. Paloma and others had gathered closer, their faces solemn. "Marco, you will carry this Old One to that warrior, who has found a good cave. Place her inside and cover her with stones."

This was the impressive man she had married. Her heart full, Paloma watched as Marco did as Toshua said, gently unstrapping the Elder from the travois, then wrapping her in a trade blanket someone handed to him. He mounted, then held out his arms for the light bundle, a woman of the high plains and grasslands who had survived her entire family.

"There is no ceremony?" Paloma whispered to Eckapeta, who shook her head, then took Paloma's hand in hers.

"No, but we never leave the Old Ones to die alone as some tribes do."

Paloma looked around at the serious faces, people who knew this woman well. "Did you know she gave me a carved bird for Kahúu's niece?" she told Eckapeta. "I will give the little toy to her when she is older."

"She told me she liked you," Eckapeta said. "I cannot say her name now, because she is beyond our reach and we don't want to call her back."

Paloma bowed her head and let her tears flow. When her vision cleared, she watched her husband carry the Old One toward the warrior waving the blanket. Toshua gestured for them to fall into line again, and the orderly march continued. She watched as they passed the men, stooping now inside one of the smaller caves. The travelers kept going; Paloma looked back until the men finished their work and rejoined The People.

Marco rode beside her, so serious now. "It is a good place. We covered her with stones."

"Will it keep out wolves and coyotes?"

"We'll let the canyon do its work, my dear."

THEY FOUND A MUCH larger cave as the sun's rule finished earlier than anyone wanted and was replaced by clouds. Wind began to blow and Paloma looked up anxiously, remembering the deep blue of the clouds, the Apaches, and their desperate ride to the canyon's rim. She wanted to leave her place and ride beside Marco, but did not know if there was some bit of Comanche etiquette she would be trampling on.

The column slowed, and she saw pleased looks on the faces around her. The women began to talk and joke together. They evidently knew this area, which took some of the tension from her shoulders. Maybe Marco would have time tonight to crack her neck and rub her back.

There it was, a cave that would hold them all, and maybe even the horses, too, if the wind proved too strong. Paloma watched as Toshua called for the flame bearer, an old fellow who kept the fire burning in some way like a slow match. Two of the warriors lit rush bundles the women had quickly gathered and tied together. They carried them into the cave, calling and holding their torches high, their lances at shoulder height, ready.

The women dismounted and Paloma followed, stifling a groan that would only have led to good-natured teasing. The little baby—oh, why quibble? *Her* baby—gazed at her out of bright eyes. Paloma smiled and made a face, and the little one chortled.

She was reaching up to lift the cradleboard loop off the pommel when her horse stiffened and started to dance. She grabbed the cradleboard and yanked it away, the child tight in her arms, when she heard a roar from the cave and watched The People scatter.

Terrified, but silent this time, Paloma flattened herself against the canyon wall beside the cave mouth. Kahúu stood beside her, clutching her baby and looking at her husband, who was trying to dismount. She thrust her cradleboard at Paloma and grabbed for his bridle, leading his plunging horse off the trail and against the canyon wall, too. Paloma stared in amazement at her skill.

"Paloma, put the babies behind you!" Marco yelled as he rode his equally skittish horse to the cave mouth and dismounted as it still moved. He took a firm grip on his lance, looking down as if wondering how to use it to best effect.

"Please don't go in there," she whispered.

Another roar, closer now, the sound reverberating against the cave's walls.

She did as Marco ordered, and propped the cradleboards into a crevice, steadying them. Kahúu had calmed her husband's horse and was helping him dismount, her eyes wild with worry for the babies and her man.

The babies were crying now, terrified as the roars grew louder. Paloma's horse was a distant memory, racing up the canyon. Her hands shook but she yanked off her cloak and threw it over the babies' cradleboards, mashing the fabric into the crevice, hoping that would quiet them.

As she did that, her hand brushed against the knife in its sheath on the back of her dress. She pulled it out, pledging in her mind to protect the babies. As she watched the cave, a bear cub ran out, and another. Her jumbled brain told her that The People probably only used this cave in the summer, when bears in hibernation were not in residence.

The cubs paused at the entrance, looking around, bawling in their terror, sounding disturbingly like human infants. She heard deeper roars and then anguished cries, and then the scream of a man.

"Please no, God," she said, ready to walk into the cave, her mind and heart on her husband.

She was shouldered aside by Kahúu's husband. He held his lance easily in his hand, steadied himself and started into the cave. He glanced back at her, made a chopping motion with his hand, and pointed to the cubs. He made the sign for food with his fingers, and gave her a fierce look she had no trouble interpreting.

She understood. No matter the outcome in the cave—this primitive contest between bear and men armed only with lances—The People needed food. The cubs bawled, the babies cried, and Paloma grabbed the cub by the scruff of the neck, hanging on with determination as the terrified animal flailed and scratched her. She plunged the knife into the animal's neck, striking over and over until it was still. Another woman killed the second cub after Ayasha tackled it.

The babies continued to wail, stopping only when Kahúu flung off Paloma's cloak and pulled their cradleboards from their stony niche. As calmly as a woman could—one whose man had just staggered into a dark cave—she opened the front of her deerskin dress and nursed them both.

Carrying the old man's lance, Eckapeta ran into the cave. Paloma wiped off her knife and followed her. The cave smelled of death and blood and animal droppings. They stood together, and waited, because all was silent.

Paloma dropped to her knees in relief when Marco and Toshua came out, carrying another warrior between them, his head drooping. The bear's claw had ripped into his thigh, but at least the blood did not spurt. His woman ran to him as Antonio ran, too, intent upon the wounded man, his beaded medical bag on his shoulder.

Paloma had not the energy to stand. She stayed on her knees until Marco reached her. He knelt, too, and grabbed her around the waist, his face in her hair.

Neither of them said anything. What was there to say? Paloma just breathed in and out, grateful beyond measure because he still lived. They stayed there as The People hurried into the cave and began to shout, the echoes weird and wonderful, because there was food now, as much as they could eat.

"I ripped my pants," he said finally. Paloma laughed.

"Now it is your turn to look like the rest of us, my *juez.*" She held him tight until her heartbeat returned to normal. "What will the governor think?"

Chapter Twenty-Eight

In which Marco finds more in the cave, and Eckapeta introduces Tatzinupi

KNIVES FLASHING, EYES INTENT, The People made short work of the bears. The fire bearer sent the children scattering to gather wood and built a fire inside the cave. After staring at the mound of bear meat and turning away with a queasy feeling, Marco appointed himself to round up the horses that had fled in terror. The old man who had helped him gestured that he would come, too.

Marco helped the elder mount his horse again, wondering how useful he would be. Before they rode from the clearing, he looked back at Paloma, who blew him a kiss and waved him on. She had taken the baby out of the cradleboard and held it in her arms.

The old man gestured to Toshua, and the two of them spoke in whispers. Toshua nodded, his eyes lively, then scratched his head as if wondering how to convey the message.

"I can manage whatever he says, Toshua," Marco assured him.

Toshua waited a little longer, obviously trying to convert what he had been told into workaday Spanish. "Señor …."

"So formal, my brother?" Marco teased.

"He, uh, hopes you give that woman lots of tipi time."

Marco blushed and looked away, speaking to the distant canyon wall. "Let the old goat know that I do, indeed. By the way, has he a name?"

"It will come as no surprise to you that his name translates as Buffalo Rut."

Marco threw back his head and shouted with laughter, which earned him stares, then smiles, then laughter from people relieved to have something to joke about, even if they hadn't heard the conversation. Paloma gave him her look-down-the-nose stare, so he thought it prudent to actually search for the horses.

They left the area at a walk, and Marco was immediately impressed with Buffalo Rut, who went from elderly man to Comanche tracker. The old *muchacho* prudently did not lean too far out of his saddle to look for tracks, wisely leaving that to Marco.

The snow showed no signs of letting up, but the tracks were visible. After a mile or so they found Paloma's horse calmly nosing aside snow and eating dry winter grass. Another mile, and the rest were gathered in.

"I wish I could talk with you," Marco said to his companion, feeling the shadows of early evening creep around the canyon and into his heart. It was that time of day when, if he had paperwork to deal with, he would close his ledgers and clean off his desk—tidy fellow—and start to wonder what Paloma had ordained for dinner. There would be cheerful conversation, maybe a glass of wine in the *sala*, and then prayers in the chapel and bed.

Funny how the memory of a lifetime seemed to recede, the longer he stayed with The People. He closed his eyes and let his horse find the way back. He would probably tell Paloma about their quick work in the cave against an enraged sow protecting her cubs, but he doubted a wife even as well-tuned as his would understand what it felt like to take a stance, lance in hand, and wait for the beast to charge. All his life, he had heard Pueblo Indian tales of the Old Ones, and even seen the curious skulls and bones of giant animals found in their colony. A sublime storyteller, his mama had told *fantasias* of primitive people—half man, half beast—who had roamed their mountains, living short and terrible lives.

"Are we any different, Mama?" he murmured. All of a sudden, he longed to be back in those Sangre de Cristo Mountains, living the life he knew better than this one. He took a deep breath. And yet he could not deny the siren's call of the life he was leading right now. Well, it would be something to think about, shoes off, Paloma in his lap, a glass of wine in his hand. It couldn't come soon enough.

He looked back at Buffalo Rut. And yet ….

AFTER A PRODIGIOUS NURSING, the babies were full and exhausted by their rare bout of crying. Paloma and Kahúu cleaned them and swaddled them with trade blankets and popped them into cradleboards, where the tight wrap reassured them and sent them quickly to sleep. Ayasha said she would watch them, while the women not preparing great slabs of bear meat for the fire had gathered to offer help to Antonio, if he needed any.

Tired down to her toes and pained by the scratches on her arms, Paloma sat on a rock by the cave entrance, her chin on her palm, her eyes heavy. She watched Antonio work quickly on the warrior with the bear claw scrape. He offered the man a leather strap to bite, but the warrior turned his head, looking faintly insulted.

"Suit yourself. You're braver than I am," Antonio said. Gently, he pulled the wound together and stitched away. The Indian began to sweat, but he made no sound.

Antonio surprised her then. When he finished, instead of walking away, he put his hand on the man's heaving chest, patting him until his breathing returned to normal. He also did not object to the mash of something that looked to Paloma like beef gravy that Eckapeta applied to the wound. In fact, he smiled his approval when she took a smoldering stick of wood from the fire, blew it out, then waved the smoke over the man.

He must have felt her eyes on him, because Antonio joined her on the rock. She didn't ask, but he pushed back the fringe on her deerskin sleeves and took another look at her scratches. He rummaged in his medical satchel and pulled out a tin of salve. He sniffed it and nodded. "Might help," he told her, and applied it to her arms.

"But you don't know for certain?" she asked, skeptical.

"It's been a while since medical college, but I remember a doctor telling me, 'Whatever it is, treat with white salve.' There you are."

She smiled at him, wondering what had changed.

He must have known what she was thinking. Mirroring her earlier position, he rested his chin on his hand and stared toward the fire, too. "They went into that cave so fearless. Did you see what happened?"

"Probably not. I closed my eyes because I was so frightened," Paloma said frankly.

"I took a lance from one of the recuperating warriors and started into the cave, too."

"You *did*?"

He gave her a wounded look, which made her smile. "I am not without some courage," he said, then smiled, too, a shy sort of smile, interesting because of the hope in his eyes, a quality Antonio Gil had lacked. "Well, a little courage."

"You *started* in?" Paloma asked, prompting him.

"Yes. Ayasha grabbed my arm and yanked me back." His voice took on a sound of wonder. "She told me, 'Medicine men do not need to fight. Your battle is different.'"

Paloma digested this, thinking of the times Ayasha had helped the little doctor, who could be so irascible. "I think she likes you, Antonio."

He made no comment. When she took a good look at this face, his eyes were closed.

Kahúu took the babies inside and arranged their buffalo robes, making her husband comfortable. Paloma stayed where she was until Marco and the old man returned with the horses. Someone, probably Toshua, had created a picket line near the cave's mouth. Paloma watched as the men cared for the horses then trudged through the snow to the cave. She joined him, ready to eat, her mouth watering.

To her heart's delight, he put his hand on her shoulder and massaged the muscles, then draped his arm over her shoulder, establishing complete ownership of her—something he never did at the Double Cross, with his servants around. This was a different man, too, and she liked him just as well.

After eating until one more bite would have signaled disaster, they joined Toshua and Eckapeta, who leaned against the cave wall, far enough back from the entrance to feel warmth from the fire. Her eyes closed, Paloma listened as Toshua and Marco organized the watch.

With no protest, she let Eckapeta lead her to a familiar buffalo robe and obeyed the woman's soft-voiced command to raise her arms. Her dress came off and she crawled between the robes, content to sleep in her own semi-hibernation. She was aware when Marco came to bed, less aware when he left later for his turn at the cave mouth.

No one spoke. Silence ruled the cave until some point in the early morning when a baby was born. Paloma moved closer to her husband.

IN COMPLETE AGREEMENT, THE war chief and the peace chief decided that the people needed one more day in the cave, eating and sleeping. The snow tapered off by mid-morning, allowing weak sunshine to angle inside. Ayasha had organized the older children in a stick game. Marco was content to sprawl on the buffalo robe and watch his wife play with Kahúu's small niece. When he spoke, and the baby turned her head toward him, his happiness was complete.

He knew he had to say something to Paloma about her attachment—no, *their* attachment—to the infant. What it would be, he did not know. He wasn't a man to put off important conversations, but his courage would fail him if he spoke now. Surely they had a few days. Such a conversation would keep.

HIS MORE PRESSING CURRENT worry was the big rip in his breeches. Toshua solved that bit of sartorial indelicacy, totally at Marco's expense. After a discussion with the men in the encampment, punctuated by laughter, Toshua motioned Marco inside the cave. He held a breechcloth in his hands, which made The People chuckle.

"We have decided that our peace chief needs more dignity. Little brother, you are one of us. Take off your rags and come here."

"Um, you could hand that to me where the cave is dark," Marco suggested, his face warm, even as he began to grasp the significance of what was happening.

"Do it their way, Marco," his sweet wife said. "Didn't you tell me this is their world?"

How true were her words. He looked at her. Her face was solemn because she already understood what was happening. He took a deep breath. This was more than a change of clothing. He was being offered entrance into a society he had feared and dreaded all his life.

"Help me, Paloma?"

She stood, already so graceful in her beaded deerskin dress, and unbuttoned his equally ragged shirt. Her eyes did get a little merry when he removed his useless breeches and the women started to chuckle and talk to each other.

"I think they envy me," she whispered, which made him smile.

Naked now, he started walking toward Toshua with as much dignity as he could manage, considering that he was a modest Spanish gentleman. To his relief, Toshua took his arm and ushered him into the welcome darkness of the deeper cave. He wondered just what he would have to do for Paloma to buy her silence about this, once they had returned to the Double Cross. He didn't think that a new dress would be enough, then remembered the red leather shoes he had promised her, in a world that seemed distant now.

"You know that in Valle del Sol, I am considered a man of some dignity," Marco said to Toshua, as they walked deeper into the cave.

Toshua looked around elaborately. "I do not see that man here," he teased, and then became serious at once. "I see instead a man of great kindness." He handed Marco the breechcloth.

Keeping his mind blank—what he was doing went against his entire life and upbringing—he put on the Comanche breechcloth. The garment was a model of economy, and he had to admit to himself that he had been envying the men on their journey. Toshua took the trade blanket from his own shoulders and draped it around Marco.

"I can't take your—"

"Eckapeta has another one for me. Don't argue."

Marco kept his boots on, knowing the sight would probably send Paloma and her friends into whoops. That was all right, too. The People needed to laugh, maybe Paloma more than most, because he feared what was coming, when they reached the greater gathering of The People.

They found a flat rock that in some distant epoch might have tumbled from the ceiling, and sat down. Toshua called out in Comanche, which in a few minutes brought a warrior with a torch. He sat with them while Toshua asked Marco what he thought about sending the man ahead to the still-distant place in the canyon where a larger river flowed and The People waited out the rest of the winter.

"He can tell the Elders that the Dark Wind has visited us and passed, and we have someone who can save The People."

"I think he should go ahead," Marco replied, "if he is willing." He had to ask what had been on his mind since the strange journey began. "I know there must be Kwahadi in that gathering who lost many friends and family at the Rio San Carlos, where my governor and many of us defeated Cuerno Verde. What will they do to us, do you think?"

"You called him Cuerno Verde. We had another name for him." Toshua said. "I will not speak it. Strange, no? We cannot agree even on names, your people and The People."

The warrior with the torch spoke no Spanish, so he questioned Toshua in a low voice, his eyes on Marco. Toshua replied and the man nodded. He spoke to Toshua again then put his hand on Marco's bare knee, giving it a shake. He spoke again.

"Tell me what he said, *pabi.*"

Toshua stood up, and the other two rose. "He said he will *not* go ahead. He said let us all ride in together as brothers. We will speak for you and your woman, even for the little man with the cutting knife who frowns all the time."

Marco felt relief settle around his shoulders. He signed "thank you."

The warrior spoke, and it looked to Marco like Toshua's turn to dig deep. So much for white men who thought Indians showed no emotion.

"He wants to say, 'You have all saved us from the Dark Wind. We do not forget.' "

They started back toward the cave mouth in the distance. The warrior with the torch spoke to Toshua, who nodded, then turned and went deeper in the cave. Marco watched, a question in his eyes.

"My brother, he said that when he went farther back yesterday to see if there were any more sleeping bears, he found something that you might want to see."

Marco heard the sound of metal on metal, then saw the bobbing torch. He gasped to see what the Kwahadi carried.

"*Dios mio,* they are branding irons!" Marco exclaimed. "What in God's name …?"

But he knew. Some raiding party—last week or fifty years ago—had used this cave to secrete branding irons. Why hide them, he could not imagine, knowing how Indians prized anything made of metal. Had the raiders thought to return later and make a bargain with some *juez de campo* in another district to the east? Death must have come for them, and no one else knew.

The warrior dropped the irons with a clatter because they were heavy Spanish brands, some so elaborate that they required more than one iron spoke. His heart sick, Marco knew what he would find.

There it was, the brand with the star and the *vega*, the star in the meadow. For years, Paloma's brand, wrenched from her family, had lain through heat and cold in a cave in the secret canyon of the Kwahadi. As he stood there in a Comanche breechcloth, he hoped they were dead, maybe even eaten by Tonkawas.

"You could leave it here," Toshua suggested. "We would never speak of it."

Marco picked up the brand. "I cannot do that."

They let him walk ahead of them to the cave mouth, his eyes alert for his wife, the treasure of his heart. When she saw him coming, she waved, the baby against her breast. He kept walking, doing nothing to hide the branding iron in his hand. What would be the point?

He knew the moment when she realized what he carried, because she set the baby down with great care and smoothed her deerskin dress—her habit back at the Double Cross. So fastidious, Paloma always made certain she was tidy when she waited in the door as he returned from a trip, or even from his office next to the horse barn.

He kept walking, but slower now, uncertain. Her hands went to her throat and then carefully in front of her. She took a step toward him, then could not move toward what he carried. With a cry of anguish, she turned and ran from the cave, ran and ran. His heart pounding, he stopped and watched as she leaped over the small stream, picked up speed and ran to the canyon wall opposite where he stood.

His heart broke as he saw her pound on the canyon wall as though she wanted to be away from everyone in it. "Please, not me, too," he said, as he crossed the stream, unsure of himself.

He stopped when she began to moan, doubled over now in great pain. He knew that pain. In his mind's eye, he knew he would always see himself lying prostrate on the graves of his wife and twins, moaning his sorrow.

"Go, and hurry."

He turned around, startled, because Eckapeta had followed him. She took the branding iron from him and walked back to the cave, her stride purposeful. He did as she said, running now to Paloma. He grabbed her and held her so tight that he feared for her ribs. With a sob, she wrapped her legs around him and wept.

He knew the world was a harsh home, but his heart told him that on that particular day—whatever day it was, because he had lost count—there were more tears shed in that spot than in any place on earth.

Marco Mondragón sat with Paloma Vega as the afternoon turned to dusk, and the cold came on. She said nothing for a long time, then she began to speak of her family. Hesitant at first, she told him of Claudio and Rafael and her parents. She had mentioned them before, but this time she told the tiny details of their life together, much like his life on the Double Cross.

"It's hard," she said finally, and leaned against him.

He debated a long moment, wondering whether to add to her pain, then realized she already knew.

"You are going to have to do another hard thing very soon," he said. "We are nearly at the great gathering, and Kahúu's brother-in-law will be there."

She nodded. "I know. Don't speak of it. I will be as brave as I can, but I cannot guarantee what I will do."

"Agreed. I will be with you."

"I know." She did something she had done once before, in the kitchen at the monastery of San Pedro, where the Chama meets the Rio Bravo. She raised his hand to her lips and kissed it formally. He did the same thing with her hand.

He pulled her to her feet. Arms around each other's waists, they walked back to The People. Eckapeta met them at the cave mouth, her eyes so kind. She put her arms around them both, murmuring words neither of them understood—except that they did. As they approached the fire, where the fragrance of bear meat rose to greet them, she pointed down.

The star and meadow brand lay in the coals. She pointed to the ground next to the fire, where someone had stretched out a buffalo robe, the tanned side so smooth, a blank canvas.

"Do it for them, and they will be at peace."

Paloma stared into the flames for a long moment. Eckapeta handed her a leather square, which she wrapped around the iron handle. With great concentration, Paloma lifted her family's brand from the fire, looking over her shoulder for him to help, because he knew it was heavy. Together they branded the robe, then Marco leaned the brand against the cave wall, where it could cool. Tomorrow, Paloma could decide what to do with it. He hoped she would not object if, when they returned to the Double Cross, they stamped his brand on the robe, too, and hung it in the *sala*.

"It's a fine brand," she said. She looked around, her eyes defiant, her chin up. "It is *my* brand! Never my cousin's! *Mine.*"

He tried to take her hand, but Eckapeta stopped him. She put her hands on Paloma's shoulders. "I asked Toshua. He said I could name you. It is my right because you have become a daughter to The People." The woman with the pox-ravaged face looked around at The People, who had gathered to watch.

"Tatzinupi. Star."

Paloma nodded, serious. She looked at the buffalo robe. "Probably we should hang it in the *sala*. Husband, I am tired. Let us go to bed."

Chapter Twenty-Nine

In which brave people speak

THE BRAND AND THE robe rode with them in the morning, tied behind Paloma's saddle. With it, a change seemed to come to the travelers. The more superstitious among them—Marco was not in that number—wanted to give the brand all credit. After all, Eckapeta was convinced that Paloma's brand on the buffalo robe had freed her family—not to put too fine a point on it—from a problem caused by The People in the first place. It struck Marco as strange reasoning, but they were obviously outnumbered. More than likely, it was just time for spring and everyone felt it.

He had noticed a change of another kind during his early morning watch. He sat at the cave mouth, leaning on his lance, wondering if his wife would object to the lance in their *sala*. Maybe Toshua could teach him how to throw it properly. That thought proved unproductive; after all, why would Toshua return to the Double Cross to teach him *anything*, once The People were inoculated and Antonio Gil had his daughter back? It was obvious to everyone that Toshua and Eckapeta were making the most of what randy old Buffalo Rut called tipi time. There was no reason for Toshua to return to the colony of New Mexico that had enslaved him. He had a wife again, and Marco understood what that meant better than most.

I'll miss you, brother, he thought, as he stared out into the canyon that had been his home for at least a month now. As he sat there, feeling more than melancholy, Marco suddenly realized that he was not cold. Granted, he had wrapped himself in his cloak, plus the trade blanket, but there was more in the air than chill. He heard water dripping. Faintly, from the soaring heights above, he thought he heard small birds, the kind that move farther south when October winds blow. They were back; spring had come to the Texas plains.

He glanced into the cave, wanting to share the observation with the dearest person in his world. She had fallen asleep in his arms as usual, but this time she had also cuddled the baby, who Kahúu had assured her would sleep all night, now that her belly was full. And that had meant he had cuddled the child, too, hand on her little head as he reached over Paloma for his share of the pleasure.

"We need to be home, my dove," he said softly to no one in particular as he sat there in the cave mouth. "Lambs and calves are coming now, and there are fields to plant. I'll be busy; you'll be busy." Would it be enough? He doubted it.

He had talked to her about the matter yesterday, as they had walked to the horses, walked anywhere just to be together. She had nodded, her face serious. He knew she understood that there was no way in the universe that the Kwahadi would ever relinquish one child. If they tried to escape with it, they would die, and not in easy ways. "I know," she had said, her voice so sorrowful.

She knew, but there would be that moment when the child's father claimed his daughter and Paloma had to actually let go of the baby she had tended so well, easing Kahúu's burden.

Why does it have to be this way? Marco asked himself. He had spent a lifetime bending to the will of God, but he thought it hard.

He stood up, shaking his head against his unproductive thoughts. And all because spring was coming.

They left at daybreak, full of bear meat. Yesterday, the women had roasted long strips of it over the fire, so there was enough to get them to the gathering. Marco thought they would ride in their usual order, but he noticed a subtle difference, one that gave him hope.

While Paloma waited to join the women and children in the marching order, Toshua gestured her forward, and Eckapeta, too, until they rode directly behind him and Marco. Old Buffalo Rut followed them with Antonio, and the young warriors rode around them all, cocooning them against whatever lay ahead, when they reached the Kwahadi gathering place.

Before they started, Ayasha joined them, her head held high. Skillfully she angled her horse next to Antonio's, which meant that Buffalo Rut fell back, a smile on his face.

Paloma noticed right away what their friends had done, and she crossed herself and closed her eyes, her lips moving. He saw no fear on her face. This was not the woman who had begun this journey with a massive grievance, well-earned, against the lords of the southern plains.

He slowed his horse and rode beside Paloma for a moment. He meant to reassure her, he told himself, but mostly to reassure himself, if he were honest. "*Oye*, Paloma, if we succeed in any measure, I might ask Governor de Anza for a small raise. What do you think?"

"I think you have noodles for brains," she replied. They laughed.

No matter their fears, Marco knew he could live another forty years and never see anything as magnificent as the canyon of the Kwahadi. The walls seemed to rise higher and higher until he couldn't look up, because it made him dizzy. Hawks circled overhead on the air currents, making little wing adjustments, gliding, gliding. Grass already grew here. The place of buttes, mesas and canyons within canyons seemed touched by magic. Maybe winter never came long to this place. He looked around with a rancher's eye, thinking what a land grant this would have been. *Noodle brains, you'd have lasted here only long enough for some irate Kwahadi to roast you over a slow fire*, he reminded himself.

He also noticed new Kwahadi warriors not of their ragged band, all on horseback, watching. "Have they been tailing us long?" he whispered to Toshua.

"Maybe since the cave."

That was not the answer Marco wanted. "Why didn't they make themselves known?" he had to ask.

Toshua leaned toward him. "Do you see the warriors with the left side of their hair cropped? That is how warriors mourn deaths. We leave it to the women to cut themselves. They have suffered from *la viruela*, as your little doctor thought. If we have *la viruela* among us, they'll see it and maybe stop us."

Marco digested that. He saw the hesitation on his friend's face. "There is more?"

"They have probably noticed Spaniards among us who are not bound hand and foot and who do not have ropes around their necks."

THEIR LITTLE CAVALCADE RODE steadily on. Everyone ate in the saddle. The canyon widened and widened, and then there was the river, tipis lining both sides, which told Marco that it was fordable. In the distance he noticed separate tipis, a cluster here and there. He also saw mounds of burned tipis. In the distance, he could not begin to count the size of the horse herd.

They had reached the great encampment.

Toshua scanned the village, too. "Not as many lodges," he said simply. "My people have suffered."

More warriors and young boys on horseback appeared to ride alongside their ragged band. Marco saw other Kwahadi running to the immense horse herd, catching their own mounts. Toshua motioned him closer.

"Stay tight now. Some may try to reach through us and count coup on you. I can make no promises."

Marco nodded. "Can I do anything to protect Paloma?"

"Trust Eckapeta."

The Kwahadi crowded so close to them now that their horses moved forward only with some effort. Marco's Double Cross horse tossed his head and rolled his eyes, fearful. It was all he could do to keep the animal under control.

A stone struck the back of his head, which made him sway in the saddle. Paloma called his name, and he heard Eckapeta calm her with quiet words. Another stone brought blood by his ear. He waited for a war club to slam him to the ground, wishing he had never listened to Antonio Gil.

A quick glance told him they were surrounded by angry men. Appalled, he kept his view fixed on that space between his horse's ears. He knew there were prayers that a good Christian saved for times like this, but all he could think of was Paloma.

"Let us dismount carefully and slowly," Toshua said to them all. "Take Paloma's hand, if they will let you."

They wouldn't. As soon as he was on his feet, Marco was pushed into the middle of a group. He heard Paloma exclaim, then someone thumped him with that war club he dreaded and he fell to his knees.

He was too foggy to know precisely what happened next, except that he heard a roar of disapproval, and then chuckles, of all things. He glanced around to see warriors ducking and whooping, and then Paloma stood beside him, swinging her brand, her eyes full of indignation. She also had the baby on her back, so no one came near. She stood right over him, ready to swing again.

All was silent. Marco rubbed his shoulder, where the war club had found its mark, then touched her ankle, wanting human connection.

He heard the creak of leather as the rest of the travelers dismounted. Kahúu quickly took her place beside Paloma, grabbing her free hand. And there was Eckapeta standing behind him, protecting him. Someone thrust Antonio among them and Ayasha knelt by him, covering his body with hers. Toshua had shouldered through the crowd.

Yes, pabi, he thought. Pray God someone is in charge and find him. I'd like it to be someone without a grudge, but I am not a complete fool.

The crowd parted and a warrior stepped forward. Kahúu raised her hand in greeting, said something and pointed to Paloma.

"Turn around, my love," Marco told his wife.

She looked at him, and he saw her lovely face. Someone had struck her with stones, too, and her cheek bled. She clenched the brand so tight that he wondered why her bones didn't come through the skin.

"He's come for my baby, hasn't he?" she said in a low voice, as the warrior, his eyes troubled, reached for the cradleboard, jostling it on her back.

Marco nodded. "Take your arms out of the loops. Slowly, slowly."

She dissolved in a flood of tears, and he knew it was not fear but love. A quick glance around told him that everyone else saw what he saw. "This is hard," she said, between great, gulping sobs.

Kahúu spoke earnestly to the warrior, her hand on his shoulder. She kissed his cheek, then gently took the branding iron from Paloma so she could do what she wanted least in all the world to do. "You must, my sister," Kahúu told her.

"Deep breath, my love," Marco said.

Paloma closed her eyes in what he knew was prayer, then became the courageous woman he had married. She opened her eyes and carefully slid the rawhide loops from her shoulders. The warrior said something, and Kahúu put out her hand to stop him.

That's it. Let her do this with dignity, Marco thought, grateful to the woman who had become Paloma's friend because they had each filled a need in the other.

With a shaking hand, Paloma wiped her eyes, then held the cradleboard close to her face. She kissed the baby, all bright-eyed but restless at the noise, caressed her dandelion puff of hair one last time, and held out the cradleboard to the baby's father.

"Kahúu, can you tell him please that I will miss his daughter as though I had lost a fiber from my heart?"

"I already have," the woman whispered in Spanish.

The warrior said something and the crowd parted again to admit a woman with a cradleboard on her back.

"His other wife," Kahúu said. "It will not do for a warrior to carry a cradleboard."

I would, Marco thought. *God above, I would.*

It was done. The woman took the baby and hurried away. Kahúu's brother-in-law made the sign for "thank you," then another sign which Marco did not know. He looked at Kahúu.

"It is hard to say in Spanish, except that it means more than only thank you."

"It will never be enough," he said.

As Marco watched in amazement, and in the dawning of hope that they might survive this day's work, Kahúu sat with them in the dust, took her own daughter from her back and spread the cradleboard across Paloma's lap, too.

A look at her husband, and he dismounted and stood behind Marco with Eckapeta.

He heard a greater creak of leather as old Buffalo Rut dismounted. Roughly, he patted Paloma's head and kept his hand there as he spoke. He signed as he spoke. He told how he had been so ill in their village and this little woman of the big Spaniard had chewed his food for him so he could live another day.

"There is much more," Buffalo Rut began, then stopped at louder voices and movement.

Marco sighed with relief to see Toshua, and with him an older man with some considerable dignity. He was no taller than the others, but he wore a cap of buffalo horns and an air of complete control. This was no peace chief, but this was not a matter of peace, but of dark days ahead. With their arrival, Spaniards had found their way into the Kwahadi canyon.

"What more?" the chief asked, after taking in the sight. "Toshua, a warrior I had not thought to see again, tells me there is healing magic among the Spaniards."

Toshua pointed to Paloma and to Antonio, who knelt with them, his eyes kind. Something had changed. For the first time, Marco thought he actually looked like the physician he was. Ayasha held his hand, her face calm, too.

The chief looked at Paloma, assessing her with wise eyes, and nodded. He gave Antonio a similar assessment. "Tell me more."

Toshua raised his head, and Marco felt his spirits rise, too. This was the Comanche who had survived, chained in a henhouse, for several months on nothing before Paloma had rescued him. The little flame that had flickered and almost gone out before his rescue by the hated Spaniards had grown into something impressive. Marco felt himself sitting taller, too. "*Pabi*," he whispered, so only Paloma could hear. "We have a good brother in Toshua." Her response was a nod.

Toshua spoke loud enough for all to hear. "You need the little man and the woman of the Spaniard. These two can save our people from *la viruela*." Toshua looked around, taking his time. "I see warriors here with only one braid, and women with scarred faces and cropped hair. There should be more children. What of our friends the Kiowa? I see none here. Is everyone hiding from the Dark Wind? Can you go far enough to hide?" He pointed with his lips. "What about those tipis over there? Are they full of the Dark Wind? And these burned piles what remains of the lodges of warriors and families? Where are they now?"

In a low voice, Eckapeta translated into Spanish. It was the only sound, beside the harsh call of a hawk that floated overhead, watching the proceedings, but more likely looking for meadow mice.

"I have never known the Kwahadi, you Antelope Eaters of the plains, to cower in fear," Toshua said. "We can change that. We have power against the Dark Wind right here."

Chapter Thirty

In which the play goes on

EVERYONE WAS SO STILL now, riveted on what Toshua had said, looking from Paloma to Antonio. She knew if she lived to be an old woman in the colony of New Mexico, she needed no more adventures. This was enough. *I just want to go home with my darling*, she thought.

She had to sit there, her head up, proud and dignified, when she wanted to gather herself into a tiny ball and mourn the loss of the baby until all the tears allotted to her in a lifetime were used up and she could weep no more. To distract herself, she thought of her kitchen on the Double Cross, the soft murmur of Spanish, the fragrance of *posole* bubbling, the welcome sound of Marco's steps at the end of the day, and the way he tapped his boots outside the door and then brought in the mud anyway, to Sancha's exasperation. She longed for the genuine pleasure of her legs wrapped around him as they made love. She wanted him to whisper into her neck and not be overheard by others—kind people, but people still—in tipis and caves.

Just a little longer, she told herself. *Patience and shuffle the cards, as my husband would say. Antonio will find his daughter and we will go home.* She gave Marco a reassuring smile and received one in return. It would not have surprised her if he was thinking exactly the same thing.

"What is his name?" Marco whispered to Toshua.

"Kwihnai. Aquila, an eagle to you, but better you call him Kwihnai." Toshua looked at his wife, who appeared enviably serene. "My woman will translate."

Kwihnai made a motion for silence. Kahúu squeezed her hand, under the cover of the cradleboard.

The chief said something. Toshua answered, then said Marco's name, which made Kwihnai stare in amazement.

"War chief and peace chief," Eckapeta whispered. "And look now, he indicates Antonio. Let us hope our little man is equal to this."

Antonio must have seen the end in sight, too. With an obvious effort, he got to his feet. With a smile, he dusted off his precious beaded medicine bag and stood there, a short man who tried to will himself tall.

Toshua pointed to him with his lips. "This man can save you from *la viruela*." He looked around elaborately again, as Eckapeta continued translating. "I can see the Dark Wind has taken a toll. Even among our friends the Kiowa?"

The chief nodded, his eyes sad.

"'How will he do this?'" Eckapeta whispered, translating the chief's words.

The same thing happened as before, and Paloma was ready for it. Antonio began to speak, his voice eerily high, showing fear impossible to hide, no matter how he tried. Toshua translated, then gestured for Paloma, ignoring the *médico*. They would do what they had done before, the stakes infinitely higher now.

This is the performance of my life, she thought, calm. *In this I honor my brave mother, who would not let me die.* She and Toshua pantomimed the agony of smallpox again, from the fever to the staggers. The People who had gathered tight in anger moved back, the better to see this. She glanced up to see nods of sympathy.

Even Antonio got into the rhythm, taking first Toshua by the arm, cutting him, planting the scab-covered thread, then bandaging him. It was her turn, and she did the same. All the while Eckapeta translated into Spanish, her voice more assured when Kwihnai offered no objection.

It was a simple play. When Paloma had been in the Santa Fe home of her uncle Felix Moreno, they had all gone to a *milagro* in the plaza in front of the governor's palace. A traveling troupe from Mexico City had performed a sinner's view of hell and what happened to those who did not confess their sins or pay alms to the church. She remembered little imps with pitchforks and wings on their backs, flitting through the terrified crowd, poking and jabbing. Somehow, the actors had created the mouth of hell, with flames made of waving strips of red cloth. It was one of the few times her cousin Maria Teresa had clung to her, uniting them in fright. Paloma had nightmares for weeks.

This little scene in the canyon was nothing to the fires of hell, but The People had never seen anything like this play of death and suffering, which climaxed when Antonio cut their arms, and according to Eckapeta's translation, let in the Dark Wind.

Everyone gasped and drew back. Toshua nodded meaningfully to Paloma, and she stepped forward, smiling to show all was well. She made the sign of the sun rising and setting, gestured five days, then went about her business as usual, gathering eggs—what they thought she did, she had no idea—and sweeping her floor. She even grabbed Marco's hand, pulled him up, and gave him a great kiss. Then she rubbed against him, lifting her deerskin dress, which made everyone laugh.

"Oh, Paloma," he whispered.

She was in charge now. She held up both hands to stop the laughter, and gestured with five fingers again, while Toshua took up the story and Eckapeta translated.

"After five days of good life, the Dark Wind wants out," Toshua's woman said. "The suffering begins, but it is smaller this time. It does not kill."

Paloma continued her pantomime, lying down in the dust at the feet of warriors who might, at the very least, kill her. She suffered with fever. Marco did not fail her. He knelt and wiped her face, raising her up and signing "food." Kahúu helped, too, wiping her legs, turning her over and cleaning her like a baby, as Paloma lay in the dust and prayed God was watching their performance with sympathy.

Toshua stopped speaking and raised his hands. It was hardly necessary, because he already had everyone's total attention. As Marco gasped in surprise and Kahúu covered her face in relief, Paloma sat up, smiled, and stood. She did a little *paso doble*, and Marco joined in. "And they think *we* can't dance," he whispered to her, which made her smile.

"The Dark Wind is gone after five days more, and it will never return," Eckapeta said, triumph in her voice now. "This is what the little man and ... and," she stopped and looked with great pride upon Paloma, "Tatzinupi, my daughter, can do for The People. They will not fail you."

The sun had passed its meridian now, and the air was cool, but Paloma dripped with sweat. She shook the dust from her clothes and wiped her arms, noticing the second cut on her other arm, the one she had insisted on to convince their ragged friends a month ago.

"Follow me, Toshua," she said, and gathered all her courage and walked to Kwihnai, the war chief. Silently, she pushed both her deerskins sleeves to her shoulders so he could see identical cuts.

"Dear chief, I have amazing power," she told him, her head up and her voice unnaturally high. She had noticed that the Kwahadi sang in high voices to honor the gods. It couldn't hurt to do the same with war chiefs. "*Twice* I have been cut. So has my man, the big Spaniard. The Dark Wind trembles and runs from us. Do any of The People suffer from the Dark Wind at this moment?"

The chief listened carefully, and made the sign for yes.

"Let me and anyone else who has driven out the Dark Wind stay the night with them. We will be alive in the morning, and we will do this cut for each of you, so you and your people will be safe. Yes, you will suffer in five days time, but it is not a suffering unto death."

Kwihnai stood in thought a long time, not a man to rush into anything, evidently. He gave her a shrewd look then, and gestured to Marco.

" 'Let me speak to this man of yours that you like so well,' " Eckapeta translated.

Marco stood next to her, taking her hand. He bowed, one leg forward like a Spanish grandee, then gave her hand a little tug. With her own flourish, she went into the deep, deep curtsey she had performed once for her almost-husband when she accepted his proposal, and thought never to do again. The People seemed suitably impressed.

He spoke into her ear. "See there, you had another occasion, my dove," he teased. She laughed and jostled his shoulder.

The war chief smiled briefly, and then he was all business. "Spaniard, tell me why would you do this thing for people you hate? Three years ago, your war chief, and maybe you, fought us. Why should you keep The People alive?"

It was certainly the question of the century. Paloma put her arm around Marco's waist, pleased that there wasn't a tremble in his entire body. Or hers, now. They were in so deep that there was no need to fear. What happened was in God's hands.

Marco glanced at Toshua, indicating without words the necessity that every sentence be translated correctly. Toshua nodded. He stepped forward and put his arm around Marco's waist; he, too, was committed.

"I am the man who lives behind stone walls. You know of my place. I have fought you, it is true," Marco began simply. "I do not lie. I only wish to live in peace in Valle del Sol. This is where my loved ones are buried. I never want to come here again, even though your canyon is beautiful. It is *your* land. Can we not divide our lands and live in peace? Why is this hard?"

"If you help us, you would like us to leave you alone?" the chief asked.

"It would be a beginning," Marco answered. "All I ask is a chance."

Paloma heard Antonio clear his throat loudly, interrupting the mood. The war chief frowned.

"There is another reason, and our little medicine man reminds me," Marco continued. "Once we have satisfied you by showing you that we cannot get the Dark Wind and we mean what we say, we will tell you."

Kwihnai nodded and gestured to the older warriors. They gathered around him, leaving Marco, Paloma, and Toshua on the outside.

"You could have mentioned Pia Maria," Antonio began.

Marco grabbed his shirt, lifting him off his feet. "I am doing the best I can to keep us alive," he whispered. "Little by little." He shook the doctor, whose eyes were starting to bug out.

He started to say more, but the crowd of warriors separated and surrounded them again. Kwihnai had made his decision. Marco released the doctor.

Kwihnai gestured toward the distant tipis. "Go there tonight. If you are alive in the morning, we will let in the Dark Wind."

SILENT, WORDLESS, PALOMA, MARCO and Antonio started toward the three tipis. Antonio rubbed his throat, but wisely chose to remain quiet.

Could you develop some wisdom fast enough? Marco thought.

"You know it takes more than one night with *la viruela* to cause symptoms," Antonio began finally.

Perhaps I hope in vain, Marco thought, weary of the man.

"The point is, The People don't know that," Paloma told Antonio, much kinder than Marco could ever be. "Incubation is not something even Toshua understands." She managed a small laugh. "I barely do." She leaned against Marco's shoulder as they walked, noticing that The People had fallen way back. "What will we find ahead?"

"That which we have seen before," Marco replied. "Be brave a little longer."

His dear one nodded. "You will owe me red shoes and a coral necklace when we are home."

"I was thinking more in terms of emeralds and rubies. Perhaps you can bathe in mare's milk like Cleopatra."

They laughed together, which made Antonio stare at them.

"Wait up there, my children."

Marco turned around, touched to see Toshua and Eckapeta walking toward them. Ayasha held Eckapeta's hand. She carried trade blankets and a buffalo bladder full of water. Their arsenal of medicaments was puny, indeed.

"We cannot really do anything," Marco reminded them gently.

Trust Ayasha. When she spoke so softly, he prayed that someday he would have a daughter like her. "We can do as you say, señor. We can begin here."

Chapter Thirty-One

In which Antonio wins and loses

THIS NIGHT IN THE tipi with the dead and dying was not Paloma's worst night, by any means. She knew it was not Marco's. As she looked at the others, she knew it was not their worst night, either.

To her astonishment, Antonio took charge and assigned them each to a tipi. He went about his work more quietly and efficiently than she had seen at any point in their acquaintance. She could call their association nothing more than acquaintance, even after several months. She knew he was a man desperate for his daughter, and she understood that. She also knew she never wanted to know more about him; he was that kind of person.

Still, Paloma reminded herself that Ayasha had no trouble helping Antonio. She had observed them on the final part of the journey to the Gathering, watching how they rode together, each so aware of the other. She even thought Ayasha was teaching him the language of The People. Paloma herself was certainly more proficient in sign language now, even more than Marco.

She spoke about Antonio to Marco while they cleaned the dying as best they could and tried to give sips of water to those beyond water. "He is a complete mystery to me, but if Ayasha likes him, then he must have qualities I am not aware of."

"Poor Antonio," Marco said, many minutes after her comment, long after she thought he would respond. "Some people are just not well-liked, no matter what, and then when they are, it's a shock." He managed a wry smile. "Truth to tell, Alonso Castellano is a man like that. He has few friends, but you know, I always liked him and would like to be his friend again."

"I do not think even my cousin is his friend," Paloma said. "I wonder how they have fared, and the people of Santa Maria."

"Does it seem to you like they all belong to another world?"

She nodded, too tired to say more.

By dawn, it was done. One *pobrecito* remained alive in their tipi, but only just. When she and Toshua looked in, Eckapeta shook her head. Worried what she would find in the third tipi, Paloma was touched to see the order Antonio and Ayasha had created there. As they watched in sympathy, Antonio sat back on his heels finally and told Ayasha to stop. "We can do no more," he said simply, and Paloma agreed with him.

Weariness itself, Toshua beckoned Marco and Antonio for a conference. They squatted outside the tipi while the women drew closer to each other. Their words were soft, until Antonio stood up and declared, "I cannot," and left the two men.

"You know what they will do," Eckapeta said.

"I know," Paloma said, her eyes on the men when they drew their knives and went into one tipi and then the other. There was no need of their merciful services in the third tipi. Antonio and Ayasha stood together, silent, until Antonio walked away from them.

"I did not know he had a tender heart," Eckapeta said, her eyes on the solitary figure.

"He didn't when we started this journey," Paloma replied.

Too tired to move, they huddled close together in the cold morning air, waiting for someone to come by—not too close—and see that they lived.

Marco was as comforting as ever, opening his generous embrace to Ayasha, as well. "A man has two sides, after all," he said, kissing one on the head and then the other.

They sat in silence, listening to the small birds and the lowing of cattle, stolen from one rancher or other in Texas or New Mexico. "I should copy the brands," Marco said idly.

"With what?" Paloma asked. "Don't be a *juez de campo* now, because I would just about give my right arm—no, *your* right arm—for a piece of beef cooked just so."

He laughed softly at her little joke.

When the sun's rays finally struck the broad meadow surrounded on all sides by towering canyon walls, Kwihnai and two of his elders walked toward them. Toshua stood up immediately and hurried to them, but not too close, on the little doctor's advice.

"He's telling them to send a man who has a pockmarked face to check inside the tipis and see what we have been through. He's also asking for new clothes," Marco explained. "I told him to do that. We need to burn everything: the tipis, the dead and our clothes."

"I wish I could keep this dress of Kahúu's sister."

"I wish you could, too, but on the bonfire it goes."

The warriors left, sending back an old man with a ravaged face, and Buffalo Rut, also scarred. They carried with them an armload of clothing and a torch. Eckapeta, Ayasha, and Toshua stripped and threw their clothes into the first burning tipi. Paloma retreated behind the second with Marco. She took a long look at her beaded dress, sighed and threw it into the tipi as Buffalo Rut applied the torch. Antonio changed alone.

Paloma watched Marco, quite practiced now, adjust his breechcloth. "I could almost start to think you enjoyed dressing like this."

He grinned at her, the first genuinely pleasant smile after their long night. "There's a certain freedom," he told her, "a nice swing to the jewels. *Ay de mi!* Paloma, leave me alone!"

She blushed when she heard Toshua laugh from the other side of the tipi that was now a bonfire.

I could sleep a week, Paloma thought, as they walked to the encampment. Smoke curled from tipis and the dogs growled over scraps. She heard women talking, horses neighing. Once the little *médico* explained his terms, The People would line up for inoculation and their work would be done. Antonio would retrieve his daughter and they could go home.

Eyes nearly closed, Paloma sat with Eckapeta and Ayasha, women apart now, because they had powerful medicine against the Dark Wind. Had they not survived a night with the disease? Antonio Gil spoke and Toshua translated his feeble Spanish, just in case Kwihnai didn't understand everything.

By now Paloma knew a little of the language, but she knew more of human nature. The look on the war chief's face could have mirrored Marco's a few short months ago, when Antonio explained his devil's bargain. But there it was; as Antonio Gil had bent Marco to his will, so he trapped and cornered the war chief: inoculation for The People in exchange for his daughter. Antonio gestured the height of a small child, touched his own light-colored hair, folded his arms and sat back with less triumph on his face this time, maybe even some doubt.

The chief rose and spoke to other men, who went among the tipis. Paloma cried out to hear women shrieking and moaning and knew that someone's heart was breaking. True, the child had been stolen from the doctor and his wife, but during the intervening years, Pia Maria had become part of someone else's family.

"I know Antonio wants his daughter, but that means another woman must suffer," she said, turning her head into Eckapeta's sympathetic shoulder. "I cannot bear this much sorrow!"

She closed her eyes, opening them when she heard Marco gasp, "*Dios mio! ¿Qué es esto?*"

Paloma stared as she felt the blood drain from her face. "*Two?* Good God, there are two!"

She hurried closer, but no quicker than Antonio and Marco, as the war chief dragged two crying girls forward, both obviously blond, even through the grime she associated with the Kwahadi, and both of similar age. She glanced at Antonio, watching in horror as his mouth dropped open. He simply stood there, looking from one weeping child to the other. The mourning of their Indian mothers made Paloma want to cover her ears.

She clutched Marco's arm. Still Antonio did nothing. Surely he knew his daughter. As she looked from the doctor to the girls, both crying and struggling now, Paloma suddenly understood a greater evil. "Marco, he …."

Her husband had reached the same terrible conclusion. "He doesn't recognize either child," he said, his voice strangled, as though the words were so wrong they couldn't be uttered. "Good God, Paloma." Marco clutched her shoulder now, his grip nearly painful, as realization struck him as it had her. "That beaded medical bag. Didn't you say—"

"It was for someone taller." Paloma could barely say it.

She could not stop the bitterness welling inside her, as two women in the encampment and their relatives raised a huge lamentation for their adopted daughters, standing there in tears, clutching each other. She relived their own terrible journey, and all for what? Before Marco could stop her, she darted forward and slapped the back of the doctor's head, counting coup.

When she struck him, he assumed that subservient crouch she had not seen in weeks. She gasped to see it, and pulled her hand back, fearing contagion of another kind. At least he turned around to look at her, his eyes bewildered.

"Well? Well?" Kwihnai demanded, struggling to contain the little ones who wanted their Indian mothers.

"I do not recognize either of these children," Antonio said. "My daughter is not here."

He turned away, his face calm now.

Paloma raised her hand to strike him again, but Marco grabbed her. "Who *are* you?" she asked, leaning forward. "In God's name, who *are* you?"

THE ANSWER WOULD HAVE to wait. Shocked, Toshua grabbed the crying girls under each arm and returned them to their Indian mothers, who snatched them and ran. He exchanged a long look with Marco, a warning that the *juez* was quick to heed. Paloma may have been paler than a ghost herself, but they had to act. "Get your medical bag and begin. Quickly. Eckapetha …."

Her face calm, a woman well-acquainted with disaster, Toshua's wife was already lining up children and mothers who needed inoculation. A glance from Paloma to Kahúu sent the Kwahadi mother flying to her tipi for the medical bag she had taken for safekeeping yesterday, when the adventure in the encampment began.

Marco watched his wife will herself calm in that masterful way he could only envy. She found a place to sit and someone brought up a small table that must have come from some ranchero's house. Ayasha ran up with a cloth, probably from another unfortunate hacienda, and the inoculations began. All was silent. Ashen, shaking, Antonio tried to join her, but she shook her head.

"Wait until you are calmer, you dreadful man," she said quite distinctly. He turned away.

His heart in his mouth, Marco sat cross-legged with the war chief, Toshua next to him, their shoulders touching. He could not have said which of them needed more reassurance.

"Just tell him that the doctor's child is not here. That is all we know, and it is no reflection on the Kwahadi," Marco said, when he had gathered his composure around him like tattered clothing.

The war chief nodded philosophically and offered them strips of beef—stolen from someone's cattle herd and dried against the long winter. In turmoil, Marco forced the food to stay down. Kwihnai finally took his turn in the line. By now, Antonio had begun to work beside Paloma, but not too close.

They finished within the hour. The chief requested another rendition from Paloma and Toshua of what would happen next. They provided it, to the general amusement of the camp, even though Marco could see that his wife had unraveled the final thread of her equanimity. She went through the playacting, then sat down, stunned. He put his arm around her and she turned her face into his shoulder.

"Five suns," the war chief said, his good humor evident. "You may leave now with the little man who shakes and crouches like a slave. Toshua and Eckapeta will know what to do when the Dark Wind needs to escape."

Marco nodded. "We will do as you say, Kwihnai, but may we ask for an escort across the Llano Estacado? It remains a mystery to me."

Kwihnai nodded, a generous man, now that he knew his people were safe. "I will provide one, and you will promise me never to return." His eyes were kind as he looked at Paloma. "Your woman is tired and your eyes are heavy, too. Sleep first."

Marco looked at Antonio, who could not meet his gaze for long. "The little man who shakes will share a tipi with us."

"I—"

"Now, Antonio. Now."

Chapter Thirty-Two

In which a scoundrel does a noble thing, perhaps for the first time

IN THE PRIVACY OF a tipi, Paloma lay with her head in Marco's lap, too weary to keep her eyes open, her nerves so tightly wound she knew she would never sleep again, not ever. She could not bring herself to look at Antonio Gil. Toshua and Eckapeta joined them, Ayasha close behind.

"Who *are* you?" Marco demanded of the man who stood before him. Out of the chief's commanding presence, Antonio had regained his eerie calm. "Tell us!"

She had never heard his official voice so stern. Heaven help the man who lied to this husband of hers.

"Leo Flynn. Señor, I—"

"I will ask and you will answer. What have you done with the doctor?"

Paloma opened her eyes when Antonio—Leo now?—shrieked. Quicker than a finger snap, Toshua had sliced a strip of flesh from the doctor's cheek, only a small strip, but peeled with such precision that Paloma vowed never to ask him another question about his life before she met him.

"That should be enough, *pabi,*" Marco said, striving to keep his voice conversational, even though Paloma knew Toshua had startled him. "Anto … Leo … *Where* is the doctor?"

"Dead somewhere in Texas." Leo Flynn started to cry. "I'm going to bleed to death!"

"Not before you tell us the truth."

Her eyes troubled, Ayasha handed him one of the cloth scraps left over from the inoculations.

"Begin and do not stop until I tell you to," Marco commanded.

Leo Flynn's story came out in fits and starts, how he had come from London to Georgia, a colony for debtors, under an indenture. "I was to work for Dr. Gill seven years; then I would be free," he explained.

"How odd," Marco said. "Keep going."

The story he told was much as he had related earlier, how Dr. Gill ran afoul of the British and was forced to flee to Natchitoches eventually, on the Texas frontier with his wife Catalina.

"And you followed him?"

"Had I a choice?" Leo replied, with a flash of irritation that made Toshua pull out his knife again. Leo gulped. "We ended up in Los Adaes, a Spanish possession, as I am certain you know. Pia Maria had been born in Natchitoches."

Paloma thought Marco could have been kinder when the poor man asked for a drink of water and the *juez* ignored him. Looking injured, Leo continued with a tale of increasing drunkenness and desperation as Dr. Gill, damn his hide, gathered enough money to hand over to land speculators without a single credential to recommend them.

"Dr. Gill was always going to make his fortune farther west," Leo said, making no effort to disguise his bitterness. "What could we do but follow? His wife by vows, and me by a damned document."

He stopped, his head down, and Marco thrust a gourd of water in front of him. He drained it eagerly.

"All along, you had been learning a real physician's skills?" Paloma asked.

"It wasn't hard. Set a bone, purge and bleed someone. I didn't like it—too much stink and pus—but when did he ask me?"

"*Pobrecito,*" Marco said sarcastically, "my heart bleeds for you."

Paloma gave her husband a little shake. When Marco spoke again, he at least sounded more civil. "And?"

"We lived near Los Adaes then, in a one-room *jacal* with sand fleas and cockroaches. Mrs. Gill had decided to leave him, take Pia, and return to her father. The day she was going to sneak away, the Comanches struck. The doctor and I were treating diarrhea in the garrison at Los Adaes." He paused, his eyes weary as he passed his hand in front of his face. Paloma knew that gesture, because she had done it many times herself, trying to wipe out a view that would not leave the brain.

"We came back to horror." Leo glanced from Toshua to Eckapeta, their expressions unreadable. "I have already told that story."

"Keep going."

"Surely we could leave now, but no! Dr. Gill returned to Natchitoches and told his father-in-law what had happened. Señor Rosas was understandably beside himself. He offered the doctor a huge amount of gold to find Pia and bring her back to him. *He* would keep his granddaughter, and the doctor would go back to Georgia. That was why we went onto the plains."

"For money," Marco said, his voice troubled now, the anger gone. "Not for love of his daughter?"

"For money," Leo repeated, his voice more firm. "That was Anthony Gill."

He was silent. Marco sat back, as if exhausted by so much greed and deception. Eckapeta passed around a wooden bowl of dried meat and they ate. When they finished, Leo continued.

"That vile man had the worst luck. We joined ourselves to as foul a group of traders as you will ever see. The doctor promised them part of the gold he was going to collect, so they suffered us." Leo turned his face away then, his sorrow palpable. "When they could not find women, he let them use me. God damn him to eternal flames forever."

Leo said it in a low voice. Ayasha was in tears now. Toshua and Eckapeta looked at each other, shocked.

"Did *you* kill him?" Marco asked, his voice kinder, speaking into the great silence.

"I wanted to! Before God and all the saints, I wanted to! I am a coward; you know that." He managed a dry chuckle, but his eye consigned the real Dr. Gill to unimaginable torture. "The doctor and the head trader got in a brawl over the turn of a card, and Anthony Gill, that bearer of bad luck, received a knife through his bowels for his pains." Leo rubbed his hands together. "I am happy to report that he lingered in agony for some days."

Chilled to the bone, Paloma moved closer to Marco. With a shudder he did not try to control, her husband passed around a bottle of good brandy that Kwihnai must have liberated from another rancher no luckier than the doctor.

Leo took a long swig and sighed. "I was all for turning back. We had almost run out of trade goods and winter was coming. But no, the traders decided *I* should become Antonio Gil. We would recover his daughter and still get the money." He shrugged. "Maybe it wasn't a bad plan." He gave Paloma his attention. "You were the only one who noticed that the medical bag obviously wasn't made for a man of my height. Dr. Gill was a head taller."

"Much good that did," Paloma said dryly. "I didn't put anything together, did I?"

"We continued, and then *la viruela* struck. I watched the traders die and felt only delight, even though I was alone." He folded his arms. "You know the rest. In my mind, I knew I had to become Dr. Gill and continue the charade."

"There is more," Marco said, after a long, uncomfortable silence. "I am a *juez de campo* and I am trained to watch people, to study them, if you will.

You're lying right now, and you were lying in the gathering with the two girls. I know it."

Leo threw up his hands. "You are so determined to have the whole story?"

"I insist."

Leo looked at Paloma, and she saw the sympathy in his eyes. "Blame Paloma for my sudden reformation."

"What are you talking about?" Marco demanded, sounding like a man whose last fragment of patience had just blown away.

"I? What ... how ...?" Paloma stammered.

Leo held up his hand to stop them, not taking his eyes from Paloma. "Pia Maria is the shorter of the two girls we saw earlier. Señora Mondragón, of all the people in this tipi, you know why I said nothing."

Paloma swallowed and turned her face into Marco's arm. "It was the weeping women, was it not?" she said, her voice muffled. "You couldn't bear to do to them what Kahúu's brother-in-law did to me."

There was a catch in Leo's throat. "I could not. It isn't in me anymore."

Paloma held her hand to her mouth so she would not sob out loud. Marco put both arms around her.

"After all, who could say if I would ever get Pia Maria back across east Texas?"

"No, that was not in the devil's bargain, was it?" Marco said as he cradled Paloma in his arms now.

"No. I thought at first that I would tempt you with the gold from Pia's grandfather, that which tempted the traders," he said, with a rueful shake of his head. "I was not two days in your presence before I knew you would never be so dishonorable."

"Well, thank you," Marco said, his voice heavy with sarcasm.

"It's more than that. You don't know Señora Gill's father; I do. He is a lying cheat who beats his slaves. Who can say how he would really treat a child who has, for all intents, become a Comanche? Pia Maria is better off here, with a mother and father who love her. Who paid twenty buffalo robes for her."

"Thank you, Leo Flynn," Paloma said, as she swabbed at her tears. "You have done a good thing."

He gave her a genuine smile, one of the few she had ever seen from him, and it was directed at her. "Dear lady, do you remember what you told me, even before this journey began?"

"No, I ... no."

"You told me that the more time I spent with you two, especially Marco Mondragón, the better I would become. You were almost right, except that I believe the credit goes to you."

Marco started to laugh, a low laugh that began somewhere down deep and seemed to spread through his whole body. "Señor Flynn, you are a cheat and a rascal, but you are absolutely right," he said when he could speak. He raised Paloma's hand and kissed it. "My love, you might be *my* star in the meadow, but obviously I am not the only person becoming better through your influence."

Paloma covered her face with her hands, unable to look at any of them. "I wish my cousin Maria Teresa had been so susceptible," she whispered, for Marco's ears only.

"We'll try again with the Castellanos when we return home," he promised her. "My star. Tatzinupi."

"I just want to go home."

"And so we shall. Leo Flynn, we will get you back to Valle del Sol. You can do what you want from there, but we have need of a *médico* in Santa Maria."

"But I'm not—"

"Oh, you are. Come, Paloma. I need to walk with you."

He held out his hand to her and she rose gracefully, happy to be away from such heavy doings. Outside the tipi, she jumped when she heard a shriek much like the first. Wiping his knife, Toshua came out next.

"What did you do, *pabi*?" Marco asked.

Paloma had to turn her head away at Toshua's wounded look. "I just gave him a matching strip on his other cheek, in case he tries to forget this little lesson." He drew himself up. "It is the Kwahadi way. We are tidy people."

THE TIDY PEOPLE DANCED that night, willing to use Paloma's promised five days of comfort, laughter and tipi time before the Dark Wind paid a visit. They danced to honor the bear that the bedraggled travelers had killed, which meant that Marco had to dance, too, pantomiming his approach and the creature's death. Paloma watched with considerable amusement, and then some respect. Her husband was light on his feet. She noticed that the Mondragón family jewels did swing more comfortably in a breechcloth. How in the world would she ever get him into breeches again? Then Eckapeta pulled her up, too, and she had to dance with another woman, the one who killed the bear cubs.

In the morning she was still comfortable in the robes with the most accommodating man she knew, thinking about a little more tipi time before the sun came up completely, when Eckapeta came into their tipi suddenly.

"Up, Paloma."

Marco groaned and started to shake his head, but Eckapeta yanked off the buffalo robe, baring his nakedness. The woman laughed to see his readiness for something other than rising and left the tipi. Whatever dignity he had possessed now shredded, Marco gave himself a moment then sat up, muttering to Paloma, "You would not do that."

"What could she want with me?" Paloma asked as she dressed.

Marco shrugged, lay down again, and closed his eyes, a smile on his face. "Better you than me," he said, which earned him a small kick from his excellent wife.

It was a beautiful morning, the air crisp, but promising warmth by midday. Paloma breathed deep; spring had come to the Texas plains. The smell of cedar campfires tickled her nose. The camp was beginning to stir. Soon they would leave—a thought that gave her more mixed emotions than Paloma was willing to admit, even to herself.

But there was a kitchen garden to plant, and she knew she would almost give the earth for a long soak in the wooden tub. She smiled to herself. Last night Marco had reminded her about the promised red shoes. And perhaps she could find a way to Maria Teresa's dusty heart. She couldn't do that here, so it was time to go home.

She asked Eckapeta where they were going, but the woman she had come to love like an older sister just shook her head. She took Paloma by the hand, the gesture infinitely companionable.

They walked until they were out of sight of the tipis and horse herd, to a clearing with a small fire. Someone had laid green cedar branches across the flames to create a haze of sweet-smelling smoke. Close to the fire, but not close enough to be burned, Eckapeta spread out a trade blanket. When she finished, she turned to Paloma. "Take off your dress."

"Oh, but ...."

Eckapeta folded her arms, not about to be deterred.

Even a month ago, Paloma knew she would never do such a thing out of doors and in the bright daylight. Anyone could wander by. Everything had changed now, and she trusted Toshua's woman with all her heart, even as she trusted Toshua. With one fluid motion, she pulled her deerskin dress over her head.

"Your moccasins, too. Sit down here and cross your legs."

"Oh, I can't .... Very well." Paloma sat, after looking around to assure herself that no one else was even near the clearing.

Eckapeta picked up the smoking cedar branch and waved it over her, singing in high, high notes, so the good spirits who helped The People could hear. Paloma looked at her, tears either from shyness or smoke running down her face.

"This is a cleansing ceremony," Eckapeta said. "I like to do this after a long journey." She chuckled. "Maybe I just like the smell of burning cedar." She touched Paloma's forehead. "You know The People are not sentimental."

"But you are?" Paloma teased back.

"Maybe," Eckapeta said, then struggled within herself. "And maybe I love you as a sister."

Paloma bowed her head, knowing that whatever happened, Eckapeta's words had already cleansed away any feelings of sorrow.

Paloma closed her eyes, enjoying the warmth of the fire and the fragrance. Eckapeta waved the branch a few more times, then set it back in the fire. She opened her eyes when the woman knelt in front of her. She forgot to be shy when Eckapeta touched each breast, her fingers gentle around her nipples. A soft pat on her belly followed, and then she was done. She had begun the little ceremony so serious, but she smiled now.

Paloma dressed, while Eckapeta spread dirt on the fire and rolled up the trade blanket.

"I will miss you, little sister," was all Eckapeta said, as she brought Paloma back to the tipi she shared with Marco. She turned away and Paloma watched her shoulders shake and her head go down.

"I will miss you, too, sister," Paloma whispered.

THEY LEFT THE PEOPLE after another meal of excellent beef from someone's herd, Marco was certain. Their friends and fellow-travelers from the little camp sat close to them, laughing and talking. Paloma had returned, quiet and contemplative, from her walk with Eckapeta. When he had asked her what had happened, Paloma only blushed and said, "Later."

Marco steeled himself for the pain when Kahúu brought her little niece by for a farewell look. Paloma probably would not have started to cry if the baby hadn't started kicking her feet and cooing when she saw her temporary mother.

When she was calm again, Paloma held out her arms to accept another beaded dress from Kahúu. "I will miss you," she told her friend. Paloma couldn't take her eyes from the baby.

"For the dress you lost," Kahúu whispered, then fled back to her tipi, her niece in her arms. Marco had to hold up his wife until she had her feet under her again.

With a terrible sort of dignity, Kwihnai made certain that Marco would never return to the canyon of The People, and never tell anyone how to get there. Marco did not flinch as the war chief took a nick out of his cheek, but only on one side.

"That is to remind you that death will come in terrible ways, if you go against your promise."

"Never," Marco said, as blood streamed down his face. "On my honor, which is as dear to me as my wife, Spain, and God. And you will honor *your* words about Valle del Sol. I am depending upon you."

Kwihnai nodded. He reached down and slapped dirt on Marco's face, making a most casual poultice. "Go now."

Now or never. Marco held out his hand, not knowing if the war chief of the Kwahadi, a proud tribe humbled to the dust two years ago by Governor de Anza, would touch fingers. "My war chief—you know him—wanted me to tell you that we have land and you have land, and there is enough for us both. Come and see him at the Taos Fair. If not this year, then some year."

Marco's heart lightened when Kwihnai touched his fingers. "Perhaps some year, if you will be there, too."

"God willing, I will be."

"Your woman, too?"

"Most certainly."

Marco mounted his horse, pleased to see his pack animals again, their old tents on them now, and food. But there were Toshua and Eckapeta, ready to ride, too. He couldn't hide his relief or his surprise, but weren't they needed to help The People through the five bad days to come?

"I told them I would remain."

Marco stared at Leo Flynn, standing so quietly beside him. Funny, he had almost forgotten about the man already. But that was Leo Flynn.

"You? *Ay caray,* you?"

"Your friends want to go," he said simply. "They will help me when they return. Also, that disgusting old man Buffalo Rut tells me there are more Kwahadi and many Kiowa who need what I do."

"Are you certain?"

"I thought about it all night," was his quiet reply. "Maybe I do not want to be known for my faulty character anymore."

"Thank you, Señor Flynn," Paloma said, and kissed his cheek.

"There is more," he said.

"There always is, with you," Marco grumbled.

He said nothing, but pointed to Ayasha with his lips. She came to his side, her eyes down, shy. "I don't want to leave her." He managed a surprisingly courtly bow to Paloma. "Ayasha can continue molding my faulty character where you have left off, Señora Mondragón. Go with God, and may you be fruitful."

Leo Flynn—indentured servant no more, now medicine man to the Kwahadi—patted the beaded doctor's bag that fit him. "Or I might show up in Santa Maria again with Ayasha." He laughed. "I also cut hair and barber."

Leo stepped back, after Kahúu's husband handed Marco his old Spanish bow and quiver, but with Kwahadi arrows now. He raised his hand in salute. Kwihnai motioned to Marco and handed him his own lance, which meant it was Marco's turn to look away until he collected himself.

Chapter Thirty-Three

In which Paloma is cleansed again

BUFFALO RUT FOLLOWED THEM up the steep canyon trail and onto the Llano Estacado, riding with them for two days until one morning Paloma woke to find him gone. She stood a long time watching to the east. Marco did not disturb her silence that day.

"I will miss him," was all she said. *As I will miss my baby, and The People, and Kahúu especially*, she told herself that night, after Marco slept.

They would have taken a punishing pace to cross the Staked Plains, except that she knew after the first day that Eckapeta told them not to. Paloma had tried to maintain their easy, mile-eating lope and heaven knows she did not complain, but she could not keep up. Exhaustion she could not explain seemed to fill her whole body.

She thought there might be contempt in the warriors' eyes, but she saw nothing of the kind. Eckapeta told her later, as she brushed Paloma's hair—her hairbrush fascinated the woman—that The People would tell stories for a long time about the woman who was brave enough to challenge the Dark Wind with two cuts, and who had stood above her man with a branding iron, ready to swing at them.

"Anyone would have done those things," she said, which made Eckapeta tug her hair and laugh.

Paloma couldn't help but admire Marco, every bit as dignified in the saddle as the Kwahadi. She even thought her modest husband was a little bit proud of his Kwahadi scar. The days were warm now and he had tucked away the trade blanket he had worn on his shoulders, during the last gasp of winter in the canyon. He had also put away his Spanish boots, because as a parting gift, one of Kwihnai's wives had made him a pair of moccasins that fit.

He was proudest of Kwihnai's lance, practicing with Toshua and the others in the evenings. When they were nearly to Santa Maria, thinking Kwihnai had only loaned the weapon to him for the journey, Marco tried to return it through Toshua. The Comanche—his friend, his *pabi*—had backed his horse away, shaking his head.

"It is yours, my little brother. Keep Paloma safe with it always," Toshua had said, including her in his gesture.

That had led to tears. Paloma no longer bothered to ask herself why her heart was heavy with tears for The People she had thought to hate and fear all her life.

As much as she knew she would miss The People, Paloma could not deny the great relief that covered her like a warm bath, when the towering Sangre de Cristos finally came into view. "Our mountains," she said to Marco as he rode beside her. "*Gracias a Dios.*"

He rode beside her more and more now. She knew she had not complained, but she had noticed Eckapeta speaking to him more than once, and then stopping her talk when she came closer. *They are worried about me,* she thought, irritated with them both. *I have said nothing and they are worried.*

A day later, their escort, including Toshua and Eckapeta, left them without a word. She had awakened from a sound sleep to find Marco missing. When she crouched out of the tent, she looked around and cried out, "Where have they gone?"

He stood facing the east, tears on his face.

"Why did you not wake me?" she raged at him, then threw herself into his open arms.

"They told me not to," he whispered into her hair. "They said it was best this way."

"Why didn't I hear them?" she asked, sad to her heart's core.

"They're Kwahadi," he said with a shrug.

"You heard them," she accused.

He had no answer for that.

The greatest difficulty came in approaching Santa Maria without alarming anyone or becoming victims themselves, since they wore the garb of The People. Marco solved it handily enough by traveling in a roundabout way to the fields of a friend of long standing.

"I will call his name and sing a *Te Deum*. Stay here and watch."

Filled with misgivings, she did as he said. A hand to her forehead to shade her eyes, she watched distant figures in the field stand, gather close, and then run. "Please, please be right, Marco," she whispered.

She watched, fearful, as Marco dismounted to face the approaching horsemen, picking their way slowly. Just as slowly, he set down his lance, removed the quiver from his back and stood there with his hands outstretched. "I am Marco Mondragón!" he shouted. "Your *juez de campo*, Juan Sandia, you horse-stealing old fornicator." She closed her eyes in gratitude to hear laughter.

The riders were Don Juan Sandia and his son Diego, men she remembered from inoculations in February. Was it only February? How could that be, when her life had changed in every way? When the Sandias crowded close around him, everyone talking at once, Marco waved her in and the journey was over.

MARCO TOLD THEM ALL he could as they rode to Santa Maria in the protective center of the entire Sandia clan. "What month is it?" was his first question. He had to know before he would tell them anything. All of a sudden, the month mattered. Half-naked in a loin cloth, and he wanted—needed—to know the month. *I am a bureaucrat*, he thought, amused.

"*Abril, mono*," Juan teased, taking liberties with the *juez de campo* because they were friends of long standing.

Everyone had something to say. Marco found himself missing the polite clearing of the throat in tipis. On the outskirts of Santa Maria, he held up his hand. "My friends, I promise I will call a meeting soon and tell everyone what happened. Now you tell me that Lieutenant Roybal is here again? Why is that?"

"Word has passed around that we have no *juez*. He'll be glad to see you," Juan replied.

Lieutenant Roybal *was* glad—overjoyed, in fact—grabbing Marco in an *abrazo*. He sat them both down, ready for a long story, which Marco overruled, after a look at Paloma.

"We are going home now," he said firmly. "I will write you a detailed report in a day or two and bring it myself. I would ask two things of you: could you send someone to Señora Saltero's to at least borrow a skirt and bodice for my wife? We daren't ride any farther in these clothes. I can surely find clothes from someone in the garrison."

At the mention of the dressmaker, Lieutenant Roybal's face fell. "Alas, *la viruela* ...."

"Then it did fall upon Santa Maria," Paloma said. "We could not tell, as we rode in."

"It did, but few died, thanks to you and that doctor, Señor ... Señor ...."

"Señor Antonio Gil," Marco supplied. No need for them to know the complication that was Leo Flynn. "Such a brave man. He has decided to continue his work among the Kwahadi, building such bridges as our governor would be grateful to know about. But Señora Saltero?"

Again the sorrowful shake of the head, followed by a philosophical shrug. "I believe she was not inoculated."

"That is true," Paloma said, her voice soft. "She chose this and we understand. Could you send that same man to Aldonza Rivera? I believe our old friend, God rest her soul, said Aldonza would be the new dressmaker in Santa Maria."

"I will."

By the time the servant returned with a handsome skirt and bodice, Marco had been clothed in breeches and a shirt and doublet that nearly fit. They would get him home to the Double Cross, and he needed nothing more. While Paloma changed, the lieutenant told him about the others in Santa Maria who had survived the Dark Wind.

Marco had to ask. "You have not mentioned Rico the tinsmith, and his wife Luz."

"They are fine!" Roybal leaned closer, ever the gentleman. "And wouldn't you know that Señora Mendoza is increasing yet again?"

Inwardly, Marco heaved a sigh of relief, wishing he could tell Leo Flynn that even a pregnant woman might live through inoculation, and her baby, too. *I cannot possibly be missing that difficult little man*, he thought, startled. *Well, maybe a little.*

"So life goes on in Santa Maria." Marco could have said something about the promise of the Kwahadi war chief never to raid the valley again. It could wait for the official report in a few days. And here was Paloma, looking like a Spanish lady again.

The lieutenant walked them to their waiting horses, grained and watered. He stopped with another frown. "Señora, you probably do not know, but there is sadness in your own family."

"I have no family, other than this man of mine," she said.

"Your cousin and your brother-in-law, Alonso Castellano." He shook his head. "Such a sad thing. Both dead of *la viruela*. Rumor says that all their servants scattered before they drew their final breaths. I only just learned of it, but I will ride there tomorrow, because something must be done. There are records to be found. Ho there, señora."

Marco grabbed Paloma when she sagged against him, holding her easily in his arms. He sat down with her on the bench by the horse trough, his arms tight around her, until she stirred and sat up.

"Such loss, such loss," she whispered into his neck.

After that news, he did not trust her to ride alone. So it was that they shared the same saddle as they approached the Double Cross, the same way they had arrived a year and a half ago when Paloma Vega—the one The People now called Tatzinupi—arrived from Santa Fe. She had offered no objection then and she offered none now.

"Thanks be to God Omnipotent," he said simply as they came slowly toward his gray-walled fortress, just the two of them with no outriders. He knew they need not fear the Kwahadi again, no matter how matters stood in the rest of the colony. That would go in his report to the governor, too. Valle del Sol was safe, no longer a target on the edge of Comanchería.

The gates swung wide at their approach, and there was old Emiliano, clapping his hands and capering about like a man half his age. His other servants came running. Marco handed down Paloma to willing hands, even as she laughed, and protested, and tried to hug everyone at once. Trece, that expensive yellow dog, came out to prance back and forth and land finally in Paloma's arms.

"Sancha is overfeeding you," she said, then looked around, setting down the little yellow dog. "Where is Sancha?"

Marco held his breath, knowing that Felicia's housekeeper had been inoculated years earlier. Still, other calamities could kill a person in this colony. Pray God, no.

Emiliano gave him a thoughtful look that said nothing of death. "She is busy in the kitchen." He came closer. "Keep a hand on Señora Mondragón when you go in there, my lord."

A question in his eyes, Marco did as his *mayordomo* said, taking his wife by the hand, then putting his arm around her waist as they walked slowly down the path through the kitchen garden, already sprouting green shoots. He knew Paloma would probably be weeding in the garden tomorrow, because she loved young, tender things.

He opened the door, ready to call out a greeting, when Sancha turned around. His knees suddenly grew weak in his borrowed breeches. Paloma gave a strangled cry and they somehow propped each other up.

Sancha held a baby in her arms, one even younger than the little niece of Kahúu. The child's hair was brown, and not nearly as plentiful as a Kwahadi baby's would be. Sancha smiled and held out the baby. "Not all died at Hacienda Castellano," she said, with a certain grim determination. "Paloma, my sweet, meet your daughter."

"One of us has to breathe," said Marco, finally, to Paloma, who stood as if rooted to the tiles.

She took one deep breath, followed by another. "If I reach out, she will vanish."

"Not this child," Sancha told her with a laugh. "You should see her tug at the wet nurse's nipple if her milk doesn't flow fast enough! She is here to stay."

Paloma looked at him as if wondering what to do. He saw the pain in her eyes and knew she was reliving her last look at the Kwahadi baby. Maybe she also saw some reassurance in his face, although God knows he was as astonished as she was. He gave her a little push forward.

She needed nothing more. Paloma held out both hands eagerly as Sancha placed the small bundle in them. With a gesture so tender that he could not help his exclamation, she touched the baby's cheek with the back of her hand. She sat down at the kitchen table, that place where all business was carried on in the colony of New Mexico, and hugged the baby close, but not close enough to wake it. In another moment, she crooned to the child, her cousin from her cousin.

He smiled as the practical Paloma took over. She did what he had seen her do to the Kwahadi baby, one night, when she didn't think he was watching. Her fingers so gentle, she carefully unwrapped the baby's blanket—good God, *their* child now—and counted her toes and fingers. He had seen Felicia do that very thing to each twin, when she had recovered from the stupor of childbirth. Maybe that was how a mother established ownership, whether the child was of her body or not. He held his breath as Paloma leaned forward, breathing deep of that baby aroma he remembered. God was good just then in Valle de Sol, a place not even the king of Spain cared about, if he had ever even heard of it.

As he watched them, Sancha took his arm. She walked him into the corridor, sat him down and whispered what had happened.

"Their servants truly deserted them in their hour of death?" he whispered, appalled. "Even those who had no need to fear *la viruela*?"

"Even them. Only one woman remained as Maria Teresa, covered with smallpox, gave birth and died. She didn't even tie off the cord properly, but wrapped the baby in a tablecloth and ran."

"*Here*? Here, to this place Maria Teresa hated?"

Sancha nodded. "Jorge Maestas, the Castellanos' nearest neighbor, found her and brought her here, because Maria Teresa—"

"What is this?"

Paloma stood in the doorway, her arms tight around her child. Marco moved over and she joined them.

"Señor Maestas sent a rider ahead and Emiliano met them on horseback," Sancha continued.

"Good God," Marco said. "No one has been back to the hacienda?"

She shook her head. "It is a death house. You cannot get a Tewa or Navajo near the place. Something must be done." She looked at him with expectation.

"I will do it." He remembered Lieutenant Roybal's promise to visit the

Castellano hacienda tomorrow, and knew he could not wait a day. "Send a servant to saddle Buciro."

Paloma put a hand on his arm, but she spoke to Sancha. "Why here? Of all people and places my cousin hated …." The baby stirred, and Paloma put her daughter to her shoulder in that tender spot.

"I do not understand it, Señora Mondragón, except that the woman said Señora Castellano called for you as she was dying. Over and over, they said."

Paloma bowed her head and Marco pulled her close. "If only she had wanted me in life," she said simply. She sat in silence, then remembered him with a kiss to his cheek, even though Sancha sat there. The Kwahadi had changed them forever.

"Go, Marco. Your family will be here when you return. Just remember that."

Chapter Thirty-Four

In which Marco finds the star in the meadow by firelight

MARCO HAD NO PLANS to share this terrible ride with anyone on the Double Cross. The sky was still light and he feared no Indians in Valle now. He rode on faithful Buciro, enjoying the familiar feel of his patient friend. The gate closed behind him. When he was out of sight of the Double Cross, he reined in and waited.

"You knew I followed."

"Toshua, I have been learning from masters for more than two moons. I will speak as we ride."

He knew how the Kwahadi felt about restless spirits. They were riding at a near gallop now to a place filled with haunts. "If you don't wish to come, *pabi* ...." He didn't finish.

"What kind of a big brother would that make me?" If scorn were a living thing, Marco knew just then he would have seen Toshua flog it in front of him.

The gates hung wide and creaking. Marco crossed himself as they passed through them, feeling his insides churn. So much for his brave words. Only Toshua's presence kept him from abandoning the whole desperate business, even if to hesitate one day meant that Lieutenant Roybal would arrive to do his duty. He dared not wait.

There was not an animal on the place, not a dog, cow, or chicken. Marco made himself think like a *juez de campo*, instead of a frightened man. In a few days he would send his men to round up what livestock might be nearby. Surely every animal had not vanished. There were reports to write, and changes to make, if need be, to protect the baby that he knew Paloma would never relinquish to her Santa Fe relatives. *And that is how business is done here*, he thought grimly. *We are on the frontier in many ways and we must bend our rules.*

At least the door to the main house was closed. He knew the stench would be overwhelming, but at least they would not find the work of wolves or coyotes inside. He tied his handkerchief over his mouth and nose, and held out the extra one he had brought along, certain Toshua would join him. Eying the handkerchief for a disdainful moment, the Kwahadi followed Marco's lead.

"We will work fast. I have to get court and land documents from Alonso's ranch office, and there is something else," he said in a whisper, as though he feared the spirits crowded close to eavesdrop and spoil his plans. "Behind my saddle I tied two torches. Bring them, please. I will go to their bedchamber first."

Marco took a final breath of good air and opened the door. The smell of death struck like a fist, thrusting him back outside, where he raised his handkerchief and vomited. He jumped when Toshua clapped his hand on his shoulder, steadying him.

When Marco's hands quit shaking, he used his flint and steel to light the torches. Holding them high, they went inside. The breeze from the open door and the flickering lights threw shadows against the walls and made the saints painted on leather dance. Toshua gasped. Marco hurried to Alonso's chamber.

His friend lay there, already melting into his coverlet, his features unrecognizable from pox and mortification. Marco pointed to the curtains with a hand that shook. "Fire it," he said.

While Toshua torched the curtain and then the bed, Marco threw open the carved chest, tossing clothing right and left. Nothing. The fire spread quicker than Marco had imagined it would. Toshua held out his hand from the doorway and pulled him through.

"Where is the wife? She did not lie with her husband?" Toshua asked.

"This was not a happy family," Marco said. He thought of the Castellanos' baby in Paloma's arms now, a child that would know nothing but joy.

He opened the next door on a sight he knew would give him the shivers and heaves for a long time. Maria Teresa Moreno de Castellano lay there, legs spread, a woman who had given birth with her last breath. Maybe Paloma's cousin truly had been braver than he knew. If only she had been kind.

In a voice he barely recognized as his own, Marco ordered Toshua to stay where he was. The Kwahadi ignored him, of course. Toshua yanked the rug from the floor and threw it over the ruined woman. Silent, except for hard breathing that betrayed his own terror, Toshua torched the bedding. He held out his hand for Marco, beckoning with impatient fingers. "Spirits are walking here," he warned.

"Let them walk." Marco went to Maria Teresa's carved chest and threw it open. As the smoke thickened, he found a small cask, the kind to hold a lady's jewels. The lid was open; someone had already rifled through it. Marco cursed the dreadful servants of these dreadful people and looked closer.

There it was, something no thief wanted. As the room seemed to swell with fire, he snatched up the necklace with a star and a V, a child's necklace. He stuffed it into his doublet pocket and ran for the door.

"You worry me," was all Toshua said.

Marco knew where Alonso's office was located. He thought of better times when he had sat there with his weak friend from childhood, drinking and laughing. The hacienda was filling with the stench of burning bodies as he grabbed the land grant parchments and brand records, thrusting some to Toshua and carrying the rest close to his chest. He threw his torch into the room and they staggered from the building. Coughing and gagging, they collapsed in the dust of the courtyard and lay there until they could breathe again.

"You know, you could have picked up that cask of jewels and carried it from the room," Toshua said. "You came away with nothing."

"Oh, no, my friend." He fumbled in his doublet and pulled out Paloma's necklace, handing it to Toshua.

"Ah. Tatzinupi, our star." Toshua handed it back. "Let's ride."

"We watch first."

"The spirits, little brother," Toshua warned.

"No spirits here, *pabi*," Marco said. At the top of his lungs, drowning out the roar of the flames, he sang "*Te Deum Laudamus*," the chant of a war chief this time.

Feeling older than the oldest man in Santa Maria, Marco sat on Buciro by the Castellano gates, until the hacienda burned to the ground. They rode home slowly.

He wanted Toshua to ride in with him. Marco told him about his new daughter, which made Toshua laugh. "After what Eckapeta told me, this too? You will be busy," he said.

They looked at each other in complete understanding.

"Don't leave us," Marco said at the place where the road continued straight to the Double Cross, and branched east to Santa Maria and the plains of Texas.

"I will think about this," was all Toshua would say.

Toshua turned his horse toward the Santa Maria road, and Marco swallowed his disappointment. He knew Toshua would ride all night and rejoin the other warriors and his wife. Maybe he would come back some day, or maybe this was their last meeting. Silent, they touched fingers and then palms. Marco let Buciro pick up the pace and get him home, because he hadn't the heart to pay attention. He stopped once or twice, certain he could hear another horse. Nothing.

Sancha must have told Emiliano what he had done. When Marco was safely through his gates, the old retainer led Buciro into the horse barn. Marco washed his hands and face in the *acequia* and went into his kitchen.

It was too much to hope that Paloma would be up still and waiting for him, but she was. She put her finger to her lips and pointed to the cradle by the banked fire. She wore a clean dress and she smelled heavenly of roses and talcum powder.

"There is a bath for you in our room and," she chuckled, "I know better than to bother with a nightshirt for you. Are you hungry?"

He shook his head, certain he would never eat again. He put the official documents on the table. "We burned it to the ground, just like the Kwahadi and their tipis of dead."

" 'We'? I rather thought Toshua would help you. You couldn't get him to stay?"

"I tried. We will see them both again." He looked at her. "How did you know?"

"You're not the only smart one."

He knew how vile he smelled, but he also knew Paloma would take his hand anyway. He stopped at the doorway. "The baby?"

"The wet nurse is in the next room. She will take the cradle when we leave the kitchen."

They moved as one down the corridor. He stopped outside the door he had not opened in years. He opened it now.

"Why ... why did you not put our little one in here?" he asked, genuinely puzzled.

"I wanted you to open the door," she said simply.

They walked inside. He went to the window, removed the bar and opened the shutters, letting in the moonlight. He breathed in the fragrance of newly turned earth. He would be busy in the fields tomorrow, catching up.

"I'll wash the bedding tomorrow and we'll move her in." She took his hand. "May I call her Soledad Estrella, after our mothers?"

"You know you may," he told her, touched. "I can put the second crib in the lumber room tomorrow."

"I think not."

He smiled. She knew. Why not? It was her body, after all. "All right, Paloma, what are you telling me?" He could feign surprise, but for how long, he wasn't sure.

He didn't think she would be shy, not after a year and a half of yearning, but she was. "At first I was not so certain. You know I missed so many monthlies when I went all those years without much food in my uncle's house, and here we were, starving again. Goodness knows, we did not eat well in the canyon until the bears in the cave."

"True. Those deer Toshua and I shot were puny to feed thirty people, and I knew you were giving your portions to Kahúu for the babies."

She didn't deny it. She opened her mouth to speak, then closed it again, giving him that down-the-nose look. "*Why* are you not surprised?"

"It was the cedar smoke and Eckapeta."

The look became more pronounced. "This *milagro* of ours happened weeks before the smoke. I think it was the night I worked up my courage to ask Toshua and Eckapeta for some tipi time without an audience."

He grinned as she took his hand and hauled him next door into their room, where the light was better. "Get in the tub and I will scrub your back."

Marco stripped and sank into the tub with a sigh that went on and on. Paloma sat on the floor beside him, her arms resting on the wooden rim. "Eckapeta? The smoke?"

He lathered up his own cloth and wiped death, grime, and five hundred years from his tired face. "She told me on the Llano, when you were starting to droop and flag." He washed some more, until she grabbed the cloth.

"Told you *what*?"

"She noticed as you sat there naked in the smoke, that the area around your nipples had turned brown. I hadn't noticed because tipis are so dark, or I might have said something. I do remember that from Felicia. Eckapeta also said the veins in your breasts were so large." He touched her cheek. "When did *you* decide that maybe our luck had changed?"

"Probably on the Llano. All I wanted to do was sleep and throw up. I still do. And *ay!* Those breasts you like so well are sore to touch." She leaned her forehead against the tub. "Thank you both for slowing the pace. I know the warriors were upset and Toshua, too."

"Not after she told them why."

Paloma laughed. "We all could have said something! My goodness."

He finished washing, as she changed into her nightgown and sat cross-legged on the end of their bed. "You realize, Marco, that we are going to be busy here in eight months or so, when Soledad is nine months old and we have a newborn."

Saying the word aloud, maybe for the first time, made her gasp and lean her head forward until she touched her toes. "A newborn," she repeated, her voice muffled. She laughed again. "Soon I will not bend this well."

"Is Soledad too much?" he had to ask, even though he was nearly desperate for his turn to hold the little one.

"She is already ours," Paloma said, her voice firm. "We will give her a good life, the best." He saw sudden fear on her face. "My aunt and uncle. Oh, no, please no!"

Marco reached for her. After assessing what he thought his wife could bear, he amended the account of the dreadful business at Hacienda Castellano. "Alonso had no living relatives. Your aunt and uncle will get my official report of the death of their daughter and son-in-law, and our condolences. It is over. Lieutenant Roybal will have no report but mine, so he will know nothing of a child."

"People here will know."

It warmed Marco's heart to know that a mother's heart for Soledad already beat in her breast, so determined was she to consider every angle to protect the sleeping baby.

He leaned over enough to touch the frown between her eyes. "Certainly our friends will know, and they will rejoice with us. The people of Valle del Sol are like that. Soon no one will remember anything different about the children of Marco Mondragón and Paloma Vega. Santa Fe is far away."

"Are you bending the law again?"

"It is my choice, as *juez*," he said simply.

She tossed him a towel when he stood up. "I'm going to miss that breechcloth," he joked, looking down.

"That reminds me, husband. I remember how you groused to me one night that *I* had a name from The People and you did not."

"Well, it would have been nice."

She yanked the towel away and pointed south of his stomach. "I can't say it in Comanche, but the women named you Big Man Down There. Now don't let it go to your head!" she said when he started to laugh.

"At least it's more flattering than Buffalo Rut," he joked, pleased.

He crawled into bed and lay there in complete comfort as his wife pulled the sheets and blankets over him. "I have missed this, Paloma."

"I, too." Her voice turned wistful. "Call me Tatzinupi now and then."

Tatzinupi. Marco sat up. "You're closest. Hand me my doublet."

She did as he asked, a question in her eyes. Watching her expressive face, he reached in the pocket and pulled out her little necklace, handing it to her.

"You went to that death house for this," she murmured, when she could talk.

"That and the land grant papers. I will keep the star and meadow brand record here. I will send the land grant papers to Governor de Anza. He will abrogate the grant and throw the land open for other settlers. Eventually—you know how slowly things move in our colony—Tatzinupi and Big Man Down There will have new neighbors."

She gave him such a look, sitting there so lovely in the moonlight—this mother of their new daughter Soledad and their baby growing inside her. *Ay caray*, they would be busy! She sat in profile to him, so he traced the outline of her face. When his finger reached her lips, she kissed it.

"*Te deum laudamus*," she sang so softly. "O God, we praise thee."

MARCO THOUGHT HE WOULD go to sleep at once, but he lay awake for an hour or more, listening to his wife's peaceful deep breathing. It touched his heart to see how her hand already curved protectively around her belly. Tomorrow there would be Soledad to hold and admire. *Has ever a man been as blessed as I am?* he asked himself.

He lay there, calm, thinking of all there was to do tomorrow. Suddenly, he knew why he could not sleep. Paloma was so deep in slumber that she made no sound when he slowly moved his arm from under her shoulders.

In case some of the servants were still up, Marco knotted the bath towel around his middle and padded down the corridor. The kitchen was dark and silent, so he crossed to the door and opened it onto the garden.

Te deum laudamus, he thought in utter gratitude. Two horses were cropping grass by the *acequia* and he could just see a flicker of light from the fireplace in his office by the horse barn. He leaned against the doorframe, content, relieved and grateful all at once. Since Paloma was going to need his help more and more, maybe he could move his office into one of the empty rooms in the hacienda itself. He didn't think for a moment that Toshua and Eckapeta would stay with them permanently, but they might like a place of their own when they visited their children.

In the morning first thing, he would ask Paloma what she thought, even though he was already pretty sure of her answer. No. He was certain.

Author's Note

FROM THE TIME OF the Spanish Conquest, smallpox or *la viruela* was always present in the Americas, cycling in severity, but never entirely absent. Notable epidemics in 1780, 1820, and 1836 stand out as particularly terrible smallpox seasons, affecting white and native alike. In the East, the 1780 epidemic added to the complications of the American Revolution.

Until Edward Jenner's world-changing introduction of vaccination in the late 18th century, that same world had relied on inoculation, which involved inserting live smallpox into a healthy body. The result, fatal in a small percentage of cases, usually produced much milder smallpox, which left much less scarring and the sought-after blessing of future immunity. Because it could be so risky and fickle, inoculation was a last resort for many.

Inoculation had been practiced in Africa and Asia for hundreds of years, with the method arriving on Europe's shores in the early 1700s. The method was refined in England and rendered slightly less risky, but it still involved the use of live matter taken from smallpox victims.

Records of the 1780 epidemic in New Mexico indicate a great worsening in 1781 and later, among settlers and indigenous people alike. Death tolls among the Comanche and Kiowa are understandably harder to quantify. Some say the Comanche suffered as greatly as any tribe, while other accounts suggest that the more remote Kwahadi (Antelope Eaters) of the high west Texas Plains escaped. If this is true—and the records are inconclusive—was it because of their isolation, or were other factors at work? For the sake of this story of Marco Mondragón and his wife Paloma Vega, I have offered just such a factor. Frontiers were fluid places and it is not unthinkable that help could come from an unexpected person, no matter how dubious and unwilling such a person might be.

Bryner Photography

A WELL-KNOWN VETERAN OF the romance writing field, **Carla Kelly** is the author of thirty-one novels and four non-fiction works, as well as numerous short stories and articles for various publications. She is the recipient of two RITA Awards from Romance Writers of America for Best Regency of the Year; two Spur Awards from Western Writers of America; two Whitney Awards, one for Best Romance Fiction, 2011, and one for Best Historical Fiction, 2012; and a Lifetime Achievement Award from Romantic Times.

Carla's interest in historical fiction is a byproduct of her lifelong study of history. She has a BA in Latin American History from Brigham Young University and an MA in Indian Wars History from University of Louisiana-Monroe. She's held a variety of jobs, including public relations work for major hospitals and hospices, feature writer and columnist for a North Dakota daily newspaper, and ranger in the National Park Service (her favorite job) at Fort Laramie National Historic Site and Fort Union Trading Post National Historic Site. She has worked for the North Dakota Historical Society as a contract researcher. Interest in the Napoleonic Wars at sea led to a recent series of novels about the British Channel Fleet during that conflict.

Of late, Carla has written two novels set in southeast Wyoming in 1910 that focus on her Mormon background and her interest in ranching.

You can find Carla online at www.carlakellyauthor.com.

Book One in the Spanish Brand Series

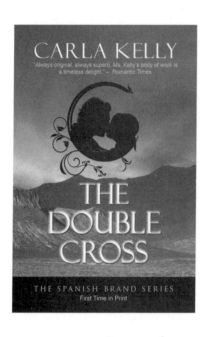

The year is 1780, and Marco Mondragón is a brand inspector in the royal Spanish colony of New Mexico whose home is on the edge of the domain of the fierce Comanche. On a trip to Santa Fe, he meets lovely Paloma Vega and rescues her from cruel relatives. Now he is determined to find out if they stole the brand belonging to her parents.

Carla's very first novel

Maria Espinosa is "La Afortunata." First she survives the 1679 cholera epidemic in Mexico City, then an Apache raid on the caravan transporting her to Santa Fe. Rejected by her sister, Maria goes to live with a ranching family living uneasily among the Pueblos and inspires a rivalry between Diego and his half-Indian brother Cristobal. When the Indians revolt, will Maria's good fortune hold?

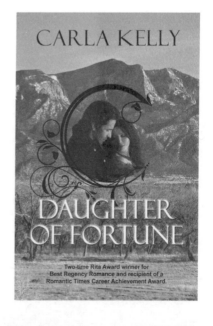

CAMEL PRESS

Camel Press Regency Romances
by Carla Kelly

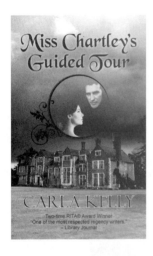

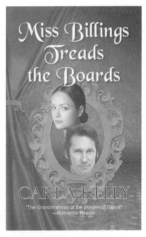

Coming Soon:
With This Ring